Praise for
A Mending at the Edge

"I love when a book illuminates a small slice of history that has relevance to our lives today—even better when it does so with interesting characters and a compelling story. Emma Giesy is a woman with flaws and attributes we all can relate to and whose journey is one that easily could have taken place today."

—JUDITH PELLA, best-selling author of seven series,
including the Daughters of Fortune series

"Jane has a gift for breathing simple beauty into the lives of remarkable historical women characters. In *A Mending at the Edge*, Emma comes off the page and shows readers an unforgettable picture of a very unique Oregon community. I love living within view of Mount Hood even more now that I better understand those who shaped the tenacious beginnings of this region."

—ROBIN JONES GUNN, author of the best-selling
Glenbrooke series and the Christy Award–winning
Sisterchicks novels

"Jane Kirkpatrick's knack for stitching history and fiction together is as skillful as the quilts she writes about in the Change and Cherish Historical Series. *A Mending at the Edge* is a satisfying ending to an absorbing series that manages to stay true to the past while relating remarkably well to today's modern women."

—TINA ANN FORKNER, author of *Ruby Among Us*

"In *A Mending at the Edge*, Jane Kirkpatrick completes the literary quilt of the Emma Wagner Giesy trilogy, piecing together the historical fabric of Emma's personal story with that of the Aurora Colony. Emma's efforts to find a house—and a home—in this communal society in Oregon once again reflect the conflict of individual and community needs represented in Kirkpatrick's earlier two works in the Change and Cherish Historical Series. Based on a solid historical framework of the Aurora Colony and the broader social, political, and cultural landscape of the 1860s, Kirkpatrick offers a story of hope and achievement that captures the spirit of giving, sharing, and receiving central to 'mending' within a communal settlement."

—JAMES J. KOPP, communal historian and board member
of the Aurora Colony Historical Society

"Jane Kirkpatrick artfully weaves this story for us, rather like Emma and the women of Oregon's Aurora Colony weave together their quilted existence as well as their personal quilting projects. Her masterful placement of the fresh-turned phrase and the graceful metaphor enriches this captivating and yet disquieting story of mid-nineteenth-century pioneer women whose lives are so very different from ours—or are they?"

—SARAH BYRN RICKMAN, author of *Nancy Love and
the WASP Ferry Pilots of World War II, The Originals,*
and *Flight from Fear*

A Mending at the Edge

Books by Jane Kirkpatrick

NOVELS

Change and Cherish Historical Series
A Clearing in the Wild
(2007 WILLA Literary Award, Finalist, Best Historical Novel)
A Tendering in the Storm
A Mending at the Edge

A Land of Sheltered Promise
(Western Writers of America Spur Award 2005, Finalist,
Best Novel of the West)

Tender Ties Historical Series
A Name of Her Own
(2002 Oregon Book Awards, Finalist, Best Novel)
Every Fixed Star
Hold Tight the Thread

Kinship and Courage Historical Series
All Together in One Place
(Readers' Choice Award 2000, Finalist, Best Inspirational)
No Eye Can See
What Once We Loved

Dreamcatcher Collection
A Sweetness to the Soul
(winner of the Western Heritage Wrangler Award
for Outstanding Western Novel of 1995)
Love to Water My Soul
A Gathering of Finches
Mystic Sweet Communion

NONFICTION
Homestead: A Memoir of Modern Pioneers Pursuing the Edge of Possibility
A Simple Gift of Comfort (formerly *A Burden Shared*)

ANTHOLOGIES
Daily Guideposts 1992
Storyteller Collection, Book 2
Crazy Woman Creek, "Women Rewrite the American West"

A Mending at the Edge

a novel

JANE KIRKPATRICK

WATERBROOK
PRESS

A MENDING AT THE EDGE
PUBLISHED BY WATERBROOK PRESS
12265 Oracle Boulevard, Suite 200
Colorado Springs, Colorado 80921
A division of Random House Inc.

Scripture quotations are taken from The Holy Bible, containing the Old and New
Testaments, translated out of The Original Tongues, and with the former translations
diligently compared and revised. New York: American Bible Society, 1858.

This book is a work of historical fiction based closely on real people and real
events. Details that cannot be historically verified are purely products of the author's
imagination.

ISBN 978-0-7394-9545-2

Copyright © 2008 by Jane Kirkpatrick

Printed in the United States of America

*This book is dedicated to the volunteers, staff, and board
of the Aurora Colony Historical Society and Museum
for their passion in honoring descendant stories
as they keep history relevant and alive.*

Cast of Characters

At Aurora

Emma Wagner Giesy	German American
Andrew	Emma and Christian's older son
Catherine/Kate/Catie	Emma and Christian's daughter
Christian	Emma and Christian's younger son
Ida	Jack Giesy and Emma's daughter
David and Catherina Wagner	Emma's parents
Jonathan, David Jr., Catherine "Kitty," Christine (the foster child), Johanna, Louisa "Lou," and William	Emma's siblings
Joe Knight	oysterman, former scout, Matilda's brother
Adam Schuele	colonist, former scout with Christian and Emma
Wilhelm Keil	leader of Aurora, Oregon, colony
Louisa Keil	Wilhelm's wife
Willie (deceased; buried in Willapa), August, Frederick, Elias, Louisa, Gloriunda, Aurora, Amelia, Emanuel	Keil children
Martin Giesy	colonist, a future pharmacist and physician, and Christian's brother
John and Barbara (BW) Giesy	colonists, Christian's brother and sister-in-law
Elizabeth	John and Barbara's daughter
Karl Ruge	colonist, teacher, toll keeper, Emma's friend
Barbara Giesy	colonist, Christian's mother, widowed
Helena Giesy	colonist, Christian's sister
Louisa Giesy	colonist, Christian's sister
Martha Miller	colonist, a woman of the colony
Nancy Thornton	painter in the Oregon City area
Almira Raymond	a member of Emma's house church
Matilda Knight	sister of Joe Knight, an original scout

Jacob Stauffer	colonist, son of John Stauffer, an original scout
Henry C. Finck	music teacher
Henry T. Finck	Henry C's son, Andy's friend
Christopher Wolff	colonist, instructor and leader of a Bethel wagon train
John and Lucinda Wolfer	colonists who tended ill people in the community
Catherine and Christina Wolfer	mother and daughter who saved the plate
Mr. Ehlen	colonist, wounded Civil War veteran
Lorenz Ehlen	son of Mr. Ehlen and friend of Andy and Kate's
*Brita Engel	a *Zwerg* and a woman in need
*Charles, Stanley, and Pearl	Brita's children
*Opal, the goat	
*Clara, the chicken	
*Po, the dog	

At Willapa Bay

Christian Giesy	Emma's deceased husband and former leader of the scouts, buried in Willapa
Sebastian and Mary Giesy	Christian's brother and his wife
Elizabeth	Sebastian and Mary's daughter
Louisa Giesy	Christian's younger sister
Sam and Sarah Woodard	settlers at Woodard's Landing
Jacob "Jack" or "Big Jack" Giesy	Emma's second husband

At Bethel

Andreas "Andrew" Giesy Jr.	colonist, Christian's brother, preacher and co-director of Bethel Colony in Keil's absence
August Keil	colonist, Keil's son sent to assist with colony business

* not historical characters

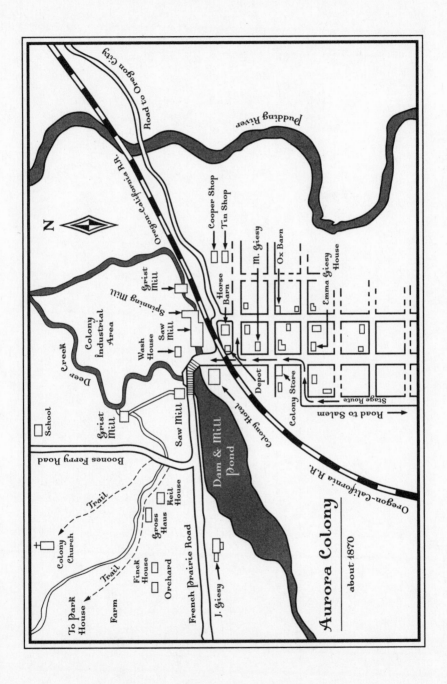

Aurora Colony

about 1870

Women are the brooms of the world—they clean houses and they clean souls. But often they get put back in the corner until the next mess needs to be cleaned up.

ALISON SAAR, artist, *Expanded Visions:
Four Women Artists Paint the American West,*
Women of the West Museum, 2000

Each community has a different rhythm.... We have our own individual rhythms within the community: ...some devote their lives to the daily maintenance of the community while others breathe life into it through their art, music, and poetry. We may find ourselves in a radically altered relationship to the community as we move to its edges or outside it entirely for brief or lengthy periods of time....

Rhythms of community can be both life-giving and stifling, liberating and oppressive.... We listen to and follow the Spirit's own rhythms as it moves with us.... We listen to the stories of other women in other communities.... We better understand what it means to be a creative, spirited community of healing, of hope, of resistance, and of transformation.

JAN RICHARDSON,
Sacred Journeys: A Woman's Book of Daily Prayer

Then they that feared the LORD spake often one to another: and the LORD hearkened, and heard it: and a book of remembrance was written before him for them that feared the LORD, and that thought upon his name.

MALACHI 3:16

A Mending at the Edge

The Hope Inside

Of all the things I left behind in Willapa, hope was what I missed the most. But memory is a flighty friend, wisping in to warm or warn when one can least expect it. I wanted to remember Christian—my first husband—and the hopefulness that we'd brought with us across the plains from Missouri to the wet Washington Territory in 1853. Remembering him recalled that good part of me, before change had rubbed me raw. After that, much had happened to take hope from life, and I questioned whether expectation was a virtue one could nurture or if once lost would never sprout again. My friend, Karl Ruge, a lover of words as I am, says that in English, *despair* means "to fall back from hope." But for my friends, I would have drowned in despair.

On this dark day, rain pounded like Indian drums on the cedar shakes above us. Through the wavy glass windows I watched raindrops splash out over the full, coopered barrels stationed at the *gross Haus* corners, a collection place for wash water. We needed to do the wash, what with all the people and mud. It was how one belonged to this colony, sharing in work and in the waiting together through storms. Out the window, I could see an east wind whipping the young walnut trees in the yard beyond. The bare branches looked like skeletons instead of as intended, hopeful sentinels standing guard over this small colony in the infant state of Oregon.

A deep roll of thunder rattled the windows in the entryway where I cluck-henned my boys and Kate around me, holding Ida in my arms. We huddled in a corner of the *gross Haus,* the three-story building being built by Brother Keil (I refused to call him *Father* Keil as do most others in our communal society). We shared the house with two dozen others, all longtime members. I'd found safety here. But I never knew when that fragile calm might be shattered. The smell of wet wool filled my head as cloaks and coats draped every railing or chair or blue bench, drying out. Colonists from the low-lying areas drove wagons here when the rivers began to rise early in December, adding still more numbers to an already-crowded house. The *gross Haus* rose up on the highest knoll of the village, like a castle of old, visible from a great distance. Of course. It was Keil's house.

The aroma of sausage and beans bubbling in the large pots in the kitchen reached my soggy senses. Someone lovingly prepared a meal where hunger served as sauce. But just as quickly, the scents reminded me of my family still in Missouri, family where the threads of connection had been strained since I'd come west. I'd received no letters from my parents since my decision to leave Willapa and come here with my four children. Well, we hadn't all come at once. I arrived first with my friend Karl Ruge and my daughters; my sons were brought to me later by their uncle Martin Giesy, a tactic of safety we'd all felt necessary. But my sister Kitty had written from Missouri to say they were coming to Oregon, so things would change. Dared I hope they would change for the better?

My cheeks felt cold, and Kate's six-year-old upturned nose looked red as a summer rose. The children would probably collect sniffles with so many people huddled so closely together. Andy especially had to fight off frequent illnesses. Failing health affected our days—our entire lives, in fact. We'd lived the past years not far from the Pacific Ocean where we'd seen days of downpours, and some said that our part of the wild endured ninety inches or more in a year. Coughs arrived with the weather. I'd thought it would be better here in Oregon, but the past days of January 1862 had yet to reveal that a sun did shine somewhere overhead or that rivers in Oregon really did know how to flow within their banks. Not very hopeful, that thought.

I'd reentered this community for the loving embrace it promised, the kind built on grace and faith, not domination or control. Embraces can constrict. Other members of my husband's family had taught me that.

A few log houses, a stage-stop barn, a grist and lumber mill, and some board homes composed Aurora, the village the colonists had been building since 1856. The structures clustered in a swale, like eggs in a chicken's nest. Deer Creek and Pudding River helped define its tree-lined borders. A quarter mile from the houses ran a deep ravine, and near the top of that hill, Brother Keil had built his house with a view looking out over his domain. Other colonists had been assigned farmland farther away. A few had settled nearer the Willamette River some eight miles west. Most of us this winter were staying in the yet-unfinished Keil house, high above the creeks and flooding waters.

Another crack of thunder. Kate shivered against me. "We don't hear thunder so much here," Helena said. She's the older sister of my deceased husband, Christian, tall and formidable, and her observations usually come out as dogma. But now she fidgeted with the braids formed like a crown on the top of her head, and she startled at the rumble too. It was the first time I'd seen Helena look even the least bit flummoxed.

"I like the sound of it," Louisa told her cheerfully. "It reminds me of Missouri." Louisa is Brother Keil's wife and the mother of their eight living children. "I haven't seen any lightning, so that's a good thing, *ja*?"

"*Ach,* you find cream in even stale milk," Helena told her, brushing her hand in the air as though she brushed away flies. Still, they spoke as old friends, family perhaps, as women accustomed to sharing differences that really didn't matter.

I hadn't found anything wrong with Louisa's tying thunder to a good memory from Missouri. Problems only arose if you stayed wrapped inside the comfort of old thoughts, refused to unbind yourself to move forward.

Rain pounded like hail now, pelting nearly horizontal. I patted Kate's arm with reassurance.

"*Ach, Jammer,*" complained one of the bachelors, as close to cursing as he'd get in this mixed company that included women and children.

"I hope it doesn't break those windows!" another said. Glass was precious here and perhaps not all that practical. Brother Keil had promised that eventually all would have glass windows, though first, we needed houses. A minor detail to him, a throbbing desire to me. I so wished for a safe place, a home of my heart, a place where I truly belonged and was accepted as I was.

Ida began to cry, and I unfolded myself from the cluster of my children. "I must feed your sister," I told them and moved out of the corner, across the pine flooring dotted with colorful rugs, and headed down the stairs to the kitchen, where I could nurse her in the presence of women only. The children began to follow, the boys included. I turned to them, Ida on my hip but clawing at my bodice. "Don't come down those stairs, now. Wait here. I'll be fine and so will you."

Kate and Christian stopped, nodded their heads in agreement. Andy, the oldest, glared at me, his arms crossed over his chest. He didn't turn around as the other two had. "Don't come down these steps," I repeated.

I wished I felt more hopeful about my relationship with him.

Ida squirmed and fussed as I took the narrow steps, then crossed under them into the kitchen area. I looked up to see if the children had moved away, and they had. They were like hinges in the midst of all the changes, swinging toward security by clinging to me, then pushing away for independence.

A row of windows bordered the ceiling and looked out onto the sodden ground, but the room felt gloomy. Rain painted everything dark. Even my quilted petticoat couldn't ignore the chill. Thank goodness a fire glowed in the fireplace. It spit and snapped with raindrops racing down the chimney. I could smell fresh bread nestled against the brick firewall, baking in the bank of warm ash. Women bustled about, so I pulled a chair into the wide hallway and sat in front of the blue cabinet built from floor to ceiling. It had glass doors, of course. We waited for houses, and Keil had our craftsmen build fine furniture for him and order in new glass. I folded back Ida's Nine Patch quilt from around her face, helped her find my breast, and nodded to the other women working at preparing pork and beans. Along with bread and peas, potatoes and what fruits we'd dried, ham and beans were our staple food this winter. The chickens hadn't produced since November.

I silenced the chatter in my head to focus on Ida and give her all she needed to be calm and eat. My younger daughter would be seven months old before long and had spent most of her early life in turmoil. We'd made our escape from her threatening father, leaving nearly all we owned behind. She'd adjusted to living huddled with so many others while I worked, cooking and washing and mending. I also worked at holding my tongue.

I'd come to Aurora in good part because those few I trusted thought it best. Worn down and hopeless, I'd leaned on them. It had been a good decision. Still, I lacked confidence in the choices I'd made since Christian's death. Grief, I've learned, has many siblings—guilt, anger, fear, unworthiness, separation from those who love us, resistance to change. They clamor for attention in times of trial, and sometimes I heard those brothers and sisters of grief speak louder than the call of comfort that can come from family and friends.

Ida suckled eagerly. Of my four children, only Ida could I nurse; wet nurses and the goat's milk had rescued my others. I should have found it hopeful that I could feed this child and that I fed her in a dry, safe place. But too much had happened. Time, like a good chalk, had yet to erase the stains I carried on my heart.

"*Ach,* someone comes in through the root room door," one of the kitchen women said. She had disgust in her voice, as though the intruder should know better than to drag his muddy boots through the food larder instead of stomping and removing his brogans at the covered porch outside, above us. I felt the gush of wind carry the scent of roots, which were hung to dry in the rafters behind the hallway door. Wood slammed against the doorjamb. "I will tell him to go around," she said as she moved past me.

For a moment I had this twinge of premonition. It could be Jack Giesy, my second husband, come back. He had a claim on me, though not on my heart. Brother Keil had sent Jack packing last fall, but I knew Keil could change his mind. At the sound in the root room, I wondered if perhaps he had.

Ida fidgeted, her blue eyes wide, and she stared at me as she let her hands flop away from my breast. My only child of the four to have blue eyes. If I ignored her, she could make me pay, with her new teeth coming in. I smiled nervously at her, brushed her walnut-colored hair, the same color as mine, but with dozens of tight curls instead of my strands pulling loose from my bun. I shushed her as my fingers lifted those ringlets. "It's all right," I said. "You go ahead and suckle now. Mama is with you." I tried to relax as I plotted my escape route up the stairs if Jack came through the door.

"What are you doing in here?" I heard the kitchen woman say, and I swallowed hard, started to stand. "Soaked like a swimming kitten you are. *Ach.*"

I craned my neck to see who followed her in.

"Andy," I said when I saw my almost-nine-year-old son. Irritation followed relief. "Didn't I ask you to stay upstairs? And why on earth would you go outside and get all wet rather than use the stairs anyway?" Water dripped off his chin, puddled at his boots.

"You told me not to come down the steps," he said. "I wanted to do what you said." A raindrop like a tiny pearl hung from his long eyelashes. His dark eyes twinkled with a hint of guile. My head began to pound.

Ida sat up then. Her eyes moved to the popped cornball Andy held in his hand. She reached for it. "And where did you get that?" I asked.

"At Christmas, remember? *Herr* Keil gave them to all the children. I saved mine."

I wondered if some of the cornballs might have been kept back in the root room and if he'd lifted one as he walked through. It didn't look soaked. I didn't like him lying to me or being disobedient. *I must not think these bad thoughts about every little thing that happens. He might have had it in his coat.*

"Someone will need to clean up the mud mess in the hallway," the kitchen woman said. Under her breath as she passed by me she added, "Some people need to keep better control over their children, *ja?*"

"I'll tend to it," I sang out to her. To Andy I spoke firmly, "Go get a broom and sweep up this mud. Now."

"That's women's work," Andy said.

"So is disciplining a wayward boy." He dropped his eyes. I softened. He'd been through so much. "You see we're fine here, nothing to worry about. Get the broom, and then maybe you can go into Brother Keil's workroom to see what medicines he's mixing." I nodded toward the opposing door. "Go on." Then to Ida I said, "Finish up here." I pushed Ida's face back to my breast. "Mama has things to do."

My son moved off, and I heard Brother Keil welcome him in. Relief flooded me. Only later did I remember that Andy had failed to sweep up the dirt. I vowed he'd do it later.

I patted Ida as she ate. How could I not feel hopeful with a baby growing fat at my breast? Oh, I once had wishful thoughts and a profound belief that I could do all things necessary for my children, alone. But belief in one's own strength is not enough. Firm wishes held out like hope are not enough. I'd had high hopes for my second marriage too, but I'd come to that union like the mule who wore blinders when it plowed, unable to see what frightening things could catch me unaware.

Jack Giesy always had his problems and was never a steady man, but I'd failed to see that until he threatened my children's fate and, *ja,* my own, leaving me bruised and broken in more than my bones. Toward the end, I'd had to keep him separated from Andy, most of all, Christian's son who thought he'd have to rescue his family by doing harm to Big Jack.

Now here I was, settled in Oregon, in a tentative embrace of those very German American colonists who had once rejected what my first husband and I—and colony scouts—had been sent out from Bethel, Missouri, to do. We'd found a new site in the west, but it was not to Keil's liking, and so our group had split. I'd once rejected them too, refusing their help after my husband's death. Finding the balance between strict molds and a singular support, that was what I longed to find, and I would. I resolved that I'd remember myself back into a hopeful state, where I saw the possibilities instead of the disappointments. Soon, I prayed, my parents and brothers and sisters would arrive from Missouri and we'd have a grand reunion. I'd have a house of my own. I'd raise my children, keeping them close. My husband would stay away. I'd contribute to the colony and be known for more than being contrary. These were my wishes.

My fingers ached still from Jack's wrenching them the year before. Ida curled her small fist inside mine.

Another whoosh of the root cellar door. *"Ach,"* I shouted to the kitchen women, "it's probably my other *Kinder* following their brother. I'll see to them."

I placed the Nine Patch over my shoulder and open bodice and hiked Ida on my hip. I scrunched the mud on the floor and approached the root room door, rehearsing what I'd say to these urchins and what to do to hold Andy accountable for being a poor model for them.

Root smells and damp earth greeted me. My eyes glanced down to the height of the eyes of my children, or at least where I expected them to be. I saw, not foreheads, but knees.

When I looked up, I stared into the dark, brooding face of Jack Giesy, the husband I'd hoped would let us be.

"Aren't you pleased to see me?" He angled toward me like a snake, as though to put his arms around my shoulders and his daughter, sucking us in. Rain dripped from his felt hat. A half sneer marked his face. I recognized it as a look that formed a prelude to his outbursts of rage. Who knew how long he'd been nursing some perceived injustice that he thought could be remedied by bullying his way in here?

I backed up. My hands grew wet. My heart pounded. Ida fussed. I saw movement behind Jack. Someone short had slipped through the door, slammed it shut with a thud. *How could Andy have gotten behind him?* He'd give fuel to Jack's fire. *Please, may it not be one of my children!*

Jack reached for Ida then, his daughter; but I twisted, holding her head pressed into my chest. "Don't touch her," I hissed. My jerking from him caused me to stumble. Jack stumbled back too, I thought from the force of my words.

Instead, a small stranger pushed her way around Jack. She waddled from side to side to stand between us. The size of a child, she wore the face of a worried woman.

She pulled on my skirt. "I know you can help me," the high, breathy voice said. She grabbed my hand, thumped a startled Jack on his thighs when he tried to move around her to grab at me. He groaned, struggled to catch his balance as she fast-walked out toward the rain, pulling at my skirts. I pushed past Jack, covered Ida's head, and scurried along.

I had no idea who this woman was or what she needed. But in the midst of my dread at seeing Big Jack, she'd sliced through my despair and somehow seen hope inside me.

2

Spinning Straw into Gold

I'd heard of small earth men, as they were called, in German stories such as *Rumpelstiltskin*. They bargained for a child by helping a princess turn straw into gold. They were magical people, part of a fairy tale. I'd never met one, only seen pictures of them as part of circus acts. Karl Ruge said the Indians thought such small-statured people were mystical, with a close attachment to the divine. Some people didn't like them. They claimed the little people made them nervous, judged them solely by appearance. The *Zwerg* I'd read about were short men with long white beards. But here stood a woman, indeed, with a wide forehead and long, thick dark hair chopped at the nape of her neck. I had never been this close to a being so…different…and despite the tightening of my throat for fear of Jack lurking behind me, her presence in that small root room had brought me strange comfort.

My comfort was short lived as Big Jack followed us outside.

"Don't run away from me," he said, grasping my shoulder, spinning Ida and me around.

"Leave me be." I struck at his arm, which he lowered, no longer a threatening fist.

"What do you think, Wife?" he whined, his palms raised in surrender. It was part of his pattern to intimidate, then snivel and cajole when he remembered there was a witness. "I maybe could see my daughter and my sons? That's all I want. To be a good father."

"You were asked by Brother Keil to leave," I said. My heart pounded in my ears, but my voice sounded steady, even loud against the muffle of wet grass and trees. The little woman still tugged on my skirt. "And they are not your sons."

"I was asked to hold my temper, to do no harm, and I plan none," he said. He removed his hat and smoothed back the hair that curled behind his ears and at his neck. He needed it cut, something I used to do for him before all that had happened between us. The drizzle caught in his beard. "There were hard freezes in Willapa," he said. He cleared his throat. "I thought I'd seek warmth here in Aurora. You'd maybe not begrudge a man comfort, would you?"

We will talk of the weather, then, as though we are old friends getting reacquainted.

I pushed Ida's head farther under the quilt. I should get her out of the drizzle, though people in this western country looked more casually for shelter than in Missouri, where one rushed to get out of the weather. Here, rushing and scrunching up your shoulders against the rain offered scant relief, just an aching neck.

"You've no time for aweather chatter," the little woman told me. "I have a sick baby in the cart under the front porch and—"

I turned to her. "Let's bring him in, then."

"Along with two others."

"I'll take Ida back inside while you go and get them," Jack said. "I maybe could help. That is my daughter you're carrying, *ja?*"

I slipped behind Jack, fast-walked back into the root room, and nearly stumbled over Andy, who'd been listening at the door. "Get Brother Keil," I told him. "Go." His eyes got round as coal, and I knew he spied Jack beyond me. "Go now! Do as I say."

Andy came to himself and scooted ahead of me into Brother Keil's workroom while I marched toward the kitchen, grateful to see that Louisa Keil had come down to check on the status of the ham and beans. "Louisa," I said, intercepting her. "Please, take Ida for me. Stay in the kitchen. There's a…problem in the root room."

"Her boy comes in there all full of mud," the kitchen grump told her, hands on her hips, a spoon held out like a bird's broken wing.

"That's not the problem," I said. "And we'll clean it up, I promise. It's Jack."

"*Ja*, sure," Louisa said. Her eyes held concern as she took my child. I buttoned up my bodice. I loved it that Louisa didn't question me further.

Behind me I heard, "What's this?" Keil's voice boomed as Jack came back in. "Oh, Jack Giesy. It's been some time since we've seen a Willapa Giesy."

These men forget so easily.

"He comes to make trouble," I said.

"*Nein.* I make no trouble," Jack protested. "A man needs a dry place and a moment or two with his family. Is this such a bad thing?"

Brother Keil tugged at that tuft of white beard at his chin. "*Nein.* You come inside, then. The draft pushes against the lanterns and scrapes the wall," he said as Jack moved toward the stairwell. I hesitated. *Leave Ida so close to Jack?*

"Remember, Louisa," I warned. She nodded and headed up the stairs. I'd have to trust her.

I slipped past Jack, pulling the quilt tighter around my shoulder like a shawl.

"And where do you go, Sister Giesy?" Keil called out to me.

"She's helping me," the little woman told him. She'd followed me back in. Keil looked down. Her protruding forehead hid her eyes.

"And who might you be?"

"Brita-witha-one-t Engel. Are you coming?" she dismissed him, pulling on my skirt.

"*Ja*, well then, I guess that is all right that you go help another," Keil said to my back, as though I needed his permission for anything at all.

The rain now let up and turned into a soft mist that dribbled through the slats of boards on the porch. Huddled back as close to the house foundation as they could get were Brita's children. Two boys stood by the two-wheeled cart. Their coughs nearly covered the soft murmuring of a baby. Brita lifted the infant, and I scooped up the younger of the two standing children. The older boy was about my Andy's age, though taller than his mother. She told him to bring the cart, and he pulled it after us, coughing all the while, as we headed back into the house through the root cellar. I could see my breath in the air. We'd have snow by morning.

I knew change and challenge waited for me inside the *gross Haus,* but for now I felt grateful to this Brita for giving me a meaningful diversion. Her troubles rose above my own.

Brita spoke to her boys in German mixed with English words, and she interspersed *"danke"* with her English "thank you" to me.

"It's what anyone would do," I told her, holding the door so she could pass in front of me, followed by the tallest child pushing the cart before him.

The baby cried now, a weak wail. "I've no milk for her," Brita said. "The cave we stayed in flooded, and the goat ran off with a thundering, a final brick to bring my chimney down."

"I can wet-nurse her," I heard myself say. "But we have cow's milk and goat's. And this one?" I nodded my chin to the child I held. His cough sounded wet and rattled.

"He throws up cow's milk. It's why we got the goat. He's so tired from acoughing." She pulled at my skirt again, and I realized that Brita couldn't see the face of the child I held unless I squatted down. She wiped spittle from the toddler's mouth. "Poor Stanley," she said. "So sickly."

"Let's see what Brother Keil might have to offer for remedies."

My eyes adjusted from the darker root room to the lantern-lit hall. No Jack in sight. I heard musical notes from the horns coming from the highest level of the house. Band members dealt boredom a blow by practicing a tune or two or took a work break from finishing the upper floors. Andy's head stuck out from Keil's workroom, then slipped back when Keil entered the wide hall. Louisa came back down the steps, patting Ida's back. The red trim of her quilted petticoat swirled a flash of color as she stepped. *A furbelow, from Louisa?* It was a bit of stitching spice I had never noticed before. *Why do I notice such insignificant details when my world is spinning apart?*

Charles, Brita's older boy, left the cart and sat down on the bottom step, holding his head in his hands. Dark circles framed his chipped nails. They disappeared as he clutched his dirty blond hair. He held himself in a wracking cough. Brita placed a handkerchief to his mouth, comforting him. I saw green mucus there.

"Let me see your tongue," Brother Keil said. Charles lifted his head, opened his mouth. I was vaguely aware of people standing near the kitchen, though I didn't see Jack's profile. I cast a glance toward the workroom; it stood empty. *He's upstairs with Christian and Andy and Kate. I should have warned them. I need to protect them.*

"Does your chest hurt? *Ja,* I figure as much," Keil said when Charles nodded, an action that began another round of coughs. The child in my arms, maybe two or three years old, also coughed now. I wondered if the warm room didn't aggravate their symptoms.

Keil opened one of the doors in the large blue cabinet and took out a vial of dark liquid. "Pulsatilla," he said. "It should help the cough. Then we get you some food and a dry place to rest, but no sleeping on the left side, *ja*? You'll be better then, in the morning."

I knew about the juice compressed from that flowering plant. Martin, Christian's brother, used it for a toothache once, and after Christian's death, he'd given it to me and said it would help me be less sad. I don't think it did, but then nothing save grace and time could have helped me. I hadn't known pulsatilla would stop coughs. I'd always treated my son with dulcamara, carefully measured, as it could be dangerous. But he got better in the warmth and worsened in the cold and damp, unlike this child. That Andy hadn't yet contracted some winter's ailment was a gift in itself, which I'd just then thought to be grateful for.

"We should put the family in a separate place," I said. "Maybe keep the coughs from spreading."

"Nein," Keil said. "The boys can go with the other men. The one you hold, he is a *Junge*?"

"They stay together," Brita said, moving in that side-to-side gait to stand before him. Despite her small size, she acted fearless in front of Keil. "With their mother."

My own children and I were clustered together in the evenings in this wide hallway at the behest of the Keils, but during the day my boys were urged to spend time with the older boys and men staying at the upper floors. Now they couldn't, not with Jack there.

A fiddle joined the horns. I heard a concertina.

"Can't they rest here with us, in this corner area?" I said.

"I said to send them to the men now. Go. It will be better. We must have some sort of order in this household. I am still in charge."

"If they remain here, Charles can step into the root room sometimes, where the cool air might make him feel better," I said. "I'll gather up some quilts and they can settle on the floor, not spread the coughing through the rest of the house."

"That's a good idea, Husband," Louisa told him. She nodded to me that we should exchange children, I taking Ida from her while she comforted Brita's middle child. Her willingness to support me against her husband both surprised and comforted me.

"She needs goat's milk," I told Louisa. "It would be best if they are close to their mother."

"It's a strange, new place for them, Husband," Louisa told him.

"*Ach*," he said, dismissing us. "You women do what you will. I have more important matters to attend to than sick children," and with that he turned back into his room, as unpredictable as a household goat.

Jack bounded down the steps then, and I realized too late that I didn't want Brother Keil to leave. My taking umbrage with him might have upset him, and now that the accommodations for the Engels had been decided, I had my own troubles to contend with.

"I have the right to see my daughter," Jack said.

"You put her in harm's way, so I don't think you're owed anything more than to gaze on her face, which you are now doing. You didn't like the responsibility of me and the children. You have a farm that ought to have gone to my sons, but you have it. I left everything for you."

"Emma," he began, took a step toward me. I backed up, clutching our daughter between us. She stared at him with wide eyes. "A woman is meant to be with her husband. He has the right to discipline his wife. Scripture says she's to surrender to him."

"Surrender to a husband who treats her with love. You have a habit of referring to the portions of Scripture you prefer," I said, "and inter- preting them so they support you."

"As do you."

One of Jack's manipulative tools was his ability to hit a target with his piercing darts, making me question myself and thus giving him room to maneuver. But not this time. "We are not a matched team, Jack. I regret that I offered up our marriage bargain at all. Not only for what it did to hurt my family…but you too. It pushed you. Ida is the only good thing to come out of it, *ja*? But let's keep her from being pulled and tugged at like a flighty kite. She needs…a solid place to be, safe. She needs to be here."

"Which is why I've returned."

"You're not staying."

He reached to touch her head. She leaned back into my chest but allowed his caress. I shivered and she fussed.

"I'll build a house for us," he said, removing his hand from her hair. "One without the memories of Christian in it, so we maybe could have our own life, put the pieces back together, Emma." A cunning boy's look came to his face. He smiled and raised his eyebrows, as if he were asking me to put my skates on and join him for a swing around the frozen ponds beside the Pudding River.

For a moment I wondered if we could. Maybe he had changed.

But then I saw Andy on the landing, his arms crossed over his chest. It would never work. "The pieces of our puzzle never did fit, Jack. It was a labyrinth of loss."

Behind me I heard the rustle of Brita and her children, the chatter of women in the kitchen. Louisa giggled at something I hoped had nothing to do with us. Everyone could hear our marital discussion. The safety found with others also robbed me of needed private space.

"We could be together again, and with Brother Keil and others close by, I won't be tempted to let you twist my good nature into something foul." He smiled.

"Take her, would you?" Brita said, at my knees again.

"What?" I said, turning to look down.

"Hold her for a moment, please? The…privy makes an urgent call."

"But—"

Brita was already waddling out through the root room. The weight of the second child in my arms brought me back.

Jack said, "Your Kate is as short and squat as that *Zwerg.*" His insult was the perfect nail to hammer my decision tight. Having Big Jack Giesy back in my life on any terms was nothing short of insane. I'd have to ask Brother Keil for wolfsbane to calm me down, or be sent to an asylum if I even considered moving into a house with Jack Giesy. It wasn't worth the price. I slowed my breathing, grateful for the children that weighed against my chest.

"No, Jack." I looked at Brita's child in the crook of my arm as I talked. "You should do what Brother Keil said weeks ago. Leave us and stay gone." He grunted, and I looked up at him. His face clouded again. Somehow the presence of these children in my arms, the music from above, and the smells from the kitchen all served to remind me that I was not alone. The presence of the others didn't have to be an anchor to hold me down but could be a raft to buoy me up.

"You take in vagabonds and circus imps and their kin but want to send me out into the rains? Not even Doctor Keil would do that. No. A divorce is wrong."

"I haven't said I'd divorce you," I told him. A divorce would be one more thing that might separate my parents from me. In this country, regardless of the circumstances, divorced men always got the care of the children. No, I'd never choose divorce and risk that!

Brita returned and took her infant back into her arms. I didn't know her story yet, but she had a way of intervening at the perfect moment. "You said you could awet-nurse my Pearl," she said.

"*Ja,*" I told her. "As soon as I get Brother Keil."

I entered Keil's workroom without knocking and asked him to step out. Patiently, acting calm, I explained again my plight, my need to be free from Jack's pressuring presence. Getting other people to do what you want takes effort. You'd think after my years with Keil back in Bethel, trying to get him to let me go west with my husband, I'd have learned how fatiguing that is. It's a woman's necessity, to name her desires and then find ways to achieve them by meeting the needs of others. I remembered how my uncle, the ambassador in France, wrote of having to think in such ways, organizing certain gestures, looks, and words, pulling them together to create a new image, like disparate fabric pieces forming a quilt. It was all such a puzzle, this living.

Keil looked over my shoulder at Jack, then finally spoke. "He's calm, Sister Giesy, despite a justified distress at being separated from his wife. If he lives with the bachelors and stays away from your boys, he can stay." I opened my mouth to protest, but Brother Keil quieted me. "I decide these things, not you, Emma Giesy. All are welcome at my door."

He looked at Brita and her brood, nodded his head as though to assure himself that all really were welcome, and then he returned to his room.

Jack grinned. "So. I have license to convince you, Wife," he said. "In my timing." He tipped his hat at me in a rakish way, then took two steps at a time up to the main floor. I heard his boisterous laugh as he brushed at Andy's hair when my son ducked beneath his hand and descended the steps to me.

What could I do? I'd need to keep the children constantly within my sight, hen-clucked around me, have them stay in the wide hall near the kitchen where Brita had joined us with her coughing sons. I'd need to wear vigilance like a cape.

"I don't like Jack's being here, Mama," Andy told me later, as we settled in for the night. Christian nodded his head in agreement as he slipped into his bedsack.

"I know. I don't either," I whispered. "But Jack won't hurt you as he did before. There are always people around. And you needn't worry over me either. I'll be fine. We have friends."

"We had friends before, but they didn't help," Andy said.

"You forget Karl," I reminded him as I pushed the cloth beneath his chin. "He helped us. And so did Martin."

Andy nodded. "But I can't be with Martin with Jack up there."

"When the weather improves, building will begin again, and maybe Martin will have his own house soon, and you can go stay with him sometimes. Or maybe your *Opa* and *Oma* will arrive from Missouri and we can live together with them. Maybe Big Jack will leave. Maybe Brother Keil will build *our* promised home. Any number of things will happen to change, Andy."

"So far, most of what's changed has been bad."

"That's the way the walnut rolls sometimes," I said. I brushed his straight blond hair from his eyes. "And besides, we're here together. There's nothing bad about that."

———◆———

Sleep did not come easily for those huddled on the floors in the hallway. Outside, the weather turned beastly cold, and the mighty Columbia and the Willamette River froze over. Adam Schuele, one of the original scouts, made his way to the *gross Haus,* and I heard him and Brother Keil arguing. Such close quarters made privacy a treasure. Adam had given his all, yet Brother Keil kept him now at arm's length. I wondered if Keil held a grudge because Adam hadn't joined the colony in Aurora but had remained instead for a time to help Christian and me and the other scouts still in Willapa. When he left, he'd returned to Bethel, not come here. He'd only recently shown up in Aurora. These acts of independence bothered Brother Keil, though I wasn't sure that's what brought on the intense voices behind the closed door. I closed my ears and thought of pleasant times past.

After the Pudding River went back into its banks, oval pools of water clustered in the low-lying areas and froze into perfect skating ponds. The cold kept us mostly indoors. Men bundled up to feed the animals or to bring in hams from the smokehouses. They couldn't heat the mills up to work, and the logs froze together. The men around Aurora stayed indoors, weaving baskets or using builder's sand to smooth the banisters. They set up a loom in the parlor area. Jack stayed in the house with the rest of them, rarely venturing outside, keeping me and the children stuck in the hall, where I told them stories or made up puzzles to keep their minds clear.

We all bundled up to race to the privy and, shivering, returned.

We did hear of Solomon Durbin in the town of Salem taking a team of sixteen horses with three sleighs attached and driving them across the frozen Willamette River. Someone took a photograph celebrating the winner in a contest to see who could handle the biggest sleigh and team.

"Men," I said, when Helena mentioned the competition and the lengthy sleighing season in the usually temperate valley. "So cold they can't work, but not too cold to compete."

"We women aren't so competitive as that," she agreed.

Through the winter, Brita looked after Ida and Christian, my younger son, while I helped in the kitchen, contributing to the colony as I'd agreed to. A few of the women spoke asides about "extra mouths to feed" or of an "invasion of *Zwerg*," but most of the colonists lived out their belief that it was worthy work to make another's life better than their own: the Diamond Rule, the luster of our Christian faith.

At night, I listened to Brita's stories that made my past and current trials look like puppies playing. She had endured a life of jeers and jokes over things she couldn't control: her small size, her pointed ears, her waddle-walk. One night she quietly told of the death of her husband in a circus fire and her journey to bring her husband's children north from California. They'd lived in a cave for a time, only to have that refuge washed away in the floods. So much loss seemed more than a person could bear, yet she had.

In the *gross Haus,* with the cacophony of coughs from Brita's brood, my own sons soon took ill, and I spent the spring doing what I could to comfort them. Both Martin and Brother Keil drew remedies from the blue cabinet we slept near.

Jack's presence on one of the floors above us cast shadows over my days. I could encounter him on our rushes to the outhouse. I had to serve him meals at the long men's table. At any time his dark looks might turn into actions. I listened for intruding steps in the night, planned activities based on smidgeons of information gleaned at the table to guess where Jack might be. Uncertainty fatigued as much as the hard work of doing the laundry for dozens.

I prayed for my parents' arrival. They'd be the stakes on either side of my family, safe and separate from Jack. I longed for my own home, with locks to restrict unwanted visitors. I hoped that Brother Keil would keep his word and soon build me a house.

"This is such a beautiful day," Brita announced one spring morning. We were bending over, planting beans in plowed fields of black earth.

"It is." I stood and stretched my back. "You're such a hopeful person, Brita, despite all the tragedies you've faced. How do you do it?"

"You can't always get what you want in this life," Brita said. Her smile filled her wide face. "But as any wise *Zwerg* knows, a hopeful soul learns to spin gold from the straw she's been given."

3

A Closer Weave

May 4. I wore Brother Martin's felt hat to keep the sun from my face while dipping water from the barrels to feed the bean plants. Helena clucked her tongue at me, but a hat opens the face while a bonnet is a blinder, and I have enough of those in my life already. I intend to weave a straw hat for myself.

June 10. I wrote to my parents. They've long supported Keil, and I wonder if our staying in Willapa instead of going with him is the reason they do not contact me. I'm trying to find the perfect stitch to hem my need for them while not sounding as though all my edges are frayed.

Dear Parents, Sisters, and Brothers,
    Several days ago Brother Keil received some letters saying that none from Bethel will come to Oregon this year. For me, no news, not even an answer about the letter Brother Keil sent to you in the beginning of this year, where he said it would be helpful if Jonathan would come and take over my personal business. I would have written sooner to you, if several of my children had not taken ill, Christian and Kate. Now the little ones, thanks to God's blessings, are healthy and very active again, but it took many months before they recovered from the nasty fever.
    Dear Parents, I am willing to obey and respect all orders which you gave me personally and the advice for my children's well-being, but you will forgive me if I ask what

*delays you after such a long separation and bitterness for
which I have no explanation? I long for a peaceful reunion
with my good loving Parents, Brothers, and Sisters. How to
arrange that I do not know. But I hope that Brother Jonathan,
if not on his way already, will arrive this summer and will
give poor Keil relief. He has so many worries, the whole town
surrounded, some wondering if our communal ways are a
challenge to them, and Jonathan could help relieve him of
me and my children at least. Most of all, I am grateful for
the daily love and devotion that Keil and his whole family
have shown to me. I wish you to come not for my benefit but
his, when he has so many continuous responsibilities to carry
already. He is hoping my family will give some relief to ease
the situation.*

*Many hearty greetings to my good Parents and my Broth-
ers and Sisters, to my Friends, and everyone who knows me in
Bethel, who remember me lovingly.*

Live well and keep on loving. Come soon.

Your obedient Daughter and Truly Devoted Sister.

*P.S. I almost forgot, Big Jack has been here since Epiphany.
I'm hopeful he'll leave soon as Andy stays with me and goes to
school. I am doing what Brother Keil says to do. Greetings to
little Louisa. We think of her often. I remain your loving
Daughter and Sister,*

Emma Giesy

That summer, while waiting for my parents, I churned butter or toted water from the spring, carrying questions about what I'd done to upset my family so that they'd stopped writing to me. I had left Jack, yes, but I hadn't divorced him. There were only one hundred divorces in the whole territory, or so Karl Ruge had told me when I once broached the subject with him—just in passing, of course. I'd explained to my parents why I'd left him. My brother Jonathan had urged me to come to

Aurora long before I even married Jack, and here I was now, so the problem couldn't be that I'd come to Aurora to stay. They'd always supported Keil. I'd thought my being here would please them.

The crops had been late coming on, as we'd had a very cool spring to follow the hard winter. The wheat crop promised to be smaller than normal, and I supposed in some ways Brother Keil might have been glad that the Bethelites would not be coming this year from Missouri. Feeding them—and housing them—once they arrived promised to be a major task. Yet he lamented their delay as I grieved my parents' silence.

Thousands of new settlers had come into the valley the previous winter, but few of them spoke German. They came from the Ohio Valley and farther east, and some from the rebellion states, so Brother Keil said he felt "surrounded" by those who might see the world differently. People seemed threatened by our sharing of resources. I'd thought that was the point and part of why we invited others to learn more about us, why we helped people as we could, to introduce them to our ways. But I suppose we did want to change other people's ways at least a little; we just didn't want their presence to change ours.

I'd listen to railroad talk at the long dining room table where we served the men. More than thirty thousand miles of tracks marked the country now, and Congress had authorized the Union Pacific Railroad to build from Nebraska to the Deseret country of Utah, where my aunt lived. That rail line would meet up with one being laid eastward from California. More people would come…but apparently not my parents.

"We'll get a spur through here one day," Brother Keil said, as he motioned for Louisa to bring him more coffee. "That will bring us work for the men and industry for Aurora." His wife hustled to him, fluttering over his comforts. Her constant deference to him was not a good model for her daughters, in my opinion, or for other colony girls either. But every now and then she resisted him. Perhaps she'd found that balance a marriage requires. I didn't like eavesdropping on other people's lives. Oh, how I longed for that home of my own!

Big Jack took his seat in the middle of the men, and I kept my eyes averted from his. I worried over our crops he'd left behind in Willapa.

Who farmed it now? Why didn't he go back? I'd give him no satisfaction by asking.

The men nodded in agreement that the railroad would be a good thing for Aurora. I shook my head in wonder. Keil had sent us west nearly ten years earlier to find a new colony site, specifically to avoid the bad influences that a railroad would bring. Now here he was championing it. I'd never understand the thinking of men. Sometimes Brother Keil's enthusiasms centered more on economics than on living a faith-filled life. We didn't even have a church building yet and held a service only once a month. I thought that a loss, even though I took issue with a few of his points of view on religion. Well, perhaps I took issue with his views of economics too. After all, he'd belittled Christian's and my plans for farming oysters as a way to survive in the Washington Territory, and yet it had served us well—until Christian's death.

Again my thoughts turned to Christian. How I missed his strength and vision. I understood Louisa better now, since we had both suffered the deaths of loved ones dearer than skin. *Ja*, she hovered over her husband, but she did not judge me that I failed to hover over the husband I'd been left with. Well, the one I'd poorly chosen.

If my parents would come, if my brother Jonathan could help me build the house and use his good business mind here, the entire colony would benefit. I had to press that point to my parents when I wrote next. They believed in generosity and in the work of Keil's communal society. At least they always had.

I think Brother Keil secretly liked to have us under one roof. He puffed up, sitting at the head of the long table, and faked chagrin when he was called out by local people seeking medicinal help. He'd sigh and say, "*Ach*, the demands," as he pushed himself away from the steaming food, while the women scurried to gather up his tailored coat and bag, several vying to go with him to serve as nurse. If Louisa was in the kitchen, Helena answered his every beck and call, bringing him his pipe or tobacco twist.

"Catie," Brother Keil called out to my daughter as she sat stitching. "Ah, you do such fine work, Catie."

"I'm Kate," she corrected him. But she beamed with pride at his recognition of her efforts.

"*Gut,* very *gut.* You'll make a fine seamstress one day. I'll show you special stitches if you'd like. I was trained as a tailor, you know, *ja?*" He patted her hair and didn't look at all chagrined when I frowned at him, though he did take his hand from her head.

To the young girls and those of marriageable age, Keil told stories, tweaking their cheeks and patting their shoulders as though they were recently out of their pinafores, instead of young woman harboring hope in their hearts. Most of his stories were about women being in service to their community and their Lord, about how they found happiness through these means rather than in marriage. It was a theme he'd been increasingly harping on even though it hadn't worked to keep Christian from marrying me. Now he urged celibacy even to married people. I thought it was renewed effort to keep us all available for the work of building the colony rather than our faith.

I watched to see if Louisa noticed his flutterings with the serving women. There might not have been anything untoward occurring between them, but he did sometimes let his hand linger longer than I thought necessary at a woman's waist when he moved through a crowded group to his seat at the table. I watched looks pass between two mothers when one of the daughters ducked and quickly moved away from Keil as he attempted to pat the braids on her head. And once I thought his face turned pink when a mother slapped his hand as he reached across her to pick up an oatmeal cookie from the pan in the kitchen. Her reaction said more about what part of her anatomy his hand had brushed than about his taking the cookie.

Louisa didn't appear to notice these little indiscretions. If I'd have mentioned it, she'd have defended Keil as she always did. They had found a way to be together all these years. She tittered and laughed overly much at his jokes; in return he allowed her to do *Fraktur* lettering. Each evening she put coals in the pan to make the flannel sheets warm before he slipped into them. I hoped she warmed up her own side of the bed, since she had a bad hip that pained her in the cold weather. When I asked her once, she looked surprised and said, "*Ach,* we don't sleep in the same bed. The hard floor works best for me and gives the good doctor fine rest, what he needs to be fresh to serve so many."

"Many of us colony women sleep alone," I said.

"How else do we wives get so much done," Louisa said, "except if we've had a decent night's sleep?" She didn't see the humor in what she'd said.

I never saw Brother Keil do helpful things for her, at least not the way Christian had for me. I don't think he ever made a gift for her, though I saw him tailor a dress for Aurora's doll, the daughter for whom he'd named the town. Christian had given me gifts of his tinwork, a chatelaine to hold my needles, for example, and a real pearl taken from an oyster. And once, when we were both young, he'd given me a ruffled petticoat that said he understood more than anything else my need to be unique in the midst of so many common threads.

Keil scoffed at such frivolities between a husband and his wife, as I recall. But Christian's gifts had fueled me as coal to a fire. They helped me endure our separations and warmed over the chill of words sometimes spoken in haste.

Even now, as I lifted the chatelaine from the chain around my neck, I could almost feel Christian's presence. My throat tightened. I blinked back tears and stepped back into the kitchen, wiping my eyes with the edge of my apron. I thought my grief had spent itself, but I'd cried more since being here than in those first months after Christian's death.

Of course, the greatest gifts Christian gave me to remember him by were our children. They were his legacy, the one I was meant to take care of.

At the close of the evening meals, while we served men desserts piled high with sweetened cream, several of us women washed the heavy dinner plates. Painted with tiny tea leaves, each one was different, though they were clearly a set. As I wiped them dry, I watched Louisa follow Keil to their quarters on the first floor. He said something and she laughed. He laughed too. *I shouldn't judge what happens in any other couple's bedroom,* I decided. It was a fault of communal living that stitched a married couple too close beside others, without a proper sash between them.

I carried the dishwater out to put into the barrel to be used on the floors later. I sometimes wished that I shared Louisa's oblivion and acceptance. Instead, Keil's actions drove me to think of how to get my girls out from under his roof before my Kate became old enough to notice.

I walked a narrow path, though: Keil might be willing to build my house only if Jack moved into it with me.

I began to wonder if moving elsewhere might be a choice, if I should take that train to some faraway place and begin again. Perhaps I could find employment with a family in Portland, cooking while caring for their children and maybe my own. There were wealthy families there who might want a German maid.

"Emma," Jack said, catching me on my way back into the house. Twilight lingered in the August evening. I stood rigid as a churn paddle at the sound of his voice.

"What do you want, Husband?"

"I've discovered a puzzle," he said. He chewed on a toothpick. "I thought you maybe could explain it to me."

"I've no spare time for puzzles, Jack Giesy. They expect me back in the kitchen to work, where you should be off to as well. Earning your keep."

"*Ja,* earning is the puzzle." He tapped at the air with his finger. "I understand you earned a ten-cent piece for one of your paintings at the fair last year." I nodded agreement before the wariness hit. "A wife's earnings belong to her husband. You must remember that, Emma. What did you do with your profit?"

I swallowed. "They were given over to the common fund," I said.

"But against your ledger page, *ja,* Emma? So you can buy against it?"

"I've only gotten things for my children."

"Not women," he said. "They shouldn't have a ledger page."

Haven't I seen other women's names in the store book? Perhaps not. "Helena has her own page," I risked.

"No, she doesn't. But if she did, it would be because she is a single woman, Emma. Brother Keil let your page slip by, because you behave like a widow when you're not. It's my earnings you'll squander if you select a ribbon in exchange for it. I thought I'd let you know that I know." He yawned then. "I encourage your work, but don't assume you are making gains from it. You'll have to see me if you care to spend it from now on. I'll see to the ledger page to make sure it reflects the truth, so you needn't worry over that detail. Have a good evening, Wife," he said as he turned to go into the house.

I had forgotten the laws of this land. I didn't even own the clothes on my back; my husband did, along with my earnings.

I waited until I was sure it was safe, returned to the kitchen, and made my way to the wide hall to be with my children. I envied Brita for a moment, despite her challenges and losses. She at least could work for herself.

"He's a good one, that Martin," Brita said. We sat together and carded wool brought in from one of the Giesy farms. It was a soothing thing to do before we bedded down. "And your Andy likes him well too. Follows him around when he feeds the chickens on the way to the store to work." I'd noticed that too and sometimes felt saddened that my son preferred the company of Martin to me.

"Seems a waste," I said. "Martin should go to school and become that doctor instead of helping to run a store. Then he could really remove the weight from Brother Keil's shoulders. Maybe then we'd get more homes built."

"Perhaps Brother Keil doesn't want help," Brita said. "People often say one thing and may even believe it, but then they do things that make getting what they wish almost impossible. I should know. I've had a habit of such myself."

"How could that be?"

She shrugged. "I didn't want to be stared at for my…size, but then joined the circus where they paid me to endure the insults. I got the very thing I didn't want."

She wasn't alone. I had wanted independence from Christian's family in Willapa after his death but then made a poor marriage that left me even more dependent on others. Our minds moved our bodies into the strangest places.

Brita didn't want to join our colony or be a permanent part of our family. She had other hopes, and someday before long, she'd move on, she said. Until then, she was grateful for the work in return for the shelter. The colony women assigned tasks to her, including caring for the children. While she looked after my Christian and Ida, keeping them out of Jack's way, I helped cook at the new Aurora Hotel, now serving the stage route. We'd located it in the old house that had been the Keils' first home, at the base of the hill. I wasn't working for Jack, I told myself, but for my children. I checked the ledger and saw I still had a page in my name, but Jack had posted *tobacco twists* on the debit side. I didn't notice any other pages with a woman's name on it, not even the single women.

Karl had opened school in the toll hut, and Andy and Charles, Brita's oldest, were there during the day. When I wasn't at the hotel, Brita was still there, scrubbing pans nearly as large as herself or raking white linen tablecloths across washboards, so the guests would feel pampered when they ate with us. Brother Keil proposed that such exquisite care would make customers stop at our business, even though they were but a half day's ride from their destination in Portland. What but fine German food and excellent service could make them forget how tired they were from riding the stage all the way from Sacramento?

So far, the stages stopped at our site, and we sent people off filled to the brim with our biscuits and bratwursts. I made sure the colony goat was milked so Pearl would be fed, since I'd weaned Ida. While we worked, Brita would tell stories of unusual things, such as chickens that laid blue eggs.

"They're from someplace very warm in South America. I saw them with my own eyes. Sailors from ships sailing into San Francisco had them. Prettiest birds, with no tail."

"That can't be true," I said.

"It is. They're acalled"—she hesitated, trying to remember—"Araucana. Brown and reddish with sprinkles of blue in their feathers. But no tail. Shortened. Like me." She grinned, her mouth nearly filling her lower face.

"Ach," I said. "You tease."

"I don't. You look for them. They'll come this way."

Perhaps because she was an outsider, I found it easy to share laughter and my longings with her. I didn't have many women friends. Mary Giesy was a Willapa friend, but there'd been strain there. Jack had lived with them once. I suspected she thought I'd treated him unfairly by leaving.

"My father would stand for me if he were here," I told Brita one day. "He'd tell Jack it was time to go back. Or my brother Jonathan would."

"Family stands for you," she said. "My family what took me from the orphanage couldn't have been better to me. They chose me, even when they could see what they was agetting."

Family stands for you. It hadn't happened that way for me. I wanted to make it so for my own children.

I enjoyed cooking at the stage hotel, away from Keil and Jack. Some of the guests teased me, and while I was a mother and a married woman, I saw nothing wrong with smiling and letting people know I enjoyed making spinach salad the German way or peeling potatoes or serving freshly made blackberry pies. Food prepared with unhappy hearts causes indigestion, so I wanted to be sure such didn't happen to my guests. I thought of them all as *my* guests, and doing so made my frustration with Jack's power over me less draining.

I eavesdropped on guests' conversations when I refilled their coffee cups or brought out the bread puddings for their desserts. They spoke openly of events happening far away. Gold had been discovered in the mountains east of us, and people expected a rush as they'd had in California. Quite a lot of chattering went on when Stonewall Jackson and General Lee defeated the Union forces at Bull Run for a second time. Someone boasted that Colt was producing more than one thousand guns a day for the war effort, and a new kind of gun had been patented that had ten barrels and could fire two hundred fifty shots per minute. Admiration mixed with worry on men's faces at this talk of the Gatling gun, as they shoved my hot potato salad into their mouths. "At least the army abolished flogging last year," one of the men said, to bring a lighter note.

Keil had sent letters back to the Bethelites, telling them to be careful what they spoke about there. He declared that we were Unionists, one and all, and they should be too, though quietly. A part of me wondered what it must be like for the men to be silent about something that mattered. It was a new path for them, a path we women knew well.

One evening, a lone man with a limp stepped off the stage, settled at the table, and said he was from Missouri. I saw the others show new interest. Missouri was a state of widely divided loyalties, which had seen abolitionist battles even before the war began. Keil had urged the Bethelites to send the young men west, where emotions didn't run so hotly, or so he thought. But we'd heard that Oregon had raised the first cavalry of six companies preparing to enter the war. Maybe the boys weren't safe even here.

"I come from Virginia, first," the man said. He needed a shave, or perhaps he planned to grow a beard. At his table, the men moved away ever so slightly at his mention of one of the seceding states. So far, the people we'd encountered from South Carolina or Virginia had been civil, and we'd heard of no altercations resulting in forced duels or, worse, deaths. But we were wary of arguments, even so far from the fighting.

"Where are you heading?" one of our colony men asked him, and he hesitated.

"Is there a welcome here?"

I watched as the men cleared their throats, diverted their eyes. I waited for someone to say something. Didn't we open our doors to everyone in need, isn't that what Brother Keil had always said? *Isn't that why Jack is still here?*

"We're a Christian community," I said. "Everyone in need is welcome."

I heard a woman gasp from the kitchen. Then my name was called.

"It isn't a woman's place to make such statements," Lucinda Wolfer whispered to me. She acted more upset that I'd spoken than that I'd spoken the truth. She'd come out from Bethel with her husband, John, and two daughters, first to Willapa, but then she'd followed Keil to Portland and on to Aurora. I hadn't noticed in Lucinda the gossipy nature that plagued some women, even though she now chastised me for answering that Virginian. At least she hadn't corrected me in front of the others. "Father Keil determines who's in need and who should be offered refuge. Don't let Louisa or Helena know you said such a thing or even spoke up at all."

"But I was only being welcoming."

"Something a woman should not do in our communal ways."

Just one more thing defining what a woman could do in a family by what she wasn't supposed to. I still had much to learn.

4

And It Will Change

September 6. Dried blackberries on the rooftop. Covered them with muslin to keep the birds away. Filled four baskets. Now have fifteen baskets of dried berries, various kinds.

September 8. Made tomato figs. Used brown sugar Louisa said that I could have. Exposed them in the summer sun. Will take some with us to the fair. Still no plans for my house. Still no word from my parents. My dear Kate now wants to be called "Catie," spelled differently and because Brother Keil calls her that. He influences my children too much.

October 1. We learn of Antietam and the twenty thousand killed there, counting both sides, and well we must. The battle moved into the north but without a win or defeat or so the telegraph tells us. Such is the news of warring.

The vine maple asserted itself through the green with its vibrant red, marking a seasonal shift. We finished harvests, dried fruits and vegetables. Colonists spoke then of the produce they'd bring for exhibit at the state fair. Sometimes in the cooling nights when I curled up with my children snuggled around me on their mats, I felt like carded wool, thick and full of tiny seeds that needed constant combing to get the blemishes out, so the wool would be useful one day. This distance between me and my parents stuck like a burr I couldn't card out.

Begin to weave. God provides the thread. Louisa wrote out the German proverb in her *Fraktur* lettering and hung it in the hotel. I read it every day. My mother had shared it with me as a child. Where was the thread of my life? I wasn't weaving a thing.

"The rats have gotten into the butter," Lucinda Wolfer told me. She showed me a butter block from the octagon cool house, where we kept butter immersed in spring water until we took the blocks for trade. The one she showed me had bite marks and tiny scrapes I took to be where the mold had been held by the rodent's claws. I was surprised the rat had gotten into the water, though I supposed they did swim. I wondered if all of the butter might be contaminated.

"When I have my own place," I told Lucinda, "I'm going to build a buttery at the river's edge, with the sides deep enough down that the rats can't penetrate."

"*Ja,* I have plans for when we build a house too," she said. "But it'll be some time, my husband says." She stared at the rat bites. "We could cut it off and take the remainder to Oregon City and trade it across for butter there," Lucinda said. "It won't hurt anyone if they don't know about the rats."

I laughed. "I can see you explaining to the shopkeeper why you're trading butter for butter. He'll go to the storeroom, change the wrappings, and give you back the same rat-butter you'd brought. After all, 'It won't hurt anyone if they don't know about the rats.'"

Lucinda laughed with me. "*Ja,* I could see that happening in Oregon City, all right. Well then, we'll scrape off where they've bitten into it and use it ourselves. But I'll get another today for our sauce. The idea of eating what the rats left…" She shivered.

We finished up, and that night, after the children were in bed, I imagined my house and its buttery. It would be a double house, not like the Missouri "saddle bag" houses, which were two houses built completely separate and joined by a common middle section. They called the hinge section a "dogtrot" used by both households. Keil's house was somewhat similar to that design. Mine would have no dogtrot. It would have two entrances at the front and two fireplaces downstairs, one in the kitchen and one on the other side of a shared stairwell. The stairs would be enclosed, so people could sit in the parlor while others went upstairs or down, no one being the wiser.

Upstairs there'd be bedrooms on either side of the stairwell, and a hall wide enough to allow trundle beds or cribs for toddlers. Two families or maybe more could live in the house and come and go as they needed, without bothering the other. But they'd be close enough that if one called for help, the other would hear it. There'd be front and back covered porches. And I wanted glass windows, to let the light in and to let me see what dangers might be lurking on the porch. Maybe the Wolfers would move in with us. Maybe Brita. My parents and brothers and sisters.

I got up and found paper that had wrapped one of Ida's birthday presents, now carefully folded for reuse. On it, I drew the plans, deciding that even if Jack never left, even if my parents never arrived, I'd push to have my house be the next one the colony constructed. There'd be a buttery, and I'd find a way to keep the rats out.

———

Brother Keil had a number of entries for the state fair. He'd prepared his strongly medicinal Oregon grape wine once again. He entered dried fruits too, including peaches. He'd gotten the peach trees from a French Prairie farmer who'd brought them to Oregon in the late thirties from the California missions. The leaves made fine green dye for our wool. Several of the young men had worked some of the bulls to halter, so they could show them entered under the Aurora Colony's name.

The animals trailed along behind us as we rode in the wagons, shaking their big heads of the flies. Brother Wolfer sat astride one of his finest horses to enter in the race. We Aurorans didn't have much stock to speak of, so I wondered about the likelihood of an Aurora horse winning a race. I liked the calming murmur of a horse as he nuzzled his velvet nose up against mine, and I wondered why we didn't have more of them in Aurora. I guessed that Missouri mules were our choice because they were such good workers. Always it was about work.

Louisa took her *Fraktur* pieces to show. Some of them reminded me of the punch paper kit patterns, models they were called, that we girls were taught to stitch. "Trust God for Every Need." "God Bless This House." Simple words of wisdom that our fathers would show to interested suitors as indications of our proper training. The words were drawn on paper cards with holes for where the threads should go, and we stitched right over them. I thought that Louisa's *Fraktur* with letter flourishes would make a lovely model for my Kate, and she'd be ready soon to do such work. She had already stitched on a quilt with Aurora Keil. I wondered if my parents still had the paper models I'd made, which I'd hung over the main room door. Thinking of my parents saddened me yet again. I pitched the thought away.

Several women had knitted socks with actual heels in them, rather than the plain straight tube. Very inventive, and more comfortable for a man to wear inside those heavy brogans. We entered skeins of hand-dyed wool, all perfectly carded, dyed, and spun. We had well-fed sheep that offered up their wool. *We.* I said that often these days, *we* of the colony.

I'd had no time to draw or paint in these past months, nor the interest, so when Louisa asked, I told her that I didn't plan to go to the fair, that I had nothing to enter. "You need to come with us, Emma," Louisa told me. "As you did before. Didn't you have a fine time at the fair?"

"But when we came back…there were problems, remember? Jack showed up. We argued…"

"*Ach, ja,* but he is already here now. There'll be many of us together when we come back, and he can do you no harm. He's staying behind. Come with us." I must have grimaced, or maybe I rubbed my fingers as I did when anxious. "Emma. You can't allow past things to keep you from possible pleasantries. It won't be the same. It can't be. You're older and wiser, *ja?*" Louisa said. "You make it different this year. Have a pleasant time with your children. Listen to the band play." She drew in her breath. "I can work an entire day of beating rugs, knowing I will hear music at day's end." She clasped her hands and heaved a happy sigh.

The girls were eager to go, and so were my sons. "We can't buy anything," I said, relenting. "We have no money." I didn't add that even if we did have money, Jack would decide how to spend it. They agreed they'd ask for nothing. We took Charles and Stanley and Pearl too, along with my four, and Louisa and I baked and cooked for us all. With other families from the colony we walked or rode the nearly twenty-five miles toward Salem. We'd spend three nights and be there for the entire second day, always said to be the best.

On arrival, we spread quilts on the grass where we ate and would later sleep beneath a canvas tent. I hoped we'd have plenty to feed the hungry Aurorans with some left over to share with others. Our food would attract people to Aurora, more than Keil's medicinal wine or a winning horse. Sharing food would bring us notice. Selling sausages on a stick would bring in cash as well. Being at the fair had purpose for us colonists, more than just fun.

Women walked arm in arm, in and out of the exhibit barns, and I heard the band warming up. It always amazed me that the tiny piccolo could be louder than the large trombone, its piercing tone uplifting while searing through the drums and bass. Being little didn't mean being ineffective or unnoticed. Brita showed me that.

I walked through one of the tents where someone had brought rabbits in a cage to show. I had Ida on my hip. I pushed Pearl in a cart I'd rigged for her, and she slept now beneath the shady basket weave above her head. I'd seen an Indian woman carrying a child in a board with a woven shade and did my best to duplicate it. I talked to Ida about the bunnies, and she leaned into me, excited and frightened at the same time. Next to the rabbit vendor, foiling my idea that there'd be no surprises, stood a man with odd-looking chickens…without tails.

"They lay blue eggs," he said. Several people around him scoffed when he showed us the shell. One man accused him of dyeing it with blackberry juice. "No, no," he insisted. "This is the color she lays."

I tried to remember the name of the bird Brita had said: *Araucana*.

I must have said the name out loud because the man turned to me. "That is the name!" He pointed. "The woman knows this is true! Yes! The bird has blue eggs, sometimes green."

People moved closer then. I did too. The eggshell was sky blue with tints of green. The chickens strutted. They wore their rust and ebony, ivory and turquoise feathers as though they knew they were unique. The vendor had three birds, and just as Brita had said, their tails looked chopped off. The vendor said they came from South America and were for sale.

"How much would one be?" I said.

"Maybe twenty dollars."

Someone said, "You aren't in the gold fields now."

The vendor responded with a sheepish grin. "Maybe fifteen?"

The eggs would be interesting things to show people and to serve at our hotel table. We'd save the shells for Easter etching...

"I'll buy one," I offered. "But for five dollars, no more." I fully expected he'd come back with ten, but he didn't.

"Sold," he said.

I swallowed at my success. I didn't know how I'd pay.

People wandered away. The vendor pulled up a basket of reeds, opened the cage, and put one of the chickens inside it, laid the flat strands on top. I could see the chicken through the separation in the reeds. Her tiny eyes met mine. I decided to call her Clara. She'd fill that empty place in my heart that Opal, our goat, had left when I'd come to Aurora with nothing but my children.

"You have coins?" the vendor said.

"I don't." He frowned. He'd be upset if our transaction had sent a paying customer away when I couldn't come up with what I'd offered. "I intend to pay with...food." The word came into my head. "I'll bring you food for the time you're here, baked myself. Berries I dried myself. Strudels."

"Fresh bread?" I nodded. "Hmm. I don't really need food," he said, moving to put the chicken beneath his vendor bench.

"Everyone does. That's how your chickens work for you, *ja*? Keep

Clara for me. I wouldn't name her if I didn't intend to pay for her, would I? And before the afternoon is over, I'll bring you a basket of food."

"Five dollars' worth," he said.

"Five dollars' worth."

The chicken would be a communal one. Her eggs would only add to the notoriety of the colony. Keil would like that. She'd pay her own way. And since I'd baked the goodies I planned to trade, I'd pay my own way too. I put Jack's claim aside. Such are the ways we tell ourselves stories. I gave this one a happy ending.

———◆———

Louisa and Brother Keil wandered over the fairgrounds, Louisa a step or two behind her husband. She didn't appear to mind. I wished she did. I watched to see if he took special notice of the women in their finery, and he did, tipping his hat at them with a smile. He was always the showman. A few tall, handsome Indians rode fine horses toward the racetrack, followed on foot by women in their regalia. Young girls strutted by, pretending not to notice the boys who stared at them, as if they hadn't come to the fair just to walk by those boys. One of the colony musicians strode past me carrying his *Ophicleide,* a wind instrument that twisted like a snake up into a bell, running from the ground to well up past his dark hat when he sat to play it. The brass finger keys gleamed in the setting sun, like buttons on a uniform, against the smooth wooden horn.

My boys ran with a kite, Charles at their heels; enough breeze lifted the diamond fabric high in the air. While Ida and Pearl slept, I took out my sketchbook to capture the boys' exuberance.

The act of moving lead across the paper soothed me. I'd forgotten that I took joy in capturing what lay before me. In my mind rose my mother's sharp words about my drawings—she said they had no practical value—Jack hadn't liked my drawings either. *Not here, not now. I must think on good things.*

I kept drawing. I smelled stick candy stiff with peppermint that someone carried past me. I wished that I could bring that scent to paper. I listened to the rhythm of voices around me. I heard a Spanish-sounding man—Portuguese, someone said he spoke; French and English. Brits and Scots and Irish, mostly men, and the clicks and swishes of the Chinook language spoken by the natives gave a mix that made me feel as though I belonged in this interesting if not always predictable world. My sons laughed, and my heart caught in my throat with the sheer joy of it. To see them happy, healthy was a gift beyond measure. *I can see God in this.*

"You're smiling," Lucinda Wolfer said as she plopped down beside me, her skirts billowed out enough to make me wonder if she'd reinforced her petticoat with wild rose limbs. We Auroran women didn't wear hoops as did women on the outside, but we weren't averse to being inventive in our effort to be fashionable.

"Jack is more than twenty miles away. That's cause for smiles."

She nodded. "Watching the *Kinder,* that's restful too, *ja?*"

Kate ran over and plunged without asking into the food basket. "*Ach,* no," I said. "You wait until we're all ready to eat."

"But I'm hungry, Mama."

Kate's constant state of hunger probably explained why Jack's comment about her being a "fat little Kate" had so buttressed my resolve against him.

"Come here," I said, placing my drawing things beside me. My days were well-sewn patterns, and we had scant time for impromptu tying of loose though important threads. I opened my arms to her, and she fell into them. I nuzzled her neck, knocking her straw hat from her head, and in her effort to retrieve it, we both fell backward onto the quilt.

"Mama," she laughed. "You bottom-upped me!"

"So I did," I told her. I helped her stand, brushed at the hem of her dark dress. Her stockings had begun to slip, but she didn't seem to mind. Once I'd wondered if she'd ever laugh again, ever feel safe again, and here she giggled like a normal child. If Brita had been able to come, perhaps she could have set aside some of her bad memories of fairs too. There was no bearbaiting here, and with new friends present, perhaps the memories of that devastating circus fire could have healed a bit.

Beyond our quilt, Andy and Charles had their heads together now, looking at something they held in their hands. A frog perhaps, or maybe a grass snake. The kite lay askew, leaned against their knickered knees. Charles's presence had tempered my son, and while I saw less of Andy when he was at school, following Martin, or off rolling hoops with Charles, I enjoyed hearing his laughter. Now they gathered string for another run with their kite.

I was glad I'd come. Hesitation didn't always mean that what followed would be worrisome. Plans could prevent some difficulties. I should have hesitated more before I married Big Jack; I knew that now, but I hadn't. At some point I'd have to forgive myself for that.

Christian called to Kate then, and she grabbed at her hat, bent to kiss my head, and went running, all thoughts of food forgotten.

"If only all our hunger could be assuaged so easily," Lucinda said. She patted my hand.

"I've some biscuits and strudels I need to deliver," I said. "Some of my preserves and a few things like that. Would you care to come with me?"

"Where are you taking them?"

"I've made a trade for us."

"We could use some Buena Vista pottery. Are you trading for a kraut jug?"

"*Nein.* Colony food for a chicken who lays blue eggs." Lucinda raised her eyebrows. "*Ja,* blue eggs. Think how lovely they'll be on Easter."

"Are you trading rat-tasted butter?" she asked, her eyes laughing.

"No butter. Some beans, but mostly our baked goods. Five dollars' worth," I said.

She never asked if Brother Keil had approved such a purchase. She knew no woman would propose such a thing unless she'd been granted our leader's permission.

———————

When the wagon pulled up the grade toward the Keil house, I had a moment's hesitation yet again, remembering our return from the fair last year. Big Jack had been waiting for me. He'd struck at me then, in front of everyone, and Brother Keil had sent him away. As we walked up the steps to the *gross Haus,* I wondered if Jack would be there this time. It'd be like him, to recall the same event and maybe even attempt to reenact it. Maybe take any earnings from me he thought I might have.

I had to set aside these loathsome thoughts. They did nothing to improve my life and kept me from enjoying the new memories from the day.

Martin met us on the steps. "We need to talk," he said.

"What's happened?"

He shook his head, nodded to the children as though they ought not to hear. He helped unload the wagons and carried Ida in while I brought Pearl. Charles and Stanley chattered to their mother about everything they'd seen. Martin returned, lifted Christian, who had fallen into a sleep so soundly that he could be lifted, carried, and laid down without missing a beat of his snoring.

"Did you have a good time?" Martin whispered to Andy. *Martin sounds so calm. He can't have bad news.*

Andy nodded, and Kate began telling him in her boisterous voice about the monkey who sat upon a wooden music box, then started dancing.

"We need to finish unloading," I told her. "Settle down now." I scanned the area, looking for Jack. All I wanted was to know what Martin had to tell me.

"I'll get Clara," Kate whispered. She ran back out to see if she could lift the basket with the chicken in it by herself.

I had to help her. We set the basket next to her, as she cuddled beside Pearl and Ida on the mats that Brita had laid out for us all. I'd have to build a movable pecking cage for Clara in the morning.

When I came back out to the wagon to get the last blanket twisted around the food basket, Martin stopped me. "Jack's gone back to Willapa. He says 'for good.'"

I caught my breath, put my fingers to my throat to keep me from crying out with joy. "Could my life be so blessed?"

"Karl talked with him on the bridge. He said he'd had enough time in Aurora. Said he's going back where having an ale or two isn't considered demonic."

"Truly," I said. I sat on the lowest step, removed my bonnet. It was like him to do the unexpected. I was so pleased I hadn't wasted hours in anticipating how he could mess up our return. "That's it then? I'm…free," I said. *Can it be?*

I knew I wasn't totally free. I was still married to Jack Giesy. But as the days went by without Jack around, I realized that ambiguous position provided a certain safety too. I was not a woman who'd be sought after by a man. Even if I were, I could easily put off such an adventurer by saying that I was a married widow. That alone ought to confuse a suitor and send him looking elsewhere. I'd already attempted to blend one family into another without success. I had no wish to try again. I could devote my life to caring for my children. If I wanted to hear a man's voice or smell a pipe, I could visit Karl Ruge or walk up Keil's steps to the main floor, where bachelors congregated in the evening, making music, talking.

Jack had taken up so much space in my life that I could hardly imagine a day without worrying about his next move, without defending my children from him. But maybe life did offer strange twists that turned us around like a top. *Ja,* they did.

Late that fall, Henry C. Finck arrived from Bethel, bringing his five children including ten-year-old Henry T (as he was known). The child squinted at the vials in the blue cabinet, reading each label aloud and telling any who would listen what the name would be in Latin. He was precocious, but his love of learning could make him a good pal for Andy.

"We will have the best, most wonderful Christmas this year," Louisa crooned. "*Herr* Finck is a genius with the music. We'll have choirs and a Pie and Beer Band too, not only the Aurora Band. There'll be music for those left behind when the band travels off to dances and such. And he's a widower too, Emma. You think of that."

"Nothing to think of," I said as I stitched. "I'm still a married woman, remember?"

"*Ach,*" she said, waving her hands at me. "I so easily forget."

"If only I could."

A rooster crowed while we served the men their suppers, reminding me that no one had said anything about how I'd paid for my chicken. One of the bachelors said, "He's looking for that Clara of yours, Sister Emma, the one that looks like she was tossed out of the creation oven before there was time to put tail feathers on her."

"She's the way she was intended to be," I defended to the men's laughter.

"She does stand out."

"As Emma likes to," Helena said. She set a plate of ginger cookies on the table and wouldn't meet my eyes.

Everyone liked the blue eggs. They liked the idea of the colony having such a unique chicken. But Helena saw it as yet another way I was being a separate dish in a community that honored blended stews. The colony owned the chicken, this I knew, but I did name her and did build the cage for her. Perhaps Helena was threatened by my having something attached to my name instead of the chicken's belonging to us all.

I thought about that the rest of the evening. The next morning I took Clara out and put her with the other chickens, scratching for worms behind the Keils', and prayed that the hawks would resist the delicacy.

———◆———

As the rains began again that year, Brother Keil arranged for Karl to read Scripture to us twice monthly, but he himself stopped leading worship. Louisa hinted it was his gout that pained him. During worship, we women sat on one side of the big upstairs room, and the men sat on the other. Karl sat at the head, his back to the fireplace. I liked hearing the words but wished we could have sung more hymns as we had back in Bethel. Still, the band sometimes played. Brother Keil liked band music.

After our meetings, I found I wanted to talk, to make the readings relevant for how we lived in Aurora, and not just focusing on way back when the words were first written. When we were in Willapa, Karl and I could have talked like the old friends we are. But here, people clustered around us in the *Haus* and there was no time to speak freely as friends. Karl spent days at the toll hut, but I didn't feel right about visiting him. It wouldn't be "seemly," as Helena was fond of saying. That's what she told me about discussing the readings too.

"It isn't seemly," Helena said, "for us to discuss Scripture, without structure provided by a religious leader."

"My husband will feel better soon," Louisa said. "Then he'll lead us as he has before. Instead, let's use this time together to stitch or card."

In the back of my mind I remembered a scripture about people "hearkening together," but I couldn't name it. I'd look for it in Christian's Bible and then make my case again. If I ever got my own home I'd have a talking time there, or at least invite others to come. I might ask my mother for that verse when I wrote her next. She might respond to a question of faith, if not to my plaintive calls for them to come west. I sat down to do it right then.

———◆———

In November, Brita left us. "It's atime," she said as she folded her children's meager things into the middle of their quilts and blankets. I fidgeted, agitated, maybe envious at her ability to set a goal and meet it. She'd decided some weeks earlier to help a neighbor outside of the colony, in addition to assisting at the hotel. That's where she'd been working the night we'd returned from the fair. The people Brita had gone to assist weren't part of the colony, and so they paid her with currency, even a greenback, said to be in great circulation back in the States. Her new employers worked her hard, and she returned to the *gross Haus* exhausted each night. But she could keep her earnings. She'd make better wages at the Durbin Livery Stable in Salem, once she moved there.

"Aren't you worried about working with such big animals?" I asked.

"I'm just cleaning stalls," she said. "It's warm and inside work, and there's a room my children and I can stay in. I'm close to the ground, so my back doesn't ache as another's might. Besides, there's asoothing to be found around a breathing animal like that. If a dog or chicken or goat is company, why not a horse?"

"But Pearl..." I said.

"The Durbins like to have babies about. The boys can help with feeding and such, and I hope to make enough to send them to school. I'm not a saying it's forever, but for now, we'll be together, and I'll be putting money aside for when the new Homestead Act's set up."

I hadn't heard of this and said so. She told me of the act, which would give one hundred sixty acres to anyone over twenty-one who was willing to farm, build a cabin, and stay for five years.

"I'm saving money so we can buy seed and other things we need," said Brita.

While I had been imagining a house with two sides to share with her (though I'd never expressed it), she had proceeded with dreams of her own.

Andy regretted Charles's leaving. He'd found a real friend in the blond-headed boy. "He was my lookout, Mama," Andy told me. "So we never were surprised by Big Jack."

"His leaving is good timing, then," I said. "Jack is gone. See how God provided for us, all we needed?" Andy nodded, though I could still see the loss in his eyes.

"I'll look out for you," Christian offered. Andy shrugged, but Christian didn't seem to notice. Christian had his big brother back. "Andy's more in-trusting than Stanley or Pearl," my younger son told me.

"The word is 'interesting,'" I said.

"That's what I said," he defended. "In-trusting."

"Well, maybe that's a good word too," I said.

Ida, too, noted the change in our hallway constellation of stars.

"Pearl gone?" she'd ask, her personal doll somehow come up missing. When I explained that yes, Pearl was indeed gone, my youngest child brushed aside the mending I worked on, pulled herself up onto my now-empty lap and demanded in her small but charged voice, "Mama, hold!"

And I'd held her, my chin on her head as she leaned against my breast. "Mama holds," I said. I'd hold my impatience in getting a home, hold my sadness at Brita's departure. Most of all, I'd hold out hope that my parents would join me one day. Until then, holding my children safely was a prayer I lifted up for myself. All families need the glue of someone to hold.

5

Seeking Meaning

December 12. Kona coffee sells in Portland along with crushed sugar. I've no need now for the sugar breaker Christian had the blacksmith make for me. I have happy plans for holiday cooking. Food to heal the sorrowful souls. Clara has stopped laying eggs.

December 13. I let the flour dry on the back of the range all night. My cake rose higher than expected. Perhaps it is a sign of good things to come.

Only Kate appeared oblivious to the departure of Brita's family. The Keil girls pampered Kate the most of all my brood, and they continued after Brita left, playing hiding games with her, letting her go with them to gather eggs or feed the goats. Aurora, who was nearly thirteen and looked more mature than that, showed Kate how to stitch the paper model "In God We Trust," and my daughter insisted they were "wise words" when she showed it to me. A twinge of guilt tweaked me that I'd taught Kate neither how to do the stitches nor nurtured her spiritual life to help her find those wisest of words. The Keil girls were doing it for me.

"It's lovely, Kate," I said. "But why did you sign it 'Catie'?"

"*Ja.* Father Keil says that's my name."

"It's not the one your father and I gave you."

"I like it," she said and pooched her lower lip out in protest.

I loved her independence but resented Keil's latest intrusion into my life. It was probably nothing worth arguing over, I decided. "Well,

I'll still call you Kate," I said with more assurance than I felt. "And that'll be that."

———— ◆ ————

When the annual sickness came, I took a deep breath. This was how our winters wore on. But now I was among people who could help me care for my children if they became ill, as they had that first hard winter. I could be hopeful. Everyone had sniffles. It was part of living.

"The people your little *Zwerg* helped out are ill now," Lucinda Wolfer told me.

"She isn't my little person," I said, "any more than anyone else's."

"*Ja, ja.* I meant no offense."

"Besides, they were healthy when Brita left."

I knew that Brita had worked hard steaming the bedclothes because she told me of the demanding work, the tubs so tall she stood on stools to stir the clothes with an oak paddle.

John Wolfer, Lucinda's husband, that kindhearted man, asked Brother Keil if he shouldn't go and help another family across the Pudding who suffered from the illness, even though it might be smallpox. "It's the Christian thing to do," John said.

"*Ja,* it is that." Keil was on his way out the door to help another household, and he had already been by to treat John's friends. Martin, too, had begun visiting the sick, and more than once Andy asked if he could go along to help. I'd refused him that, fearful of what he might contract. Andy'd scowled as he used to, arms crossed over his small chest and his leather shoes kicking at the sideboard. "You're prone to sickness," I told him. "It wouldn't be good."

"They've had what medicine I can give them," Keil told Martin and John as they stood before the blue cabinet. Both healing men were filling their leather medicine bags. Andy glared at me with darkened eyes. "It's mostly tending now. You'll need to wash the linens, John. Use soap but don't breathe in the steam. Keep the windows open to air things out, and don't get too close to them. You understand? And always wash your hands afterward. We know now that helps. That doctor who came from the States in '52 with wagons to Portland made everyone wash their hands and boil the water, and they lost not a soul, though cholera raged around them. You wash your hands." John nodded and left by the root room door.

"I hope this isn't smallpox," Brother Keil said to Martin. "It could race through Oregon as it did of old." Brother Keil had taken to wearing a frock coat he had tailored himself. It was the fashion now, but it still surprised me that he'd take the time to be in style. He checked the stitching on the cuffs.

"We'll do what we can," Martin said. He touched Andy's hair. "Your mother's right. You stay here and keep those sniffles from getting worse. When you're better, you can help."

Andy looked up at me. "When the sniffles are gone." His face relaxed, and the kindness of his heart, wanting to help others, showed through his eyes.

John Wolfer traveled back and forth to assist the ill family but finally returned to stay when the man and two of their children died. The man's wife and another child appeared unaffected.

"You did your best," Brother Keil told him in the workroom. I could hear them as I tended the children in the wide hall. "And you've not become ill, so this is good. If the cold weather comes, it'll freeze out the disease."

"We can hope," John told him.

I wanted us to do something that wasn't weighted with illness and loss. I'd begun to realize that I grieved Brita's leaving. In the past when my heart felt broken, I'd slammed the door on it, then opened it later to a slug in the garden named Jack. This time I wanted to recognize my sadness and do something thoughtful rather than impulsive. I looked for a happy task. I decided to begin furnishing the house I didn't have yet. I found four, empty wide-necked bottles and solicited Louisa and Lucinda Wolfer's help.

"We really have so many other things to do," Louisa said.

"But music makes you happy, and making these glasses will make me happy."

"Drinking glasses?"

I nodded. "Put the leather thong around here," I directed. "That's where we'll want the top of the glass to be, right at the base of the neck. Now I wrap a good cord twice around the bottle."

"Have you done this before?" Lucinda asked. She looked doubtful.

"I watched the men do it in Bruceport," I said. "And because it takes three, I got to help. I remember the details."

"Let's pray you do," Louisa said. She straightened her apron and set her feet, as though she was readying to catch a pig before it ran between her knees.

"You hold this end of the cord, and, Lucinda, grab the other. When I say so, take turns pulling back and forth on your cords as fast as you can, but keep the bottle straight."

"I don't understand how this will get you a glass," Lucinda said.

"The bottle will heat up where the cords are pulled," I said. "Then when the glass is hot…I'll grab hold of it to know…I'll drop a stream of cold water where the cord is, and when you remove the cord, the bottle will break just above the leather, and I'll hold a glass in one hand and a candlestick holder in the other. It's *gut*!" I sang out.

We set about our tasks, the leather thong marking the top, me with the cold water ready. Louisa pulled first; Lucinda pulled back. They seesawed and we laughed until the cord smelled hot. "Reminds me of a taffy pull," Louisa said.

"Now?" Lucinda said.

"Let's get it good and hot," I said.

A tiny trail of smoke rose up, and I lifted my apron bottom to hold the bottle. With my free hand I dribbled the cold water, set the ladle down, then took hold of the top.

"*Ach, Jammer!*" I said, shaking my hand of the stinging heat.

"Emma," Lucinda chastened. "Are you burned?"

I shook my head no, reached for a quilted pie pad, and held the top as the glass separated like a yolk from a perfectly tapped shell. "My first furnishings for my new home," I cheered.

"Well, I'll be," Lucinda said. "Who would have thought? I've turned a tin can into an apple corer by sticking it into hot coals to cut off the top, but I've never turned a molasses bottle into a drinking glass."

"You are such a clever woman, Emma," Louisa said, smiling.

"Someone told me once you had to spin into gold the straw you were given," I said. "Let's see how many more we can make. Some for the colony, of course."

———

Two days later, Lucinda became ill. She was followed by Brother Keil's son Elias, a big, strapping boy who helped with the animals. And then Gloriunda Keil's giggling lessened. Aurora lay panting beneath her mother's cooling forehead rag. Louisa, Keil's oldest daughter, complained of headaches, and then the cough came. Amelia took on suffering next, her frame as slender as a spring sapling overwhelmed by quilts. We were tending them all at the *gross Haus*, steaming linens, making sure none of the healthy children were nearby to breathe in the harmful mists. Spoonfuls of laudanum got handed out like candy to help ease their discomfort. I feared that the blue cabinet would soon be empty. I wished again my children were in their own home, away from the spots and the coughs of so many.

Even more, though, I was afraid that the Keil children would die. The Keils had already lost a son, Willie, who they'd carried across the plains in his own casket and buried next to my husband in Willapa. Brother Keil had preached on more than one occasion that a child's death spoke more to the sins of the parents than about the child. I'd never understood such thinking, and to speak it at a child's funeral seemed as cruel as the death itself. I ached for Louisa, who went from bed to bed to comfort them. Five children ill. She took few moments even to eat, spending all her time and energy attempting to get her children to sip beef broth and hold it down. Reddish spots formed on their chests. Their youngest, Emanuel, Louisa relegated to our hallway area, since he showed no signs of illness. Frederick Keil, already a young man in his twenties and not coughing, stayed with the bachelors on the top floor. I thought his mother might have appreciated his assisting her, but it wasn't likely he'd offer and Louisa wouldn't ask. She'd already lost one son to illness.

"Those ugly boils," Louisa said. I'd just come downstairs from the bedroom where Lucinda convalesced.

"Don't they mean that the pox is taking its course?" I asked. "Isn't that a good sign?"

"Oh, I pray they'll get well now," she said. "I do." She said it with a wail. "What could I have done to bring this on? What?"

I reached to touch her hand. We Germans weren't known for demonstrations of affection, and the wartime Sanitary Commission urged people not to touch another's clothing during times of illness, but comfort sometimes required an abandoning of the rules.

"You didn't do anything," I told her, relying on my understanding of the gift of grace. "Illness…happens. It isn't brought on by a parent's behavior or as punishment. How could it be as punishment? We've already been forgiven for our many sins, remember?"

Louisa shook her head. "*Nein, nein.* There is reason for everything. Look at Job."

"But not everything is reasonable," I said. "Christian's death wasn't reasonable, drowning to save another who saved himself. Your Willie was too young to die, too good, and yet he did. That's not reasonable, it just is."

"*Ja,* that's why I fear this. My husband believes the sins of the father are given to the children."

In this case I thought Brother Keil couldn't place blame on the sins of the *mother.* Surely he wouldn't. But I knew Louisa heard it that way. She'd carry the blame. We all did when someone we loved was in distress, wondering what we might have done differently to prevent it.

I stood beside her, my arm around her waist now. She was taller than I was, but she leaned for comfort into my smaller frame. Her ribs felt as thin as knitting needles. I wanted to say something to encourage her. I tried to remember what Karl Ruge had said after Christian died. I'd trusted that someone who cared for me on this earth could be the hand that reached out to keep me from falling. Then a psalm came to mind. *"Behold, the eye of the LORD is upon them that fear him, upon them that hope in his mercy.... Our soul waiteth for the LORD: he is our help and our shield."* I recited it softly to Louisa.

"*Ja,*" she whispered. "I'll hope that God is merciful to end our suffering." She cried then, against my shoulder.

To end suffering. Theirs and my own. I prayed for an end to the suffering of my friends. Our own healing often came when we prayed for others. Karl had told me that too. After a time, Louisa dabbed at her eyes and put the cloth in the basket where we kept all used linens.

"We can transform things," I told Louisa. "We stitch tiny scraps into comforting quilts, spare and splendid in their beauty. We make glasses out of old bottles. We take sad times and find the threads of wisdom there and weave it into the next generation. We're alchemists, we women," I said. "We change things."

"*Ja,* but Eve turned a lovely garden into a place of separation," Louisa said.

"We need to think of hopeful things, Louisa." I took a deep breath. "For now," I said, "let's trust that God will change us through our prayers, *ja*? We'll pray the sicknesses of hearts and bodies will pass over and only small scars will be left behind."

On November 27, we learned that Solomon and Isaac Durbin's livery in Salem, where Brita had gone to work, had burned to the ground.

On the same day, my parents arrived.

They stepped out of the ox wagon on a cool day with misty rain beading onto our wool cloaks and dresses. I'd come out of the house through the root room door to bring in a bucket of rainwater, breaking loose the lace of ice around the edge. I looked up, saw the wagon, and recognized my mother. I was speechless. Raindrops tap-tapping on leaves filled the otherwise still air.

My mother walked to me, wrapped her arms around me, and patted my back, not long enough for me to be the first to let go, but firmly enough.

"You look well, Emma," she said, surprise in her voice. Then, "*Gut.* That's *gut.* Where are your children?" She looked around. "Ah. So, this is your Andy." She pointed with her chin, past me to where the children had once again followed me out. They must have seen the wagon through the main floor windows.

I gathered up words. "Say hello to your *Oma,*" I told Andy, pushing him forward to his grandmother. Andy shook her hand. Kate curtsied, without my even telling her. "This is Christian," I told her, introducing my younger son, who had turned four in April. "And Ida, the baby, is inside. We should go in, to get out of this weather."

"Jack's girl," my mother said. Water misted off of her felt bonnet.

"My girl," I corrected.

"Your Christian has his papa's eyes. Kind eyes. Well, all the brothers and sisters have his eyes, don't you think so, Mr. Wagner?" It's what she called my father. "Ida has brown eyes too?"

I shook my head no. My father nodded agreement to my mother's words. He hadn't reached out to hold me, and so I held back too, my fingers making circles against my thumb pads. I couldn't have borne it if I'd reached my arms to him and he'd stood rigid as a backsaw, cutting through my hoped-for warmth. I was glad I held a pail in my hand. Then my brother Jonathan greeted me with a bear hug, around bucket and all. "Sister," he said. "You finally made your way to Aurora."

"You too," I told him. I smiled. "Has it changed much?"

"*Nein,*" he said. He gazed around. "Jack told us where you'd be staying."

"You fooled me with your grand words about Aurora," I told him, ignoring the reference to Jack. "You described an Eden here, but it isn't."

"*Ja, ja,*" Jonathan said. "But Eden is in the mind too, Sister. So it becomes what you make it, *ja?* What your mind's eye brings to it."

" 'I think myself happy.' "

My mother nodded. "From the book of The Acts," she said.

"It can be done, Sister," Jonathan said, "with faith." He held his index finger up to the air like a teacher giving me a good grade. "It can be done."

I was reintroduced to my younger brothers and sisters then. William had been four when I left Bethel; he was nearly fourteen now and towered over me as he asked if they could carry things inside.

"*Ja,*" I said. "Go right in through there. Ask for biscuits in the kitchen. I'm sure you're hungry, *ja?*"

He nodded and moved past me. Louisa, sixteen, stood slender and pale. She held her head at an angle, and one eye drifted off to the side as she smiled at me. Johanna, eighteen, nodded and said with no nonsense, "Sister," then took Lou's arm, following William inside. Kitty, as she called herself, was twenty and had always complained in her letters about the size of her hips, but I envied her robust roundness. Beside her, I felt insignificant as a string beside a rope. She was lovely. Her eyes held adoration, and I felt my face grow warm.

Another woman I didn't recognize stood beside Kitty. She stood back from the crowd. Her dark hair parted in the center, and her skirts billowed out from a waist as thick as a walnut trunk. *How can Kitty think herself big compared to this woman?*

"This is our foster daughter," my mother said. "Christine's her name." She curtsied toward me, her back as straight as a ladle. Her skirts made a hush as she bowed.

"Your...foster daughter?"

"I wondered how you'd look after all this time," Kitty interrupted. She'd closed the gap between us, grabbed my narrow shoulders, and held me at arm's length, then pulled me into a closer hug. "And now I have two older sisters. Isn't that grand? You look young as a twig," she said. "You've been married twice and me not even once." She rolled her lower lip out, the way Ida did when she didn't get her way.

"*Ach,* Kitty," my mother chided her. "How you worry over nothing."

David Jr. was twenty-two and, like my oldest brother, Jonathan, a grown man with a full, dark beard. He stood beside the team, absently rubbing the harness. Both of them began gathering things up out of the wagon, David Jr. saying he'd take the ox team to the barn if I'd direct him.

I pointed toward the ox barn down in the village, then said to my mother, "I didn't know you'd fostered a child. A person. Taken in a child when you haven't even written…

"Christine." I nodded to her, my stomach flummoxed indeed.

"She had a need; we could meet it," my father said at last.

"Yes. Of course," I said. "That's what we Wagners do."

In the midst of my confusion, I still managed to warn them then about the illness. It was everywhere in the country, but at least here we kept precautions in the *Haus.* I thanked Kitty for writing to me and hoped I didn't sound wounded that my parents hadn't. I invited them to sleep inside.

"Oh, we'll stay in the wagon," my father said. "So don't drive it away, David. It surely can't rain like this all the time." To me he said, "We're used to the wagon. Slept in it while visiting your aunt in the Deseret country."

"But there's room here," I insisted. Then thinking that maybe they didn't want to stay where I was, I added, "Or you could stay with the Snyders. Or at Adam's, though he lives a good seven miles out. You boys could bed down with the bachelors on the top floor." I couldn't imagine them spending one more night in that wagon. "I wish I had a home for you to stay in," I said. "But there were more important things happening here than building a house for me." I said it cheerfully. I didn't want them to think I complained. "Then the illnesses…," I said. "No one has had much interest in doing anything except nursing the sick."

"Another reason for us to go elsewhere," my father said.

William had come back out, holding a biscuit. "Oh, let the children spend the night inside," my mother told him. "And I'm going in out of this rain to see Louisa and Helena at the very least."

"And to meet Ida," I told her.

"*Ja*. To meet Jack's Ida." She sighed but patted my arm as she walked by. Christine, my new sister, followed close behind.

Inside there were greetings all around. Even Keil came out of the sickroom where he'd been attending his ailing children. He held my father in a bear hug. Neither man spoke a word, and they cleared their throats and looked at the floor when they released each other. *They hold affection for each other, so it's something I've done that kept my parents from coming here.* Amelia, looking somewhat improved, descended the steps and hesitated. Frederick's face lit up. He'd not taken ill, and neither had Emanuel, but it is a weight, I think, to be healthy while watching those you love suffer.

"She recovers," Keil said, nodding his head toward Amelia.

"You can stay here," I assured my family.

"*Ja*, you must, David. We have much to catch up on," Keil said.

"Well…you boys bunk for the night in with the bachelors, as your sister suggests," my father told them. "Your mother and I will remain in the wagon."

"Just until we build you a house," Brother Keil said. "It is so good to have you here, David. *Ja*, this will be good."

My father grunted in that way he did before he said something he thought might be disagreeable. "We'll stay until we find our own property, Wilhelm."

"You're not going to live in Aurora?" I blurted.

"We'll do better on our own."

Keil took that poorly. Perhaps he was already worn down by the smallpox; or perhaps it had something to do with old memories, like the time when Adam Schuele had returned. He wore a puzzled look when he turned away. He said nothing more, walked back toward his workroom.

"Jonathan will stay. He's prepared to help manage the store," my father called after Wilhelm. "But we are too many to add to your burdens here, with the children ill and all. We'll make our own way. Perhaps find land to homestead."

I didn't think Keil was listening. But I was. "Would you…that is, would you allow me and my children to come with you, then?" I asked. I'd spoken a thought out loud and heard it myself for the first time. It wasn't good timing.

Keil reentered the room, his eyes boring into mine. "We have not made life here good for you, then, Sister Emma?"

"*Ja*. I mean, no, you have been very good to me and my family. But as my father notes, many mouths to feed are burdensome."

"What should we do with these, *Frau* Giesy?" One of the newer girls came down the steps carrying dirty linens, unaware that she was interrupting.

"Steam the linens well. Maybe put some lavender in the water to make it smell pretty for the Keil girls. Don't inhale the steam."

"*Ja, Frau* Giesy," she said as she hurried out to the washroom. Her red and green coverlet offered bright color in an otherwise drizzling day.

"You should think twice about leaving," Keil said to me. "This communal place has served your family well. Or do you so easily forget? Did you not request a home?" He stared at me.

"You promised me a home, but—"

"I've had things on my mind, *ja*? Are you so impatient and self-centered as to begrudge a man that? What more can we do for you!" He turned and closed the door to his workroom.

I wanted to remind him that I'd worked very hard to pay my way here, only to have my husband assume my earnings. I'd waited a long time for a home that didn't appear any closer to being constructed. Now here was my family. How could he object to a family gathering itself together after so long a separation? But of course he was right: I was thinking of myself and my family, and not the suffering of his.

I looked at my father. I felt a hopefulness that even without knowing the why of our separation, my family would stand with me. I was not alone.

"I'd say you were settled in well here," my father said. "You seem to be able to direct people." He nodded toward where the girl had passed by with the linens. "And Keil obviously thinks your being here is of use.

I wouldn't want to interfere with your successful arrangements. We'd best find a place apart. Come, Mrs. Wagner," he told my mother. "We'll get us biscuits and warm up by the fire and then settle in for the night. Christine, Daughter, you're welcome too. You're family."

My *sister* nodded at me, then followed them into the kitchen. I tagged along behind, like a beaten-down puppy.

6

An Elevating Purpose

My friend Lucinda Wolfer died just a few days after my parents arrived. The smallpox from the family John cared for had made its way to his very own bed. Grieving with John and Lucinda's family kept me from pursuing Brita's fate at the burned-out livery in Salem, but it also took my mind from the unease between me and my parents.

I wished we'd had a church where we could hold ourselves together in our grief. I missed the bells and almost told Helena so. She had so much wanted the colony to build a church before we built a single other dwelling. I hated to think it, but she was right. In Bethel, the bells had rung out for glorious occasions, but also for funerals. It was a fitting requiem for lives lost, the bells tolling like the years, a reverberating silence when the last clang had rung. Lucinda had been a good friend, and I felt that somehow the tiny *Schellenbaum* bells tinkling in its standard in the drafty room were not enough to tell the world of our great loss.

"I've found ways to not worry so much over the unexpected," I told Karl one day when I brought hot soup to him at his toll hut. During the winter months, after school, I risked wagging tongues by taking sustenance to him before dusk. Boiling the onions to arouse more flavor from the potatoes, I remembered my mother saying that as people grew older, they longed for intensive tastes. I had to skip over puddles and walk on the spongy grass and balance my hand just so, since my fingers hadn't healed well after one of my bouts with Jack. Still, I kept the soup kettle level.

"All my worrying over what I'd do when Jack came here, or what he'd do while he stayed, came to nothing," I told Karl. "He up and left—

after reminding me that by law, he deserved all my earnings." I took a deep breath to wash the disgust from my voice. "I'm sure John Wolfer followed Martin's and Brother Keil's advice for caring for the ill, but Lucinda died anyway. My parents finally arrive, but there is still this strain between us. It doesn't seem fair, any of it. I told Louisa that not everything had a reason, but I'm having trouble believing that myself today."

Karl nodded. "*Ja,* it is good to come to that place. Death and uncertainty are a part of our lives. We wrap our grief with good memories of what encouraged us; they remind us that we live through such things. In the unpredictability, that's where the Spirit comes to bring us comfort."

"I wish the Spirit wouldn't wait until I'm miserable," I said.

"*Ja,* you hear His voice in the calm too, not just the storms, but we have to learn to listen." I looked at the tin ladle I'd brought with me from the hotel. It had an emblem, a leaf, at the back. I recognized it as one that Christian had made. I'd found it, now among the common drawer utensils. I'd considered keeping it out for myself but didn't.

"What is left to do then is to find meaning, Emma, not a reason. To live a life despite worry or planning against disasters. Things will happen. Worse would be to let fears of death or disappointment frame our days. We are placed here with desires. *Ja,* desires," he affirmed when I lifted my eyebrows. "It is part of our journey to discover what those desires are and then to find a way to live them fully as intended. That's why we listen."

"I only wish suffering weren't so much a part of living," I sighed. "Surely that's not a desire for life."

"That's what family is for," Karl told me.

"Family is for suffering?" I asked. "Well, that explains a few things."

"*Nein, nein.*" He laughed. "Family helps us through our suffering."

I considered that, then replied, "I'm not sure my family understands that's part of their task. I'd hoped that with them here, my life would be easier. But instead…"

He whittled as we spoke, though I noticed he had a Shakespeare book open on his table. Next to it lay a soft journal called *The Atlantic Monthly.* He never said I'd interrupted his reading, but then, he wouldn't.

"Each day events that trouble you can draw you closer to Providence, Emma." Karl always came back to Providence's place, never passing judgment, though, when I failed to recognize it on my own. "Can you see God weaving through your confusion?"

It was a difficult question for me to answer. He'd asked me that before, when Jack arrived and then was sent away. I did think I'd seen protection, with friends who had reached out to me, with my having the courage to risk leaving Willapa to come here. There my husband's family had stepped away from me, drawn a veil over what they didn't want to see. Here the colony had kept us from Jack's harm. The Aurora community had allowed me back, even opened their hearts to me, in that reticent German way of touching with a nodded head more than embracing arms.

"God is there, Emma, present at the end of a thread, pulling us toward Him. And if we ask ourselves in every situation how He is working in that experience or even our worry or disappointment, then we can feel that tug on the thread."

"I suppose I'll know that it's not me, hung up on a twisted twine that will simply break if I pull back too hard?" I said and smiled.

"*Ja.* You'll know. If you let yourself."

"There's grace in that thread, I suppose."

He handed me a wooden doll he'd carved for Ida, then bent to slurp his soup. "*Gut,*" he said. "Just the right amount of pepper too."

I left, strangely reassured. Only later did I remember I hadn't asked him what it might mean that my parents had fostered an adult child. I probably couldn't have said it without petulance pouting from my tongue. Maybe God was in my forgetting.

———◆———

The suffering of the Keil children did eventually end; but for those who cared about them, our suffering did not. Nineteen-year-old Elias Keil died first, followed by Louisa. She was eighteen, close to the age of

Kitty. Amelia suffered on, but Gloriunda died the same day as Louisa, just short of her sixteenth birthday. And then Aurora, amiable, adorable, admirable Aurora, passed away on December 14. Aurora, the dawn, was thirteen.

Kate was inconsolable. She was nearly six now and old enough to feel the pain of loss, especially of her friend Aurora.

"She's sleeping, Mama. Wake her up." Kate hiccupped from all her crying. We stood at the doorway of the Keils' large room, on the second floor above his workroom. I had my hand on her slender shoulder, keeping her from entering. Louisa knelt at Aurora's bedside, still as a blue heron. That bird quilt Aurora had stitched now lay across her, the reds and blues splashing in each block like spring birds against a stormy sky. They moved as through the air across Aurora's still form. Soon we women would help wash the body of this latest child to die, and wrap her in the loving folds of quilts, and then place her in the ground. My mother and sisters would work at my side. I'd sent them word.

Though she insisted that Aurora was sleeping, Kate must have known it was more than that. She cried so hard, but still she hoped. I didn't want Kate worrying about going to sleep or fearing she might not wake up when she went to her mat. "No. She's not sleeping, Kate. She's died," I said.

"Is it like when the tomato died because we didn't water it enough?"

"Something like that, only she didn't die because of anything you or I or her mama and papa didn't do."

"Is she with Papa?" To this I concurred, grateful that once again I believed in the words I'd spoken to my daughter about when we'd see the Keil children again.

"What's heaven like, Mama?" Christian asked me later.

"We don't really know," I said, brushing his blond hair from his forehead. Kate sat up, turned her head to me. Her eyes were swollen. "But let's imagine that for our beloved Aurora, it's a place where young girls quilt, all day long, because she loved to stitch, remember?" Kate and Christian both nodded their heads. "And she never has to take any stitches out, and there's always enough material to make the perfect block and border; always another one to piece together, with each one telling Aurora's story."

"Are there people around?" Kate asked.

"Chattering like squirrels. Outside a choir is practicing, and Aurora is healthy and well and happy, surrounded by those who love her, who sit and stitch beside her."

"When I see a quilt, I'll think of Aurora," Kate said.

"When I see birds, that's when I'll think of her," Christian said. "She liked birds and got mad at me when I brought one down with my sling shot. I didn't mean to. Well, maybe I did, but she sure got mad."

"Remember the good things, Christian. She'd like that."

We buried the Keil children in a fresh graveyard on the hillside above the *gross Haus*. Lucinda had been buried in the Aurora Cemetery, in the dip of the valley, but Keil wanted his children closer to "where the church will one day be."

Louisa clasped in her arms the bird quilt Aurora had so beautifully stitched. "She worked so hard on this," she said. "See here, where she poked her finger. There's a little bloodstain on the pink bird. I forgot to tell her that it would have come out with her own spittle on it. No one else's will take blood from wool, only the one who poked herself." Louisa's lips trembled. "Here's where she made a mistake and started over." She fingered tiny white stitches that formed a *V* against the madder red block. "So many things I never got to tell her. Or Elias or Gloriunda or Louisa." She whispered that last name. "Oh, Emma." Her eyes grew large, and I could see that the reality of her own death became clearer too, with the unnatural outliving of her children. As I held her, the rough wool of Aurora's quilt brushed against my cheek.

Brother Keil did not preach his usual sermon about the sins of fathers being passed on to children. He could barely speak at all, his grief so raw, his throat constricted by his tears. Louisa stood beside him in the cold, holding him up as she balanced at his elbow. The cardboard of her black bonnet sagged to hide her face. Twenty-two-year-old Frederick stood on Keil's other side, while nine-year-old Emanuel huddled against Louisa's skirts. Amelia still wasn't completely recovered and remained at home.

The band played a funeral dirge made all the more morose by the accompaniment of drizzling rain. John Wolfer, still reeling from his own great loss, Karl Ruge, and several other men, including my father, carried forth the scriptures for the day. Adam Schuele stood off to the side. Whatever rift had split him and Keil was still continuing, but he'd put it aside to grieve with his old friend. I looked around. We were not alone in our sorrow. So many in the outside community beyond had died of the pox as well, and I wondered if they had such arms of comfort to surround them.

Every death brought Christian's back for me. In mourning him, I'd turned inside, hoping to mend the tears in my heart alone, praying there'd be no more sorrow. But there always is. Loved ones left. Friends departed. I'd have to dare to make new ones. I'd come to see that it was the mark of our character, how we let others be the patch in our lives when we felt the most torn apart. If only I could remember it.

———◆———

In the weeks that followed, Brother Keil walked the halls at night, came to his workroom, and puttered there until early morning. His face wore a vacant look, and when people requested aid, he sighed heavily and sent them looking for Martin. He didn't come out often to the blue cabinet near where we slept to select vials or healing potions nor put any new concoction inside. Instead he stayed in the room, surrounded by healing herbs that did little for his soul. I wondered if he blamed the herbs for failing to heal his children, or if he blamed himself. Or God, the way I once had. He never said.

He discouraged Louisa from entering his workroom, but did allow Helena to come in once or twice. Louisa would look expectantly at Helena, who shook her head sadly when she came out, often carrying a pot of tea that had cooled without his having tasted of it. In the morning, if he did leave his workroom, Keil's eyes would be rimmed in red.

Helena finally coaxed him to join us at the large plank table for a meal one day in January. He ate but failed to brush breadcrumbs from his beard and the frock coat, now stained. Louisa tried to talk him into changing it, "to brush the soil, Husband." But he resisted, rubbing the frayed edges of the hem. He'd worn that coat when he nursed his children, held their frail bodies to his chest. Perhaps he thought that taking it off would break the bond he still felt with them.

I remembered wearing Christian's clothes after he died, and the comfort of that scented cloth.

Men came to ask Keil about the mill contracts or the purchase of horses or selling a wagon or an order for barrels. They left shaking their heads and talking of his "hollow eyes." If they had some question about finances or land, they found him disinterested. "Do what you will," he said, waving them away with his hands.

Even my father was unable to rouse him. He came out of the office and told my mother it was like "talking to a post."

"Maybe you and Adam Schuele together could get him interested," I said.

"We're in his craw, old Adam and me," my father said.

While Keil grieved, my father, David Jr., and William spent their time scouring the area for the perfect land to purchase. Somehow my family had means to buy, without the colony's help. I wasn't sure how my father had arranged that—he must have sold property back in Bethel or had private contracts we'd never known about—and so far we had yet to be alone so I could ask him. His silence, with his presence so near, was almost worse than when we'd been separated by a thousand miles. At least then I could make up reasons why I hadn't heard from them: the letter had gotten lost, Lou's health took much of their time, they were busy helping manage things at Bethel. Once here, I could see that my wish to bridge our differences was not a bridge he wished to cross. I had thought I'd find a time to sit with my father and chip away at the wedge between us, but his physical presence hadn't opened that door. I'd have to open it myself.

We did not celebrate Christday that year. No sweets or treats, no band playing songs to make our feet tap. Even the boys' and girls' choirs did not practice their singing. The Feast of Epiphany that others in the surrounding community might celebrate in January was a day like any other in Aurora. Our community felt like a backwater—water swirling in one place. Only a flood would wash new water in and remove unwanted debris.

In the spring, Henry C. Finck decided to plant an orchard at the far edge of the village, up on a point not far from Keil's house, but on land deeded to the musician rather than the colony. Like my parents, he seemed to have independent funds. He and his children set about planting apple starts he'd purchased from Luelling. He had a dozen varieties, from yellow bellflower to Rhode Island greening and my favorite, rambo. He had plans to sell the apples in California. But every day, he came by to visit Brother Keil, encouraging him with talk of music. He said they ought to order bells for the church that would be built one day. Keil apparently said nothing, and Henry C would come out of the room, and if another man was waiting, they'd talk for a time.

Henry C and Karl Ruge spoke of education, since they were the only university graduates at the Aurora Colony. Keil had hoped Christopher Wolff would come from Bethel and bring his university expertise, but so far, he hadn't. They had camaraderie at least, Henry C and Karl. I served them hot coffee with cinnamon buns swathed in butter and envied their discussions, while most of what we women explored as we sewed or sipped steaming black tea was mundane, the merits of yeast over saleratus or the best cork bluing recipe to use.

Even though Brother Keil and Louisa still had each other, they slipped past each other in the wide halls, sometimes without even nodding their heads in acknowledgment. Once or twice "tailor Keil" entered our sewing room, where we women stitched on quilts or patched and mended. He had a fine eye for design and had always encouraged us to make dresses without such full skirts, so we would not catch our hems on fire at the hearths. He approved our hiking the hems up into our apron waistbands too when we worked. Again, for safety. He sometimes nodded at Louisa's stitching, and I saw her beam at his notice. *Was I ever so needful of recognition from my husband?*

None of us knew what to do to help Brother Keil and, in so doing, comfort Louisa.

Jonathan had already moved into the Keil and Company Store, which was still being run out of one of the log buildings. He'd begun taking over the bookkeeping. There'd been a bit of a tussle with the existing shopkeeper over Jonathan's role. Both men had asked for an audience with Keil, who'd said something like, "Jonathan was here before. He knows what to do," and that had been taken as the proper transition of authority, at least on my brother's part. Jonathan had opened a ledger page with my father's name on it and written, *Brandy, yds. of hickory, tobacco for Jonathan* on the page. My father was taking from the common fund, so he must have planned to contribute to it as well.

I asked to see my page and saw more debits than entries. Few of the former were mine.

"Someone has to do something," Helena said one afternoon. We sat in the Keils' room, where Helena and Louisa spun yarn. My mother and sisters knitted, and even my foster sister, Christine, sat there. Her hands clicked needles as fast as my sister Johanna's. I noticed Johanna's kind smile and how good she was with Lou, quick to respond when my sister had one of her quaking episodes. I could see that Johanna'd been good help to my mother.

I supervised Kate with a sampler and mended Andy's pants. He'd torn them when he and Christian had climbed down the banks of the Pudding to watch logs float by. When I chastised him about the river, he told me they looked for crawfish to serve at the hotel so it wasn't all play. I'd warned them to avoid the rivers, but the Finck boy, with his new ideas and adventurous ways, had set my sons to doing risky things, even when he wasn't with them. He hadn't grown up around Keil and didn't hold the same reverence for him that most young people in

Aurora did. Water had always been a fright for me, one that increased after Christian's drowning, but I wasn't sure the boys listened.

Kate raised her sampler to me, and I leaned over to guide her little hands. Ida played with a wooden duck Martin had carved for her. At least today my boys were with Martin, at a new building finally going up. Martin had suggested a pharmacy be built, more central to the colony, one that he and Brother Keil could stock and distribute from—if Brother Keil ever showed any interest again. Martin and Helena, brother and sister, had argued in their quiet way, as Helena insisted that the church should be next.

Earlier, when I'd gone to the site to watch the latest house going up, I noticed Frederick Keil there, sweat dripping from his brow. He grieved the deaths of his brother and sisters with a hammer in his hand. I'd seen Kitty bring bread and cuts of ham out to Frederick. They were of an age together. Frederick was a good boy and might be a match for my sister. She blushed with the young man's attention.

Together, Kitty and I had walked back to the *gross Haus*. I wanted to talk to her about Frederick but hesitated breaking into her happy spell. Then we'd begun our stitching, spinning, and weaving in the presence of Frederick's mother, and it didn't seem the time.

Brother Keil was in the workroom below us. He'd placed a mat there, and Louisa said he now slept every night on the hard floor, as though "paying penance." I hoped she'd resumed sleeping in their softer bed and had given up the hard floor herself, but I noticed the bed in the room where we worked did not look slept on. The quilt frame was kept by a pulley above the bed and lowered when we began work, double stitching so many of the rows. Perhaps it was too difficult for her to sleep in it, since her girls had died among the quilts.

"If only more Bethelites would come out. Perhaps Henry C will write them and encourage them to come. Or do you let them know of how things are here, Catherina?" Louisa directed her question to my mother.

"Or those from Willapa," Helena said. "They could come here. They're much closer."

"We tell them how it is here," my mother said.

"*Ja.* If people returned to our folds, then Dr. Keil would become interested in living again, I know it." Louisa's eyes pooled with tears.

I worried more about her than Brother Keil. He could lock himself in his workroom, but Louisa still had the daily obligations that never went away: meal preparation, laundry, tending to the children, endless work. We couldn't give Louisa the things she needed most: her children back or her husband able to share in her mourning. Louisa kept on, wearing herself thin. Her arms sticking out at the end of mourning-dark sleeves looked like Clara's legs. Keil was…neutralized in his grief. He was bread without yeast. It didn't need as much watching.

"Jonathan helps with the ledgers, doesn't he?" I asked. "I see him and Brother Keil smoking their pipes together. Maybe that helps him, Louisa."

"And the music, the choral practices, those ease him, wouldn't you say? 'Music washes the soul of the dirt of daily living,' " my mother finished by quoting an old German proverb.

"He needs an…elevating purpose," Helena announced. She placed her needle into the batting. The movement caused the scissors at her waist to clink against the quilting frame. She stared out into the room. "Pipes and music will not do it. Something to engage his mind so he is not thinking of his loss so much, that's what he needs. A task to remind him of God's faithfulness despite the darkness of the days he experiences now." She inhaled as though to orate: "I remember after I made my decision not to marry, I needed such an elevating project."

Her supposed fiancé had been a bridge builder. I thought to say something about a bridge being elevating but bit my tongue instead.

"We should begin the church. That's exactly what we need now. I've thought that for a very long time."

"Perhaps we should telegraph them," Louisa said. "The Bethelites. There's a way to do that now."

"Better we get the Giesys and Stauffers to all come from Willapa," Helena said. "They can help us. My brother John can be here within days from Willapa, instead of the months it would take Missourians to get here. Surely they will listen now to our needs, with Father Keil so mournful and without Emma there to restrain them from doing what should have been done long ago. Oh!" She touched her hand to her mouth, as though suddenly aware that I sat before her. She'd spoken out of habit. She dropped her eyes.

"*Ja,* I was so powerful, I could keep all the Giesys up there against their will," I said. "*Ach!*" I'd poked the needle into my finger. Kate looked up at me, a question in her eyes. "I'm fine," I said. To the others I said, "I didn't keep Adam Schuele there. Or Karl Ruge. Or even Martin. They're all here now."

"*Ja,* we don't talk so much about Adam," Louisa said.

"I didn't mean, well, I guess I did mean it," Helena said. She clasped her hands in her lap. "None of them listened to me or Father Keil when we were there for Christian's burial. That would have been the right time to make the necessary change, and Father Keil was hopeful of that, or he wouldn't have made such a lengthy trip."

"He would have," Louisa said. "He loved Christian like a son."

"But they hung on," Helena continued. "Martin even said it was in part because of you, Emma. They didn't want to abandon what you and Christian had so wanted and worked for. Even my mother stays there in part because of you."

"Not because of me," I protested. "She and Andreas took my son and came here, remember? And Adam Knight left, and so did Adam Schuele. They went all the way back to Bethel. I didn't hold them there against their will."

"Will you never let my mother forget that? My parents meant no harm in bringing Andy here," Helena said. To my mother she said, "Did she tell you that my parents kidnapped her son? Goodness, it was such an affair. They were trying to help, give Emma room to take care of her other children." Back to me, she said, "You were with child again, after all, waiting for young Christian to be born and had your hands full. It would have been a better thing for him to have lived with them."

"Well, your mother has your sister to look after her and your brothers," I said. "There's no reason for her to come here." I felt my fingers begin to rub against each other; I took a breath, felt calmer.

"*Ja, aber,*" Helena protested, "we need to be all together now, as the disciples in the book of The Acts: 'They were all with one accord in one place.' My brother John could handle finances. Just until Father Keil is restored," she hastened to tell Louisa. "The Stauffers would help at the mill—"

"My Jonathan is doing a good job taking care of finances," my mother said.

"Perhaps Emma's being here will make it easier for the Giesys to come now," Louisa said. "You could be right, Helena."

"They haven't come yet," I reminded her. "I've been here more than a year. If I were so busy holding them hostage, why wouldn't they have come if they'd wanted to?"

"People sometimes don't notice that their shackles have been removed," Helena said, "until someone else points it out to them." She picked up her needle. "I'll point out to them how much better we fare here."

I didn't comment. At Willapa everyone had a single-family home, not like here where we crowded together like piglets in a piggery, where maybe that had caused the Keil deaths.

"You should ask them to come, Emma. Now is the time."

"It would be my good fortune that only Jack would listen."

"That wouldn't be good," Louisa agreed.

We worked together in the quiet then, me piecing my red wool blocks into a quilt pattern that put the blocks on edge, as though the squares were diamonds. It was a unique design, one that had come from my imagination as I was thinking of the Diamond Rule. My sister Lou had commented on how pretty it was. Kitty had said it reminded her of a symbol on a deck of cards, at which Helena had gasped. The point took extra doing to get to a sharp edge, but I found that the concentration required to make that perfect edge took away some of the irritation of the conversation.

"Let's invite Sebastian, then," Louisa said. "He and Mary and the girls. Sebastian helped construct the mill there, didn't he? He's a good hand with a hammer, and that's what we need now. Good hammer hands."

I swallowed hard. *No.* Mary and Sebastian were our old neighbors, and I suspected that Jack lived with them once again. Their exodus could spur Jack to come back here with them. I took another stitch at that red square edge. I poked my finger with my needle and sighed. Only my own spittle would get rid of the stain.

7

An Open Door

March 26, 1863. My birthday! Christian would have brought me an oyster shell or maybe some small treasure of tin. Instead, I will bake myself a pudding using carrots in place of eggs, well boiled and mashed and sent through the sieve. It tasted good in January when the hens stopped laying. Lighter than any egg pudding I've made.

In March, we traveled by wagon to Salem for the reopening of Durbin Livery Stable. My parents didn't go. They'd been staying with Adam Schuele, my father's old friend, and attending events far away proved too much trouble, my mother said. Jonathan took their wagon and my children. I rode or walked along when my *Hinterviertel,* my backside, became tired. In the distance, we could see tall poles being set for the telegraph wires that would come right through Aurora. "We won't have to go to Portland to communicate with Bethel now," Jonathan noted. He appeared quite pleased with Aurora's continued entry into the wider world, with no worry over the prospect of the outside contamination that had once brought us west.

Andy acted glum during the entire trip. He poked at Christian's shoulder with his fist, not so hard he hurt him but enough to annoy his younger brother, who'd whine so I'd turn around. I pointed my first finger at him and scowled.

"Stop it now! This is a fine outing your uncle is taking us on, and we don't need to be upsetting his ears with your antics."

"He hits me, Mama," Christian complained.

"Andy…," I warned. "You mustn't hit the boy."

"He took my cap and stuffed it in the straw," Andy charged.

"Christian…?"

"He poked me."

"Andrew Jackson Giesy, you are older. You are wiser. You cease. This instant."

"Or you'll what?" He set his jaw in defiance. I could feel heat come to my face, and my palm opened as though against my will. I swung back to strike his cheek, but then Andy mimicked me: "Mustn't hit the boy."

I stopped myself, my arm in midair, turned around, clasped my hands in my lap. *What have I almost done?*

"They raise your dander, Sister," Kitty said. "Just being boys, *ja?*"

"Naughty boys," I said.

"They're bored. It's a long trip," Jonathan noted. "You don't spend much time with them, I notice. They are always with Martin."

I felt my face burn. "I'm busy doing," I said.

"Some might say you should be doing with your boys," Jonathan said.

"Do you say that?"

"I'm just supposing."

"Today they should appreciate the outing. They have much to be grateful for, and they fail to notice it."

"Children are students of their parents," he said.

"What are you saying?"

Jonathan shrugged his wide shoulders. "I don't hear you saying so much about all your blessings, Sister. Maybe all they hear of is the disappointments. It's what they remember, then."

"I've had my share," I said.

"*Ja,* you can be right about your past, Sister, but hanging your hat back there only lets sun burn your face today. I don't see you tap your feet to the band music here. You don't dance anymore. Have you made little wooden shelves, like you once did? You must be a good steward of your trials, as well as of your gifts."

"I'd never considered the tithing of my trials," I said. "Who would want ten percent of misery given to them?"

"You tithe the lessons learned from suffering," he said.

"My brother the philosopher," I scoffed.

"Happiness doesn't appear to have been invited to Emma Wagner Giesy's house," my sister sang out.

"Emma Wagner Giesy doesn't have a house," I sang back, off-key, of course.

We rode without speaking, my attention now on Ida, sitting quietly beside me. Kate daydreamed out the wagon back. She looked to the past too, it appeared, her eyes always on the distance. The boys still bickered, but I heard no more howls. Kitty began teaching Kate a round. *When was the last time I danced? When was the last time I wanted to sing?* I remembered Sarah Woodard of Willapa talking about her Indian friends, the healing ones. They asked these questions of ill people, to assess how far they had fallen from doing things that pleased them and brought them healing. Singing and dancing, working with wood, and painting brought me comfort, but I wasn't doing them. I quilted, yes, but less because I found solace in the act and more to get the quilt top done. Was that what my sons saw in my life, a working woman, tending her children, avoiding one husband, grieving another, pursuing her parents, but always working? I turned to look at them. The boys and Kate were old enough to witness some of my struggles. Was Jonathan saying I needed to share more of my joys as well?

I couldn't even name a present joy. Perhaps that was the heart of the problem, the place where I needed to begin.

"I love spring," I said to no one in particular. Then to the boys and Kate, I said, "See the buds on the trees? They're different trees from those we had in Willapa. Not such big firs or cedars here. Remember when we used to play that game of how hungry we were, telling each other what we'd eat?" Kate shook her head. "It was when we walked Andy home from school. You, dear Kate, were hungry enough to eat everything in our house," I reminded her. "And, Andy, didn't you want to eat the tree?"

"I don't remember," he said. He'd stopped punching Christian.

"You ate the tree," he said then. "So you'd have toothpicks in your mouth when you were finished."

"That's right. You've such a good memory."

"I ate the cow. And Kate said we could wash everything down with the river."

"See, you remember it all." It pleased me that he recalled a difficult time that we'd converted into something fun. "I like that."

"What did I want to eat?" Christian asked.

"You were so small you did somersaults, or tried to. And by the time we'd eaten everything in sight, we were home."

"That was before Big Jack," Andy said.

"*Ja.* It was before him. Just like now, though. We're going to a new place to have a good time for the day. Your uncle drives the wagon; we have food packed to serve people, so we won't need to eat fence rails," I added. "And we will see Brita and her family again—I'm sure of it. When we come home, you'll have aunties to entertain you. It's a grand day. One to remember."

"And the sun shines," Kate said.

"So it does."

"So we can wash down whatever we eat with spring water instead of a river, right, Mama?"

I smiled at her. She began singing Kitty's round. This happy thinking could be catching.

———◆———

I had never seen the old Durbin Livery Stable in Salem, but the new one was grand. Horses grazed on the short spring greens behind the planed wood building. Two of them stood with their heads over each other's necks, as though chattering. Several more nickered over the half doors of their stalls, which had been newly whitewashed. The horses liked all the activity of men and women arriving, their liquid eyes following the women dressed in their finery. Sometimes one whinnied low when a woman stopped to pat her gloved hand at a soft nose. The parasols didn't frighten these animals, a sign they were trained to be with happy, dancing people.

To celebrate their rebuilding after the fire, the Durbin brothers had organized a cotillion party. Tickets were four dollars for the dinner, but Jonathan had managed to get several gift tickets since the colony band was to play. Brother Keil had come out of his cave to sit at one of the tables. Louisa had remained behind, feeling a bit under the weather, or so she'd said. Sometimes I suspected she liked it when she had time to herself in that big house she had to share with us all.

We colony women had been asked to prepare cold foods—fried chicken, carrot loaves, dandelion salad, and jars of pickled cherries and tomato figs—and baskets of doughnuts and breads made with our hops and potato yeast.

I watched to see if Jonathan danced and which woman he might choose. My brother had shown no interest in any woman that I could see. I wondered if he'd left a sweetheart at Bethel. He kept his nose to the ledger books, as I kept mine to my children and work.

Today I looked forward to seeing Brita. She'd been here to help rebuild after the fire so maybe that gave her a chance to put memories of the circus fire behind her for good. Something about her perseverance inspired, and I'd missed that once she left. I hoped she'd put her homestead plan into action too. My father hadn't said a word about the Homestead Act, and my mother told me he didn't really intend to use it. "He wants to purchase a place with a dwelling already on it," she said. "Most of those places have better land than what's left for the Homestead Act." I wasn't being included in the search. I pitched that loss away. Today, as Jonathan had encouraged me to do, I'd be grateful for what was.

Helena served the table where Brother Keil sat with some dignitaries. People raised happy eyes to me as I brought steaming platters and cold dishes. Here I could eavesdrop without appearing like a gossip. And we didn't need to wear our bonnets here. We'd donned straw hats we'd made ourselves, so our faces were open to receive their kind smiles.

"Oh, you'll like these pickled cherries," I told one frowning man, who said he'd never heard of such a thing. "The cloves and cinnamon and vinegar combined will pucker up your lips so quick, you'll collect a friendly kiss from your sweetheart there, *ja?*" I nodded to the woman seated beside him, who fanned her blushing face at my words, while those at the table laughed with good humor, then dove into the cherries. They nodded assent and pointed with their fingers for more as their mouths puckered.

When we'd finished our serving, we stood at the edges and watched the dancing. People loved to dance in this Oregon State, and the swoosh of their dresses brought back good memories of Missouri, when even young girls learned the *Schottische,* that slow waltz, by standing on their fathers' shoes to be "best girl" for the dance. It was how my father had taught me. How I wished Christian and my father could have been here to teach Kate.

I made sure not to make eye contact with any of the men standing loosely at the edge. They'd be bachelors, and it would not be good for them to think I was available, though I stood with the single women. As I watched the dancers move around the smoothed plank floor, I realized I did miss dancing with a man. But couple dancing was a thing of my past. Maybe after everyone had eaten, Kitty and I could swing around the floor, for the women often coupled up while men smoked their pipes. Fewer men than women attended in any case, a reminder again that our states were at war and young Oregon men were off training for battle.

"Would you care to dance?" It was the voice of a stranger, a man not much taller than I, but well formed.

"I don't much," I said.

"Oh, go," Kitty told me. She pushed at my elbow. "It's only a dance. I'll watch the girls."

Wasn't this what Jonathan urged me to do, participate more, just enjoy?

So I did. He was a jockey, he said, who rode horses in races when he wasn't working on nearby farms. When asked, I told him I was a mother, a cook, and a wife.

"Your husband's at war?" he asked.

"*Nein.*" It was all that I said. He nodded politely at the dance's end, bowed at his waist, then turned to leave. I complimented myself on experiencing a moment of joy, until I met a glare sizzling across the dance floor from the eyes of Brother Keil.

———

I hadn't seen Brita anywhere among the crowd. While others danced, I took Ida by the hand to wander by the stables. Kate and the boys were being watched by Jonathan and my sister. A breeze brought the unmistakable scent of horses to my nose, and Ida said, "Horses?" I nodded yes. Brita had been hired to work the stalls, and it was there, far from the dancing, that I found her.

I crouched to her height, and we held each other for just a moment, our shawls wrapped loosely at our shoulders. Pearl sat playing on a blanket in an empty stall, and Brita took her toddler's hand as we walked and talked. Ida held my hand too and attempted to skip, her dark curls bouncing. Men sauntered outside to smoke their cigars, while in the distance women fanned themselves, warm from their dancing exertions.

"I'd show you our quarters," Brita said, "but they've stacked ice blocks there right now, to have them closer for the party. Once this is over, my life goes back to normal."

I couldn't imagine what normal was for Brita. She was raising children who within a very few years would be bigger than she was. Charles already was. I saw the boys together at a distance. They threw rocks at some sort of target in an open field. I remembered how close I'd come to striking Andy for his sassiness and was grateful that I hadn't. For Brita, there'd be no physical means to keep her children under control. Jack had tried to control me that way. I suppose Brita had learned faster than the rest of us that size wasn't much help in keeping one's children in check. I could still grab Andy's ear, but he hated it, and I didn't like doing it. I needed to find some tender way between us, instead of arm twisting.

Brita acted as though nothing could impede her way, not even a fire in the place where she lived and worked. She hadn't heard that the family she'd served in Aurora had lost their father and two of their four children of smallpox, nor had she heard of Lucinda's death or the Keil children's.

"I'm sorry to hear," she said. "It's good that *Frau* Keil has you there, then, for comfort. It appears Mr. Keil is recovered." She nodded toward him, leaning into some discussion with a well-dressed man, Helena close by his side.

"This is his first outing since the children died," I said. "And I'm not sure I'm much comfort to Louisa, but my mother and sisters bring her nurture."

"Your family came? But that's good. I'm surprised you even remember me, with your whole family with you now."

"You're memorable," I said. I was pleased to see her smile. We walked awhile, and then I said, "Brita, tell me all you know about that Homestead Act."

If it surprised her, my change of subject, she made no mention of it. She sat down on the tongue of an unhitched wagon. I could see that she'd stitched up her skirt hem with tiny, even stitches.

"Go off to the courthouse. Find land that hasn't been aclaimed and claim it. Build a house on it and stay there five years and it's ayours. I've got a spot far south of Salem. It's not open, so I'll have work to do to clear it for planting."

"Even women can do this?"

She nodded. "The land is yours in even shorter time if you're a veteran, if you're coming back from the war. They wanted to give aspecial help to soldiers. But why would you do that, Emma? Didn't they promise to build you a house right there in Aurora? And your family is there now."

"I wonder if that will ever happen. Brother Keil mourns the deaths of his children so deeply he rarely comes out of his workroom cave. When he does it's for something…promotional. Certainly not to build a woman a promised house. Helena wants a church, and that makes good sense. Part of me feels selfish, wanting the colony to build me a home when there are others who need them too. Sometimes I wonder if the trials we've faced have been because we haven't taken time for gratitude and worship, just as Helena says."

"It would be difficult to build a house on your own," she said.

"You're planning to do it."

"But if I had someone close to help me, I'd accept the help."

"I never told you, but the house I want will have room for two families. We could make them totally independent or have one kitchen that we both used. Have a good roof and a place for people to be private, but within a shout should they need help. I'd thought maybe you'd join me there, you and the children, but then you left."

I wanted her to say she'd return. It would give me a reason to push for the house daily. We started walking again, out across the meadow. I slowed my pace, partly for Pearl's shortened steps, but more for Brita, who still moved by shifting her weight from side to side. She finally stopped, picked up Pearl, and bounced her lovingly as she faced her, her daughter's legs around her waist.

"Your double house idea is lovely," Brita said. "But I'm not the one to live on that other side."

"Because you want your own home."

She nodded. "Though when I first came for help, that house you describe would have been a good place to collect myself again and get my children settled down. Not that the hallway by the blue cabinet wasn't a restful place," she hastened to add. "But a house with only one other family around would abeen better. It's a fine idea, Emma."

"But?"

"People like me must be prepared in case someone pulls the rug from beneath our feet. I want to know that I made the rug I stand on and laid it in the house with my name on the door. I want to know that it is my home and that I'll leave when I choose, and not when someone else says I must."

"I'd never ask you to leave, Brita."

"It wouldn't be your home, though, Emma. The colony would have the house, and they could do with it what they pleased. That's the other side of sharing everything."

"One's own place" was a slender thread of the colony life that others could snip off. Still, no one had ever been expelled from Keil's colony. Even back in Bethel the Bauers had built ten businesses right inside Bethel after they'd said they no longer wanted to be a part of Keil's communal ways. Keil had left Bethel, and it might be yet another way Keil kept control over us colonists here, promising things but never delivering. I'd have to get approval from him to use the house, even if he authorized the two-family design. "Maybe Keil will determine who would live on the other side."

"Unless you were strong enough to stand your ground," Brita continued. "That's the only way a woman, even a small woman, can have what she wants. You got to care deep to step over people's open-mouthed gasps that you'd dare something so outrageous or that it could ever succeed."

"How did you ever get so wise, Brita?"

She laughed. "Ah, the fire-eater taught me all that."

———————

Spring turned into summer, slow but steady as the milk that dripped into the lumps that formed cottage cheese. Still no word about my house. Still no movement toward the church. My parents kept themselves distant from the village. I began thinking about work I could do to make a living apart from the colony. Maybe Jack wouldn't know where I was, and an employer would assume I was widowed and eligible for my own earnings. I wasn't sure that the colony would want me around, working for them, if I found another place to live. It was acceptable for Henry C, the music master, to live within the village and yet earn money from the outside that he said he would use to send his son to Harvard one day. He never took a dime for lessons given to colony children, and Jonathan said he believed in the communal ways of sharing. But a woman? I doubted they'd pay me for my cooking or sewing. Truth told, I did have much to repay them for. They'd rescued me and my children two years earlier. Still, by the time I found land to build on, what I contributed in work to the colony ought to make things even with what they'd given to me, Clara the chicken included.

Two years I'd been here. It was a year already since Jack left the second time. I decided to ride along one day when the men delivered butter to Oregon City. They'd stop at Solomon Weil's pottery shop there too, to make trades. I asked and they let me off at the Clackamas County courthouse. "I just want to check on something for Jonathan," I told the driver, never quite sure if he'd report to Keil or not. It wasn't a total lie…just a half truth. I'd let Jonathan know of my results of looking at land maps and deeds. I sought unclaimed land that had already been surveyed. Most of it was far from Aurora or any other place where my children could go to school or where I could find employment. Maybe I'd have to do what Brita did, first find a paying job and then save up enough so that all I needed to do was work at proving up my land within those five years.

If I began this fall of 1863, I reasoned, my Andy would be fifteen by the time it was mine. I'd need his help to do it. But Andy needed to be in school. And how would I do that? We'd be as we had been in Willapa: isolated and alone. Still, throughout the summer, I rode to look at various sites. When I rode with my sons, no one asked any questions of where I was going. When I came to the barns alone, the men would frown as I asked for a horse or a mule, as though without children around a woman was somehow up to no good. I gave no explanations to them. Let them wonder.

The search took time, what with fitting it in between the constancy of colony work. And I had to feel strong enough, when I went alone, to endure the disapproving looks of the men.

To gain such strength, I'd begun reading the Scriptures again. Karl had recommended it, and once, before Christian died, I'd found the time of reading full of peace and wisdom. I'd deprived myself of both by ignoring those words. My sister Kitty had preached Scripture to me in her letters. At least that was how I'd seen them. I'd lifted her words and carried them as weights, instead of as the wings she intended. But then that psalm had come to me to comfort Louisa and to remind me that once I'd found nurture in the psalms and other scriptures too. Kitty loved the psalms and even taught the group of us a psalm to sing while we worked. It was a part of her, Scripture and song, and they weren't meant to make me wear a cloak of guilt just because I didn't experience faith the way she did. One summer morning, I'd been reading in the book of Revelation: "Behold, I have set before thee an open door, and no man can shut it." The words spoke to my heart, and I decided to take my little man, Andy, with me to see if we could find that "open door."

Andy didn't seem all that happy to go with me. I wanted to talk about what I proposed to do and how it might affect him. I asked Kitty to look after my other children, so I could devote this time to my older yet more distant son.

"I promised to help Martin sort out the new shipment," he said.

"Martin will do fine without you for a few hours."

"I don't like that old horse they always pick for me either. He tries to bite me whenever I bend over."

"Don't bend over near him, then."

"Martin teaches me things, Mama. Important things. I should stay and help him." I reminded him that Martin wasn't his father and that I, as his mother, would decide how he spent his time. I too had things to teach him. He said he didn't care to spend his time riding around anyway, and he didn't know why I wanted to live someplace else either. "I like Aurora, Mama."

"*Bitte,* don't make this difficult, Andy."

He crossed his arms over his narrow chest.

"I'll take care of the horse," I said.

"That I'd like to see," he sassed. I didn't reprimand him. Instead, I decided to do him one better.

———◆———

"Is that dinner, Mama?" Andy asked as we walked toward the barns for our afternoon excursion. I'd told him there'd be a delay because I had something special to prepare. He nodded toward the basket I carried. It was a colony basket, made from ash and oak and brought from Bethel. The cover fit tightly to keep flying bugs out, but the weave let air flow through. Inside I had cold ham slices and bread and several hard-boiled eggs in blue shells. But I also had a very hot baked potato, just taken out of the coals.

"Dinner and a surprise," I said.

When we arrived at the barn, one of the men saddled the mule and then led up Andy's mount, the horse he didn't like. "Mama...," he began.

"That one bites, so be careful," the stableman said.

"*Ja,* so I'm told," I said. "Give me a moment." To Andy I said, "Act like you're having just the best time." I showed them a pocket I'd made, and put the hot potato in it. Then I tied the pocket around my waist, with the hot tuber at my backside, making sure the horse was busy munching and not paying attention. "You watch." I led the horse down the fence line and tied him loosely to the rail. I gave him plenty of rope to move his head. I chattered about the weather as the man placed the saddle on the horse's back. And then I deliberately bent over to check the stirrup, my backside toward the horse's head. The potato was hot enough that I could feel it through my dark calico dress and petticoat.

"*Ach,* be careful," the stableman warned.

I heard the tug of the rope and the horse twisting his head, and I knew he'd be reaching to bite the potato in my pocketed *Hinterviertel.*

"Mama..."

"Shush now," I told him in a singsong voice. "We're just chattering away here."

I felt the pocket move. The horse grabbed and bit into the hot potato.

The animal twisted his head back. I heard the halter rings rattle against the rope, followed by the thump of a half-eaten potato hitting the ground at my side. The stableman chuckled low. "A hot *Kartoffel* never had such a bite."

I straightened, fussed with the leather, and then found a reason to once again bend with my *Hinterviertel* toward the horse's biting end. The horse twisted his head but did nothing. "I doubt he'll ever do that again," I said, standing up. "He'll think he did it to himself too, if we don't make any real notice of it. So, are you ready to ride with your mama?"

The stableman smiled as he walked away, shaking his head. Andy nodded and mounted up. I thought I saw appreciation in his face. "You outsmarted him, Mama," Andy said.

"Yes, I did."

Martin wasn't the only adult my son could learn from. Perhaps I'd opened my very next door.

8

Acting as Though Hopeful

Andy and I had a grand day out riding. I'd made a map, thinking maybe my father would be interested if I found a good piece of property, even if it couldn't be a homestead claim. Being with my son made me grateful: we had a roof over our heads, and we had family around us, though neither fit the image I'd planned. Serenity settled in my mind while we rode. I could accept the present experiences while still pursuing something different and, hopefully, better.

Andy spoke with animation about his time with Martin and his pharmaceutical activities.

I asked, "And do you want to work with apothecary things, be a healer of sorts?" Then thinking I should not just ask questions but state my thoughts if I wanted to influence my children, I added, "Healing would be a good thing to do."

"When someone needs their leg cut off, I want to cut it off," Andy said. I raised my eyebrows. "When someone breaks an arm, I want to set it. And if—"

"You...want to cut off limbs?"

"Only to help people, Mama." I heard the disgust in his voice. "If there's infection. I want to heal and fix things. Make it better."

"That's *gut*," I said. "Very good." This was a change from the time when he'd wanted to hurt Big Jack. "It would take both strength and courage to do such work," I said.

"I have both."

"You say that very firmly for one who is not quite ten years," I said. I shook my head, and he raised his eyes in question. "Your father and I headed west ten years ago. The years slipped past me like an otter sliding down the Willapa River's banks." As we rode, I pondered silently. What did I have to say for them? More important, what did I want the next ten to look like?

"I'm old enough to know what I want to do when I grow up," Andy said. A slight breeze lifted his straight brown hair, and he pushed it away from his eyes. He rode without a hat and squinted into the sun. He had new boots on. I hadn't purchased those for him. Martin must have. Or maybe my father. *Had he needed shoes and I'd failed to see it?*

"You want to be a doctor in ten years then, *ja*?"

"Is there a way that can happen, Mama?"

He lifted those sable eyes that caused my throat to tighten. Oh, how I wanted to be the person he saw, someone who could do anything to make her children's lives better than her own.

"Only Karl Ruge and the music master have university degrees here. But they could prepare you for a university. While you study hard now, I'll try to find a way to send you later." I thought perhaps my father might help pay for his schooling. Or maybe the colony could, but I didn't propose either solution. Better not to lift up hopes that would only be later dashed.

We found ourselves near Adam Schuele's farm and reined our horses down the long lane. Keil had given directions for a road to be built from Aurora to a Giesy farm, a road that bypassed Adam's farm altogether, making it difficult for Adam to bring his goods to Aurora. I hadn't realized the convolutedness of this trail until we'd ridden this less-traveled road.

I hoped we'd see my parents here.

Adam greeted us with a bear hug. He raised hogs, and the pungent scent of the pigs rose to my nose despite the distance of the pens from the house.

"What brings you here, Emma?" Adam asked. He could use my first name because we'd been through so much together that first winter in Willapa.

"I thought maybe I'd see my family," I said. "And we're thinking to find a homestead plot, my son and I, so we're riding and beholding."

"Like father, like daughter, wanting to live somewhere outside of Aurora." Then, "Didn't I hear Keil had agreed to build you a house?"

"Did he, Mama?"

"With his children's deaths, he's been morose and not interested in much of what's going on. I'm afraid our home isn't very high up on his list," I told Andy.

"The Homestead Act is a good thing. I considered it myself."

"You and Keil…quarreled," I said, risking the intimacy.

"He thought we scouts made a mistake." His hands quivered as he pulled a chair out for me. He was aging like my father.

His words burned at my stomach. I'd been a part of that so-called Willapa mistake too.

"*Ja,* well, that is his loss. He's envious of what we had there in Willapa, building a new place different from what Aurora is, everyone with their own home in their own name instead of Keil and Company."

He looked wistful. "Those were good times, *ja*? We took care of you, Emma, as your father asked us to. And you took care of us."

"My parents, they've—"

"They didn't want to come out here at first," Adam said. "But they tangled with August Keil and Andrew Giesy when Wilhelm sent that son back to Bethel and told that Giesy to help your father manage affairs in Bethel. Then leaving seemed wise. But I don't think they wanted to deal with what might greet them here, either." He'd been hulling some berries when we came in, and he handed a few to Andy now. "I told your parents not to come, to stay there where land was in their name and not Keil's only. But they wanted to help family." He smiled at me. "And Jonathan is a big Keil supporter."

"They didn't want to come here—"

"But they did. For you."

"But then why aren't they here for me?" How much could I tell him? And in front of Andy. "My parents are…" I looked at Andy. "We should be going," I said. "Thank you for the spring water and the berries. Will we see you on the Fourth of July? The band will play. Maybe there'll be a horse race."

"Of course," Adam said. "But you ask *Herr* Keil again about your home. Maybe you can get him to sign a statement, Emma. Wilhelm believes in the written words he signs. You remind him that your Christian paid back the money loaned to him by the colony to buy your Willapa land. That's right, *ja*?" I nodded. "Get it in writing, and you can have your colony house without fear of its being given to someone else before you're ready to give it up. *Ja,* that would be better for you and your children than trying to homestead on your own."

Adam was a good man, a calm and faithful man, not unlike my Christian. Perhaps my parents resented that I'd begged them to come, causing them to leave their home in Bethel for this…this distant colony with tangles in the threads that should have joined us together, instead of separating us further.

Adam ruffled Andy's hair, told the boy the story of his birth, and boasted that he'd been one of the first to greet my son in this world. Andy's sparkling eyes told me he enjoyed the attention. We spoke our good-byes. As we rode back, I thought of Adam's words. If I pushed for the house, got it in writing, rather than try to homestead, Andy could continue to go to school and to learn from Martin, and maybe, just maybe, I could convince the colony to send Andy to medical school when that time came.

"Get it in writing" was what I remembered three days later, when we learned of Adam's death. He'd collapsed on his way to attend the Fourth of July picnic in Aurora, 1863. I resolved I'd make my home a memorial to Adam, to the scouts who had been my family, and to Christian too. I'd dedicate my home to making other lives better than my own…if I ever got a home of my own.

———

Keil didn't attend the funeral, so Karl Ruge spoke the blessing. My parents and brothers and sisters were there to mourn Adam, and of course, my brood did too. Few others attended, and I wondered if perhaps it was the hold Keil still had over people, muting even their wish to openly grieve someone who no longer held favor in Keil's eyes. I'd filled two of the glasses we'd made with blooms from the herb garden. I placed one on Adam's fresh grave, then walked over and put the other on Lucinda Wolfer's grave.

I chose the next day to see Jonathan. "Has Keil said anything about my house being built?"

"What brings that up?"

"I spent some time with Adam before he died, and we talked about it."

"I'm surprised Adam would be interested," Jonathan said. I thought he bristled a bit.

"And the answer is?"

"He picked a site. But he hesitates. He wants to be fair."

"Fair? After what I've given? The colony owes me a home. I'm widowed because of the colony."

"*Nein,* Sister. There is another way to see that. You had separated from the colony."

"Separated, yes, but my husband continued to act as though we belonged to Aurora, and he repaid what the colony gave us to make purchases in Willapa."

"Some still stay in Willapa, and Brother Keil knows that is in part because of Christian's decision. Money for all those purchases has not been returned." He shrugged his shoulders. "I wouldn't demand the house, Emma. There are many others who would like a home built for them, and they might resent your receiving one before them."

"*Ach!* Then I'll go homestead," I said.

"*Ja.* I hear you're stopping at the courthouse in Oregon City."

"I meant to tell you. I just forgot," I said.

Jonathan sighed. "You can't homestead, Emma."

"I can find a place. Women alone can do this," I said. "Single women and widows are allowed. My friend Brita is going to do it. She has acreage—"

"If they are heads of households. But you aren't. You can't homestead, because you're married still. Unless you're thinking of getting Jack to homestead with you…or maybe…a divorce."

A fly could have buzzed in and out of my mouth without my noticing, I was so aghast at his words. *How can I keep being surprised at the boulders on my road?* Women bore the brunt, no matter how dangerous it might have been to remain married to some brute. Women were left to fend for themselves and their children, to pay for the rest of their days for the poor choices they once made. Women suffered whether they stayed married, chose to live with the disgrace of divorce, or dangled dangerously in between.

"I don't want a divorce," I wailed. "I want a home."

"You could find someone else to file for you, I suppose," Jonathan said. He'd leaned back in his chair, the front two legs lifting. He now dropped them down with a plop. "But that wouldn't be legal, and there'd be no way to protect yourself if they decided to write you out of it someday in the future."

"Papa…?"

"Papa's looking for land with potential that can support his family. He doesn't want to depend on the colony. He's wrong in that, but that's his way."

"I'm not the head of the household."

"Not in the law's eyes," Jonathan said. "I'm sorry, Emma." He patted my hand, offering comfort. "Without Jack around, your oldest son comes closer to being that."

◆

My former mother-in-law, who was still the grandmother of my children, arrived in Aurora in late July. My sister-in-law Louisa Giesy,

Christian's younger sister, held her mother's hand, and they were swinging their arms back and forth in delight. John and his wife, Barbara White Giesy (I thought of her as BW), came in the wagon with their girls. Behind them followed Sebastian and Mary with their children. They'd even brought Opal, our goat.

No Jack Giesy in sight.

Louisa Keil gushed. "So good, so good you are here! Now my husband will have all the help he needs." She clasped her hands, unclasped them. Her eyes glistened with happy tears.

"John is a good head at business," BW said of her husband. "It was a good time maybe to come and help Brother Keil out. Sometimes older men with more experience can do a better job." She looked straight at me, and I wondered if she knew that my brother had been the manager and done fine work for the colony.

Everyone gathered at the ox barn. Neither Louisa nor Helena, who had joined us, acted surprised at their family's arrival, so once again news had come in and slipped past me like bats in the night. The women stepped down and shook dust from their skirts. We'd be taking them to the log hotel for something to eat, then setting yet another family up in the *gross Haus. There isn't any more room.* "From the looks of your wagons, you must be planning to stay a long time," I ventured.

"Ach, ja," young Louisa Giesy said. Her face was flushed. "Didn't you know?" She'd lost that drifting look she'd had while she tended to her mother and my children, back in Willapa. Something had inspired a change. Maybe it was the move out of the Willapa Valley.

"Louisa stays for sure," Helena said. She smiled and put her arm around her sister.

"Goodness, *ja,*" Louisa Keil said. "She's here for her wedding. It's one marriage my husband has approved."

"Who are you marrying?" I asked. People exchanged looks, so apparently everyone else knew.

"My son," Louisa Keil said. "Frederick. They've been writing back and forth for years."

"Some things don't change, *ja,* Emma? You're always a step behind," my mother-in-law chided. "But then you don't always have so much to contribute either."

I felt my face grow hot. A headache threatened. My fingers did their rubbing dance of irritation.

I turned to Mary. "Thanks for bringing our Opal," I said. "At least goats don't keep secrets."

Mary blushed. We'd been neighbors back in Willapa but hadn't communicated at all since I'd left. The goat's knees had dirt spots on them, like dark brown eyes on white legs, and she pushed her way to me, yanking against the tether. She placed her front feet on my shoulders. "Opal missed you," Mary said.

"Emma spoils her goat as she spoils her children," my mother-in-law said. "It's so good that our Jack let you have her."

I scratched behind Opal's ears, no longer ambivalent about their arrival. Except for the goat, I was wishing they'd all stayed at Willapa.

———◆———

A few days later, I saw Keil swinging his cane with more lift than the day before, so I left my post at the hotel and intercepted him on the path. He headed toward the millpond area. A tiny mist of steam rose from some hot springs in the lowlands across from the mill, and today I could smell the sulfur in the breeze. On winter mornings, the area made me think of fairy tales and dragon mouths blowing hot breath in the air.

"Brother Keil," I said. He turned at my voice. His eyes grew wider. *Wariness?*

"Sister Emma," he said. "Walk with me."

I kept his pace, which was slow, though he had long legs and we could have strode right out if he hadn't been so run down. "To what do I owe the pleasure?"

He is in one of his good moods. Thank You, God!

"I want to begin my house," I said. "It's been nearly two years since you said I could have a place of my own for my family. I've proven myself to be a good worker. I've caused you no trouble and been a help, I hope. You need more room in the *gross Haus*. It seems the time."

He sighed. "It is difficult to think of such things when my mind has been so filled with grief and the business of affairs here. And I've enjoyed seeing you and your children outside my workroom. I've hardly left our Aurora, you know." His voice caught at the name of his lost daughter. I wondered if maybe he'd change the name of the town now, since it grieved him so to speak it.

"The cotillion put a lift to your steps for a few days," I noted. "Helena was a fine encouragement there for you." *Bite your tongue, Emma.*

"What? Helena? *Ach, ja, aber* such joys are fleeting." He paused. "Like a dance at a spring cotillion, *ja*?"

Touché, as my French ambassador uncle would say.

I looked up at the crows gathering in the firs. "The Giesys offer you good support, *ja*."

"Very *gut*. Very *gut*."

"And soon you'll have a new daughter-in-law."

"A Giesy," he said. "She's a good girl for my Fred."

"It's wise to allow marriage," I said. I could have bitten my tongue again for raising a potentially contentious issue. "But the happiness of your children was always paramount. This I know." I cleared my throat. "I have a design for the kind of house I want. It will be for two families, one on each side though a two-story house. It will have two front doors."

"Helena believes we should build the church next," Keil said. I remained silent. A part of me agreed with her, but I so wanted that house! "But such a huge undertaking needs people," Keil continued. "I've had to send our boys out to work in Portland and Oregon City and Salem, because we have not enough sales from products here. So they are not available for building. I pray for people to come from Bethel and all the rest from Willapa. Maybe you could share your home with one of those from Willapa?" He turned to me, smiled.

"Not Jack Giesy," I said.

"Families are best when reconciled," he said.

"This is not negotiable."

"There is always hope within a family, Emma. You must remember this."

"Aurora has become my family," I said. "I've reconciled with it."

He found a tree stump and sat down on it, the cane now between his knees with his hands resting on it. He pushed his hat from his forehead. He motioned me to sit beside him. I don't suppose he liked having a woman look down on him. "Maybe your parents would live in your house. I have failed to understand your father's moving about the country, as though Aurora was insufficient to meet his needs."

"I have no control over my parents," I said.

"I suppose this is true. That Christine they fostered is a sturdy woman. Hard worker in the hotel. She exudes…mystery, that one. Perhaps you could have her share the house with you. It would make her travel easier. Now I understand she rides in from Adam Schuele's place."

"Perhaps. I know that I could make the house be in service to the colony, I could promise that much."

"We could use a house for the unmarried women, such as we had back in Bethel," he said.

"It would have to be twice as large," I said. "We have so many."

He frowned at me. I wondered if he thought I was being critical of his not allowing some to marry. But he moved on. "*Ja*, well, maybe we don't have material for such a big house. Those women can remain at the *gross Haus* or stay with their families."

I wanted to say, "Or you could allow them to marry," but I held my tongue. No sense getting distracted from my present doing.

"And you would commit to working here as we see fit, to giving back what we give by building you a house?" Keil insisted.

"Yes. If you'll allow me to use the house to benefit the colony as I see fit," I said.

He stared at me awhile. The scent of sulfur from the hot springs nearby filled my head.

"But there is this pressure, about the church," he said.

"I'll write letters myself, urging more to come from Bethel," I said. "I'll approach them as the wife of your former lieutenant. My little house will require few people to build it. And you'll have more room in your house for those who come."

"You don't think we are challenging God by building for ourselves first, Sister Emma?" I couldn't tell if he truly wanted my opinion about a theological matter—something so rare it was frightening—or if he was looking for new words to silence Helena.

"The church building is important," I said. "But even in the beginning, the early followers went from house to house to worship and practice their faith. More important than even the structure is that there be a time set aside to worship. As we once did, all together. Even twice a month, Brother Keil. You've let that lapse in your grieving." He raised an eyebrow. *Don't be critical.* "I mourned Christian poorly," I said. "Separated myself from everything, everyone. When I first came here, our twice-monthly gatherings in your home helped bring me back. I miss them."

He stayed silent for a long time. Perhaps I'd gone too far by offering up any personal thoughts about a spiritual matter. He wouldn't think it was my place.

"I will have Jonathan draw up our agreement, and he can begin your house," he said at last. "Or perhaps it should come from John Giesy. Maybe he should sign it."

"You ought not to bother John with such an insignificant matter, him having just arrived. Jonathan can tend to it." I felt my heart pounding. I was so very close. "Should I assist by talking with my brother?"

"I'll see to it. Of course, you'll want to write those letters to Bethel. Get them to come out. Your home will be your reward."

"There is a meadow—"

"*Nein,*" he said. He pounded the ground with his cane. "We will build it not far from the Pudding, but in Aurora proper."

"Not on the site I choose?"

"Nein."

"But is it a site that will flood?" I cautioned. "Water is a fright to me. My husband—"

"I know." He patted my knee, kept his hand there. I moved as though to brush lint from my skirt and stood. "Well, it might be closer to the slough than you'd like, but you will adapt, Emma Giesy. You always adapt, *ja*? And it will make it easier to build there. We don't want you too far out. Isolation is not a good thing for a woman. And besides"—he smiled now—"I wouldn't want Emma Giesy too far from my sight."

9

Diamonds on Edge

August 9, 1863. Louisa and Frederick's wedding day. I baked the wedding cake. Fifteen eggs (three blue), butter, sugar, three pounds of seeded raisins, serviceberries, molasses, cinnamon, cloves, and bolted flour! It rose like a mountaintop in an oven set at dark yellow paper heat. When cooled, the frosting smoothed across it like a dragonfly flitting at the river's edge. There were several other cakes but many commented mine was tastiest. Is this pride, I wonder? Or a gift received?

October 3. We have new arrivals! I fell back on the grass and sent arrow prayers upward for my house.

Brother Keil officiated at his son's wedding, and it did seem to lighten his step. Louisa Giesy's face glowed, framed by white blossoms in her hair. She allowed Helena and the rest to fuss over her. Frederick, too, appeared to have matured, wearing a tailored suit that his mother let everyone know had been sewn by his father. Several of our colony now worked in the tailor shop, and people from Salem and Oregon City came to make purchases at our growing garment industry. Trust Brother Keil to find a way to use even his son's own wedding as a way to promote our products.

Martha Miller attended, along with other single women and men of the colony. Martin was there, and Karl Ruge and my foster sister, Christine. It was as festive as Christday without all the presents.

Jonathan and my sister Kitty came too, despite snatches of malcontent expressed by my sister about the Willapa Giesys' arrival. I mostly saw Kitty at the hotel kitchen, which gave us little time to talk of family or future. But while the Aurora Band played for the wedding festivities, she and I sat on my new red and blue quilt.

"What did you call this?" Kitty asked, running her palm across the blocks. "It still looks like Diamonds on Edge to me."

"I suppose it is, but I wanted a new name, one unique to me. I call it Running Squares, and I added a few different things to make it mine."

"The wide border of squares," she noted, "with double rows of quilted stitches." She pressed her fingers against the red block in the border, then turned it over. "*CG?* For Christian?"

I ran my fingers over the cross-stitched initials. "I started the quilt before he died," I said. "Diamonds on Edge is how I felt after he died. Our Diamond Rule, about making another's life better than our own, seemed to be pushed on edge when Christian died to save another man." I sighed. "So Running Squares it is now, since I seem to be always running somewhere." She sighed.

For the wedding celebration, men placed flat boards into a square beneath the trees, and people danced and danced while we sat and watched. Festivities—weddings—were truly some of the best times at the colony, and I noticed that outsiders made their way here without invitations, knowing there'd be music and good food. Given the smiles and laughter, I wondered if they also came to be rejuvenated among us Germans, as we lived simple yet productive lives, knowing how to celebrate as well as toil, sometimes doing both at once. They didn't know the inner turmoil, the trials that strained our communal threads. We probably looked to them like a serene pastoral scene, painted and hung over a fireplace.

"I didn't even know they knew each other," Kitty said.

"What?"

She nodded toward the glowing wedding couple. Louisa carried a bouquet of blue flowers with long white ribbons hanging down, standing out against her dark wool dress. "Frederick never mentioned Louisa to me." She spoke with a tone of wonder, mixed with betrayal. "I don't know how I could not have known."

"There's no reason to be hard on yourself," I said. "Did you and Frederick talk so much?"

"When I brought the dinner baskets to the field I sometimes shared a word or two. But then this one time, he took me on a boat on the Willamette River, moving up the backwaters. He was a gentleman," she assured me. "We saw lush water plants, and the trees draped over the boat like a green veil, just so pretty with the sun sparkling on the river." She wiped at a tear.

"It sounds lovely," I said. "Though a little risky without a chaperone."

"You could draw it, I suppose. I couldn't, but you could. I'd have it as a memory, then."

"Have you ever tried to draw anything?" I realized I didn't even know what she liked or didn't, what her talents were or weren't, except her love of music. Here she was, my sister who had been so dear to keep writing to me when I'd felt abandoned by everyone else, and I'd paid scant attention to her now that she lived within touch. "Maybe I could teach you to sketch."

"It's not an interest of mine," she said. "Except to remember that day. Maybe I'll put it into a song, though what's the use of that? He's gone off to someone else."

"It's still your memory. You felt...cared for. Nothing wrong with that."

"The day was dreamy." She smoothed the quilt border over and over with her palm. She chewed her nails. I'd never noticed that before.

"Backwaters hold mystery," I said. "There's life in the water's edge, sometimes things there we never see in the faster-moving stream."

Her eyes watered. "I thought I was special." She removed a hand-kerchief from her basket and dabbed at her nose. "But all the while he courted Louisa. How could I not have known that?"

"Maybe Frederick didn't even know. Maybe he looked for a friend and found that in you. Maybe he didn't realize that Louisa would come into his life as a future wife. Perhaps his mother influenced the Giesys to come here now, and then—"

"But they'd been writing to each other!"

"It doesn't take away the fact that he was there with you that day."

"He did mention marriage." I looked at her. "Oh, not ours, no. He said his father didn't approve of marriage, that he thought it took us from the important work we had to do to live the Christian life."

"He would say that," I muttered.

"I actually agreed with him," Kitty said. "But I thought I could devote my life to the colony in the way you do, Emma, if sometimes I had happy days with Frederick, rowing a boat or sitting at the bandstand and listening with him beside me."

I didn't want to think about her view that *I* was somehow a model "single" woman in her eyes. I nodded for her to continue. "I thought my biggest obstacle to a marriage one day would be Father Keil, but it turned out to be a Giesy."

She leaned against me and cried then. I held her, rubbing her back. "It'll be better in time, it will, Kitty. This is something I know." Wounded by a Giesy; that was something my sister and I had in common.

———◆———

As I'd promised, I wrote letters back to friends in Bethel, everyone I thought might still think kindly of me. I encouraged them to come, to help us build. I smiled to myself; Christian would have been pleased, though he'd have wagged a finger at me. I was encouraging them to come mostly to ease my guilt at wanting a house before a church could be built.

The autumn turned to times of harvest. Sometimes I wondered why I was so happy when the seeds sprouted in spring gardens, as they promised hard labor come fall. In between gathering pumpkins and potatoes, we dried apples, peeling and slicing them, the juice sticky against our fingers. Some we hung to dry, stringing them with big needles onto flax. Kate helped with that, though she ate nearly as many as she threaded. Days we spent making soups of vegetables and meat, to preserve the broth. We made *Kraut* until I could smell the cabbage in my sleep. We dried seeds to be used for next spring's plantings too. Ida carefully turned each one over on the cloth, her tiny fingers barely bigger than the seeds. We dug trenches lined with straw to keep cabbages and watermelons covered for use in the dead of winter. In between we did the usual: laundering, rug beating, daily meal preparations, care of our families.

I was aware, slowly, that our women's work did allow a certain amount of laughter, a bit of pleasantry, as we exchanged stories. Perhaps I was being allowed to become a part of things here. Helena's quick tongue could calm as well as strike, and when she raised some scripture for an occasion, it was often done not with a hammer but on a platter, offering something up to nourish, if someone chose to pluck the morsel. Sometimes in the midst of stirring beans in crocks, I'd look over at the elder Louisa Keil and see her crying, and without even thinking I'd put my arm around her shoulder and just let her, knowing how memories like steam arise to take us somewhere else and how a loving shoulder can be enough to bring us back.

Even Mary Giesy had begun to joke with me as she had in years past, before Jack. She was the only woman besides me who'd spent time around Jack. I wasn't sure how long they intended to stay, for she still called Willapa home. Once she even praised a suggestion I'd made. "Nailing drying strips to the ceiling was a good idea, Emma," she told me. "I wished I'd done that years before. The mosquito netting worked well hanging from there too, with our dried apples and peaches, when I could get them."

"You hung them right in your kitchen?" Martha Miller asked. "Didn't you have a drying shed in Willapa?"

"*Ja,* good and high so we didn't bump them with our heads. It made the room smell nice. It was Emma's idea. At least I saw it at her house."

My life was a river's flow. I'd be an outsider at the edge, then move slowly into the current of influence. Perhaps I wasn't so selfish. I was able to give, to be in service, doing for others. Maybe I had more to give because I spent time at the edge, seeking to nurture myself.

All the while I worked, I prayed that I'd be doing the work of drying food and preparing for winter in my own home before too much longer. But soon after the wedding, Keil ordered construction of John Giesy's house. Frederick and Louisa's, he said, would be next.

—◆—

Fortunately, Brother Keil began to hold services again, and I hoped that would ease the pressure to construct the church until we had more people to help. "My brother talked sense into Brother Keil," Helena told us as we dried wild grapes in the airing boxes. Apparently Brother Keil wasn't going to get all the grapes for medicinal purposes. "John told him he simply must hold services until such time as we could construct a building."

"John convinced him?" I'd heard it was John Will who had approached him. But I had as well. I wondered if I should tell her about my conversation with Brother Keil. Helena and I were alone at the big red dryer, placing fruit on the flat pads.

"Oh yes," she continued. "My brother said they'd come from Willapa just to follow him and his great relationship to our Lord. He said none of us could afford to lose that connection if our colony was to succeed here as it had in Bethel. It was all about Brother Keil's great faith and how he led us in it."

Those were the very things my brother told me John Will had expressed to Keil. Helena was usurping a bit of influence, it seemed.

"Well," I said, "I'm glad he listened to someone."

—◆—

At the toll bridge, Karl Ruge let out a shout I heard from the hotel. Several of us stepped outside that cool morning, because it wasn't the usual announcement that someone had attempted to cross without paying. It was the wrong time of day for the mail run or the stage bringing passengers to eat with us. A wailing cry, then a trumpet blast, then another horn or two echoed in the air.

"What do you suppose is going on there?" Helena said, hurrying from the ox barn, her hands shading her eyes.

I watched Michael Rapp and Henry Burkholder, the blacksmith, men in their midthirties, running like boys toward the bridge. Conrad Yost came out from his post to see what the ruckus was. The young Snyder boy who'd come along on Keil's first trip out started to skip. Andy rushed by me as well. "Come, Mama," he shouted. Martin walked slowly toward us, his sleeves still wearing the straw-woven cuffs worn to protect the cloth as he worked. His forehead frowned in question. Henry C's choral class stopped their vocalizing beneath the trees, and the girls clustered together, chattering.

"What is it?" I asked, as Martin got beside us. He shook his head as though he didn't know. And then I could see for myself. I'd truly have to trust in God's timing if I'd ever get my home built.

Conflicted was the word for my feelings as I watched the first of many wagons drawn by big Missouri mules roll across the bridge. I counted twenty, thirty, forty. A light wagon pulled by mules preceded more wagons, each pulled by two teams of oxen. Then the pattern began again with mule-drawn wagons, oxen-led ones carrying cages of chickens at the sides. Behind them, dogs barked and kept a flock of thin sheep bleating forward on the wooden bridge. In the distant dust, I could hear mooing. A few rust and white colored cows with short horns shook the bells around their necks and trundled across the bridge, driven by young men riding on still more stout-looking mules or astride Morgan horses.

"They sound like the three billy goats gruff clumping across the bridge, Mama," Kate said. "Trap, trap, trap. 'Eat me when I'm fatter!' " Kitty had heard the story from Norwegian travelers in a wagon train and shared it with my children, much to their delight.

"Is the troll under our bridge?" Christian asked, his eyes the size of apples.

"Nein," I said. "Trolls are only in stories." I thought of Jack and forgave myself the lie.

Christian and Kate had joined us and Amelia Keil too. She carried Ida from the lawn beside the ox barn, where she'd had the youngest children in tow. Pox scars marked her face, but otherwise she had survived the pox when her siblings had not. She lifted Ida to my arms. My head began to ache. All these people arriving would change things again. *Poor me!* I started to think, then, *Nein. Fear must not be my master.* I would make things change for the better.

I think myself happy, like the apostle Paul. I reached for Kate's hand. "Pick up your skirt," I said. "This is a joyous occasion." And we started to run too.

There were forty-two wagons in all. Jonathan sent one of the boys up to the Keils' to tell them that the Missouri Bethelites had at last arrived. He stopped at the mills along the way, so soon all the Aurorans were there, greeting old friends from Bethel.

Joe Knight touched his fingers to his hat brim in greeting. Joe and Adam Knight were both former scouts, and their grins carried a brother's familiarity.

"Isn't Matilda with you? The women…?"

"We went to Willapa first," Joe said. "The women will come up later on boats. We'll bring them here, but we brought the cattle down overland. Stauffers are coming too. We've scooped up the Willapa contingent, Emma. We're coming here as you did."

"All of them?" I asked, uneasy.

"Ja, well." He coughed and looked down. "I was sorry to hear of your troubles with Jack Giesy, Emma." He looked me in the eye then. "But you found safety here." I nodded. "You deserve that."

"Oh, I don't know if any of us deserves anything good," I said.

"You do no one good by not taking up what the Lord provides, though." He leaned toward me so only I could hear and added, "And Jack didn't come with us."

Adam Knight reined in his horse, then, to say how sorry he was about Christian's death.

"*Ja*, that was a long time ago now," I said. It was the first time I'd characterized my loss that way—that it was a long time ago. And suddenly, it had been.

"No one wrote to say you'd be coming. Didn't you get my letters? And with forty-plus wagons? It's like when Keil came out with lots of people and us not really ready with houses for you all."

"But here it's the third of October, *ja*? Didn't Keil tell you? We wrote to say we'd be arriving. Most of us are hoping there'll be houses ready, since there are working mills here. Not like at Willapa at all."

"I imagine the important people knew," I said.

"It doesn't rain so much here as it did in Willapa," Adam Knight added. "This is the truth, *ja*, Emma? Tell me that Keil has not exaggerated in that."

"Brother Keil was right about rain," I laughed.

Professor Christopher Wolff captained this train, and he stepped down now from the first wagon. He was the one who'd read Keil's letters to the Bethelites, sent first from Willapa and later Portland. He shook his head.

"This…this is not what we expected," Christopher said. He scanned the area.

I looked to see what he saw. A few scattered houses with a smokehouse or two. Partially built commercial buildings. The ox barn and our hotel of sorts beside it. Privies like pox marks at the end of scratched paths. Tree stumps, a few corrals, a horse or two ripping at grass, a few Missouri mules.

George Wolfer stood beside him, shaking his head. "When I met an old Bethelite at the bridge, I asked, 'How far to Aurora?' and he said, 'You are right *in* Aurora.' Can this be?"

"I'm afraid this is it," Jonathan told him.

Christopher Wolff had a university degree, was considered brilliant, and had just successfully led more than forty wagons and two hundred fifty people across the plains. But at this moment, he looked as though he'd stepped in a pile of manure and couldn't imagine how he'd get his boots cleaned. I was only one step ahead of him in scrubbing at the uncertainties of Aurora under the direction of Dr. Keil.

———◆———

The wagons stayed circled in the middle of Aurora for several days as we feasted, listened to music, and put all work aside to welcome the Bethelites and hear their stories. Andy took a liking to Lorenz Ehlen, a boy of about thirteen whose sunset-colored hair waved away from his high forehead. He pushed it that way as he talked about the most exciting part of the trip.

"It was as we left," he said. "The last three wagons caught fire and burned, and we had to leave them and push everybody else into other wagons while we urged the others on. We unhitched the mules and the oxen and pushed them along."

"A fire?" I said. "Did someone not properly care for the fire starter?"

I looked to Mr. Ehlen. He was a widower who had brought along his five children. Without a wife to assist, accidents like that could happen. We sat at their evening campfire, one built the right size. Lorenz's father rubbed at his arm and shook his head.

"Nope," the younger Ehlen said. He popped the end of his lips so the English word sounded different. "The Confederates burned 'em. The antiabolitionist Confederates."

"In Bethel?" I asked.

"Nope." That pop again. "They caught us as we came through St. Joseph."

"That's an amazing story," Andy said.

"Well, Lorenz might be exaggerating a bit," Mr. Ehlen said. "He has a dramatic flair. We did have some trouble with a little fire. And it was hard to hide our Union support. But I'm not sure we can attribute the disaster to the Confederates."

"It could have been," Lorenz protested.

"I was discharged from the army with a wound, just a few weeks before we headed this way. Ought not to have worn my uniform, I'm guessing. They knew we were Unionists."

Andy pressed for more details. Christian wanted him to describe how he got his wound, then Andy asked if he could see the arm that hung useless at Mr. Ehlen's side.

"Andy," I said. "You mustn't pry—"

"It's all right. The boys should know what can happen when you stand for something. I've long lamented the practice of slavery. But when they threatened the Union itself, then I had to go to fight. But it was time for us to come and find a new place to live. Build us up a new home and restore things in the colony the way they used to be. I was tired, I think, not looking forward to the journey out. House building, well, it can trouble a one-armed man." He patted his elbow, setting the limb to swinging slowly. "Sometimes a man's not certain of a thing, but then he gets propelled forward, and he knows he has to act to catch himself or he'll fall flat on his face. Coming here was me, catching myself."

"That's not just a man's discovery, Mr. Ehlen," I said. "Not just a man's."

———◆———

Keil appeared to revive with the arrival of those wagons. He'd given directions for where people should park, pointing with his cane. Over the next few days, he had Jonathan set up ledger pages at the Keil and Company Store, as he called the communal shop, so people could get their supplies. At least we had supplies for them, though the addition of two hundred fifty-two people strained our resources, or so Jonathan said. John Giesy said we'd do fine.

Checking our own kitchen larder, I knew we'd be hard pressed. I wondered why Keil hadn't pushed us to grind more wheat, to make sure we dried more fruits and vegetables, if he knew there'd be this big arrival. Maybe he wasn't sure the Bethelites would really come. Perhaps he planned to purchase supplies from the ships. He must have cash, if that was his plan.

Keil announced with some bravado, "There is plenty of land for you all east of here. You must not worry. This is our Eden, and now we will make it a garden that will become known the world around."

Keil made a big show of assuring the new arrivals that there was enough for everyone in the storehouses: enough thread for the women, enough wheat for bread, enough land to plow. No one said out loud that there weren't enough houses, though once the Knight and Stauffer women arrived from Willapa, the looks on their faces as they gazed around spoke loudly enough.

On the final feast day, my parents came to town, word having reached them at Schuele's. My mother and sisters sat on a quilt beneath the trees, brushing flies away from the baskets of bread and slices of ham and hard-boiled eggs. My children were with them, my Ida enjoying the pampering of her aunts. I'd sat with them all for a time, watching Lou work on her sampler while Johanna hovered. Lou hadn't had a quaking fit for several weeks now, my mother said. Johanna knew what the quaking looked like, and she took it as her mission to be prepared, sometimes anticipating a fit by a certain look in Lou's eyes or the way she held her head.

Christine stood to the side with my father, listening to the new arrivals. I hadn't seen her engaged in much conversation. My father talked with Mr. Ehlen, nodding his head, and I heard "abolitionists" and "war" as words drifted from the trees. *He avoids me.* When he walked over toward the corrals and Christine joined my mother and sisters, I assumed he wanted to smoke his pipe alone. I asked my mother if she'd watch my children.

"I will," Christine offered. She had the sober face of someone accustomed to disappointment, always preparing for more. "I never had any brothers or sisters," she said. "Except you Wagners later in life." It was the most personal information I'd heard about her.

I thanked her, and while the band played in the distance, I followed my father. He tapped at his pipe burl. Mr. Ehlen had apparently given it to him, as it had *Antietam* and a date carved into the outside of the bowl. Perhaps it was where he'd received his wound.

"Have you located any property to homestead?" I thought it an innocent enough question.

"What I do with property should be of no concern to you, Emma Giesy."

"Papa," I said, blinking back the tears that the harshness of his words had sprung, "I wanted only to talk…about…where I could find you and my sisters and brothers and mother, when you settle down. I miss seeing you. I didn't mean to pry."

His eyes softened. "Your brothers work in Oregon City. Your sisters help look after the Schuele fields for now. I suspect we'll winter again with them. Except for Kitty." He scoffed. "Where she picks this new name thing up, I'll never know."

"Kitty distinguishes herself that way. Maybe to be sure you don't confuse her with Christine."

He stiffened his shoulders. "We have room enough for many children, no matter how they disappoint us."

I wanted to ask if I disappointed him, but I didn't have the courage. "It's a wonder that you would have added a child, a woman, into your family. Our family."

"She needed a safe place to be, Emma. It is the Christian way, to offer safety."

"Safe from what?"

"That's Christine's story to tell," he said. The sharpness of his words sliced like paper against a child's tender skin. I was still at the edge of my family.

"Will Christine winter with you?"

"She plans to stay with the Keils. Ask her your questions, Emma. She's a grown woman, like you, on her own."

"I don't understand this…bitterness between us," I said finally, deciding to state my case.

He tapped his pipe against the split rail, sucked on the now dry stem. He sighed. "Christine works well at the hotel, or so they tell me," he said. "I hear talk that Keil will build a real hotel soon. One where many can stay over if they wish. There is railroad talk too." He shook his head. "Imagine. Keil sends people west to avoid the influence of the railroad on our children when the tracks were laid twenty miles away, and now he plans ways to bring the railroad right through his Aurora, right to our doorsteps."

"I've wondered about that too. What is it? What did Brother Keil do to make both of you separate from him?"

"It is no concern of yours, Emma."

"I wonder if whatever separates you from him also separates...us," I said. "I've come to...understand Keil and his motives. Yes, he can bob like an apple in the water, sometimes showing his colors, sometimes making one hold his nose to approach him. But he puts whatever is earned through the hotel or our wheat sales or apples back into the colony. He buys more land so new people will have places to farm. Except for the *gross Haus,* he doesn't live above the rest of us." I spoke the words softly and hadn't thought they'd sounded too complimentary of Keil. But my father, who'd been talking to me as we had of old, now bristled.

"You defend him," he said. "He replaces faith with economics. That was never the intent." Then, "You have made your bed, Emma. You lie down with Giesys..."

"But you loved Christian. Like a son he was to you!"

"*Ja,* Christian. He was a good man. The best of the lot. My good friend. And he died."

My father grieves my husband's passing too. That hadn't occurred to me.

He paused. "And you ended up giving up Christian's land to a ne'er-do-well."

"All the Giesys aren't like that. Just Jack. I was doing the best I could. I hadn't heard from you. I wanted you to come out, to help me, but—"

"Jonathan offered you a way out. You could have come to Aurora after Christian's death, and he would have helped you. You could have sold the land eventually in Willapa, so you could buy your own in your son's name. All the scouts fared well except for Adam, and that was because of Keil. But you had to do it in your way, didn't you? After all I'd taught you about staying close to the land. As long as you have land, no one can ever take it from you, Emma."

"The Indians here would argue with you," I said.

"What? *Ach, ja.* This is true enough, but I'm not obligated to have them listen to me," he added. "If I were, they would probably ignore my advice as my daughter and son do."

It's what I did with the property that upsets him? I've behaved unwisely about the land and for this I can't be forgiven?

"*Aber* in Bethel, you belonged to the communal ways," I said. "You helped start Bethel. That was your life. That's what you taught me, Papa. I thought you were angry because we remained in Willapa, because we tried oystering as something apart from the colony. Or because I remarried. To be angry because I tried to find safe haven for my children here in Aurora…"

"Because you let a Giesy get your land." He nearly shouted. "*Ach.* Why should I expect a woman to be quick enough to outfox a Giesy? Even now Andrew Giesy, who works with August Keil to *sell* the communal land in Bethel, tries to say the property I held as my own there must go into the common fund, while August Keil operates *his* land as though it is his personally. He puts nothing into the communal pot. He hasn't since he returned to help Andrew make the sales. Keil replaced me with his son as co-manager back there, quick as a lynx. He'll replace Jonathan too, you wait and see."

"I didn't know you had trouble back in Bethel," I said. "I'm sorry."

"*Ja.* I held that land in my name from the beginning, and sold it… *Ach,* never mind. It is too easy to get under another's spell, and I suspect that's what has happened to you."

"Jonathan trusts Brother Keil," I said.

"Maybe. But we would all be better if we had land in our own names. We could still offer help to others, still be communal in the Christian way. You remember that, Emma."

"I'm a woman. Land can never be in my name."

He shook his head and began to walk away. I couldn't let him. I wasn't finished. I reached for his shirtsleeve. He stopped.

"Papa. We'll talk again, *ja*? I want so for us to enjoy the company of each other again one day. This conversation, it doesn't leave me... satisfied."

The set of his jaw loosened, and I thought the lines to his eyes crinkled as they might before he smiled. "Satisfaction is what comes from a good stew," he said.

"I make an ample one. With many pieces blended into the whole to make an altogether new flavor. You'll come to my house and have it sometime? When I have a house?"

He said nothing for a moment, then he patted my shoulder. "*Ja,* Daughter. I will one day come for your satisfying stew."

———◆———

In that second week, several Wolff wagons began pulling out, heading east to the land assigned to them. The Knights said they'd look at property in the Oregon City area, and I could tell that like my father, they wanted land of their own. Mrs. Kraus, a widow with three children, said she'd remain in the Aurora area and hope for a house. *Join the wait for the walnut to roll your way,* I thought but didn't say. Triphena Will, holding her six-month-old infant, Leonard, told her husband, "I'd like to go home now." You could tell by her crying-red eyes that she meant back to Bethel.

Then began the meetings to ensure proper posting of what people brought in from Bethel to Aurora—who would get credit for what, who would be building barns and houses, who would go to work in the fields, who would find work outside the colony but bring resources back in return for their assignment of land, which new craftsmen could begin work making the big lathes needed to turn the long pillars for the church. These were experienced builders. Aurora was the sixth colony they'd built up while following Keil. Wolfers and Wagners and Forstners had their names attached to places like Harmony in Pennsylvania and, of course, Bethel. I could feel the swirl of progress in the fall air.

With all the reconsidering, I asked Jonathan to show me my page in the ledger book. The fabric I'd purchased was noted, as was the flour I'd been given for personal use on the distribution days. I noticed Clara was on the page as an acquisition and debits placed against it. A good portion of the debits were Jack's. But my page lacked acknowledgment of what I'd brought into the colony, and after my father's words, such mention seemed important. If the colony ever dissolved, I'd want to have compensation for what I'd contributed and not—heaven forbid— still owed.

"Shouldn't there be a page that says what I've contributed?" I asked my brother.

"It's there," he said. "Your hours of labor against what you've purchased—your shoes, your thread, your coffee. That dime you gave in cash for having won the award for your drawing at the Agricultural Fair."

"But that comes out even for the first year," I said. "I'm not accumulating. And there's nothing to note what I brought in through the Willapa land. That we paid it back. Or the work I've done here at the Keils', the stage stop, the gardens."

"*Ja,* I see what you say now. You really need that in order for there to be no question about our building you a house. We need to reassure that you are a full member of the colony," my brother told me.

"There's no question but that I'm a member of the colony," I said. "Who's challenging that?"

"No one," Jonathan said. "Yet. But we need to be sure in case someone does. Your husband isn't a member, so that's the rub."

"*Ach.* My husband risked his life coming out here for those of Bethel. And he believed he belonged to the colony here, even if I didn't. The Giesys are all here. Have they brought funds into the colony? Did they sell their land in Willapa? Make the certificate say when Christian joined, then, along with his wife."

"But Jack Giesy isn't a member, Emma. I don't think you can join without your current husband."

I stared at him. "We took in runaway women and never asked their husbands about doing it," I said.

"But they did not join up if they were married."

"Brother Keil would never think to stop a Giesy who wants to join up, would he? Louisa knows I'm a member. Helena would vouch for me. I'm a Giesy, for heaven's sake. It's what drives my father from me!"

"I don't know," he cautioned.

"Will you build me a home or not?" I actually stamped my foot. This had gone on long enough.

Jonathan sighed and pulled a sheet of paper from the cubby in his desk. "Keil wants you to sign this," he said. He slid the paper across the oak to me. "I've been…hesitant to show it to you."

I, Emma Giesy, will agree to abide by the rules of the Aurora Colony as directed by Father Keil, offering up what I have to give in service to the colony. In return, the colony will provide care and keeping for me and my family including the building of a home.

"Will he sign this?" I said. Jonathan nodded. "Would you?" He nodded again. "It doesn't say anything about my being a full member of the colony."

"*Ja*, you're right about that." Jonathan looked at the paper again.

"I don't need to be an official member, but I need something else here. It must read, 'care, education, and keeping for all my children and me.' And I want to add these final words." I wrote five more words onto the tail of the agreement and slid it back across the desk to my brother.

Jonathan looked at it and inserted the first suggestions I'd made. He read my final five words. "*Ja*. He will sign, though he might wonder what you mean by 'designed for use by her.'"

"Tell him it will be for service to our Lord," I said. "Then let's get this house underway."

10

Hammers in Hand

November 15, 1863. Bryonia helps the headaches. Resting in a chair overlooking the river helps too. At night, I sit outside in the rocker and wrap myself in the Running Squares quilt. I stare at the stars and imagine each one disappearing until there is only a dark sky and I am alone beneath it but not lonely. My powerlessness disappears; my headache subsides.

November 16. I've left no room to write, having spent myself on headache notes yesterday. Perhaps it is enough to say this was a good day despite the rains.

The sounds of hammers throbbed, but not for my house, in my head.

I dressed Ida, hurried my other children to don their petticoats and trousers, hating the pain in my head when I bent over to hook up Ida's buckled shoes. Together we went to Martin, to see if he could give me some powders. I'd decided not to bother Brother Keil, and besides, I didn't want to depend on his ministering to me—nor to deal with his cloying at my asking for assistance.

Tall, slender Martin, always leaning forward, was one of the finest men I'd known. I'd trusted him and Karl Ruge to help me in my darkest hour, and it affirmed for me that while I'd made some bad decisions in my life, all of them weren't so. I admired Martin, and sometimes small movements of his hands or the way he stood reminded me of Christian, his oldest brother. I ached then in remembering.

"You'll need Bryonia," Martin said, after asking me a few questions about the onset of the headache and any other aches and pains I might have. He gave me a paper cone of crushed roots, told me how to take them, then mixed up a batch in water for me to take half the dosage before I left. My heartbeat throbbed against my eyes, and everything in Martin's apothecary appeared to have halos around it. It was early, before he usually opened his still-unfinished shop, and the lantern cast a soft glow.

"In the old country, don't you know," Martin said, "they called Bryonia 'wild hops,' and it had a way of helping coughs as well." He had me sit down, let Ida waddle around, squat, and touch the white knobs on the many drawers that rose to the high ceiling. Andy took Christian and Kate to show them the back room.

"Maybe it would work for baking instead of yeast," I said.

Martin laughed. "It would add quite a strange sensation to bread dough. I'm not sure I'd recommend it."

I hadn't been in his apothecary shop much, but I could see why Andy liked being here. A big desk sat at one end. Scents and smells pleasantly penetrated my aching head. The vials of bottles and dye packets had been placed in finely measured wooden boxes with dovetailed ends that lined the walls to make a comforting pattern. Martin had stained the wood with blood and milk, giving it a reddish cast instead of our usual colony blue. He must have made the little boxes himself.

Andy led his throng back in, showing me how he swept the floors and how Martin let him unpack the barrels when they were delivered.

"He's good help," Martin said.

"His time with you is good for him too."

I thought I saw color rise on Martin's neck. "We got to know each other in Willapa," he said. "Careful," he cautioned my son, settling some glass bottles onto a shelf. "Those will break." I noticed that Andy didn't sass him back when Martin gave instruction. He carried himself proudly, his younger brother and sister watching with admiring eyes.

"Do you ever wish you were back in Willapa?" I asked Martin.

He pulled at his galluses. "I worried about leaving John to look after my mother. Well, Louisa looked after her too, of course. I didn't mean to leave her out." He looked away. I guess my penchant for reminding people that women were citizens of equal merit had dribbled over onto Martin's plate.

"I know you didn't," I said. A raging romance had blossomed between her and Frederick Keil, so Louisa must have yearned like the rest of us. I wondered if Martin did.

"We Swiss don't intend to exclude girls, Emma," Martin said. "I know you think that," he added, when I opened my mouth to protest. "It's a way to keep you women safe, to make sure you don't have to struggle with the challenges that men have to face. Sometimes sending girls to school to learn more than simple reading and writing exposes them to…unnecessary demands on their thinking. Brain sickness can result," he added.

I looked at him through squinted eyes. "You're teasing me, *ja?*"

He looked ruffled.

"Living gives us those demands, Martin. Then we lack good tools for how to solve the problems, tools the boys get through education." I didn't mention that stretching of a woman's mind could also help to lift the monotony of her days, while she worked beside her husband or brother, plowing fields or digging up potatoes, or while she ran the piles of laundry through the hand wringer. If it weren't for the complicated quilt patterns we constructed that kept us sharp as our needles, our brains would be tied up in knots. Brain sickness, indeed! The men around me found any number of pleasant distractions in their lives. The Pie and Beer Band provided excuses for the bachelors to gather. They tossed balls around and formed elaborate practical jokes that took weeks to implement, while we women worked: cooking, stitching, doing the laundry. Thank goodness for the girls' choir at least, and Kitty's in-structing us in choral psalms.

"Enjoy your time with your sons…and daughters…while they're with you," Martin said.

"Why wouldn't they be with me? Oh, you mean when they're not in school. *Ja,* well, here my girls will be educated now that Christopher

Wolff has arrived." He raised an eyebrow. "Karl's going to be a professor again and work with him. Henry will teach music, and Karl and Christopher the mathematics and science and English. Maybe even offer evening classes in Greek and the classics. He told Jonathan he would and that women could attend too."

"Brother Keil has approved the curriculum?"

"Karl assured me that Kate and all the girls would attend school. How can a people do better than they have if they don't take advantage of teaching all their citizens, *ja*? Teaching them to think and reason. Aren't we supposed to make sure others' lives are better than our own?" I could hear my voice rise. I wasn't sure why I became so bristly by the suggestion that girls weren't as worthy as boys, that women didn't deserve to be stimulated as well as men. *Brain sickness.* I pitched that thought away.

Martin pressed his palm down as though to calm me. "In this new country, that's what we should work for, that all the children go to school. Adults too," he said. "And former slaves too, now that the president signed a proclamation for them to be freed in the rebellious states." He brushed at a smudge on his galluses, then ran his thumb up under one of the two wide straps holding up his trousers. "They aren't citizens yet, but education should be meant for all, don't you know."

"I wonder if that's why the wagons were burned," I said. "When the Wolff train left."

"I think that might be an exaggerated story," Martin said. "The conscription law wasn't in place when they left Missouri, and that's when the trouble arose, at least in New York. Negroes have signed up to join the Union forces now, even though they don't need to. The rest of us, we can get out of going to war, if we have three hundred dollars. I imagine they can too, if they have the money."

I hadn't realized there was such a way out, or what the cost might be. "You're of age," I said. I squinted up at him. My eyes hurt so. I heard Ida pounding with something on the other side of the counter.

Martin leaned over. "Ida," he said. "Play with this." He took a soft leather ball from a shelf and gave it to her to toss. Her pounding ceased.

"*Ja*. John and Wilhelm and I have had discussions," he continued. "I want to go to the Wallamet University, in Salem. I hope to do so this fall, but…there are other expenses the colony undertakes now, with so many new arrivals. And the conscription requirements, well, I have no children, of course, so I am a logical man to go."

I shook my head slightly, wishing immediately that I hadn't.

Martin thought I was disagreeing with him about it being logical that he would go to war as he insisted that the bachelors were the most likely to be called up to serve. "We need you here, Martin."

He ran his thumb up under his galluses again. "Maybe if I were gone, Wilhelm would find new reason to engage with the colony, not be so distant as he's been."

I wondered if Martin was tired. He'd taken on many of Keil's patients, and now there'd be even more to serve. He wouldn't be able to go on to school if his days were taken up with mixing potions and pills, and if Keil stayed locked in his workroom, who would offer healing herbs? Once I'd felt competent using herbs myself, but I hadn't kept my sons from being ill, and no one was interested in having a woman treat them anyway.

"He's come back into his own, what with the Bethelites here," I said. "You help him. Better you should go away to school instead of to war. That would arouse the need for Brother Keil to return to his doctoring, and be a much better use of your time and contribution to all of us."

"Wallamet offers no medical courses as yet," he said. "But they do have art courses." He smiled. "Did you paint something for the Agricultural Fair this year?"

"*Ach,* that's nothing I can find time for now," I said. "I'm getting a house built, did I tell you?"

"That will be good for you, Emma." He said the words, but they lacked enthusiasm, which struck me as odd. "It is a good use of the colony funds."

I reflected that the cost of my house might cost Martin his schooling or maybe even send him to war, or some other man as well. Maybe that's why he hadn't shown much regard for my home. Perhaps I was being selfish in wanting my own house. *"The desire accomplished is sweet to the soul,"* the proverb said. Surely that meant that having a desire lacked sinfulness and that achieving it brought sweetness.

I tried to get Andy to come with me as I left to nurse my headache further. He insisted Martin had more work for him to do. Kate and Christian begged to remain too, and even Ida looked at me, yearning in her eyes. I allowed only Andy and Christian to stay. I needed Kate to help me with Ida. We girls had work to do.

———

All winter long I said, "This is the last": the last Advent season of anticipation that we'd celebrate while living in the hall of the *gross Haus* beside the blue cabinet, the last Christmas when *Belsnickel* would bring us gifts to tuck beneath the evergreens of the *Tannenbaum,* the last time I'd catch my breath when the root room door opened and I smelled that wet earth and remembered the day Jack Giesy returned.

Karl told me once that early Christians imagined there was a golden thread, given its light by the beginning of the world. They believed that it extended to us each Advent season, so we were all linked with those who'd come before, and we carried the thread on to our next generation. So while I celebrated these last times, it was also the next time, and perhaps the first time as well, for my children, that they'd be drawn together by the thread of remembering.

Then while reading one morning, I found the verse I'd been looking for, the one to tell Helena that we women could express ourselves about Scripture without a man's guidance. *"Then they that feared the LORD spake often one to another: and the LORD hearkened, and heard it: and a book of remembrance was written before him for them that feared the LORD, and that thought upon his name."* It was from Malachi 3:16. I'd have to tell her.

On the Twelfth Day, Epiphany, a celebration Karl said the Lutherans observed, when the gifts of the Magi were given, I felt hopeful by remembering all those last times framed by next times. I was looking forward, carrying that golden thread while taking stock of where I was. The thread made me think of Brita and her words that one must turn into gold the straw one is given. I hoped to turn my straw into a house that would serve.

———◆———

I walked to the site of my house's going up. It was March and my birthday. I'd given myself the present of helping dig the basement, though with many hands, I'd not done much. Framing and standing the walls proved a more time-consuming effort with only a few men assigned. The diggers, too, were soon called off to work elsewhere. I loved the smells of earth and loam almost as much as the scent of sea, and I pitched as much dirt as I could before rushing to work at the hotel.

I'd thought that maybe Joseph and Adam Knight would be around to help, as they'd shared in building Willapa. In early December, they'd gone to meet the women coming by boat from Willapa, including Joe's sister, Matilda, a woman nearly my age. She had sad eyes, a fact that surprised me. I remembered her as a young girl with self-assurance, who thought me pushy to want Christian as my husband.

We'd embraced and she said I looked well and I told her likewise. She'd be staying at the Keils', she told me. She and my mother and the sister, Christine, arrived at the same time in the colony store. Matilda said she needed thread and calico. I was there talking to Jonathan. Matilda said something to my brother about a girl back in Bethel, and Jonathan had turned beet red. He must have had a sweetheart that I hadn't known about.

"*Ja, ja,*" my mother said. "That girl you liked so well up and married, just like that, as soon as we left, I guess. You should have brought her with you, Jonathan. I'll have no grandchildren to carry on the Wagner name if you don't get busy."

"Brother Keil discourages marriage, Mother. You know this, *ja?*" Jonathan told her.

"It seems shortsighted," Matilda said wistfully. "How will the colony grow unless our families grow?"

"We'll recruit," Jonathan said. "Bring others into our happy fold. Adopt." He nodded to Christine.

"I'm not sure how happy it is, to have so many bachelors and single women as our community calling cards," Matilda said. I laughed and she smiled.

"Maybe you should come in on Tuesday next," I told my mother, my eyes inviting Matilda and Christine too. "We're going to stitch one of young Louisa Keil's quilts."

"Matilda is a magician with a needle," my mother said.

"We can use that. And then I'll show you the progress on my house. I'm sure there'll be some." I'd looked pointedly at Jonathan.

———

They'd come then to the quilting time, but Matilda stitched in silence while young Louisa Keil chattered on about her new marriage. Then we'd all walked out to see my lot, which was all there was to see of my house in December.

I hadn't chosen this site. Keil had. He must have plans for more houses to go up nearby so I wouldn't be "isolated." Oak and alder trees, with branches hanging over the construction site, covered the lot. There were no street names yet. But my house would be at the edge of the colony. The Pudding River rushed in the distance, but I tried not to concentrate on the sound. A white frost dressed the trees beneath a clear blue sky. They'd been the first I'd shown my "home" to, claiming it as mine. No one contradicted me that day, and I was grateful.

Now, in March, my brother and Mr. Ehlen, with his one arm, pounded square nails into studs, a structure of wood lying flat, not even resembling a wall. Then together they stood it up, and I could see the outline of a room now. I noted where the stairs would go, that divided my "two houses" on the ground floor. A hole had been cut out for the stairs into the root cellar.

In the next few days, other men would come to build fireplaces with bricks Conrad Yost baked in a kiln across the river. One man was known for his stair building, a special art, and he would be there soon.

On my birthday, boards climbed up the sides to cover the wall studs, and I could imagine the rooms and what I'd see out of my windows. I'd grown up in a brick house with my parents back in Bethel, overlooking a wide community garden. Christian and I had lived in a log house (after the winter under tents). This would be my first framed house, made with the lumber cut from the mill the colony operated.

"It's going to be a dandy house," Mary Giesy said. I was surprised to see her there on this spring day, especially since it was a good twenty-minute walk from the *gross Haus*. She pulled a shawl tight around her shoulders. She'd brought dear Opal back to me. Even now the goat meandered among the workers, being shooed off every now and then, until she found some shrubs along the river's bank to chew on or a pile of wood on which to climb.

"A dandy house. Yes. I can thank Jonathan for that." I'd brought him his basket of food, but he wasn't ready to stop yet. The air smelled fresh, with damp soil and sawdust mixed with honeysuckle. The men chattered as they worked.

"Family is good, *ja*? Sometimes I forget that," Mary said. I wondered what could have caused her to forget, but I wasn't going to ask. "So you will move in here before long."

"I'm counting the days." I leaned into her. "I won't have to hear Brother Keil clearing his throat or making wind when he's in his workroom and forgets my family and I live outside his door."

Mary laughed. It was a twinkling sound. Four-year-old Salome stood to her side, hugging her mother's skirts. Elizabeth would have been in school with my Kate. Mary's skirt swirled out as she set down a basket on the ground beside her. *Is Mary wearing a hoop?* "I hear it is a two-family house you designed. Very practical. Efficient. Communal."

"The German way," I said.

"And inventive. So, your way. Emma's way."

I couldn't tell if she spoke with a sense of appreciation or if something darker loomed behind her words.

"It's come at a cost," I said. "I was separated from my boys, you remember. And Jack—"

"I'm so sorry," she blurted then. "Oh, Emma, I should have been more aware. I should have listened to what we were thinking inside, when I saw you grow scared as a rabbit. We… I have prayed that I would never again remain silent when someone looks at me the way you did those months. If a child jumps when I approach, the way Andy and Christian did when they stayed with us, I will act, Emma. I will not remain silent. I didn't want to see it." Her voice broke. Salome moved away from her, still holding onto her mother's skirt. She looked up at her mother, whose bonnet covered her face so I couldn't see her crying, but I could tell she was. Her shoulders shook. "Can you ever forgive me, Emma?"

Only Christian had ever asked me to forgive him. It wasn't a human being's role, was it? I put my arms around her. "There's nothing to forgive, Mary. We all do the best that we can. If you could have done differently, you would have. As would I. I'm working at forgiving myself for the things I put my children through. Even Jack. That's all the forgiveness I can muster, or should. You have nothing to be ashamed of."

"Oh, I do, Emma." She whispered the words and looked away. Then more firmly she said, "Poor Jack." She wiped at her eyes. "He mopes around, works at the mill some, takes his charcoal and makes drawings."

I bristled at her apparent compassion toward Jack. "I'll not go back with him, Mary."

"No, no, I didn't mean… I just…" She took a deep breath. "I say the wrong things. I see pain and disappointment everywhere and wish it weren't so. I disappoint so many." It felt as though she spoke of something else, but I didn't know what. "Sebastian says we'll be returning to Willapa soon."

"After all this time, I thought—"

"I want to stay here," she said as she grabbed at my arm. I heard a note of desperation in her voice. "But I miss our own house and having the rocking chair to myself without having to wait until Barbara is out of it." I had a matched chair to Mary's that was still in our home back in Willapa.

"Tell Sebastian you won't go back," I said.

"*Ach*, I'm not you, Emma. It's better that we go. Sebastian, well, all the people make him…nervous. And Jack's back there. Sebastian feels an…affinity to him. Family and all."

I didn't want her to leave. She was as close to a friend as I had, someone who'd been through the good times and bad. Those were treasured people not easily found. With effort, we could recover a closeness once lost.

"I brought you a birthday present," she said then, making her voice cheery. She reached into the basket. "It's one that I pieced myself. One of the good things about the Keil birthday celebrations each year is that it reminds me that your birthday is nine days later."

I untied the string and folded papers I'd reuse for my oven when I got one, one day.

"Oh, Mary, it's beautiful!"

It was a Mariner's Compass quilt, with the compass rose pieced like golden threads pouring out of a central core toward the edges.

She picked at a loose thread I couldn't see. "I knew you liked bright colors, and the compass rose looked like a sun to me, with its yellows and the sky beyond all filled with stars. I hoped it would remind you of the good things of Willapa and not the bad. I wanted to show the good direction you took for you and your family when you came here."

"I shall use it only on Sundays," I teased. "It will keep me going in the right direction."

She couldn't have known about Christian's compass words, about being sure we found that compass in our lives so we could always find our way, nor about the golden threads that call us back to our place of remembering.

"I'm so pleased you like it. I was afraid you might not take it from me, because of how hard it was to help you, and then how much I didn't."

"Mary, you did what you could. It's all any of us can do."

I marveled at my own generosity, that I had treasure enough inside of me to give away. "This came from you. It's a gracious gift for my home. My very own home. Of course I'll accept it."

"And for your birthday, Mrs. Giesy," Salome reminded me.

Mary smiled now, and I remembered that impish look. "On my birthday. Right, and smart you are," I said in Swiss, and Salome giggled. "By the way, Mary, are you wearing a hoop?" I asked.

She laughed with me then as she brushed at the tiny pleats on her bodice, as though there might be a loose thread, but there wasn't. "Don't tell," she said then. "But I used hazel brush. All those branches growing beside the Willapa were good for it. You can bend them just so." She showed me with her hands, then lifted the hem. "And Sebastian doesn't even notice that my skirts are stylish."

"Will you teach me how before you leave? Could we use blackberry branches?"

"Blackberry branches for what?" Jonathan asked, approaching.

"To cut switches for fishing," I said quickly, and Mary smiled. The secret was made all the greater in sharing it with a friend.

———◆———

"I didn't expect you to literally build my house," I told Jonathan. Mary and Salome had left, and he and I sat, not on the beautiful quilt Mary had given me, but on the red and green wool coverlet I kept for picnic purposes. *Picnic purposes. That I have a blanket for picnics is another hopeful thought.* Mr. Ehlen worked at a peg. "Brother Keil permitted you to work out here instead of on the books today?"

"John's taken over most of the book work for the colony," Jonathan said. "So I had time." He didn't sound disappointed. "I'm still assisting in the Keil store. Keep those ledgers. It will be less pressure."

"I wasn't aware you were under pressure," I said.

"*Ja*, well, you don't know so much about everything here, Sister," he said. "John has good experience. The best man should be chosen."

My entire family was being moved to the edge of things, into the backwater of the colony. "Did you want to stop doing all the work you were doing for Keil?"

He shrugged, wiped pretzel crumbs from his very dark beard. He had thin lips revealed by his lack of mustache. Most of the older colony men wore no mustaches with their beards, a holdover custom from the old country when soldiers wore them and persecuted our ancestors. "Keil is a good manager. He needs to surround himself with the best people. I was needed for a time, and now I step aside. It's the colony way."

"Well, I need you," I said. "I wouldn't have this house going up if it weren't for you." I hugged him.

"Your Giesy name, Sister. That's what has given you a house. You should hang on to it. In these parts, it carries weight."

"Maybe. But I notice my house is being built on a site I would not have chosen. The bank is steep beside it and all covered with brush. I don't want the children going down there, but they'll want to explore. Maybe I'll have to build steps."

"It will give you new memories to live around water." He reached for a bread roll. "And we can build a fence if you like. With a gate to keep anyone from tumbling down the steps. Ida and Opal especially."

"I would like that."

"Put the goat to the side hill. She'll keep the brambles down. And there are springs. We hope eventually all the houses can receive water through wooden troughs. And you have a root cellar, don't forget. You can store cool water there and your butter. For now, you'll have more privacy to do what you want, Sister," he said. "Think of the site like that."

"What makes you think I'm going to do something that needs privacy?"

"You have a penchant for the unusual. After all," he said, standing and stretching and nodding toward the front of my house, "you got that chicken that lays blue eggs and a house with two front doors."

I moved into the house in early June. Before she left, Mary gave me the rocking chair that had come from Willapa. "I'll get its mate from Jack when we go back home," Mary said.

The boys ran up and down the stairs. Kate asked if we'd cook in the fireplace or if we'd get a stove one day, and Ida waddled through the house to the back porch where Opal was tied, out of reach so the goat wouldn't knock her over. Clara clucked on the porch rail; my bantam chickens and rooster pecked at the ground. Well, they weren't *mine,* but only in my care.

"It's all ours, then, Mama?" Christian said.

"For as long as we like," I told them. "We'll have beds one day. And I'll finish making a table from the lumber scraps. We'll slowly add furniture," I said. "My work time will go into the ledger book, and we'll be able to purchase as we need."

"The bachelors say it will take you a long time to pay for this house," Andy said, "unless you've worked out something special with Brother Keil." He added a strange twist to his words, suggesting thoughts beyond his years.

I felt my face grow warm. "I'm glad you'll be spending less time with the bachelors," I told him. "They don't always have the best information."

My father surprised me on a mid-June morning.

"Did you bring all these with you from Bethel?" I asked. Chairs and bedsteads filled the wagon bed.

"*Nein.* Your brothers and me, we made them. We brought nothing with us from Bethel we could make here. It saved on the animals."

"But this is so…unexpected. I…thank you."

He nodded. "I remembered that when you got your headaches sometimes, you liked to sit outside in the cool at night, all wrapped up in your flannel. You said the stars soothed your eyes. This big wide bench, you can leave that outside, *ja*? It'll be a good place to rest."

I ran my hands along the back of the blue bench. So smooth, and its offering, a balm. "I didn't know if you knew I'd moved into the house."

"Jonathan told us, and about his demotion."

"Does he call it that?"

"Like you, he is a buttress to Keil, doesn't think Keil can do any wrong."

"I wouldn't put me in that same barrel with my brother, at least when it comes to everything good about Keil. But I do think he has suffered with the deaths of his children. He isn't the same as he was, Papa."

"*Ja*, deaths do change people." He stared at me, then looked away. "But he's still more willing to make decisions based on economics than on faith. I suppose I should be grateful for that. He's sold land to us, by the river."

"Where the hot springs are?" My father nodded. I couldn't imagine why Keil would agree to sell land so close to Aurora, with one of the colony mills included. Maybe Keil needed cash to provide for all the new arrivals. Some had been here a year almost, but we still talked about them as "the new arrivals." Maybe it was his way of getting my father into Aurora at last.

"Are you all going to live there?" The property I knew of included a smallish log house too. There'd be bottom land for crops.

"We thought we'd live with you, Emma," my father said. "In your new house."

I was flummoxed for a few seconds, then said, "Truly? I would love that! I had no idea that you'd—" Then I saw the twinkle in his eye.

"*Nein*. I tease you," he said. He brushed the braids curled on either side of my head. It wasn't the traditional way our women wore their hair, with buns at their necks, but a style I'd seen in a *Godey's Lady's Book* that made my face looked fuller. "You have enough with four children to provide for. We'll build a house eventually." As though this moment of intimacy was as unexpected for him as for me, he pushed his hat back, set his hands on his hips, and scanned my house. "I am curious," he said, "about all your grand plans with your two front doors."

"I'd forgo them if you came to stay in my house."

He shook his head no. "We'll visit. Your mother and sisters and brothers and I, we'll stop by more now. But it's better that we stay at our own place, not one that Keil has a claim to. I worry about that for you, Emma."

"I have a written agreement, Papa. He can't move me out unless I want."

"Words on a paper are only as good as the man—or woman—who writes them." He cleared his throat, adjusted his hat again. "There was a time when I followed Brother Keil from Pennsylvania to Missouri. But Keil changed along the way, and now those of us who claim him in some part of our lives, now we each have to make up our own mind about what place he takes at our table, and when we'll sit down with him. A man has to stay loyal to his own beliefs and his God, and not to a man he thought embodied them."

"Yes, Papa."

"*Gut.* You think for yourself, Emma. That's good." My father unloaded a chair, urged me to sit in it, then continued. "For some, Keil buys a way out of the war conscription. And to some he says it will be a good thing for them to support the Union by going to war. Some he pays one thousand dollars to, so they will work at the woolen mill in Brownsville or Salem or the shops in Portland, but bring the pay back here. There is no guarantee they will even bring their money back here. It's risky. Keil doesn't ask any of the men who once advised him. He's in a powerful position, Emma."

"I have a signed agreement."

"No lawyers ever see the agreements signed. Not even yours. Do you have a copy? No? I thought as much. So if the agreement is broken, there'll be no way to enforce it. Even so, I hope for your sake that you are not wrong about Keil."

"I do worry over Jonathan being sent to fight. And David. Thank goodness William is still too young," I said.

"With the grist mill, if we need to, we'll be able to buy a replacement for David."

"So many houses need to be built," I said. "We could really use another lumber mill."

"That, and here is one thing that a Giesy and I can agree on, even if it is Helena Giesy: the church should be built soon, where we can all worship and pray, or even more will surely lose their way. Don't lose your way, Emma. Don't sit in that rocking chair of yours and forget who brought you here."

"I won't, Papa." I felt drawn to him, grateful for his presence. "Thank you for the furniture, the bench especially. And I won't be rocking in that chair much either. I'll be busy doing. That's who I am. And I'll make you proud, Papa. I will." I was suddenly certain I could.

11

The Art
and Compassion

June 15, 1864. Encouraged Mr. Ehlen to make more Aurora baskets to sell and showcase at the fair. They are so tightly woven they could hold soup. How he does this with one useless arm is surprising indeed.

July 31. Work on the church begins! They'll build a big hotel as well.

August 15. I visited Wallamet where Martin wants to go to school. Perhaps I do too one day.

The men decided that the thing to do was to build a dance hall at the state fairgrounds in Salem. Keil must have concurred. They were urged on by Henry C, of course. With his presence, the renown of the band had grown. Sometimes there were articles in the newspaper and interviews with the reed players or the brass boys, as I called them. The young boys, including Finck's son, enjoyed the music as much as anyone, though I overheard him telling Andy that the popularity of brass bands in this Oregon country surprised him. "To me it sounds like cats being thrown into a thrashing machine." I covered my mouth so as not to laugh out loud, then soberly suggested that he might find a different description, as we Aurorans loved our dogs and cats. Young Finck merely snickered. We women often commented that music was a good diversion from the boys' pranks and silliness, and much safer. Still, building a dance hall, and at some distance from Aurora proper, would be quite the undertaking.

While the men worked there, of course, the start of the church was delayed.

I supposed there were discussions with Keil about it. While we chopped onions at the hotel, Helena told us that when the band had played at French Prairie in February, it had been so popular that talk began about having a permanent structure at the fair, where the band could perform and charge a good ticket price. It would bring in needed revenue while the concerts at the Park House would be more promotion than anything.

"Will they haul lumber from here?" I wondered out loud.

"Oh, I imagine so," Helena said. "We'd want to showcase our Aurora lumber mill."

After a Sunday gathering at the Keils', we women sat together again, and talk of the dance hall returned. Scissor snips acted as background music to our chatter.

I said, "We'll need to bring food for the workmen. I'd like to help."

"Oh, my husband has that all organized," Louisa told us. "The single women can do it. You have your little ones with you and a house of your own to run now, and with that new stove, you might not know how to cook over an open flame anymore."

"How does that new stove work?" BW asked. "That must have cost a pretty penny."

"I'll pay for it," I said. "I've taken tatting to the store for sale to grow the common fund. The man's shirt I tailored should bring a good price. And the stove works quite fine. I can use it for the food we need for the dance hall workers." I sounded defensive even to my own ears.

"We'll take Kitty and Martha and the young girls with stamina to cook out there and lift a hammer as well, if they need to," Louisa said. "No need for you to disrupt your plans."

I'd been snipped short like a too-long sash.

It was true that I'd been enjoying my house. Each of the children had bedsteads now, and straw-filled mattresses with charming coverlets either my mother or sisters and I had made. The Pudding River ran within its banks, and I could barely hear its rustle above a hooting owl that serenaded outside my window at night. I had a perfect view of Mount Hood too, the snow like a white cap covering its top. My brother David had woven red and purple and yellow and green yarns on a wagon wheel, forming a round rug that lay in the center of the kitchen area. It had a compass look to it and fit well with Mary's quilt.

My mother had brought a set of dishes for me too. They'd been in one of the chest of drawers my father had made for me. My father had understood the importance of china treasures to a woman, unlike Catherine Wolfer's son. That grown boy had broken nearly every piece of Flow Blue china she had, smashing them against rocks near Laramie when he discovered how she'd "taxed" the animals with excess weight. She managed to save only one small butter plate, burying it in the cornmeal the rest of the way west. The story was a small reminder of how a son could direct his mother without interference from any other man. Remembering Andy's sometimes glowering looks at me made me fidget in my chair.

I pitched those thoughts away.

I hadn't wanted to have my ledger page get too heavy on the debit side without finding a way to make additions to the given side. So I'd made contributions. My stove wasn't a luxury. It helped me be busy, doing.

I'd found the stove advertised at Oregon City and thought it foolish not to claim one that didn't even have to be shipped in.

The children and I lived in one half of the house, using the kitchen as our gathering room and sleeping in one of the two rooms upstairs that were on either side of the stairwell. The boys had the north room, the girls had the wide hall, and I took the large room that looked out onto the trees and the distant cooking smoke rising from Aurora's houses. I'd give it up when needed and turn the boys' large room into two, taking over half for my own. But for now, I had space for the spinning wheel my mother had loaned me until they had space to set it up, and for my baskets full of yarn and fabrics. One day I hoped to have a sewing machine as I'd seen in *Godey's Lady's Book*.

I kept the downstairs parlor for guests, should any arrive.

There hadn't been many. But I knew they'd be coming; I just didn't know who or when…or if Louisa and Helena would have words with me about it. I figured going to the fairgrounds to help cook for the men would be an opportunity to discover those who needed my house but didn't know it yet.

"Maybe if one of us more seasoned went along to Salem while they built the hall, we'd be better able to plan for the fall, when the band must be there the entire time to play," I said.

"Oh, your sister, that new one, Christine, she's interested in going. She can let us know how it went," Louisa said. We were again squeezed into the Keils' house, even though I'd invited the group to use my parlor.

"Besides, I might be going," Helena said. "I can surely keep track of all the items eaten and how much we used each day."

"But they've started building the church, Helena," Louisa protested. "I thought you'd want to be here to make sure the churchmen were tended."

"Well, maybe Emma could do that," Helena said. "With her young children, she'd be able to stay nice and close to home that way, now that she has a house and isn't galloping around the country looking for land. She could feed the churchworkers."

I felt my face grow hot. "As the colony has need of me," I said, "place me wherever you wish. I'd be honored to be a part of the church building this summer. I know my father and brothers intend to help. It could be a lovely family gathering."

Being agreeable, I found, threw them off. I didn't even react to Helena's jibe about my looking for homestead property. But I was surprised when Louisa said after a time of quiet, "Well, Emma's right. The church is surely the more important structure we should tend to."

"Yes," I said. "A dance hall is just that, after all. A place for dancing feet. You love the music, Louisa. Why don't you go and be with your

husband? Brother Keil will be there, surely. There are always many con-
tacts in our capital city."

"*Nein.* I think he plans to supervise the church."

"*Ja.* I heard him say as much," Helena said. Another quiet moment
filled with the tiniest sound of needles pushing through fabric. "Then
perhaps I should stay. To help Emma, of course," she hastened to add,
when Louisa frowned, considering.

"I'll be fine tending things here," I said. "You could both go to
Salem, though travel can be so dreary." I gave an exaggerated sigh as she
moved her hip, then stretched her leg out in front of her, twirling her
ankle like the whirl on a white pine. No one said a word about her
revealing her striped stockings too.

We continued our work for a bit. "There is also voting here later
this month," Helena reminded us. "At Millers' house. We'll need to
help Martha."

Martha wasn't much younger than I, but she tended her father's
household well, and that's where the men voted. I thought I should ask
her to our quilting time, though this was Louisa's prerogative, since it
was her house.

Louisa shifted weight from her bad hip to her good one. "*Ja,* maybe
Dr. Keil will want to be here for that voting, as well as the church's
going up, so maybe he'll see how things start on the band hall and then
return," Louisa said.

"You should go, Emma," Helena said after a moment of silence.
"Louisa and I can remain here to assist with the more-demanding tasks.
They hope to finish the pharmacy, and there are several other houses
being readied." She hesitated before adding, "I've heard too that *Herr*
Keil wishes to begin building on a real hotel. He wants it three stories
or more, with a huge porch on the front for the band to play and a balcony on the rooftop where they can serenade the train. It'll be not far
from the company store and the pharmacy, the center of our growing
community."

"For stage customers?" I asked.

"The rumors about the railroad bear truth."

"You do cook up fine food," Louisa said. She apparently didn't want to talk about the railroad and her husband's new route to commerce and fame. "And maybe your boys could stay with Martin and your girls with your parents. Or maybe Kitty could watch them while you're there. Or that Christine. *Ja.* That would be a good plan."

"I'm sure the boys would enjoy time with Martin."

"You're so accommodating, Emma," Helena said. "Though I did think you'd want them with you."

"Times have changed," my mother-in-law said. "I remember when you protested mightily being separated from your sons."

My throat constricted. *If I trust the colony to leave my sons here, then I am a lax mother; if I protest others tending them, then I am shamed for not understanding the gifts others offer.*

"Whatever is best for the colony," I said.

Louisa concluded, "We older women will stay here while the young women—and you, Emma—can go help them build, if you're willing."

"I'm just happy to serve," I said. I'd check later to see if I meant it.

———————

Because it was to be a dance hall, musicians who were also carpenters were selected as the best builders. Based on the number being sent to work, we women prepared hams and breads ahead and took the food with us. I hoped we'd have leftovers that we could sell to those who came by because of curiosity and the call of aroma. We'd present the best side of our colony to outsiders, the welcoming, loving side. We might have quarrels and tensions within our midst, but we had much to give away. It was the communal way: looking after one another, putting ourselves beneath the needs of others, and silencing for the outsiders those issues festering within. Like any family, we could appreciate virtues of generosity, even while irritations wedged at the edge.

Matilda Knight joined us; Christine did not. I wasn't sure whether that annoyed Helena, but when I asked Christine if she'd like to come, she declined. No one questioned her right to do so. My true sister Kitty came along, and I was grateful, since I wanted both Kate and Ida with me. Martin had agreed that Andy and Christian could remain with him during the day.

"My home is perfectly suited for you all to stay there," I told Martin, "so the boys can sleep at night in their own beds."

"It wouldn't be right, my being there when the woman of the house wasn't, don't you know," Martin protested. Color spread against his neck, nearly as red as my Running Squares block. He pushed at the straw cuffs of his shirt.

"*Ach,*" I said. "How silly to leave a house empty while others are bundling up together. I have nothing you could catch, and it would be convenient." *Andy wouldn't be listening to the gossip of the bachelors,* I thought but didn't say.

"*Ja,* well, maybe then we will."

Fortunately, Martin was not the stubborn kind.

Andy jumped up and down at the thought that he'd be remaining with Martin. "Here I thought you'd be upset that your sisters get to go," I said.

"I'm upset," Christian told me. "Who will keep Andy from punching me?"

"Martin will," I assured him. "I'll speak to him. And to you, young man." I pointed my finger at Andy. "For someone who wants to grow up to be a healing soul, you should start with your brother. Smartness mixed with unkindness makes a sour sauce." Andy lowered his eyes. I was glad to see shame on his face. "And, Christian, you don't want to become someone who tells tales on others either. Or who expects to be punched just to complain of it. Notice things. Watch. When your brother thinks you're in his way, he'll give you signs. Look for them and before he hits your arm, you take your slingshot and go outside and hit targets. Or find one of the men making harnesses and ask about their work. Offer to help Brother Ehlen with his baskets. *Do* something. Don't wait for Andy to do it *to* you."

"Yes, Mama," Christian said.

"I'm leaving you boys with Martin this one time, but if I hear there are problems, then that will never happen again, understood?"

Both boys nodded in unison.

Once I'd dreaded leaving my sons behind. Now I was content. They were content. Martin was a good friend. I allowed myself to savor hope.

———

The journey to Salem took the entire day. At the fairgrounds, we women set up our food tent in the dusk. We'd be sleeping in the wagons, but we unloaded the heavy crates we'd packed with ham and eggs and bacon and bread. I'd fixed a cooler of sorts, helped by Daniel Steinbach, an arrival from Bethel. Inside a box we'd placed straw, then set a smaller box within it. In the space between, we placed ice chunks and covered them with more straw. The butter and cream kept cool, and once we made up our dressings for greens, we'd keep the leftovers in the cooling box too. We made tables with sawhorses and boards, "planed right in Aurora Mills," as I told anyone who asked. I built up a fire while the girls found a water supply. I watched them pumping water from a hand pump, splashing it at their feet as they filled the pails.

Kitty and Matilda Knight and one of the Schwader girls came along. I felt my older age with the need to keep an eye on both my little girls and these young women too. I hoped to have more time with Matilda. I wondered why she remained in Aurora while her brothers had left. I looked forward to discovering her mysteries. Except for Matilda, the girls were too young to marry, I decided. There was plenty of time for those commitments later, if only they could grasp that. If only Kitty could. She'd been talking with misty eyes about a Bethel widower. Becoming a twenty-two-year-old stepmother to a twelve-year-old didn't seem like the wisest of decisions. But who was I to make an assessment on my sister's interests or of what troubled Matilda, if anything did? Aside from Christian, I'd certainly not done well making my choices.

Up until now, I haven't done well, but I'm doing better.

Matilda was a natural with children. She and I were the same age, but I had seniority since I was a mother. I was glad she'd had time in Willapa this past year. She used her stories from there to thread her way into Kate's life, talking about oysters and mentioning the Giesy stockade, where Kate had been born during that winter when so many of us had huddled together under that one cedar roof. "I was born where everyone could see?" Kate said. She pinched her nose. "Mama!"

At eight, Kate acted as though she knew everything there was to know, but she still lacked that self-control that would keep her from stating things better left unsaid.

Matilda laughed. "*Ja, aber* your mama had a blanket for a private place, and your papa was there to welcome you, that's the story I heard from Jacob Stauffer." John Stauffer had been a scout, but I noticed whatever Matilda said about Willapa usually included Jacob, who'd come out later. "It's a good story, Kate," Matilda continued. "To be born with family all around is a blessing."

After the men finished their meals, we cleaned up and got ready for the next meal. We barely had time to eat, and what with watching children, cooking, and serving, I felt tired indeed. Maybe I was too old to be doing these fair things, traveling from home. At the last minute Brother Keil had chosen not to come along, so at least we didn't have his directives to respond to. Eventually, we women might have time to ourselves.

I wanted to visit Durbin's livery, hoping to track down Brita. Once the brothers drew me a map, making quite a show of using what German they knew, and said it would be a long trip. "Several hours walking by foot," one said. "Almost as long riding," added the other. "But we can rent you a horse."

"I probably can't do it this time, then," I said. "But I'll keep the map."

I walked back out toward the fairgrounds, disappointed. I passed the post office and decided that I could write a letter and tell Brita we'd be coming back again for the fair, and ask if she could meet me then. I'd do that before we left.

Giving up on visiting Brita, I was free to make a detour toward Wallamet University, that place where one day my son would go to school if I could make it happen. It was a good hike from the fairgrounds, and I was glad I'd not brought the girls.

The several-story brick building rose up like a castle into the blue summer sky. It had been around for at least twenty years, based on the size of the trees growing beside it. There were classes in session. At least I could see people moving behind the windows. Martin would come here to school one day. My Andy too. I thought I should see what kind of school it really was, assess its value for Andy. I looked at the sun. I had time. I walked up the steps and went in.

My eyes adjusted to the wood-lined halls, the dark coolness a pleasant respite from my August walk. The doors on both sides were closed, but I could hear voices from beyond. A large staircase beckoned and I stepped up, my leather soles like breaths of air brushed against the oak. A door stood open. I moved toward it and watched a woman ease around the room, her long skirt swishing as she bent to comment to the female student who held a paintbrush in her hand. *A painting class!* Around her, other eyes lifted from their easels to hear what the woman said.

"You can see through the portrait that the paint is but a vehicle to bring the subject into focus in ways she might not otherwise appear. Paint captures an idea, while a daguerreotype seizes a moment." I looked toward the front of the room to see the model, a young woman wearing a shoulder-exposing gown, a velvet necklace at her throat, and her hair done up with curls and combs. My eyes moved to the student closest to me who had already completed her portrait of the model. To me, the model looked warmer on that easel than she really was sitting in the sunlight that highlighted her pale cheeks. *Paint is but a vehicle for our experience.* I thought the words, but I must have spoken them out loud, for each woman turned to me, including the instructor.

"May I help you?" she asked.

"*Nein.* No. *Ja.* I didn't mean to intrude." I started backing away.

"This is a third-level course," the woman said, "for our more advanced students. We're always welcoming other artists, if you'd care to join us."

"Join? No. I was… I sketch. My son is interested in medicine. I don't live here. I'm so sorry."

She extended her hand to me the way a man does. "I'm Lucia Jordan, instructor. Perhaps you were seeking the registrar? There are always openings."

"I…*ja*. The registrar."

For a moment I put myself there in that room; I imagined my hand holding a brush, stroking the canvas with reds and blues and greens, painting the sea I remembered, the faces of my children. I sank into the images I could make that would bring me joy. I could turn my parlor into such a painting room. Like Brita, I could follow my desires; I could.

"Please, don't be shy." The instructor stood beside me, urged me through the door.

Before me was a dream I'd had for years, ripe for the plucking. I turned and ran down the steps to the sun outside. Taking a painting class would do nothing to make another's life better than my own; certainly not my children's.

———————

After the first night at the fairgrounds, the smell of fresh sawdust and hammering brought out several local men who asked questions, gave the carpenters advice, and bought up our wares. They came back each day, they said, to watch the progress, but I noticed they ate more each time, and they brought others with them. By the third day, we'd gathered up a crowd, and after serving the men their dinners, I could see that we might run low on food. I'd been selling sandwiches to this ever-growing gallery, especially in the evenings, when the band quit building and played. If Keil had been along, he'd have sold tickets. As it was, we were making money with our food sales.

"Looks like we need to make some purchases," I told Kitty. "Do you want to go to the market, or do you want me to?"

"I'll go with Kitty," Matilda said. "I'd like a little break if you don't mind." Matilda had been a faithful tender of my girls, and I wanted her to have time to relax. I handed Kitty the list and told them to hurry back, for it looked like we'd have a crowd for dinner, and very likely several would stay after to listen to the music.

I wrote my letter to Brita, then decided rather than give the girls another outing the following day, I'd mail the letter myself. With the girls in hand, we walked from the fairgrounds on a dirt path, then on the boardwalk toward the post office in the back of the apothecary store. We didn't need to go as far as the shops where Matilda and Kitty would be filling their baskets. My girls trudged along, not happy to be taken from their grassy play area near the building site.

"We won't be gone long," I said. "And we might have an adventure."

"What's adventure?" Ida asked.

"It's Mama's way of making us forget that our feet hurt," Kate said. I gave Kate a warning look.

"My feet hurt?" Ida asked, looking down at her scuffed toes. I'd need to get the shoemaker to fit her for a new pair, she was growing so quickly. Her right foot looked larger than her left. I wondered if I could talk the shoemaker into making a separate shoe for each foot instead of making both from a single mold.

"That lady hurts," Ida said then. She pointed to a woman standing in the shadow of the postal/apothecary building.

A cowed-looking woman, she sank against the brick wall, her bonnet sagging at the top. Her dress was plain and the sleeves threadbare. Her small hands had knuckles red as strawberries and just as large. And she was crying silently, without even putting her hands to her face to stop the tears.

"Don't point," I told Ida as she pulled back on my hand, forcing me to stop in front of the woman.

"Mine," Ida said. She offered the woman a wrinkled white cloth, pulled from the pocket I'd sewn onto her apron.

The woman shook her head no.

"For me," Ida told her. "Take it for me."

She must have seen Ida's disappointment, for she accepted the offer.

I'd been that tearful once, that hopeless. I'd never worn threadbare clothes, but my soul had been tendering too, disintegrated and shattered as old silk from the caustic things of life. That was how this woman looked.

"Can I help you?" I asked. Then I remembered that I would as easily have answered no when someone asked if they could help, but I would accept the offer if it meant I could do something good for someone else. That was probably why the woman had taken Ida's handkerchief at the second offer.

"There's little you can do to help," she said.

"Are you waiting for someone? We're here mailing a letter, but we could wait with you if you'd like."

The woman again shook her head no. "There's no one here waiting on me. Only my children talk to me, and they're on the Clatsop Plains, far from here."

"I know where that is," I said. Something about that area, which wasn't too far from the Willapa region, rang a bell, but I couldn't recall what it was.

She lifted her head and with challenge in her voice said, "What do you know about that?"

"I used to live on the Willapa River," I said. "I remember hearing of the Clatsop people. It was a long time ago. Very wet winters." Her shoulders relaxed. "I didn't get out much."

"One finds that a common thing for women of that region." She had gray eyes that shone clear and kind now, and looked right through me when the tears had been dabbed dry.

I saw Matilda and Kitty walking along carrying their baskets of food. They waved at me from across the street. A voice nudged at my insides. "If you've nowhere to go right now," I said, "maybe you could come back and help me. We have to cook up a storm for some men building a dance hall at the fairgrounds."

"I don't dance," she said. "It's against my faith."

"I know many who share your views. We Germans love to dance, though. And the music is lovely. Surely your faith allows you to listen to the music."

"Music has seen me through my...some difficult times," she said.

"Perhaps our music will cheer you then, Miss...what did you say your name was?"

"Almira Raymond," she said. "But I don't think I'm a miss anymore, not with nine children. But I'm also no longer a...missus."

"Even though we're widowed," I said kindly, "We're still missus or, in my language, a *Frau*."

She turned away from me. "I wish I were a widow," she whispered. "It would be better than what I am."

12

Transplanting

August. Too much happening to write often here. I'm busy doing.

Almira walked back with us to the dance hall. My fingers did their rubbing, announcing I was nervous. Well, I'd invited a woman I didn't know and who had a certain challenge in her voice to spend the evening with us. It might have been impulsive, but I saw it as an act of kindness. She needed something, and I'd heard this inner speaking that quieted when I extended my invitation. Compassion and food were all I had to offer. The provision of safe harbor must come first, before one can accept that others mean kindness. Ida's genuine offer of care must have given her hope.

We walked past rhododendrons, plants I'd seen bloom in the spring on my side hill near the Pudding, shadowed by tall trees. Someone in Salem had transplanted them to grow beside their porch steps, so they looked like tamed plants, ones that had always belonged there, rather than wild.

"Those plants give off such showy blooms in springtime," Almira said. "I didn't realize they could be taken from the forest and would still grow."

"It's surprising what can be transplanted," I said. I saw it as a hopeful sign that she noticed. When I was at my lowest, I couldn't pay attention to anything lovely; my mind trotted like a dog in frustrating circles.

"That could be said of more than just plants," she said. "Though one wonders if the second soil is really ever as good for it as the first."

"It's different, I've found, but not necessarily bad." Ida held the woman's hand as we walked, and I thought Almira flinched when my daughter first touched her, but she held Ida's fingers lightly, obviously wanting to please the child. Still, her hands must hurt, the knuckles were so red.

"Your daughter reminds me of my Annie," Almira said. Her eyes watered again.

Something made me tell her that I had left Willapa under difficult circumstances. "I've transplanted myself in a new place, Mrs. Raymond. Or been transplanted, I've never been certain."

"Please. Use my Christian name, Almira. I'm not…well, I'm not married," she whispered. She wiped at the wetness pressed out of those gray eyes. She had tiny brown spots on her cheeks and at her wrists, and when she spoke she sounded like the women from cities in eastern states. "So you're alone here? With your girls?"

"We've come from Aurora, the Christian colony east of here. I'm not alone anymore. I have two sons who stayed behind and friends to help. We're here for a short time, while a few of our men build at the fairgrounds. At the colony, we all work as we can and contribute to the common good." She frowned, but I thought it might be more of a squint against the sun. "Are you familiar with Christian ways?"

"Oh yes," she said. "Quite."

She spoke it as though it was the last thing she wanted to say on that subject.

At the building site, I served her tea. She shook as she held the cup, and so I urged a biscuit on her and a slice of ham. She was very thin, wrists the width of Kate's. My older daughter had gone off with a Schwader girl to oversee the dance hall progress, but Ida stuck by Almira's side as though she'd discovered a forgotten boat and would need to keep her in tow.

"You're very kind," Almira said. "I didn't mean to impose, and I shan't trouble you beyond this lovely supper. I feel stronger now."

"It's hardly a supper," I told her. "We'll begin preparing that now, and if you're up to it, we could use the extra assistance. You can see we've quite a crowd."

"I'd be pleased to," she said. She rose, then lost her balance and drifted down the way a sheet does when unfurled onto a bed. She collapsed in a heap beside the wagon.

Matilda and Kitty ran forward to assist me help her.

"Is she sick? Who is she?"

"She's tired," I said, hoping that was true. "Let her rest."

"I found her," Ida told them. She pointed her finger in the air as though to dispute anyone's claim. "She's mine."

———————

When the meal was complete, served, and consumed, the musicians revived themselves with music. We'd also brought taffy we'd pulled, with paraffin in it to keep it from melting in the August heat. The girls and Matilda and I had prepared stick candies before we left Aurora, and those we sold now for a penny, along with the taffy pieces. "We're making money, hand over stick," Kitty noted as she handed yet another young man the striped sweet. She'd fluttered her eyes at him as he'd taken the candy and turned back to the band.

It stayed light until nearly ten o'clock on this summer night, but soon the music would end and the crowd disperse. They'd have to pay to hear the band at the fair, so this was a treat for them. Perhaps it added to our food sales, since they hadn't parted with money for a ticket. The musicians improvised and joked with their audience.

I heard a startled cry behind me. Almira awoke, looked around, her left hand rubbing the knuckles of her right. "I need to go," she said. "I need to…" She looked around again, lost. She didn't seem strong enough to consider leaving. As the crowd lessened, I told her, "You're welcome to stay here with us. We sleep in the wagons. It's not too uncomfortable, as you probably noted; but in the company of so many, we're safe enough out here beneath the stars." She shook her head no. "You'd be doing me a favor," I said. "Ida will put up a fuss if you go now."

She hesitated and then said, "Perhaps, well, just for the night." She removed her bonnet for the first time. She lay down again, and Ida snuggled in next to her, as if the child had found a large doll to claim as her own. Almira was separated from her family, but it appeared that tonight she'd found safety in ours.

———◆———

In the morning, the workmen put finishing touches on the dance hall door, placed the lock, and stood back to admire their work. In less than two months, we'd be back for the fair, and oh, what a grand time we'd have! I'd probably not be allowed to come back to help with provisions, though the nearly twenty dollars we'd raised in these few days would say much about the market for our German delicacies in Salem.

Almira hadn't moved all night, though I'd heard her call out twice as if in a bad dream. She still lay flat on her back, hands across her chest, casket ready should she expire in the night. Ida had wriggled and wiggled her way, so that she slept now with her head closer to Almira's knees than her face. I lifted her carefully from Almira's side. The woman breathed so shallowly that I had to look twice to see if she did. Her bodice barely lifted. The stitching on her threadbare dress was finely done.

I had one last thing to do before we headed back to Aurora. I told the men I'd be back in an hour or so. Matilda agreed to watch the girls. When I returned, Almira was awake. "I have a suggestion for you, Mrs. Raymond...I mean, Almira," I said. "At the colony we have a doctor and another man who specializes in apothecary. Your hands might improve from Arnica montana. It's this cream, but I know that sometimes mountain climbers eat the plant's roots to ease their aches or help with bruises. I'm sure we can get—"

"I don't need medicines. Discomfort is what I deserve. And I have no funds." She'd begun brushing at the thin calico and looked around as though to pick up her bag, but she had none.

"But you *can* pay. By exchanging work. It's how we do it in Aurora. We're a communal society."

"Men take many wives there," she said, throwing her shoulders back in strait-laced disapproval. "Is that how I'd be asked to pay?"

"Oh, no, no. In fact, our leader is more discouraging of marriage than not."

"That's a certainty," Matilda said. I looked at her, wondering if she'd say more, but she continued putting baskets back into the wagon.

"And certainly only one family per household is our goal, but we're short of housing. People do stay with each other, but only until they can be moved into their own homes."

"You'd have room for me?"

"We'd make room."

"I sometimes wake with nightmares. And my past... You might not be accepting of me if you knew."

"We all have secrets we'd not care to share," I said. "The book of The Acts marks our lives helping each other in wilderness places despite what we've done to end up there," I said. I told her of the Diamond Rule. "It's not up to us to condemn. I'm widowed, but I'm also separated from my second husband," I said. "Yet I'm welcomed there." I wondered if that was true, decided it was.

"I've nothing to offer," Almira said. "There's no way I can make another's life better than my own, not after what I've done."

Ida stood beside her and again reached for Almira's reddened hands. "Maybe to begin with, you could look after my children. I have two boys at home too," I said, "so while I'm cooking at the Pioneer Hotel, that would help. Ida has a leavings doll I've made her from the leftover scraps, but it's not enough some days to entertain her."

Now some could say that asking a stranger to look after the lives of the most precious suggests questionable judgment on my part, but there was something about Almira that didn't worry me. Ida had accepted her immediately. And she didn't look like the kind of woman who would have nine children without being married. She might have been divorced, but those were rare indeed in the region. Something different must have happened to Almira. She might be a strong-willed woman who was perceived as stubborn or contrary, with a husband who resented her strength. I could understand that.

"Maybe for a time. Until my strength returns. And as long as I can contribute." She paused before asking, "Will you have to ask Brother Keil's permission to have me stay at your home?"

"I don't see why. I'm only following our Diamond Rule."

Matilda interjected then, "My brother says that Brother Keil sets the tone for everything. 'He who provides the food gives the orders,' he says."

I hadn't thought of it that way—that food was the force that held families together or forced them to separate in search of it, but there was a truth to that. I'd heard stories of fathers saying to their adult children, "So long as you put your feet under my table, you'll follow my rules." That must be what they meant. My father might have said that to me if I'd moved in with them.

"She'll be taking care of my girls so that I can work at the hotel or do my seamstress work," I said. "That way she's contributing, and so am I. You arrive at a fortuitous time," I told Almira, feeling awkward talking about her with Matilda when she stood right there. "We'll be building a great deal, have more people now to feed and clothe. And your arrival helps me personally. I'll let Brother Keil know that." I wondered whether to tell Matilda the rest of it, then decided to go ahead. "I'll need to work extra now, to pay off my instruction fee anyway."

Matilda looked at me.

"I signed up to take an art course at the university," I said. "And I didn't ask Brother Keil's permission for that either."

———◆———

I walked behind the others on the way back to Aurora. It gave me time to think. Keil would consider it frivolous and yet…as prayerful words took us through to God, why couldn't paintings take us to God's presence? Karl had told me once that there were those who said Saint Luke had not only been a physician but a painter too, an artist who painted portraits not of God, of course, but of God incarnate, God on earth: portraits of the living Christ.

I had forgotten Karl's telling me that until I stepped into that classroom the second time. Miss Jordan was teaching another class. They were painting human forms, but landscape scenes and still-life paintings formed a border around the outside edge of the classroom, a halo around the work the women painted. In the center was an iconic painting done on wood. It showed the Virgin Mary holding her Son as an infant to her face, her right hand clutching Him close while her left hand reached out as though seeking. I'd seen pictures of this before in books, but seeing it there among the other paintings brought tears to my eyes.

Paintings were ways through, the way music was, the way the parables were, the way I sometimes felt when I stitched and worked my fingers to create new fabric forms. I wanted to paint one of those icons to have in my own home, one I could sit before and calm my muddling mind into prayer. It was that hope which had propelled me to take such a drastic move as registering for the course. I hadn't paid for it yet. But I would find a way. My hope was that the agreement signed by Keil and me, permitting all of my family to be educated, would include me. I'd paint, sell the paintings, and use the money to make repayment for the course. Maybe I'd have enough left to put toward Andy's schooling too.

The beginners' course was taught for a week at a time, once a month for three months. I'd have to make arrangements for the children, trust that my work at the hotel wouldn't be missed, and get Keil to agree that this course was in service to the colony. It could be a difficult sell.

I pitched that thought away.

Maybe the pieces could help decorate the church. The craftsmen would be working on the altar. Perhaps some color would be welcomed on the church walls. Meanwhile, an iconic painting could offer comfort to those in need, like Almira. She'd become very important to me. This must have been how Christian felt when he'd brought someone into our fold. Christopher Wolff had been recruited by Christian. So had

Karl Ruge. Both men brought goodness to us all through their artistries, their intellect, and their service. I anticipated that Almira was only the first of many who would bring goodness to us all, and I was now a part of that.

"You're so brave, Emma," Matilda said as she stepped back to walk with me.

I laughed at that. "Brave? *Nein*. Foolish maybe, or a coward. I'm afraid of doing everything the same each day. I'm more afraid of dying before I've found out why I'm here than I'm scared of rubbing Brother Keil the wrong way. I'm not going to change the world, the way I once thought Christian and I might. But little things each day can make a difference. Besides, Keil ebbs and flows like the ocean. I'll catch him when the tide is out."

"Does he? He seems so...stern to me."

I'd forget at times that those newer arrivals from Bethel had been without Keil's physical presence for nearly ten years. He was almost a legend to many of them, until they faced him here. They'd gone on without him, making decisions, living their lives. It must have been difficult after all that time to find themselves somehow subservient to him, this man who wasn't any kind of god at all; a man who picked his teeth of meat, just as we all did.

"Sometimes he's willing to bestow goodness on us; sometimes he withholds. I never know which it'll be, so I may as well do what I think I ought to and hope I can convince him later if something strikes him wrong. It took me a while to get my house, but I got it. Even the stove, though I'll be some time paying for that!"

"I heard Barbara White Giesy say that was quite an extravagance."

"She would," I said. "But I'll bake good things for the colony, so I'll be giving back. And I didn't ask Keil for permission, and when it arrived he didn't tell me that I couldn't keep it. I'm sure he knew it was delivered. Sometimes we just do what we think we must."

"Well...," she said.

I waited for her to tell me more, and when she didn't I brazenly asked, "So what is it that you think he'll deny you?"

She blushed and shook her head. "Nothing," she said. "Nothing."

It was late when we arrived back at Aurora, but I didn't feel tired or restless. Stars were beginning to pop out of their dark closets, so I expected to see lamplight from my house. I didn't. I didn't think the boys would be in bed yet. It was summer and the air still warm, and playing outdoors was something they both loved to do. I set the lamp I carried on the table in the kitchen and walked to the back porch. No one was there except Opal, who bleated me her welcome. We'd built a pen for her, and she put her feet up on the railing. "Later," I told her. "I'll scratch your head later." The chickens had been put in for the night.

Both Kitty and Matilda had planned to spend the night with the Schwaders in their log home, but since it was late, I invited them both to stay with me. With Almira, they waited inside. Kitty lit the kitchen lantern so when I came back in, it was to a warm light.

"Where are the boys?" Kitty asked.

"I suppose they're still with Martin." I gathered up quilts for Almira and Matilda and Kitty and settled them in the parlor. "You're my first real guests," I said. It was too warm for a fire. That was probably why the kindling I'd placed there before we left hadn't been burned. Perhaps they'd eaten elsewhere so they didn't have to bother cleaning my dishes. "They'll be here before long."

I got the girls ready for bed and tucked them in upstairs. Ida tried to convince me to let her sleep beside Almira again, but I assured her she'd be there in the morning. She listened to me and fell fast asleep.

I came down the stairs and went through the kitchen out to the front porch, so I didn't have to bother the women sleeping inside. I sat there on my father's blue bench and waited for my sons to come home.

No need to be worried, I decided. I was adaptable. I knew that circumstances sometimes intervened to break up well-laid plans. Martin must have decided it was easier to sleep at Keils' with the boys than to prepare meals and whatnot for them in my home. I could understand that, in a way. Men didn't much like to cook a meal, and even though it would only have been mush for breakfast, something Andy could have fixed for them all, Martin was probably accustomed to a big bacon-and-egg breakfast that he'd find at the Keils'. Or for all I knew, they were fixing breakfasts for all the workmen building the church. I'd find out in the morning, I decided. I came inside, ran my fingers across the iron stove, blew out the kitchen lights, then carried my candle upstairs, well after what must have been midnight. I heard Opal bleat in the night and felt nearly as forlorn as her cry.

———

In the morning I heard the rooster crow and realized someone was already up, fixing the fire and preparing coffee for us all. When I came downstairs, Matilda smiled and admired the smooth pine floor I'd oiled myself.

"Your boys are sleeping in?" she asked.

I didn't respond. "I'll go on over to see how progress is coming on the church once the girls are awake. Want to come?"

"My brother expects me back. I can take the stage, he said."

"Oh, come with us," Kitty urged. Since her braids were neatly wrapped around her head, I knew she'd been up for a time too. "We can walk you back to the stage later."

"I wouldn't want to miss it," Matilda said.

Almira was slow to rise, and when she did, she asked to remain in the house with the girls. She commented on the stove, said it was a fine one. "It must have cost a pretty penny," she said. "More than twenty dollars."

"Twenty-five dollars. I'll be working long years for it, but it makes a fine bread."

She sighed onto the chair. "I haven't had a safe place to just sit," she said. "Not for a long time."

I wasn't sure if I should leave her here alone in the house, though I didn't know why not. I had no reason to think she'd take anything from me. She had an eye for the price of things. I hoped I wasn't being taken advantage of. And then I chided myself. I had offered her assistance and then so quickly began creating criteria I thought she should meet to receive it.

"Yes, you stay," I said. "Ida and Kate will enjoy not having to go anywhere after their long trip home."

Besides, if I did have to confront Martin about the boys or Keil about Almira, I could do that without the girls listening.

The three of us, Kitty, Matilda, and I, walked past the store. I looked in at the pharmacy, but no one was there, and the workmen had stopped building on that structure. I suspected that was how the building would go on now, moving from place to place, framing walls, then waiting for the bricks to be fired across the Pudding, then making the roof ridges, pounding the lumber to close in the walls and the rooms, putting on shingles. In between they'd work on the church, the largest structure we'd ever built from our lumber.

It was a quarter mile from the village to the Point, the place where Keil's house and the church stood. I hadn't been up this way for a while, so I didn't recognize the house going up below the creek.

"John Giesy's house," Kitty told me. "One of the finest, like Keil's." The path past it went up a steep ravine toward the fir grove. We were perspiring by the time we reached the Keil house. Kitty said she'd need to rest there. She loosened her apron at the waist and sat down on the steps. She chewed on her nail. "Go ahead. I'll catch up," she told us, as Matilda and I walked on toward the church. Men and boys congregated there, so I assumed I'd find my sons there too. Several of the men who'd been building at the fair were already at work here with their hammers. I imagined they'd gossiped about Almira Raymond, wondering who she was and why she had returned with us. Men tried to say they didn't gossip, but I remembered Christian always had more news than I did at the end of his day. As we approached, I heard Matilda gasp.

"Are you all right?"

"Yes. *Ja.* It's a surprise," she said. "The Stauffers are here."

I knew Jacob Stauffer. He was the son of John Stauffer Sr., a former scout who'd settled in Willapa. I wondered if John Sr. had moved his family here, then, but I didn't see him. Only Jacob.

"You met Jacob in Willapa?" I said.

She nodded. "We talked. Nothing more." Her neck showed reddish blotches, and her steps hurried up the hill even though it was the steepest part. "I used Mrs. Stauffer's oven. It's very good. You can regulate the heat well. O. B. Twogood sold it to them, a shop in Oregon City. We went by there when we came here. Such fine things for sale. Have you been there?" She rattled on, giving no room for answers.

"Ah," I said. "What time did you say you had to get back to the stage?"

She didn't say.

I waved my hand. "Jacob Stauffer," I shouted. "It's good to see you."

He turned to see who'd called his name and waved back to my raised hand, and then I watched his eyes move to Matilda's. He grinned from ear to ear, dropped his hammer on a pile of lumber, and walked full stride our way.

"You know Matilda Knight," I said when he reached us and removed his flat-top hat. A small dog trotted behind him.

"*Ja,* sure," he said. "We stopped at your brother's in Oregon City on the way down. He said you'd gone to Salem."

"He told you I was in Salem?"

"To help with the cooking. I worried I might miss you."

"You did? You worried you'd miss me?"

She repeated nearly everything he said, and I recognized it as that loving duplication of our hearts. Excitement welled up in her face. Jacob bent absently to pat the dog's head, but he never took his eyes off Matilda.

"I didn't know how long you'd be there. Or if you'd find work in Salem and maybe not come back here at all. Your brother said you were hoping to move out on your own perhaps, not be a burden on them, though he claimed you weren't that at all."

He removed his hat now, kept turning it over in his hands while

Matilda clasped her palms behind her. By the way she stood before him, she might have been fifteen years old instead of over thirty.

"Matilda's thinking of catching the stage back to her brother's soon. Maybe you could walk her there," I suggested.

"*Ja,* sure. Or maybe talk her out of it." He grinned.

"That would be good too," I said. I decided to add, "You can live with us, Matilda. There'll be work here. You're good with a needle. You said so yourself. Keil's opening a tailor shop for noncolonists to have work done."

"Opportunities," Jacob said.

"*Ja,*" she barely whispered. "But I'd better go back and talk with my brother. See what he says."

I watched them walk side by side down the hillside. Jacob put his hand out once to catch her when Matilda slipped but chastely put his hands to his side when she was steady again. Matilda would have to work it out herself, I decided. I had to find my boys.

And find them I did, right in the middle of the building activity. Martin was there with them, of course. He'd supervised them as I knew he would have, but still it annoyed me that he hadn't stayed at the house so they'd have been there when I got home.

"The boys were good, then, Martin?"

"Very good," he said. "They're fine boys, don't you know." He didn't face me, but rather stood next to me, looking out at the construction. They'd made little progress in the few days we'd been gone, but they'd begun, and sometimes that was the hardest work of all.

"You didn't stay at my house," I said. "Didn't I tidy it up enough for you?"

"*Nein.*" He cleared his throat. "Brother Keil...said otherwise."

There was no tease in Martin's voice.

"Well, I'll take them home now, then."

He stood silent next to me. I heard a crow caw in the trees. "Sister Emma, Brother Keil would have a word with you."

"We talk often."

"About the boys."

I felt my heart start to pound. "You said yourself they were good boys."

"*Ja.* That they are." He cleared his throat, and I thought his face looked pained when he turned to me and said, "It is for the best, Emma."

"What's for the best? What are you talking about?"

"Transplanting is often good. Just remember. We only want the best for all of us, to make each life better than our own."

13

Puzzle Pieces

I could see my sons in the distance, their small frames moving about like happy goats, jumping over piles of lumber, chasing friends, letting playful dogs pull at their pants. They stayed out of the close construction area, so they weren't being a nuisance. They looked fine. There had to be some reasonable explanation for why they hadn't been to see me yet and for Martin's odd hesitations and foreboding tone as he sent me off to Keil.

"I'll find Brother Keil, since you say he wants to see me. Is he back at the *gross Haus*?" Martin nodded. "Fine. I'll speak to my sons and then talk to Keil. Would you take the boys home for me after that?"

"Ah…," Martin said.

"Mama!" Christian shouted.

I waved. Christian started to run toward me, but Andy stopped him. *What's that about?* The boys waited for me to reach them as I walked farther up the hill.

"Hi, Mama," Christian said. "Did you see me jump over that pile of boards?"

I nodded, and he leaned into my skirts and I hugged him. "You look like you're having a good time, Andy," I said. He nodded but didn't speak. I motioned for him to let me hold him too, and he allowed it. I felt stiffness in his shoulders, though, and he broke the embrace first. "Martin's going to take you home in a bit. We need to catch up." I wiped at a smudge on his cheek with my thumb.

"He'll take us home to Keil's house," Andy said. It wasn't a question.

"Why would you say that? We have a home now. You have your own rooms. I know I have the quilt top stretched over your bed, but it's up with a pulley. It's out of your way. Think of it as a colorful night sky over you. We'll put it in the parlor before long. Would that be better?"

"I don't mind the quilt there, Mama," Christian said. "I like to see all the threads sticking out."

"Uncle John and Uncle Martin think we should stay with Uncle Martin now," Andy said.

A hot poker seared my heart. "Oh they do, do they? Well, we'll have a talk about that. Meanwhile, you stay right here while I go talk to Brother Keil."

Christian's face wore both confusion and fright, so I calmed myself, controlled the tremble in my voice. "It's going to be fine, Christian. Mama will be back shortly with this all straightened out. Did you have your breakfast already?"

Christian nodded his head, but Andy stared at me. What sort of thoughts had been put into his head? Not by Martin, surely. I trusted Martin.

I turned and smoothed my apron. I yanked at the pocket I'd tied at my waist. John Giesy was now deciding who should raise my sons? Would these Giesys never let me go my own way? Hadn't I given in to the ways of the colony, so my sons would be safe, so all my children would be raised well? Hadn't I done everything they'd asked of me?

I slipped on the steep path leading to Keil's house. I straightened. Kitty still sat on the steps, fanning herself. "What's the matter, Sister?" she asked. "You look as though you've seen a snake."

"Nothing," I lied. I stomped up the steps past her, opened the double doors, and immediately took the steps downstairs. That's where Keil would be. In his workroom. Plotting and planning. Maybe John Giesy was with him, and I could confront them both.

"Sister Emma," Keil greeted me with a large smile. "You've come back. I trust you had a good time at the fair?" He stood. "Though I know it wasn't quite the fair time yet, but soon, *ja*? Our new dance hall will be well received."

I reached for my pocket and nearly threw the sack of money at him, money we'd raised selling extra candies and sandwiches to the gawkers watching the dance hall go up. "Nearly twenty dollars," I said. "I realize the colony provided the goods, but my sister and I made the candies, and our labor counts for something. We women worked while there, and we were selling things. That too should count."

"*Ja*. Such things count." He picked up the bag and poured the coins out onto his workbench. He placed them into a neat pile at the edge. A few greenbacks stuck in the bag. He pulled one out, turned it over in his long, slender fingers, placed it back down. "*Gut*, Emma. You did *gut*."

"Yes, I think I have done well. So what's this I hear about John Giesy suggesting that my sons come under the supervision of Martin? To live with him here, with you? Is that true? Why would you wish this, when I now finally have a home for them? A good home."

"Ah, Sister Emma," he sighed and sat down. He motioned for me to sit as well, but I stood. "A man's influence is essential, Emma. You know this to be so."

"I'll see that they spend time with Martin and you and my brother. Even their other uncles, John and whomever else. My father lives close by. But my sons need their mother."

"Who likes to be off doing things," Keil said. I must have looked puzzled, so he added, "Off looking for a place to homestead. Liking to travel to cotillions and dance, though she is married yet to another. Once living far away in Willapa, just to be away from here. Who gets herself an unusual chicken and a stove at colony expense."

"Those were part of my duties! Louisa and Helena suggested I go. My own mother-in-law thought it a good thing to do. I would have stayed here. I only did it for the benefit of the colony. All of it, everything I have, goes back in service."

"Looking for a homestead?"

"But I settled *here*. You built the house for me, here."

"It's clear that you are not fully committed to the colony, Emma. You've taken on the attitude of your father more than your brother, and the agreement, well, that says more than anything that you aren't truly willing to be subservient to the community. It's still you, Emma, doing what you think is best, over the good of the community. You purchase a stove, rather than add to the ledger side for things needed for your sons. You've let others look after your children…as you did these past days. You welcomed in that *Zwerg*." I opened my mouth to defend Brita, but he held his hand up to silence me. "I said nothing about your taking in that circus person. But now I learn you've welcomed someone you lifted from the streets of Salem. We open our doors to others here, Emma, but they must share our common goals. I wonder if you really do. You're more interested in an intriguing world with strangers than in spending time with your family or raising your sons."

I never should have let the boys spend all that time with Martin. I'd thought it would be good for them, but now I could see that my willingness to be separated was interpreted as disinterest, self-centeredness, or, worse, neglect.

"I only want the best for my sons," I said. I sat down now. I shook. My arms felt weak as weeds and just as useless. "The community… You said this would be a safe place for us. And the house… It was meant to give my children a better life. To ease the burden on those staying here, in your home. So I could take care of them as a mother should."

"You tell yourself a story, Sister Emma. The house was always for your benefit, but you wrapped it in the needs of your sons. We knew it was to separate them from the colony influences. I suspected this, but John Giesy confirmed it. This is how you thought in Willapa too, *ja*? To separate is best, you might have told Christian. To separate is healthy. You told them that being independent was for the benefit of all, but it was for you. Isn't that so?"

"*Nein*," I whispered. "I never intended to keep my sons from family. I haven't since we've been here. I let Barbara and Andreas travel with Andy. I've complied. Can't you see that? Why would you want to take their care from me?" My throat ached. I thought I'd gotten what I wanted here: safety for my children and me, protection from Jack Giesy.

Even my hope that my parents would move west had come to pass. I had my own home. But none of it was turning out as I'd planned.

"The colony will educate Andy and Christian. That's more than your own parents are able to do, *ja,* since they won't join the colony? You'll see the boys, of course. They'll have time with you. And we'll protect them from Jack's temper, and you too. In fact, Jack left because he knew Martin would be raising your sons. They are not Jack's sons, so I doubt he'll pursue interest in them, beyond what he asked for in return for leaving. Your girl, perhaps. We'll protect her from him as well, so long as you remain here. And where else would you go, Emma?"

His voice sounded far away.

"Martin's had nothing to do with this, by the bye," Keil added, "except to agree. But he will have a place for the boys as soon as the pharmacy is finished. Until then, there's still room for him and the boys to stay there. It will justify my paying the conscription fee for him as well, a side benefit so he won't have to go to war. He'll attend the university this fall too."

"Martin?"

"*Ja,* he'll take pharmacy classes, but then next year or so they will offer medical classes. He will be a big help if he is a doctor. Maybe you can look after the boys between their classes and when Martin comes back home each night."

"I can provide care but not a home to my sons?"

"There is good reason."

The clock ticked into the silence.

"The reason being that one day my son, Andy… He'll attend the university?"

"But of course, Emma. Don't you remember the agreement we both signed? I have it here." It was on top of his desk. He'd been expecting me. He read, " 'I, Emma Giesy, will agree to abide by the rules of the Aurora Colony as directed by Father Keil, *offering up what I have to give in service to the colony.*' " He emphasized the last part of the sentence. " 'In return, the colony will provide care, education, and keeping for me and my family including the building of a home designed for use by me.' See, I signed it right here," Keil said. "Didn't I agree that your children would be educated?"

Offering up what I have to give in service to the colony. It was a sentence I'd remember the rest of my days.

"I wasn't clever enough, was I?" I said, looking up at him. My throat constricted like a hangman's rope.

"Oh, Emma. You got what you wanted: a home of your own. You secured the promise of education for your sons. Even for yourself, though I can't imagine what you'd study in the university, but it was clever to include yourself. And you agreed to abide by the colony rules and to offer up what you had in service to the colony. A reasonable exchange. A colony way."

"I assumed I'd offer up my *work* and my *labor,* not my heart, not my flesh and blood, not the absence of my sons from my life." My voice broke. *I will not let him see my cry!*

He'd come around to my side of his desk. He pressed his hand against my shoulder. "Next time we may both pay a little more attention to the wording of things, *ja?* So I'm not paying for something frivolous you might want to do, while you call it 'education.'" He patted my back. "I'll see you out now," he said.

I sat for a time until I felt his hand increase pressure on my shoulders. He led me like a calf to slaughter toward the root room door. Scents of onion and potato rose to me as I walked outside. My lips were dry as dirt. Keil pulled the door shut behind me. The sunshine hit my eyes without warmth. I blinked, focused. How had this happened? What had happened?

Kitty stood as I walked up the grade toward the steps where she'd waited for me. "Ready to head up the hill and watch them work?" she said. "They'll make progress, now that our dance hall carpenters are back."

"I'm going home," I said.

"You want me to watch the boys?"

I didn't dare look toward the boys. Christian might be waiting for me, but I doubted Andy was. I couldn't bear to see the looks on either of their faces, or for them to see mine, to see me cut like a too-long hem from their lives.

"I'm sure that Martin will," I said. "No…I…"

"Emma? Are you all right?"

Keil came through the front door, stood at the top of the steps. "Good morning, ladies." He spoke in English. He carried his cane, walked between us as he came down the steps, then headed up toward the church. I watched him. In the distance, he stopped where Jacob Stauffer and Matilda had stalled on their way to the stage. Matilda stepped back, and Jacob listened to whatever it was that Keil so diligently expressed to them. Jacob said nothing back, but he tipped his hat to Matilda, then made his way back to the church construction, Keil and that little dog walking behind him.

Someone else's life had just changed in an instant.

Matilda stared after them; she turned away as we approached, biting her lip. Even in the shadow of her bonnet I could see she wept. She would have moved past us, but I stopped her. "I'm going back to my home," I said. "Something has…come up. I'll walk with you."

"All right, then," Kitty said. "But what am I supposed to do now?"

"Come with us if you wish," I said. "Or maybe Louisa has some tasks for you." Martin had turned toward me, arms at his side. "Or you can tell Martin that I'll bring the boys' things over to him later today. He needn't plan to stop by to pick them up."

"But he's standing right there, why don't—"

"Tell him! Or not," I said. "I can't say any more."

"Are you ill, Sister?" Kitty asked.

I shook my head no. Her kindness could unravel me if I let the slightest thread of warmth from her wrap around my broken soul.

"Go," I said. "I'll walk with Matilda."

Matilda walked silently beside me. I knew she was troubled, and if I'd had an ounce of compassion left in me I'd have reached out to comfort her. But I felt as though I was stuck inside a bale of thick wool and couldn't push my way out through the dingbats and twigs to get breath. I kept swallowing. I stopped. I lowered my head. I was going to be sick.

———————

"Your girls are up and fed and ready to help with chores," Almira greeted us as we reached the house. Kitty had remained behind. I knew she was confused, but I couldn't explain. She'd gone off to talk with Martin or maybe the boys. I'd given her nothing to tell them; I didn't know what to say.

"Have Kate gather eggs," I said, pulling myself into the present. "And let Ida go with her. But watch out for Opal. She doesn't know her own strength. I don't want her knocking Ida over."

"Are you all right, Mrs. Giesy?" Almira asked. "I mean, Emma. You don't look well." Those gray piercing eyes.

"I need some time alone," I said. "The stagecoach should be…"

"I'm not going to take it today, if that's all right with you," Matilda said. "Your offer, for me to stay, is it still good?"

"Yes. *Ja.* There's lots of room now," I said and walked slowly up the stairs. I felt one hundred years old.

I looked about for the basket of wool I'd carded. Jonathan had built me a spinning wheel, set up on the wide hall, and I'd returned my mother's to her. This one still smelled of fresh lumber. The oils of my hands had yet to darken it. I sat now to spin that wool, grasping it too tightly at first, then loosening my grip to let it pull through my fingers. It was solid yet soft. My foot moved to the rhythm. I held the yarn in my fingertips. It was wool I'd dyed myself, red as blood from the madder root. The color didn't soothe, but the threads did. I needed something firm and familiar in my fingers, something I could hang on to that wouldn't drift away, that wouldn't be taken from me. I'd thought I couldn't be stumbled by any more surprises. I had a house, my health, good work, my girls. But none of that was enough. I'd lost my sons.

I must talk to Jonathan and see if he could intervene. My father—perhaps he'd be willing to raise my sons, or at least talk to Keil about letting me do what a mother was called to do. But these were tasks I'd do later. I was too tired now. My head began to throb.

When I came downstairs, the sun dappled through the trees, making its way toward setting. I could smell the soup that the girls must have eaten, and hopefully Almira and Matilda had as well. I didn't remember the scent rising up the stairs to me, but I hadn't been hungry. I wasn't now. I stepped out onto the porch to sit on my blue bench. Matilda was already there, her hands clasped in her lap.

"Do you know where the girls are?"

"Almira took them for a walk. I thought she came upstairs to tell you. It was quite a while ago." She had a slight lisp, so when she said "thought" it came out as "taught."

"She might have. I didn't hear it above the spinning wheel." I didn't tell her that I'd been in a trancelike place, devoid of anything but the feel of the yarn in my fingers. I sat down beside her. "You decided not to go back to your brother's right now?"

"You invited me to stay, you remember?" I didn't remember that we'd talked of it. "I can leave…" She stood up, but I reached for her hand and pulled her back down. "*Danke.* Thank you," she said. "Dr. Keil. He…he said Jacob needed to spend less time courting and more time counting his hours of work. We'd only taken a moment, and it was hardly courting. Jacob hasn't even spoken a word of interest to me except to notice I was here."

I smiled, for the first time in hours. "Oh, he's interested," I said. "Even in my stupor I could see how his eyes lit up when he saw you and how closely he stood to you, to hear your every word."

"Until Dr. Keil approached." She clucked her tongue. "I felt like a small child who'd been caught with her hand in a cookie jar. And Jacob…how humiliating to be accused of courting when he wasn't.

Ach," she said. "My brother was right. I shouldn't be here in Aurora. I should stay with them. But I thought the Stauffers might come here, since so many others from Willapa had. And I didn't want to miss him. Them, I mean."

"And so he has come," I said. "With intention to stay, since he's working on the church. I imagine he'll live with the bachelors, in that rectangular building they've put up on the Point."

"And there'll be other houses going up too," she added. "Or so he told me."

I closed my eyes and leaned my head back against the wall of my house. *My house.* That's all it was then. A house. Not a home that would hear the sounds of laughter and love and disappointment and challenge and hope poured out through the lives of my children, all together as one. It was a structure. Wood and glass and brick and an iron stove. And for it I'd given up my sons.

Perhaps Keil was right about me. My girls were off with a woman who might be a dangerous person, for all I knew. By her own admission, Almira had a "past." My judgment about people was obviously suspect, since so many of those I'd come to trust through the years weren't worthy of it. Perhaps I wasn't fit to raise my sons—or my daughters. I was a self-centered woman, a wayward daughter, a pushing wife, and not much of a friend, least of all a good mother. I wiped the tears that formed a stream from my eyes into my ears. My legs weighed heavy as anchors.

"Martin Giesy came by," Matilda said. "He wanted to talk with you."

"*Ja.* I bet he did." I opened my eyes.

She turned to look at me. "He said he'd come back later this evening, for you not to trouble yourself about bringing the boys' things. He said you'd know what he meant."

"Mama, Mama!" Ida's voice. I saw them approach and watched as Ida tried to skip, but double-stepped instead. "We made this place, in the trees, Mama. It was fun. We walked in a lab-rinse. Wasn't it called that, Mira?"

"Labyrinth," Almira said. "It's called a labyrinth."

"Lab-rinth," Ida tried again. "It looks like Path to the...to the..."

"Path Through the Wilderness? The quilt pattern?" I asked her.

"It might be best to call it a puzzle path," Almira said.

I'd heard of labyrinths, a very famous one in Chartres, France, that my uncle, the ambassador to France, had written to us about. He'd drawn a picture shaped like a mushroom cap. It looked like a maze, made out of stones laid out on the floor of a cathedral, he'd told us. One could never get lost inside it; the only choice a person had to make was whether to enter at all. There was only one way in and one way out, and Christians came to walk there to find answers, and had been doing so for centuries. There certainly wasn't a labyrinth in Aurora.

I looked up at Almira. "It's a path I made for us in the clearing," she said. "I scraped it out with a stick, and the girls and I laid pinecones to mark the paths. Then we walked it. Or I should say they ran and jumped it! It was a joy to hear them laughing. I'd made one on the Clatsop Plains too. It was the only place I found peace, though it later got me into trouble." She looked away. "My husband discovered it and claimed it was some sort of witchcraft. He scattered all the stones that I had used to mark the trails."

Witchcraft!

"I'd forgotten the comfort that could come from walking one," she continued. She had a shine to her face that hadn't been there in the morning, or at any time since we'd met. "It reminds me that I must let go of everything and follow the path to the center of my soul and then carry what I've learned there back out to the world. Walking helps my soul wake up."

Kate plopped down on the porch and leaned against my legs. "Is Andy here?" she said. "Where are those boys?"

I took a deep breath. "They're going to be staying at the *gross Haus*," I said. "For now. Martin Giesy will look after them, and Andy's going to help him at the pharmacy, and one day he'll go to school to become a doctor."

"Can I be a doctor?" Kate asked.

"No, Kate," I said. Too quickly.

"Father Keil will let me," she pouted. "He calls me Catie. He likes me."

"You can never be sure," I said.

"There are women who become doctors," Matilda ventured.

I couldn't imagine my Kate having to make her way through medical school, with men all around making decisions that excluded her. "We'll talk about it later."

Kate said, "I'm going to school this autumn, aren't I, Mama? Karl Ruge said I could."

"Yes. You will go to school, and so will Andy and Christian. You'll see them there every day." I hesitated, then said, "But I won't."

"Why not?" Ida said.

I didn't know how to answer.

14

Walk In, Walk Out

Could I fight this? I could ask my parents to take the boys, but Keil was right: they couldn't afford to send Andy to medical school. They had children of their own, and there was Lou with her needs. Jonathan didn't have his own home either, and at least Martin would eventually have a place to stay with my sons, assuming Keil wouldn't change his mind about finishing the pharmacy. Jack was no option. None of the Giesys were. It occurred to me that Martin's reticence when he told me Jack was gone was a part of this, that Jack had exacted the promise that Martin would raise the boys and not me. Anything to harm me. Karl Ruge? He'd never consider raising my sons, and what was the point of looking for anyone else besides Martin? Martin was the best of the lot. What I needed was the way to raise them myself.

I could hire a lawyer to demand my sons remain with me but at what cost, even if I could find a lawyer to take my case? I still had the pearls. I could sell them. Surely my mother wouldn't mind if I did that for such a cause. But then where would we go? We'd be out on the street in no time, and where would that leave Andy's future or the future of any of my children? No. There was nothing I could do. If I found somewhere else to live, to take all my children with me, I'd still need a way to support them, to care for them, to educate them, to give them shelter.

That night I slept frantically, dreams of fog and mist and mazes, of being lost, seeking rescue. "It is a woman's lot," some hag inside my dreams would cackle, as I wandered through the thickening forests. "Raise them to resist, and they'll be squelched. Raise them to consent, and they'll be trampled flat like wet leaves of winter. Raise them to believe they can do…," she cackled toward my face. I woke up sweating and pulled the quilt from the bed to go sit on the blue bench outside to watch the sun come up. *Teach them to believe they can do what?*

———◆———

"It's a terrible trial to be separated from one's children," Almira said. We sat at my table. She used a glass Andy had claimed as his favorite. "I gave birth to nine in thirteen years. My husband traveled. He was a minister who brought the gospel to the Indians and other settlers on the Plains. Then he took a job as a sub-Indian agent, and I thought he'd be home more. We lived far from the nearest settlement. But he brought…a woman with him." I looked at Almira. "He said she'd be there to help me with the children and the laundry and cooking, but instead, she helped move me out of my bed. And when he traveled, he took her with him."

I didn't know what to say.

"I bet you didn't have any more children after that," Kitty said. She'd joined us before heading to the hotel.

"Strangely, I did," Almira said. "I kept thinking I could keep him as long as I didn't turn him out. But after a time I couldn't stand the jealous feelings. I divorced him. Or tried to… You should know these details, Emma. You may not want to have me stay here, knowing this. My husband got his friends to testify and say terrible things against me. Only my oldest son and his wife came to my defense, but it was not enough. The newspaper quoted his powerful friends. It's hard to fight power."

"You got your children, though, right?" Kitty asked. "They wouldn't take children from their mother, would they?" Kitty still didn't know the details of her nephews' plight or she wouldn't have thought that.

"Legal care always goes to the father." Almira looked down at her knuckles that held the glass like claws. "Especially well-spoken men. I know it was a sin to seek divorce. He was right about that. My children are being raised by another woman, and I'm not even allowed to see them. A divorced woman and those rumors of witchcraft and all." She gave me a sad smile. "My being here might have made your plight more precarious."

"No," I said. "What happened to me, Keil had planned long before this. You needed something we had to give, and I am grateful you accepted."

I'd started sorting through the boys' things and putting them into bundles. Maybe Martin would let them come for supper sometimes. Or breakfast. Maybe I could make them special meals on their birthdays. Surely Martin would allow that. At least I wasn't banned from seeing them, the way Almira was. At least total strangers weren't going to read about my personal affairs in the Monday *Oregonian*.

As I finished sorting, Kate sang out, "Uncle Martin is here."

"Have him come into the parlor," I said. I straightened my dress and tugged loose strands of hair into the swirl of braids on either side of my head. I looked in the mirror. *Awful.* A mess. I came downstairs and entered the parlor.

I nodded toward the chair. He sat. "This isn't how I would have planned it, don't you know," Martin said. I'd offered him coffee or tea, but he'd declined. "I know how much you love those boys."

"I've bundled up their things. If I've forgotten something, you can send someone for them."

"The boys can come themselves," he said. "They're not going to keep you from seeing them, Emma."

"They? You're a part of this too, Martin."

"I tried my best, Emma. My arguments fell flat. Jack… It was the best solution, don't you know."

"No, I don't know."

"He would have hovered over your life here forever. We thought it the best and—"

"We. The 'we' that excludes me."

"But the boys will see you. It won't be like before, when you lived so far away."

"*Ja.* See, but not raise them; watch, but not influence them. Who'd want such exposure to an outrageous mother not capable of raising her own sons?"

"Emma," he said.

"Does that seem fair to you, Martin?" I still stood. "Doesn't it… frighten you that Keil can decide such things for other people? that your brother John could?"

"They mean well, Emma. They truly do. This way you're…free. To do those things that interest you. You have your house."

"My sons interest me!" My voice cracked. "My. Sons. Interest. Me." A coastal storm of grief swept across my heart. "Am I seen as so frivolous that I'd give up my sons for a house? How could you question that? How could…they?"

"As do your daughters interest you. Devote yourself to them now, Emma. You'll see Andy and Christian. You'll be a part of their lives. Let the community raise them up and educate them."

"The way the tinsmith or the turner is a part of my life?" I said. "Someone they see in passing? If there's a small need, then I might be allowed to fill it, but mostly I'm decorative, to look at from a distance?"

"More than in passing, Emma." He stood, tried to touch my shoulder, but I jerked back from him.

"Don't touch me." I stepped back. "I trusted you."

"And I kept your trust. I brought your boys to you. They've been here with you for two years, Emma. Safe. And they'll be here for many more. Just not the way you thought it would be, but when has it ever been what you thought it would be? Christian's death changed everything."

"Coming here changed everything."

"It was the path you took," he said. "A good path, made from difficult circumstances. See the good in this, Emma. There is some. You are making your sons' lives better than your own."

I turned away so he wouldn't see the anguish.

"I'll have the boys come by tomorrow. Christian's been asking for you. I told him, 'In the morning.'"

"No," I said. "I don't think I can face them."

"You've got to be stronger than they are in this. You're the adult; they're children. Your explanation will help them deal with this change."

I wanted Martin to have to face their questions. Let him bear the brunt of their confusion. If they had confusion. Andy showed no distress at all. Maybe that was what eclipsed my heart.

I stood with my back to Martin, feeling the coolness of the usually closed-off room. "Send them," I said. "If they'll come, I'll do my best to ease their distress."

Martin left then, and I stayed with my back to the door, hoping no one would come in to try to comfort me or ask me questions. I needed time to grab on to something firm. *Fabric. Wool. My God.*

"Come, Mama." I heard the door open. It was Ida's voice. "We'll show you our lab-rinse." She pulled on my hand. *Not now.*

"Mira says to call it a puzzle path," Kate said from behind her.

"I can't go with you now," I said. "I'm already walking on one."

———

"Did you know what they did to me?" I asked Karl, later in the week that seemed a month of foggy days.

"*Ja,* I heard some changes were recommended."

"Recommended? You think I had a choice?"

"We all have choice," he said. "If only about how to respond to the unpredictability of life."

"Oh, I suppose I should be asking, 'How do we see God in this?' Well, I don't." My sarcasm caused his eyebrows to lift.

"Ah, Emma," he said. "Life has not treated you well; but now you will have the opportunity to show your sons and daughters, even your sisters and brothers and your own parents, how you tithe your tragedies." His pipe, recently smoked, lay on the table, and the scent brought a comfort.

I had the girls with me. Ida played with one of the wooden toys that Martin had made for her. The sight of it no longer comforted me as it once had. "I was so blind," I said. "Why didn't I see this coming, Keil's maneuvering, John's and maybe even Helena's influence? I keep missing things," I said. "It's as though I never learn."

"Can we take the puppy to the grass?" Kate asked Karl. She held a plump black and white mongrel in her arms and had brought the dog in from outside.

"*Ja,* sure. I call him Potato using the English. Po for short," Karl told her. "Watch him so he doesn't get too close to the edge of the bridge. He doesn't know there's danger there." Ida dropped her wooden horse and followed her sister outside. I noticed then the bowl Karl had set out for the dog.

"Po keeps you company," I said.

"*Ja,* sure. One of the stage drivers dropped him off for me, thought I might be lonely and need a little companion. He guards the toll hut at night when I'm not there." He smiled. "Sister Louisa doesn't like dogs inside. You should get a dog, Emma."

"I have Opal and Clara. They're trouble enough."

"But a dog licks your face, he's so happy to see you, and curls at your feet while you work. He even acts apologetic when you step on his foot." He smiled.

"I don't have much time for sitting around with a dog curled at my feet," I said.

"They make you make time," Karl said.

I watched the girls and the dog through his open door. Yellow leaves from the alder trees drifted down, and the vine maple had turned blood red. Elderberry bushes and ferns painted the riverbanks in green. "You'll miss those stage drivers when you're back to teaching," I said.

"*Ja,* they brightened my days. I brightened theirs," he said.

"Won't you miss this, being in the classroom all the time when the school is all finished?" I turned to look at him.

"*Ja,* by goodness. Po and I have a good life right here. A nod to a sad face looking out of the stage window can change a passenger's day. They're dusty and tired and always running late. But the dog makes them grin. I ask after the drivers' families, and they like that. People sometimes go all day long without anyone hearing them or remembering what they said the last time they came through. But"—he put his palms out—"everything changes, Emma. Now I will teach the children again. It's how life is, *ja*? I will cherish my time with them."

"Should I fight them, John and Keil and even Martin? Should I take my children and disappear into the night? Would you help me again?"

"What is it that you want for your children, Emma? What do you want for yourself?"

I'd been asking those questions ever since my conversation with Keil. I sat down on the narrow bed Karl took his naps on. It was the only place to sit besides the chair Karl occupied. I ran my hands over the quilt that covered his bed, my fingers following the zigzag lines that stitched together odd-shaped pieces of cloth. His old worn pants, a shirt. I recognized pieces of calico in the Log Cabin quilt made from dresses Mary Giesy stitched for her girls. Mary must have made it for him when he'd lived with them in Willapa. She was a generous soul.

"When I was younger, I dreamed sometimes of being the first in a footrace, with many dozens of others coming in behind me," I said. "I imagined accolades as I crossed the finish line." I had never told anyone, even Christian, of this dream of mine. "I had visions of people clapping and cheering for me because I'd done something…grand. Sometimes, I'd wake from the dream and I could still hear their cheers echoing as I entered my day. While their voices faded, the uplift, like a hawk catching the wind and soaring toward the sun, stayed with me when I took out the ashes, helped my mother clean the lamp globes, peeled mounds of potatoes, changed my sisters' napkins. I thought I was called to something purposeful and important. The insignificant things I did each day were only a prelude to the symphony that would be my life." I picked at a piece of loose thread in the quilt's stitching. I'd bring my needle and thread next time and restitch the seam for Karl. "Now here I am. My sons have been taken from me. I'm separated from a husband whom I never should have married. What I do here every day could be done by…anyone in this communal place. There's nothing unique in it. And the daily music of my life is a funeral dirge, nothing grand at all."

I heard the girls laughing outside and happy yips from the dog in its play. The day felt hot, and perspiration beaded above my lip.

"There's something you do that is both important and yet unfinished," Karl said. I looked to see what he referred to. His eyes turned toward the sounds made by the girls. "They need your efforts, Emma. And didn't you raise your sons to be good thinkers, independent, and kind? They don't forget that. You'll still influence that in them. You'll still see them."

"Christian, maybe. He might remember me fondly. But Andy is as lost to me as his father is."

"*Ach,* self-pity does not become you, Emma." He picked up his pipe and drew on it, then tapped it as though to light it again. Instead he said, "Christian and Andrew are alive and healthy because of your care for them. Andy wants to heal people one day, and you are a part of that dream. Christian finds joy in the outdoors and in helping others. Your girls are smart and generous. These are of your doing too. Yet you have work left to do."

"But I wanted my life to mean something," I said.

"To be ahead in the race." I nodded. Tears welled up in my eyes, and I looked away, as though to check on the girls. "Was it being in front that gave your dream its boost, or was it knowing others ran with you in a worthy race?"

I hadn't thought of those distinctions. "If I'd been the only person in the dream crossing the finish line, it wouldn't have meant as much, I guess. But weren't the others there providing the applause because I'd done something…significant? Why would they applaud over something simple and mundane like sewing a patch on a pair of pants or fixing a stew? That's all I do now."

"Is it?" he said. "Maybe the people cheering were there to inspire the dream in the first place. It could be, Emma, that what we imagine as other people doing unusual things in our dreams are really just us. Maybe you were cheering yourself on."

"You think I'm self-centered too, then, like Keil implied."

"*Nein, nein.* Take no offense here, Emma. Remember how Shakespeare tells us, 'to thine own self be true'? You are uplifted crossing the line; but you are also the one making it happen and celebrating the victory, a goal line, *Sehnsucht,* that longing that will not cease. I believe such longings are given to us by God. You don't need to depend on others to say it's so."

I couldn't help recalling that vivid dream I'd had years before where Christian and I dove under the water, and I asked if he knew where we were going, and he'd said no, he'd lost his compass. I'd awakened worried. Could it have been me, feeling adrift and lost without a compass, and not Christian at all?

Sehnsucht. That which calls us toward something we cannot ignore, to return us to relationship with God. Maybe it wasn't winning or doing something grand that mattered, but rather being in a race that filled my heart and allowed me to one day hear, "Well done," at the end. It wasn't a thought I would pitch away.

———

"Go like this, Mama," Kate said. The girls had taken me to the open place where they and Almira had formed their puzzle path. Animals had scattered the pinecones, making the narrow paths difficult to follow. "Mira says after we walk it enough, we won't need the pinecones. Our feet will be like chalk and make the pattern."

"We could bring rocks. Or branches. The wind can't sweep branches good," Ida said.

"Well," I corrected. "Wind can't sweep branches very well. I don't really have much time, girls." I'd seen Jonathan earlier in the day, but he'd avoided looking at me and kept talking to the men at the store. *I ought to go visit my father and mother, at least tell them what transpired, so they don't hear it as gossip.* I'd kept myself busy, doing. It kept me from thinking of my loss. A sniggle of memory reminded me that when I didn't grieve what I'd lost, I sometimes made poor choices. Marrying Jack was one of those.

I'd think of hopeful things. Helena had asked if I was going to the fair. If I did, I had food to prepare, things to arrange, questions to answer: Should I take the girls? Would going affirm for Keil that I was easily swayed?

But I was here now, being tugged at by my Ida. I sighed. "So tell me what I'm supposed to be doing on this trail."

"Watch," Kate said. "And smell whatever we can smell. And feel the breeze on your arms, Mama. Butterfly kisses, *ja?*" Kate walked faster and was soon on one of the switches that led her back toward us.

"Listen too, Mira says." Ida held my hands but walked in front of me to stay within the narrow borders, so my arms rested on each of her shoulders. We walked a little like Brita did, waddling from side to side, with my feet in step with hers. "What do your ears see, Mama?"

"They see...birds singing," I said. "And someone's dog is barking far away."

"That's God talking," Ida said. "Mira says God talks to us when we walk."

"If we don't talk so much," Kate chided.

I didn't think God had the voice of a barking dog, but then these days, everything was open to question.

This trip to the field was a break in the routine we'd fallen into, Kitty, Almira, Matilda, and I. We rose early and fixed a morning meal for all. Then I headed for work at the hotel and Matilda stitched on an order she'd gotten from the tailor shop. She still didn't know if she'd stay, but for now, she'd found work that satisfied.

Almira had been sleeping less. In her first days with us, she'd wake up close to the midday meal and then fall back to sleep again before dark. Now she rose earlier, heated water for the laundry, on Mondays at least; then she and Kitty would swirl the sheets and towels and underdrawers with their sticks, carrying the steaming clothes to the wringer that by then Matilda would be ready to operate. Kitty would snap the clothes, then hang them on the line to dry, well out of the reach of Opal. Then she'd leave for her time at wherever she was cooking that day—at the Keils', the construction sites, or the hotel—while

Almira watched my girls and Matilda returned to her needles and threads.

By the time I arrived back in the late afternoon, the clothes would be nearly dry, and I'd take them down, folding them into the basket. The next day, we'd heat the irons and press the sheets and towels and plain, dark dresses, each of us taking a turn with the flat iron as the day and evening waned. Sometimes we took laundry overload from the bachelors staying at the Keils'. We often brought baskets from the communal laundry house to wash and iron. I noticed that Matilda looked at the laundry marks closely, and I asked her once if she was seeking out *JS* for Jacob Stauffer. She'd blushed.

Wednesdays we baked or dried berries. Thursdays we did extra gardening, which in the fall meant putting the soil to rest, digging up potatoes with our pitchforks, burying cabbage and melons in straw. Fridays we took the rugs out to beat them and opened windows and aired out the house, cleaned the lamp globes, and mended by lamplight at night while one of us read out loud to the others. Saturdays we heated water for baths and prepared whatever we might want to eat on the following day, so we didn't have to cook or fire up the stove on Sundays—at least every other Sunday. Soon there'd be the big productions of slaughtering the hogs and rendering lard, but that would take nearly all the colony and was an almost festive time of gathering, a welcome break in everyday routines.

Today was a Sunday when Father Keil did not speak, and so the girls had insisted that I let them lead me to their "lab-rinse," as Ida called it, to "have church" instead.

"I'm slowing down, Mama," Kate told me. "If we walk too fast, we miss things."

Almira had taught her well. I kept my eyes on the ground so as not to step on Ida's heels. Leaves brisked across our path. A squirrel chattered in the trees beyond. I didn't initially see what caused Ida to stop abruptly, then break away and run.

"Andy!" she shouted. "Come on the lab-rinse with us."

He stood at the end of one of the turns. Ida skipped over the pine cones and imaginary lines and wrapped her arms around him. He hugged her back and let her lead him. "You follow me, and Mama will follow you," she told him. "We go in, and then we go out. It's fun."

I thought of hopscotch, a game we'd played as children in the dirt with squares and stones. I'd played it for hours with my sisters on Sabbath days when working wasn't allowed, grateful that quiet playing still was. This walk reminded me of that, except I didn't really have to concentrate, the way you did when standing on one foot and leaning over to pick up the pebble in hopscotch. My mind could wander.

It didn't now.

I'd encountered my son for the first time since the decision had been made for him to live with Martin. Still, there was a bit of precarious balancing going on as we moved along the path.

He walked in front of me. I followed him, keeping my hands to myself.

Ida chattered, giving him instructions for listening and watching. Kate rolled her eyes at me as I looked at her across one of the lanes where she was coming back out from the center, while we still entered in.

"Now we pray," Ida told us. We stood in a tight circle at what was apparently the end of the route to the inside. We'd go out the same way we came in. "Pray for us coming in. Pray for others going out. That's what Mira says."

"Who's Mira?" Andy asked.

"Questions later," Ida said, as she lifted her finger like a teacher correcting.

Andy's eyes met mine, and I saw in them a look of brotherly compassion but of yearning too, a look so intense I swallowed. I hoped his eyes weren't mirrors reflecting mine. "We'd best do as she says," I told him, surprised that my voice carried nothing harsh or defensive in it.

Ida was quieter on the way out, and I found I could bring to mind the names of those I loved and cared for, as my child had suggested we do: Matilda and her hopes with Jacob, Almira, Kitty, my parents. Even the foster sister, Christine. I still called her "the foster sister" instead of "my sister." Brita. I added Louisa. Helena. My children, all. I could pray for those I didn't even know, those far beyond our borders: the stage drivers Karl spoke of, soldiers on the battlefields, their families, leaders making choices. That last prayer brought me to Keil and John and Martin. I sent a prayer up for even them, amazed that I could.

At the end, I felt refreshed in a way I hadn't been when I started on this walk.

Kate waited for us at the entry point. Christian had joined her. He rushed to me and hugged my skirts at my knees. I blinked back tears.

"Wasn't that fun, Mama? Did you pray for others going out?"

"I did, Ida," I said. I still held Christian, looked at Andy then back to my daughters. "You're a good little teacher."

She beamed. "We need to eat now." She grabbed at Christian's hand, pulling him away. "That's a lot of work. We worked up an ap-tite."

I smiled. I'd heard those same phrases from Kitty when we finished the laundry.

"You'll come too, won't you, Andy?" I asked my son. He'd held back. But with my invitation, he moved up beside me, and we began to follow his brother and sisters.

"Father Keil lets John Giesy speak at the service," Andy said then. "John talks of being helpful one to another." I tried not to see John as a hypocrite, speaking of goodness to one's neighbors while he inflicted pain on his own extended family. Here I'd just prayed for him, and so quickly I was ready to condemn. I sighed.

I hadn't attended either of the two services they'd held at the Keil house since this whole thing with my sons had happened.

"It's always good to be helpful," I said.

"You didn't want Martin to take care of us, I know, Mama. But you are being helpful too," he said.

"By not fighting to keep you with me? What kind of mother does that make me?"

"We're with you," Andy said. He reached for my hand as we walked. The touch of his wet fingers to my palm made me suck in my breath. *How I love this child.* "I can help Martin now. And they will send me to school, Mama. I'll be a doctor. Like you said I could be. Martin says that can happen because you let it be so. That I should thank you for thinking so far ahead. He says you sacrificed for us, that you put aside your own wishes in order to give us this chance. That's a Christian thing to do."

"Martin tells you these things?"

"He says you took a hard thing and turned it into something better. He...admires you. He tells me I should admire you too."

I watched my feet, gripping my son's small hand while my heart took in those healing words. I slowed my pace to match Andy's. My sons didn't condemn me. They didn't expect me to fight. I could lower the standard I'd carried all my life. Nothing else that called could ever be as important as this moment in time.

———◆———

Johanna and Lou, my sisters, leaned against their garden forks, ceasing their work as I approached. Both were tall and slender with hair the color of straw, the opposites of Christine and Kitty and me. They all lived in the small hut next to the mill my father had bought from Keil, and I imagined they used the common smokehouse or the storehouses of the colony for their staples. But we all had our own kitchen gardens too, and I could see they'd been digging potatoes. Pumpkins rose in a pyramid beside a small pit. They'd line it with straw and place the orange globes inside, covering them with leaves like a quilt, pulling them out as needed through the winter. Chickens scratched at the ground shaded by weeds they'd wisely let grow just for that purpose. Window boxes spilled what remained of large blooms.

"You can take some seeds," my sister Lou said as I eyed the flowers. "William grows them. Bigger than a fish head, some of those blooms."

"Is Papa here?" I asked.

"Working," Lou said. She wore that lopsided smile.

"In the mill?" I asked, nodding toward it.

"Delivering flour," Johanna said. "Jonathan came by to help him." She stared as though considering whether to say what she said next. "Papa's getting on in years, you know, Emma. You really should come by to see him and Mama more. They miss you."

"Do they? Mama hasn't even been at my home yet, and the path goes both ways. None of you except Kitty has sat at my table and let me serve you."

"All we need is an invitation," Johanna said.

"A family shouldn't have to wait to be invited," I told her.

"We've never been a typical family, now have we?" she said. She dropped her pitchfork then, to grab Lou's elbow before my sister lost her step. Johanna steadied her. I hadn't even seen Lou look like she would stumble; Johanna had a discerning eye. "Mama's inside," she said and returned to her work.

I entered and found my mother sewing. She patched my father's jeans, or maybe they were David's or William's. They were those hard canvas pants, what the miners used who came up from California. "These things wear forever," my mother said. "But you let a hole get started and pretty soon it's a cavern. You've got to nip things in the bud, like pruning a good grape vine."

"I wonder if I should try to fight this thing that John and Keil have set forward," I said, blurting out the thing that most crushed against my heart.

"Oh, and what would that be?" She raised her eyes to mine.

Can she really not know? No, she knows. Her eyes hold compassion. Surely it is meant for me. "They've given the boys to Martin, so he can raise them."

She winced, I thought, but said, "Martin's a good man."

Her words stung. I thought she'd be appalled and say so. "What choice do I have?" I began, as though she'd found fault with my actions. "If I insisted they stay with me, Keil would ask me to leave the house. I'd have to move back in with them or impose on the Schueles or… come here and move one of my sisters off her mat."

"There's always your husband," my mother said.

"Jack? Oh, Mama, he hurt me and the boys, he really did. I didn't make that up. And Andy, well, Andy hates him; I'm afraid of what they'd do to each other if they had to be under the same roof again."

She put her mending down. "Then you must make the best of the choices you have. I'm sorry, Emma. Sorry for the decisions you've had to make, and for some of them not working out well. But we all have to deal with such things."

"Should I talk with Papa about...moving in here?" I said. "Do you think that might dissuade Keil and let me have the boys again? We could all live right here."

"I wish we had room." She lifted her palms to the walls of the tiny house. "And if we came to live with you, it wouldn't make Keil let you have your sons back, of that I'm sure. Besides, your father wouldn't do that now. He's disillusioned with Keil and wishes your brother would see the problems the colony has as well. Your brother is devoted. I remember when your father was too."

"Jonathan hasn't even talked to me since this happened."

"I'm sure he will soon. He worries you'll force him into something. He doesn't want to distress John, who has so much on his mind."

I mocked myself. "The infamous Emma Giesy, strong as an ox, able to convince grown men to do things they otherwise wouldn't."

"You did talk Christian into staying at Willapa."

"He wanted to stay! He saw how it could help us all. It wasn't all me, Mama, despite what Louisa and Helena might tell you."

"*Ja, ja,* I know," she said. "And the Willapa people had good lives there, or they'd have left long before so many did." She watched me for a moment, then lifted her mending again. "Things change, Emma. Sometimes for the good, sometimes bad, *ja,* but always, they change. You fall in love; you grow old. Your sons live with you; they move away; they go on to school. One mends the edges of one's life to keep it from fraying. In due time, Emma. It will be better in due time."

"Christian said I was impatient."

"It is a Wagner trait," she said. Her smile was kind. "But so is doing what must be done for the good of one's family. You'll do that too, Emma."

Perhaps, as Andy said, I already had.

15

Wishful Thinking

September 15. First true guests sit in my parlor.

September 30. Wild geese make their way across the sky. They call to each other, they trade places, the leader tiring from the effort of pushing aside the wind to make the others have an easier flight. A new path is formed; all the while it looks as though they're in the same formation, never changing, but they are.

The knock on the parlor door sounded almost like a dog's scratch. It grew louder. I could hear it from the backyard where I had my chickens penned. I'd let them loose for the day and finished gathering up their eggs, holding the blue ones aside for Ida's and Kate's lunches. I assumed someone else would answer the door, but no one did. The knocking grew insistent. It was an early hour for visiting.

I peeked through the window to see Louisa Keil and Helena Giesy standing there, carrying reticules, wearing bonnets, and dressed as though they were attending a cotillion or something almost as formal. I retied my scarf at the back of my neck but untied my apron. It was so early. They were granting me an honor by coming to call all dressed for the occasion, and yet the early hour assumed almost a family right to intrude. I took a deep breath and opened the door. I looked a fright against their freshly laundered calico dresses.

To my smile and welcome each woman nodded, then took out a calling card with their names printed in lovely *Fraktur* lettering that Louisa had probably done. I had no receptacle for cards. I looked around. Then I took down an oyster shell from its shelf; I'd cleaned it and painted a picture on the smooth side; it would have to do. I set the shell on the small table beside the bench and placed the cards there, thanking my visitors. I directed them to the bench. I'd stuffed pillows with goose feathers and quilted the covers with pieces of the children's clothes and new calico I'd purchased at the store. I motioned for them to sit down on the pillows, because the bench was so hard. They picked up the pillows, commented on the fine stitching, and then sat, with the toes of their shoes pointing straight east and looking like dark eyes peeking out from beneath their hems.

"I'll fix tea. Or coffee if you'd like."

"You have coffee?" Helena said.

"Dried peas," I corrected. Helena liked accuracy. "I throw in a few beans I've saved from each distribution."

"They weren't too expensive for a time," Helena said. "But with the war, everything is costly, don't you find?"

"I still call it coffee." I sounded like my mother's friends back in Bethel when they'd come to call.

"Oh, no need to explain, Emma," Louisa said. "We should expect that you'd have finery the rest of us only dream about."

"Finery?" I wanted to say, "At least no one took your children from you," but five of her children had died, and such words would have been a cruel reminder.

"Your own home, Emma. Before even the church is finished," Helena said.

Louisa gazed around. "Not that furbelows aren't warranted. Didn't you have them on that petticoat of yours one time?" *She knew about my ruffles?* "Frills are a good thing, especially when you make them yourself. You should put some of your paintings up. I liked your work."

"I've done so few," I told her. I longed to tell her that I'd signed up for a class, but I hadn't found a way to bring it up to Keil, to see if he'd honor that part of our agreement. In a perverse way, I didn't want to give him the satisfaction of naming yet one more thing he'd claim I'd done for myself at the expense of the colony. Wanting to take the course felt like a violation of my sons now. How could I enjoy something when the one duty of my life I hoped to succeed at, being a good mother, was now in question? Still, it struck me as a pleasantry that Louisa had noticed my bare walls and suggested that my paintings might add charm to them.

I listened for the activities of the rest of the household while I gathered the coffee things. Everyone remained quiet. They could come down the steps and into the kitchen without ever stepping into the parlor, but no one was in the kitchen yet either. The coffee boiled. I returned with it in the glass tumblers we women had made ourselves. I'd ground the edges down so they were smooth as a baby's lip. I handed the women square quilted napkins to wrap around the hot glasses.

"So you think you'll stay home from the fair this year?" Helena asked. "That's such a shame."

I'd told no one anything about my fair plans. It must be Helena's way of making a suggestion, but I didn't know which way she wanted me to go.

"I haven't decided. And I didn't think anyone would notice one way or the other."

"It's always so festive," Louisa added. "My favorite time of year. Oh, Christday is too. And Easter. And, of course, my husband's birthday."

"Someone needs to remain here to help cook," I said.

"Ah, but Christine Wagner, your new sister, has become quite a fine cook. Did we tell you she was living with us at the *gross Haus*? She seems a lovely girl and a hard worker. I'm not sure why your parents gave her up."

"She's a woman complete unto herself," I said. "Not beholden to a father, brother, husband, or son. She's on her own at twenty. My parents likely had no say in giving her up, as you put it. She can choose to live where she likes."

"She doesn't distract the men from their work, the way some young girls can," Helena said. "Does Matilda still stay with you?" She'd untied her bonnet strings and let them hang loose on either side of her neck. "Kitty's found a place here as well, we hear."

I wondered if Matilda and Kitty were subjects of the first part of her comment. "Matilda's upstairs. We have a routine. Almira rises early with me to prepare breakfasts. Matilda and Kitty help clean up, then begin other tasks before they go off to take care of colony business. Well, Kitty goes off. Matilda stays here. As has Almira, looking after the children."

"Not all the time," Helena said. I must have looked confused. "You don't leave her alone with them, do you? She really isn't supervised, Emma. Or haven't you noticed?"

"I notice Almira is helpful with my children."

"This Almira is not whom I referred to," Helena said.

"Matilda? Her work is praised from the tailor shop. She never complains but simply does what must be done. If she is sometimes off on her own, what is that to the rest of us? She is nearly thirty."

"Still, unsupervised…," Helena said.

"Weren't you unsupervised as a young girl?" I asked. "Isn't that how you met your bridge engineer, John Roebling?"

She stiffened. "We were never alone."

"Not ever?" I asked. "Even your brother and I found time to get acquainted, standing outside the door at dances during breaks from the band. No one else could hear us talking, so I'd say we must have been unsupervised too."

"That got my brother a…spirited wife," Helena said. She chuckled, but it didn't take away the sting.

"It got him a good and steady wife and three fine children, that's what it got him. Is there some reason why you decided to visit this morning, Sisters, unannounced?"

The two women looked at each other. Louisa sighed. "We don't mean to pry. But the woman staying with you. What is her name you said? Almira. She looks after the girls?"

"She does."

"Is her married name Raymond?" I nodded that it was. Louisa gasped. "You were right, Helena. She's the woman written about in the papers."

"Suppose she is. Does that matter?"

"We're...we've become aware of her presence here among us, and it's...unsettling," Helena said.

"The colony has always taken in widows and women in need," I said.

"*Ja, bitte,* it's enough that *you* live here without a husband or brother in your own home. But to have a divorced woman staying here, influencing your girls, well, we're concerned. And with single women here as well..."

"For whose welfare? Mine? My children's?" I calmed myself. I didn't want to challenge them. I wondered if Almira's presence would allow these two women to somehow bring about the removal of my daughters too.

"We mean no harm, Emma," Helena said, as though reading my mind. "It's for your safety we've come. Sometimes the perspective of others can be useful in making better decisions." She placed the quilted napkin onto her lap and smoothed it. The coffee had cooled.

"Other perspectives. *Ja,* I'm sure you're right about that," I said. "Let me introduce you to Almira. That would give you another perspective."

"Oh no," Louisa said. She spilled what was left of her coffee. I rose and got her a linen. I thought of bringing Almira in and forcing them to meet her, to see that they feared someone out of ignorance. We tend to judge more harshly from a distance.

I patted Louisa's skirt with my linen. "You'd find her a quite refined Christian woman."

"Not if she's...divorced," Helena said. "I'm not sure you'd be welcomed here if you had insisted on divorcing Jack. Our Lord was quite clear about the place of divorce. He did not like it."

I sat with the damp linen in my own lap. "Doesn't it strike you as interesting that a woman was even mentioned in Scripture in regard to divorce? I mean, women had no...power then. Why bother commenting that loving another while one was married was the only grounds that permitted a man to divorce his wife? That verse was more about how men should behave than about women. Up until then, a woman was like a…bench." I nodded my head to the bench they sat on. "A piece of property for use by her husband. Almira's divorce, from my understanding of it, resulted from her husband's bringing another woman into his bed." I hoped I wasn't sharing a secret Almira would want kept silent. "For sixteen years she endured this. In Christ's time, she would have had some status."

"That's not how the newspapers recorded it," Helena said.

"Did you read it in German?" I asked. She shook her head. "Then maybe whoever told you what was written didn't translate it well. Besides, men write the newspaper accounts, and it's likely they would give her husband's story the greater weight, over the real facts that might sympathize with a woman."

"I hadn't thought about women being property in those times," Louisa said. "How fortunate that we don't have that to deal with here in our colony, where we're all treated the same by my husband, and where divorce happens so rarely, because he is so wise about deciding who should marry or not in the first place." It was a long speech for Louisa.

"You may think we're all treated fairly, Louisa," I said. "But we are not all treated the same." I looked over at Helena. "Some of us have greater privileges than others, it's true. You suggested that about my house. I understand that some of the men receive payments to go work elsewhere in Portland, while others work here with no hope of gaining wages for their ledger pages. And some of the women are treated with more…gentleness than others, or so I've noticed."

"Well. So," Helena said. She set her coffee glass down. I thought her hand shook.

"And some wish to marry and are refused, while others are allowed to. There's nothing in Scripture to prevent marriage, as I recall, yet Brother Keil does this."

"He does what he thinks is best," Louisa defended.

"As do we all," I suggested.

"We should be going," Helena said. "We've done what we came for, to express our concern for you, Emma, with that woman being here. That was our only purpose."

"You ought to meet Almira," I countered. "She's been so good to my girls and a good friend during these past weeks without my boys with me."

"Does Matilda intend to stay with you and this…Mrs. Raymond?" Louisa asked.

"I haven't asked her. She can stay as long as she likes, as far as I'm concerned."

The two women stood. Louisa tied her bonnet strings.

"I'm sure she's awake. She made the coffee for us. Let me call her."

"*Nein, nein.* We've other tasks to tend to," Louisa said. "Another time."

"Be sure she has adequate supervision," Helena said. "We wouldn't want anything untoward to happen while these women were within your control. Such things could speak badly for you."

"Fortunately, I'm learning that I'm not in control of anything, Helena," I said. *And neither are you.*

———————

It was Almira who insisted. "You told me you'd written to a friend, inviting her to meet you at the fair, remember? It's what you were doing when you found me. What if she came and you weren't there?"

Brita would understand; I was certain of that. Besides, I had no way of knowing whether she'd even gotten my letter, and she'd told me she didn't like fairs anyway.

"And there's the class. Doesn't it start soon?" Almira said. "Have you already missed a session?"

"That's a dream," I said.

She sighed. "I guess we aren't supposed to wish for things. Once I remember saying, after all that happened, that if I could just have a good night's sleep, I'd be happy. Now I have that, and I feel guilty that I have that little gift of sleep."

"Even the apostle Paul said, 'I think myself happy,' and that must mean that we're meant to be happy," I replied. "Pursuing something that matters is a part of our nature. I'm glad you're sleeping better, and now that you are, you can wish for new things. But I don't know if I wish to go to the fair. Too many reminders of when the boys were with me there."

"Walk about it," she said, a phrase I knew meant to walk that puzzle, to see what answers might come from my time there.

Instead I walked to talk with Keil. I kept my eyes alert for Andy and Christian. School was in session, but one never knew when the children would be studying botany beneath the trees. Music floated up from the grassy area near the Keil and Company Store. Henry C led the music class. Chris Wolff brought his lectures out under the trees as well, and I could see my Christian sitting there, his face scrunched in concentration. Chris read from the classics. Apparently, I walked too close, for Chris Wolff looked up at me and smiled, and when he did, my son looked up too.

"Mama!" He ran to me. "Where have you been?"

I squatted down to his level. "Working, as always," I said.

"Martin lets me help with the bottles, not just Andy," he told me proudly. "I'm working too."

"That's a good boy," I told him.

"Martin says we can come for supper soon. Can we?" I brushed his reddish hair away from his eyes. "Please? I'm sorry for whatever I did. I won't do it again."

I tried to keep from crying. Seeing them was so difficult for me, yet not finding ways to be with them was breaking Christian's heart. "Anytime you want," I said.

"*Ja*, by goodness," he said, reminding me of Karl. "I'll tell Martin and Andy we can come soon."

He hugged me quickly, ran back, and sat down. He waved at me once, then returned his eyes to his teacher.

Maybe the boys expected our family to be as my mother had said, sometimes with me, sometimes with their grandparents, sometimes with an uncle. Maybe that's all our family had ever been, this hodge-podge of people separated by our desires to serve. We were not unlike

Karl's quilt, composed of bits and pieces of discards, confusion stitched with comfort. Christian had never known his own father, and life with Jack had been anything but calm or restful. Maybe this conglomerate of people who were influencing him, keeping him warm, feeding his and Andy's bodies and spirits was superior to what they'd known when living with just me and their sisters. My girls welcomed strangers; the boys carried on as though their family home was the entire colony. Maybe I should accept that it was.

———

"So you want to go to the fair to cook, Sister Emma. This is why you're here?"

"In part," I told Keil. After leaving Christian at his outdoor class, I'd walked the mile up the hill and found Keil as he stood outside of the church construction. "I also wish to claim a portion of our agreement." He frowned. Several men had been hovering around him but left as I approached. He held a roll of plans, comparing what was drawn to what he saw before him. "Two bandstands around the steeple?" I said. "That'll be quite a sight from miles around. Everyone will know of the Keil church," I said.

"Aurora church," he corrected. "I didn't design the steeple to bring attention to me. I'm a humble man."

He didn't sound as though he teased, so I guessed he really did think that about himself. It surprised me sometimes, that what seemed so obvious to me about a person's demeanor could be seen as the opposite by the person. Almira was a good example. She was warm and kind and good with children, but she described herself as a sinful woman who didn't deserve happiness or joy. Keil, on the other hand, was often petulant and arrogant, indifferent to his wife and cloying to some of her friends. He made decisions that propped up certain people with thick pillows, while others suffered at the foot of the bed. Yet he saw himself as a virtuous, benevolent leader.

Perhaps that was the whole problem with me: I saw things differently. Who was I to say that Almira wasn't right in her sinful admission, or that it was me who couldn't see the goodness of Keil's colony care? People did have good days and bad days. Perhaps my judgment was as impaired, like a broken wagon tongue that ought never be allowed to pull along anything precious.

"I've come to humbly ask you to pay for an educational course that I wish to take at the university. I'd be there one week a month until the weather becomes impassable."

"Humbly?" I nodded but said nothing. "You'd be gone a week at a time? Where would you stay? You'd take your girl out of school? *Nein.* This does not seem good."

Keil had rarely indicated any concern about my girls or their education, but I saw it as a good sign that he'd give me any kind of reason rather than simply saying no.

"I have someone who would look after them."

"Ah, the Raymond woman? Do you think that's wise, Sister Emma?"

"Matilda has offered to stay as well. And Kitty. Surely you have no objection to them."

He tapped the rolled-up set of plans gently against his leg. "Matilda Knight, I'm sure, is a fine young woman. But she distracts Jacob Stauffer from his work, and he came here to be a carpenter, not to court."

"If anything, her being here makes it easier for the man to tend to his hammer and saw, knowing in the evening he might have a word or two with her," I said. "Would their marriage be so bad? Then she'd not be distracting him. And marriage seems to smother such ardor, or so I've noticed." I'd often wondered if it was the amount of saltpeter we used to preserve our meats that made separation of the sexes so easily accommodated.

"Work. That's what we're to do here, Sister Emma. Just as with you and Christian, you got little done your first year because your husband looked after a family. I didn't send him out to have his family to worry over."

"His family was on his way before you sent him out," I said.

He frowned, appeared to count months. "*Ja.* That was not known though. So, we should finish the important buildings before I approve any more marriages. That's what I told Jacob Stauffer. He understands."

"Matilda will be here for my girls while I take the class."

He gazed off toward the construction site again. Wild geese flew across us in their V formation, that sure sign of fall.

"Three weeks away is too much time. Martin is taking classes, and it is hard for him going back and forth. It would be even harder for you, Emma, a woman with children to raise."

"But the agreement—"

"Is that I will provide your education, and so I will. But I must have some say over the costs and conditions. That is only fair and reasonable, *ja*?"

"Will you limit my son's medical education as well?"

"*Ach,* Emma. Calm down now. Your son will be a doctor in due time. But you do not need to become…what is it you wanted to take a course in?"

"Painting," I said.

"Hardly practical." He lifted his hands to the sky. "As fleeting as geese."

"Great paintings soothe us," I said. "They're like music, *Herr* Keil." It had been years since I'd used that title with him. "Or fine furniture sanded to silk or a steeple that spirals into the sky. They can all help our spirits reach to higher places, to honor God. Even a luscious cake covered with whipped cream and strawberries can inspire. A painting does that too."

"Come up with another way to try to learn your painting then," he said. "A course away from here is not acceptable. Now, now"—he raised his hand to silence my next protest—"but you can go to the fair, Emma, if you wish. We have need of cooks, and you did so well with the building of the dance hall. Why not put your talents there? Of course you'd have to take the girls. It wouldn't be right to leave them alone with…the women you surround yourself with. Go along now. I'm a busy man."

Why not go? Defy Keil by leaving Matilda and Almira in charge. I could look for Brita and I'd cook. But I'd also talk to that instructor. Perhaps there were teachers who, like peddlers and those who sharpened knives, traveled from town to town. Maybe I could find one who would travel to Aurora. I may not get all I wanted, but there would always be another path to take. I just had to watch and listen to know which way to go.

16

Plots and Plans

September 30. We tended to the hogs today, all of us working together to finish before those going to the fair could leave. I heard grumbles from some of the men that Keil had once again locked himself inside his workroom and wasn't there to cheer us onward. When he's working side by side with others, the community moves steady as the river. But otherwise there is froth, and the people grumble.

Louisa and Keil, Helena, John and BW, newlyweds Frederick and Louisa Keil, and dozens of others left for the fair. The band would play and earn a tidy sum, as well as bring more renown to our community. My parents went too, taking Lou with them, according to Kitty, who stayed in much closer touch with them than I did.

I didn't go; I couldn't risk what might happen to my girls if I left them behind.

I hadn't planned on what did happen while so many were gone.

It was a Sunday, and with John and Keil at the fair, there was no church scheduled at the Keil house. Karl might have led services, or even Martin, both of whom had remained behind. Martin stopped by especially, he said, to tell me the boys would like to have more time with me. He asked if it would be all right if they spent the afternoon on Sunday. *All right?* I suspect he had studying to do and wondered if I might not work out a regular plan with him, to have the boys on Sunday afternoons so he would work. This first day had to go well. I had grand plans.

I wanted to do things I knew the boys might like, and involve the girls too. We'd roll hoops for a time. Maybe pull taffy. It was cool enough we wouldn't have to put paraffin in the sweetness to keep it from melting. I'd roast a chicken later, as I'd had enough of pork for a while.

I still had one ham left from last year—I'd wrapped it with sweet grass hay after giving the meat a good soak. We'd smoked dozens of hams, and bacon and sausage, but that one I claimed. I put a date and my initials on the bag I'd made for it. When we got ready to eat it, I wouldn't have to soak the slices to get rid of the pepper taste, because the hay sweetened it so well. Dozens hung in the smokehouse. We rendered lard by the buckets for making our pies. We'd washed, cleaned, and dried casings, then stuffed sausages for days, and I couldn't stand to look at another casing squeezed to the brim with pork and spices and chopped onion. We'd even run out of entrails, we had so many hogs to prepare, and several of us had made casings out of cloth. They were draped like thick ropes, round and round in the smokehouse, and it would be a few days before those sausages could be eaten. I guessed the good Lord made it that way, since no one cared about eating pork right after the work of slaughtering and rendering and stuffing. By the time we'd put the more disagreeable thoughts of the pork from our minds, the hams and sausages would be ready, and so would we.

That Sunday I busily prepared stick candy and my special gooseberry pie. We'd be eating chicken, or maybe a nice venison roast, if one of the Indians who made their way through the region knocked on my door. I often traded with them, giving them butter or sweet candies and, depending on the season, a ham or a sausage ring to take with them. These Indians, though tall and well fed, did not have the same pride in their eyes as the Shoalwaters who had helped us those long winters ago. Disease defined these Mollala or Calapooia people, the sicknesses reducing their numbers to mere scatterings of peoples. I'd probably not see them today anyway, as this was a season for hunting, and they traveled far from this Aurora region for that.

All through the preparations, my spirits were lifted in anticipation of my sons' visit. Kate and Ida rose earlier than normal, tramping down the stairs in their bare feet with their nightclothes still on. Almira was up and gave them their oats, putting dried berries into their bowls, and milk she'd gotten from the goat. It was going to be a grand day. We had plenty of time to enjoy even the preparations. Then the actual event we would savor.

We both turned to the light knock on the kitchen door.

"We know it isn't Louisa and Helena," I said.

"They're at the fair," Almira noted.

"And they prefer the parlor door," I said. I hadn't told her that they'd left as soon as I suggested they meet her, but I did let her know that they'd expressed concern about her being with me. I wasn't sure whether to keep such news to myself, but I decided that secrets seldom helped a person. People needed information to understand what was happening around them. I didn't want Almira to encounter Louisa and Helena on the path somewhere and not be prepared for their looks.

"Maybe Andy and Christian are here already," Kate said.

"Yea!" Ida shouted and clapped her hands as she went to the door. "Oh," she said, and let Christine Wagner in.

As always, my foster sister combed her dark hair back so tight into a bun that her eyes looked narrow inside her puffy face. She carried a basket of fresh-baked goods, and as she handed it to me, looking over the head of Ida, she said, "I know it's early and you've probably got plans. But I wondered if I could sit for a bit in your parlor."

I'd spent fewer than ten minutes with this woman, always at the hotel or at Keils' and never with so few others around. I hoped one day we'd talk. Maybe about how my parents fostered her and how she felt about that.

"Well, of course. I'll fix coffee and bring it in to you myself."

"If you please, I'd like to be there alone."

Why not go to the woods or sit in Keil's root cellar if you want to be alone?

"I guess that's all right. But won't you have breakfast with us first? We're late getting around, as you can see by my lazy girls here." I patted Kate on the top of her uncombed but still braided hair with its flyaway strands. "This is your…Aunt Christine," I told her.

"I 'member," Kate said. She hid behind me. Christine was a large woman, though she didn't use her girth to intimidate. She looked soft as dough rather than solid as a smoked ham.

Christine didn't acknowledge the girls. "I've already eaten. I need a moment to sit. Without...distractions. Then I'll be on my way." I noticed that she spoke English without a German accent.

I took her back out onto the porch, opened the living room door, and let her step in. The room looked bare in the morning light. The chair I'd painted yellow gave the only color. I really did need to find things to hang on the walls, maybe wainscot the side walls or put up short shelves for more plates. The room felt cool to me too, and I wondered if I ought to light a fire. But when I suggested that, Christine said, "Oh no. It's always so warm at the Keil house. This is just right. Thank you. I won't be any bother. Thank you. I can't thank you enough."

She moved into the room as though she walked on stepping stones across a stream: careful, full of caution, yet with purpose. She took a chair that faced the windows and porch but was on the far side of the room. She nearly sank into the pillow I'd set there.

"Are you sure I can't get you something? Water? A pretzel?" She looked so tired, her eyes sad and sunk into her round, smooth-skin face.

She shook her head. "This is all I need, right here."

"All right, then," I said and backed out. I closed the door behind me, entering through the kitchen door once again.

"These are good, Mama," Ida said. She held one of the biscuits from Christine's basket. Kitty awakened and skipped down the steps into the kitchen without encountering Christine. I smiled to myself. My house design worked well: privacy for the parlor and activity for the kitchen. I just hadn't expected my foster sister to discover the uniqueness of my design. Matilda and Almira joined us, and I told them about Christine's visit.

"Quiet. That's what I longed for when things were going so badly," Almira told me when I repeated Christine's request. Almira held one of the tin serving spoons Christian had made. "I'd try to take a walk in the afternoon, but there were always babies clinging." She swallowed. "Not that I didn't want them with me, but sometimes, for a few minutes, I needed to be alone. I wanted not to be responsible for them, for what was happening in my life. I took to walking at night. I wanted to be...still." Tears welled up in her eyes. "I've sat there, just as she is now, in your parlor, Emma, while your girls rested or played outside. You and Kitty and Matilda, gone. It's one of the greatest things you gave me by asking me to come home with you. A little peace. I know that's why I can sleep now. And I can get more done when I'm awake too."

"Every woman should have a place for herself," Matilda said. "Even when they marry."

"Especially when they marry," Almira said. "You keep that in mind, Matilda."

"I'm coming to believe that marriage isn't in my future," Matilda said. We all looked expectant, but she said nothing more.

"That makes two of us, then," Kitty said.

After the girls were dressed and we'd all finished our oats and milk, I opened the door from the stairwell to see if Christine needed anything. She wasn't there. She'd left a note, though, that read, "I'd like to come back again, but this time to stay."

———————◆———————

The boys arrived before I could think further about Christine's request; and though I asked Martin to join us, he declined. It was just as well. It would be awkward with him around. Andy said he thought I'd gone to the fair. "It's nice you stayed," he added.

"I'll miss seeing Brita," I said, "but I wanted to spend time with you and for you to have time with your sisters."

"I'm glad you weren't too busy," Christian said. He ran up the stairs and found the wooden chest next to the rocking chair in the wide hall. I'd put some of his winter clothes in there, and a hoop he and Andy could roll along with a stick. I climbed the steps and watched as he surveyed his old room, now taken over by his sisters and the women who lived here. "There's a lot of girls here," he said.

I laughed. "*Ja,* there are."

He sniffed the air. "It smells like girls."

"That's the lavender," I told him. "It makes everything smell nice. All the girls doesn't mean there isn't room for you, though. You're always welcome to come and…even stay, you know." *I probably shouldn't make such suggestions; it might confuse him.* I didn't want that.

"Martin says sometime I can sleep in my old bed here. Maybe."

I felt that burn in my stomach at the idea that someone else could decide for me about my child's wishes. "Whatever Martin says," I told him. I didn't want Christian in the middle of this edgy time, but I knew my voice held some contempt, because Christian glanced up at me in the sideways look he had.

"We're going to get a dog," Kate told him, as she skipped up the stairs.

"We are?" Christian and I said in unison.

"I don't think so," I continued. "A dog won't get along with Opal or Clara. Who told you that?"

"Karl said Po needs people around. With him teaching now, the dog gets into trouble and chews things, and he'll get into the potato fields or be trampled by horses or et up by the hogs."

"That's *eaten* up by hogs," I corrected.

"We can save him, Mama."

I couldn't save anyone.

Christian said, "Martin can't have animals in the store because of all the medicines and such. A dog would be fun to have. We could come and play with it, couldn't we, Mama? Me and Andy?"

"Why, yes, you could," I said.

"And we could take the dog for a walk on our special path," Ida told him. "And we'd let you teach him, Andy, when you came here." My older son had climbed up the steps now too. "If you wanted. You too, Christian."

"A dog's a good friend to have," Andy said. "Better than a horse that wants to bite you—until he learns better." Andy smiled at me, and it was the warmest light. Christian continued chattering about the dog, and I knew I'd have to talk with Karl. But just like that, having a dog around was suddenly a brilliant idea.

Martin came to pick them up later, and they went to him with reluctance, at least I thought so. Christian chattered like a squirrel telling me some story he'd forgotten to share before. Even Andy didn't push to leave. I confess I appreciated seeing that in them. But I also knew I had to make this transition easier between Martin and me, or he might find a reason not to let them come again. "You be good and listen to Martin," I told them. "I'll see you again before you know it. Andy might need new shoes," I told Martin, who nodded.

"I'll tend to it," he said.

"Or I can."

He hesitated. "*Gut.* We'll do this together, then," Martin said.

I expelled breath I hadn't realized I'd been holding.

The day after the boys' visit, I went looking for Christine and found her hanging laundry on the line at the Keils'. I told her she was more than welcome to stay with us. We had room, but I was curious about why she'd made the request, and why now.

"I'd rather not say," she said. Her dark eyes looked down. Small brown spots speckled the backs of her hands, freckles that matched a few on her face. It looked like she'd tried to cover them with powder. "The Keils have been very kind to me here, and I'll continue to come to cook for them, but I want…fewer people around. Does that make me self-ish?" she asked.

"I'm not the one to ask about that," I said. "People are always commenting about the things I want, saying they're to dress up myself."

"I'm better able to think when I'm alone. Time to read or maybe to mend or even listen to the birds."

"Or children laughing," I added.

She looked away.

"There are several of us living in my home, though," I reminded her. "We won't be able to assure you of that very quiet time as you had the other day."

"It'll be more time than at the Keils' and…with just women. I'll do my share. I'm not asking for charity."

"You can help, but part of why I wanted the house is for charity, to give to others what they might need and couldn't find anywhere else. It's why I have the double doors."

"It was rude of me to leave without saying good-bye."

"You proved that my design worked." I smiled. "Do you want me to tell Louisa that you're moving here?"

By the look she gave me, I thought she'd take me up on that offer, but she shook her head no. "I need to do hard things myself," she said. "It'll make me stronger."

Four days after Louisa and Helena returned from the fair, the two arrived again, complete with calling cards. "What did you say to Christine Wagner while we were gone, to make her want to leave?" Of course, Louisa held me accountable for Christine's request. Louisa told us she'd been less than amused when Christine spoke to her, then left at the end of the work day and walked to my home, with her few personal things bundled up in a tapestry bag.

"I said nothing to her, except to answer her question."

"We have a perfectly good place for her," Helena said. "She's been a fine influence among the younger girls too." She twisted then smoothed the ribbon holding her scissors at her waist.

"That won't change. She'll only be here in the evenings."

"And when she isn't working."

"I suppose it will be more difficult to assign her tasks in the evenings if she's over here," I noted.

"We didn't work her all the time," Louisa defended. "She wasn't a servant or, worse, a slave, for heaven's sake. She could have left any time she wanted."

"Apparently, she did," I said.

They sipped their tea in unison.

"I don't think your gathering up women like this is a good thing for the colony," Helena said. "Surely Dr. Keil did not intend for the house he built for you to be used as a plotting place for disruption in the colony's routine."

"A plotting place?" I laughed. "A woman has moved. There's nothing sinister in that."

"One would have thought that having your sons live elsewhere would have...tempered you, Sister Emma," Helena said.

I wouldn't dignify her words about my sons by responding to them, though I felt my face grow hot.

I stirred a spoon in my glass, biting my tongue. Oh, how I wanted to challenge these women's righteous indignation!

"I still think you should put some paintings on your wall," Louisa said. She pointed to the two open areas on either side of the brick fireplace.

"What?"

"Some color. Don't you think the walls need color, Helena?"

"Your husband thinks that paintings are frivolous," I said.

"Does he? Well, then, maybe the bare walls are best," Louisa said. She adjusted herself on the chair. Her hip must be hurting her yet again.

With a simple stitch, Louisa could be sewn into her husband's opinion. I suspected that the concerns she and Helena raised had more to do with Keil's wishes than with any real issue of theirs about Christine Wagner's moving to my home.

"I'm sure you're aware," I said, "that we have an agreement, your husband and I. That I am to use this house for the betterment of the colony, and so I am. Christine will continue to work for you and contribute. The rest of us living here do too. Matilda works for the tailor shop. Kitty works at the hotel, as do I. Almira tends to my children so I can work. You have nothing to worry about."

"Oh, we're not worried at all," Helena said. She stood and tightened her bonnet strings. "We thought that you should be."

———◆———

"What did they say?" Almira asked when I returned to the kitchen.

"*Ach,* something about my stirring up plots to disrupt." I slammed the three-legged spider onto the stove, and Kate and Ida both jumped.

"Mama," Ida said. "Be gentle."

"*Ja,* gentle." I took a deep breath.

"Because I'm here," Almira said. She sighed. "I've brought you disgrace."

"Because I'm here," Matilda countered. "*Herr* Keil wants me to go so I won't disturb Jacob's work. That's it, isn't it?"

"I'm not even interesting enough to be a suspect," Kitty said. "I can't imagine I have anything to do with it."

"It's me," Christine said. "I've put you all at risk."

"No one is at risk," I said. *Why do we women always assume we're the origin of problems?* "What could they do to us? Move me out… Take my…" I looked at the girls and at the faces of the women. "They wouldn't. No one would defend that action because they're girls." I hoped that Ida and Kate couldn't put the pieces together, understand what we talked about over the top of their heads. "John Giesy wouldn't be interested enough to get in the middle of such a scene, especially with no one coming forward saying they wanted…well, you know."

"Could they keep you from seeing your boys?" Almira whispered.

"So long as Martin has them, I don't think so. I even think I might see them more with Martin's going to school than if he weren't. We're going to work together at this. He said so."

"Still, they threatened you," Matilda said.

"Not such a big word as that. Just a little…chastening. I can live with that. I've experienced it often enough. I'm stronger now than I was." I removed the spider from the stove, the three legs balanced perfectly on the smooth surface. Keil and company couldn't make me think of myself as they saw me, just because they said it. "In fact, they've inspired me. If I'm going to be accused of plotting something, I may as well do it. They'll have a hard time convincing anyone that I've disrupted the colony with my kind of doings."

"What do you plan to do?" Kitty asked.

"For the moment, make apple dumplings and eat them ourselves, without sharing a one with the rest of the colony."

Kitty giggled. "Is that all?"

"No. But it's what I'll do at this moment. The real plotting will come later, after we have our sustenance." I smiled. A few paintings were forming in my head. I felt as invigorated as the day when the boys came to visit. Maybe even more.

17

Stories with Hopeful Endings

November 7. The girls complete their stints of morning stitching. When Kate finished hers today, she said, "I am full of enthusiasm!" Would that my life would be so.

December 1. Today Louisa tells me that they saw Brita at the fair last fall! She came by the dance hall seeking me. I feel bad now that I didn't go. But the past is past. I will write to Brita again and apologize. At least she'll know then why I wasn't there, as Louisa said they did not tell her, not wanting to be "gossips."

I had things to do. Perhaps because I felt unable to bring about all that I wanted in my own life, I looked at others' to see what I might do to advance theirs. That cleft beneath my heart, where I'd once daily tended to my boys' needs, felt empty, and I hoped that I could fill the space in part with something meaningful. I wondered if Helena and I might not share a motivation in this kind of thinking, but quickly pitched that thought away.

Finding out where Jacob Stauffer stood in relation to Matilda proved my first order of business. Was the man a serious suitor? Was he reluctant to express himself because of his concern over a woman's sensibilities? I suspected that a lot of talk about "sensibilities" was a way that those in power kept women in their place, acting as though we needed protection from the outside, cruel world. Our colony was both our family and another world. And like a wool coat, at times both warm and scratchy. We'd be more joyous if people were allowed to fall in love and hope to marry, without the consternation of achieving approval from Brother Keil.

I suppose I ought to have asked Matilda first, but I didn't want her sensibilities to overpower her. Her cautious side might choose to primly point out to me that in due time, if Jacob were truly interested, he would speak to her of marriage and then they'd secure consent from Dr. Keil. If Keil refused, they could always leave Aurora, but leaving this place had its difficulties; I was witness to that.

But I knew that life is short, and Matilda was already nearly thirty. If she was to have a marriage, which she said once she'd never expected, then there was no time to waste.

Our gathering had taken on new people: BW, my sister-in-law, and Barbara, my mother-in-law, had joined us too. I was a little edgy with their presence, never sure of their intentions. And I supposed if I'd thought about it, I would have waited to bring up the subject of Jacob and Matilda until it was just our little group. But my in-laws always made me act in ways that surprised even me.

"How does Jacob like his work detail?" I asked Matilda.

She blushed, and lowered her eyes so she didn't see the stares of BW and Barbara Giesy.

"Jacob's been peeling bark from oak trees, for the tanning factory to use," I told the women.

"It's hard work, but better than felling the trees," Matilda said.

"He seems a kind man," BW said.

"He's very gentle with children," Matilda added. We sat in my parlor on a Sunday afternoon. Christian and Ida were in the kitchen playing with jacks. I could hear their groans and cheers. Andy hadn't come, and Kate joined us with the stitching. Rain and wind had their way with the windows, but we were snug inside. It was late November, and for days the skies had been as gray as the bottom of a duck and just as soggy.

My mother-in-law had brought her piecework for a Friendship

quilt, something she'd heard about from relatives back in Pennsylvania. I'd been surprised by her request to join us, especially since this was the Sabbath and I assumed she'd think we shouldn't be working. I considered changing our routine for her and my sister-in-law, but the truth was, we weren't "working." Piecing quilts or helping one another stitch wasn't work. It was quiet, contemplative time, made all the more spiritual if the quilt we worked on would be for someone other than ourselves. I gave Barbara Malachi 3:16 and commented that we created remembrances together on our Sabbath afternoons, something Scripture permitted. If she wished to join us in doing that, she was welcome in my parlor.

Apparently those conditions were acceptable, as both women had arrived with piecework in hand. Now my mother-in-law was showing us a copy of *Godey's Lady's Book* that she'd brought with her. It described ways we could print verses on our fabric or stamp the letters of all our names. We decided on names.

"We might ask Louisa to write each one using her *Fraktur* lettering," BW said. John's wife had hair nearly as white as Barbara's, the mother-in-law we shared.

"I doubt Louisa will ever join us on a Sabbath afternoon," Kitty said.

I glanced at my in-laws, but they didn't exchange meaningful looks. They just kept stitching.

"Well, we could ask," Kitty suggested. "She might not join us on the Sabbath, but maybe on another day. We wouldn't always have to stitch at the Keil's. Your parlor is very inviting, Sister."

I didn't want a competition! "So, Jacob is good with children," I said, urging us back to the subject at hand.

"He has a droll sense of humor and sometimes teases me about a subject," Matilda said, "but I always think he's serious, so I give him reasons why he might not want to think that way, and he laughs. I know then that he just said the words to see me get all rattled. He said he likes to see the 'spark in my eyes.'"

She placed her needle into the soap square where she kept it, saying it made the needle go more easily into cloth. "He enjoys working on buildings," she continued. "He has a fine eye for finish work, where the banisters are smoothed or curlicues of wood fit into the corners. Back in Willapa, I saw some very nice chests he'd constructed in their family home."

"I suspect he doesn't get to do much finish work here," I said. "They must have two dozen buildings started and in various stages of completion, but not enough for a family to move into a finished house."

"Our men do the best they can, Emma. You mustn't be so critical."

"I just stated facts," I told BW. "No judgment intended."

"Jacob says that's discouraging, but he still likes the work. He likes to grow things too."

"I want to talk to him, then, about making some shelves for me," I told her.

"Didn't you make your own shelves in Willapa?" Barbara asked. "I heard that from Jack."

My stomach knotted at the mention of my husband. "*Ja.* Little shelves I made myself. I'm thinking of more like a…cupboard. Maybe on either side of the fireplace."

The women turned to look at the brick.

"A painting would be nice there," Kitty said. "You used to draw portraits, Emma. How come you don't do that anymore?"

"No time," I said.

"You could do that now, instead of quilting," Kitty continued. "Or hang up your painting you did of Christian, at least."

"I'm not sure I could look at his picture every day without feeling sad," I said.

"You're a married woman, Emma. You mustn't hang on to the past so," BW said.

"Your children might like seeing it," Christine pointed out.

Kate nodded agreement.

I hadn't thought of that. "I'll consider it, but I still want cupboards, and I'm going to see Jacob about them. And maybe Mr. Ehlen. He makes very nice baskets."

"And music reeds for the band's clarinet," Kitty said. "Kate told me that," she added when I raised my eyebrows, wondering where she'd gotten such news.

"I could put one of those baskets beside the hearth and fill it instead of a cupboard with dried weeds, I suppose."

"I like Mr. Ehlen," Kate said. "His arm is so interesting, how it swings like that. It's like a leash attached to him. Lorenz plays with us girls at school, along with Andy. He doesn't act all smarty the way Henry T does, because he knows Latin and Greek and his father is the music instructor. Andy knows those too, and he's not smarty."

"That's good," I said.

Kate worked on a tiny needlework of a dog's house that I'd drawn for her. I'd made the house with two front doors, like our home, and had promised her that on the back I'd paint a picture of Po, Karl's dog. I hadn't quite given in to having the dog move into our house as yet. None of the colonists let dogs sleep in their homes despite how we all indulged them with special crackers and such. When both sides of Kate's needlework and my drawing were complete, we'd put it on a leather thong and she'd wear it around her neck—something special I hoped Louisa or Helena wouldn't find too worldly. We might even make a few as Christmas gifts with other subjects: flowers or fruit.

"I think cupboards there would fit," Matilda said. "You could put a basket in the bottom shelf and still have room for china or one of your oyster shell paintings. Yes. A cupboard would be nice."

"That's what I'll do then. First thing tomorrow I'll have a talk with Brother Jacob Stauffer, and we'll see about a marriage," I said. "I mean, a cupboard."

I thought Matilda would faint, with the color that drained from her face. "Oh, you can't, Emma. You mustn't say anything at all about marriage. Father Keil won't permit it, and besides, Jacob might think I put you up to it, and what if he's horrified by my pushiness? He could leave. I might never see him again."

"Wouldn't it be better than this...waiting and wondering?" Almira said. "Sometimes not knowing is much worse than knowing and having to live with the next step. I hate not being able to take that next step."

"There's always a next step to take," I said. "Even if it's just to get your mind clear about what matters."

"Then having the courage to act on that," my Kate said. I stared at her. She stitched as though she didn't even realize what she'd said. *Are these words I often say out loud? Well, they are good ones for a child to remember.*

"I'd be mortified beyond belief if Jacob wasn't really interested in marriage; and what if he were, and then Brother Keil said no outright to him? That would be so humiliating for him. I can't imagine Jacob's defying him."

"It would be good not to defy the leadership," BW said. She would defend her John.

"He comes from sturdy Stauffer stock," I said. "He can think for himself."

"Emma, maybe you should let the Lord decide Jacob and Matilda's course. Maybe there's a reason He hasn't brought them together," BW added.

"*Ja*, his father defied Keil and stayed in Willapa. As did John," Matilda added.

"I find men sometimes need…guidance to bring what they want to the surface," I explained. "They're so…deep that they sometimes don't realize what they want or need until we women rub off the hard surface to get to that soft, all-important inside."

Silence filled the space, broken only by the sound of needle pushing through cloth.

"It's a good idea to find out where you stand," BW said finally. "But it's also true that there's a risk. She should know that."

"Anything worth having is worth a little risk," I said.

"Another one of your facts," BW noted, "not meant as judgment?"

"*Nein*, it is a judgment, one we must never forget if we're to live with abundance. No flower ever blooms unless it's willing to risk wind and rain while it reaches for sun."

—————

The very next day, while the rain wept like a widow, I donned my rubber slicker and trudged up the hill to Keil's house, where I imagined Jacob would be. The men weren't doing much construction with the weather so foul, so they practiced their music and sat around working on miniatures and wooden toys. The turners continued to turn out furniture in the village shop, but at Keil's, the men told each other stories they neither believed nor remembered, apparently, because they kept repeating them through the years, laughing in the same places as though they'd just heard them. I stomped mud from my feet, slipped off my wooden shoes, and pulled up my dark stockings before entering the *gross Haus*.

It really was like a hotel, I decided. No one ever knocked at the front door. Who would hear it? Who would know to come to the door? I wondered why I'd been so intimidated by Keil's Elim, the *gross Haus* of Bethel when we lived there. I was young then, a child of seventeen. Behind Keil's Elim walls, decisions had been made about my life over which I had no control. The irony was that back then, I'd still made things happen that had changed many lives, including my husband's, including my children's. Here, despite Keil's power stripping me of the presence of my sons, it seemed Keil had less influence over men than he'd had in Bethel. Other men pushed to make decisions, and made them, when Keil attempted to slow progress by disappearing behind his workroom doors, lost in one of his moods.

Today, I didn't need to be concerned with Brother Keil first. He'd already changed my life here in Aurora. It was Jacob who mattered.

Once inside the hallway, I felt immediately steamy beneath my slicker. Christine was right. They kept the house very hot: fireplaces blazing, so many people.

It was Christine who came up the steps. "I thought I heard someone come in," she said. "Are you looking for Louisa?"

"No, Jacob Stauffer."

"Ah," she said. "I remember." A smile formed at the corners of her mouth. "Would you like me to go get him for you?" Her tone said she hoped I wouldn't. Her face looked pinched yet flushed. Probably from the work she'd been doing in the kitchen.

"I can climb those stairs as well as you," I said. "I assume he's with the bachelors?" She nodded, and I started up the three flights.

I did knock on the door at the top floor.

"Who is it?" A male voice said. A fiddle stopped playing.

"Emma Giesy," I told them. "I'd like to talk to Jacob Stauffer."

"Oh, *ja,* now you're in trouble, Jacob," I heard muffled laughter behind the door. The teasing continued, with sentences I couldn't quite make out, so I said, "I'm old enough to be his mother. Must I act like that to get you to send him out here?"

"You're not old enough to be my mother," Jacob said as he opened the door. He turned back to cast some sort of look at the men who laughed, then closed the door. He moved us into the hall, so we stood in front of the window that offered frangible light as it continued to rain. "What can I do for you, *Frau* Giesy?"

"I've some work I'd like you to do at my house," I said.

"One of the few houses finished."

"Not totally. There are things to do that I'd like you to take care of for me. I'm not sure how I could pay you. Brother Keil might not think the work I want done is…worthy of an exchange on the ledger. But perhaps I could launder your clothes or patch them—"

"*Fräulein* Knight does that for me. Sometimes." Just the mention of her name brought color to his neck.

"I'd not interfere with whatever arrangements you have with Matilda Knight," I said.

"Oh, no arrangements. No, *nein.* Nothing like that. Maybe your gooseberry pie. Now that I'd trade some work for."

"Would you now? And my…bread. I could bake you a loaf of fine crusty bread."

"Those would do," he said.

"Can you come by after your workday today?"

"*Ach.* This isn't work I do here. It's filling up time. You offer a much better way to do that. Eating gooseberry pie, I mean. And doing what I must to earn it."

"Of course, that's what you meant," I said. "Shall we head back together now?"

"*Ja*. I'll get my slicker and maybe my hammer. I may as well begin the finishing now."

Begin the finishing: wasn't that what my life was about now? It was a thought I could latch on to.

———◆———

Later, back at my house, I came upon Christine as she finished her bath. She'd been so quiet in the kitchen, I thought she'd gone up to the bedroom. I hadn't heard her talking to the girls across the hall. Kate said she was hungry, and I had a piece of cold salmon in the icebox (something else Helena probably thought a furbelow) that would be good for her to eat, instead of the sweets my daughter craved. I moved lightly down the steps.

The door was ajar. I was certain no one was in the kitchen. But when I opened the door fully, Christine stood there unclothed, her feet in the copper tub we reserved for bathing. She stared at me, then we both looked at each other, startled.

"I'm sorry," she said.

"No, it's my intrusion."

She reached for a flannel sheet she used as a towel, and when she turned, I could see that scars like spring branches mapped her back.

———◆———

Jacob spent several days building my cupboards in place. He'd done the work, a fine job of it too, and took extra time, I thought, to smooth the wood with beeswax. He told me I should only build them part way up the brick sides, so that one could still see the craftsmanship of Brother Yost's brickwork above it. He worked only on days when someone besides Matilda was there. "I don't want to compromise *Fräulein* Knight's reputation," he said. Almira chaperoned them, along with my girls, now that the weather kept all children out of school. Almira had them stringing dried berries and popcorn for the *Tannenbaum* we'd be trimming as Christday approached. She reported laughter between Jacob and Matilda, and quiet conversations, and long periods of silence during which she assumed Matilda tended to her tailoring and Jacob gave elbow grease to his beeswax efforts. Whenever she peeked in, she told me, "They were like two pegs in a puzzle who never got closer than their own set place."

I'd baked the promised pies and bread, and then Jacob had gone back to his other work, without a word to Matilda about their future.

I'd thought that where interest and opportunity intersected, action must follow. Surely there was interest on Jacob's part. We women had all agreed about that. And I'd provided opportunity.

We were in the kitchen when Almira said, "You have to be explicit with men. They don't see things the way we do."

Matilda said, "Maybe marriage isn't in Jacob's future. For years I never imagined it would be in mine, and I was fine. Until I met him." She blushed. "His life before he met me was probably full and well ordered, and he doesn't see any need to complicate it with a wife."

"My parents picked my husband for me," Almira said. We all looked at her. "He was tall and articulate and had a passion for Scripture, and my parents were certain that my marrying him would mean marrying up. Of course, they had no idea that he had already accepted a call to come to the mission field, a long way from Virginia. I think he saw in me a strong young girl who could survive in the wilderness, alone, more often than not. I'd be away from my family, with no one to complain to if things got difficult. Otherwise, he might have married some young, pretty thing, but I met his needs. In the beginning." She swallowed and looked away, and I wondered if she thought of the girl who was central to the divorce.

"We do meet their needs," I said. "It's part of our duty. But it's their duty to meet ours too. Once the marriage is blessed. Christian was that kind of man. It's a good thing about the Giesys. At least some of the Giesys."

"Tell the story of meeting Papa," Kate said.

"My papa story too," Ida said.

"Oh, you've heard it a dozen times," I said. I avoided looking at Kitty, hoping she wouldn't point out to Ida that Ida's father wasn't the same as Kate's. I hadn't actually made the distinction to my girls. I wasn't sure Ida even knew who Jack was in her life. "We're working on getting Matilda and Jacob together," I said. "Let's see how we can do that."

"Matilda should be like Sleeping Beauty and prick her finger with a spindle," Kate said. "Then Jacob could come wake her up."

"With a kiss," Ida said. She made a face.

"Who is Sleeping Beauty?" Almira asked.

The girls filled her in, including the bloody details. "The king had banned all the spindles, because the frog had told him his daughter would prick her finger and fall asleep. Mama says he tried to cheat fate. But some old woman didn't hear them, and she kept spinning and the princess—"

"Who was a curious sort and who loved a little risk," Kate interrupted.

"Found her," Ida finished. Ida didn't have all the details down, but I was grateful once again to Karl for securing German books for them to read, written by the Grimm brothers, even if the stories held sadness in them.

"*Sleeping Beauty* is a story of wishes fulfilled: the king and queen got the daughter they'd longed for, and even though they lost her for a hundred years, the princess was eventually rescued by her prince," Kitty said. "It's such a hopeful story." She sighed.

"Have you already kissed Jacob?" Kate asked. Her eyes grew large.

"That's a very personal question," I told her. "And not polite to ask." Matilda smiled. "I have not."

"I hope you don't have to wait a hundred years, Matilda," Kate said.

"No matter what happens," Matilda said, as she looked around at

us as though memorizing each of our faces, "it doesn't mean I haven't
already been rescued by love."

———————◆———————

"Christine," I said. "Sit with me." I patted the bench beside me, covered with one of my quilted pillows. Everyone else had gone to bed,
and she'd stepped across the stoop between the kitchen and the parlor,
likely to see if the room was empty. I noticed that since I'd walked in on
her, she'd kept constantly to the company of others, had taken no time
to sit in the parlor alone, and was never alone with just me.

"I can come back later," she said. "I see you're reading." She nodded to the Bible I had in my lap.

"It was my husband's. Sometimes I like holding something I know
he once held." A clock I'd purchased from the store ticked as it sat on
Jacob Stauffer's finished shelves. "Join me," I said. An oil lamp cast
shadows across the woven rug.

I wasn't sure how to broach the subject, or if I even should.

"You're wondering about the scars," she said as she sat. "You've
been kind not to bring it up."

"I wouldn't have known if I hadn't interrupted your bath," I said.

"I've appreciated your not asking."

"But now I am."

She fidgeted with the chatelaine that hung from a ribbon around
her neck. "Helena has a keen eye, and I knew if I stayed there, before
long in the evenings we shared, she'd notice and ask questions, maybe
even have me expelled." Her black eyes grew suddenly large. "You aren't
going to do that, are you?"

"Because you were once beaten? No. And I don't think Helena
would ask you to leave for that reason either."

"She might one day learn about something else," Christine said.
She paused. "I had a child," she said. "I left it on the doorstep of a
church in Shelbina, where I lived. I never returned to my father's home
after that. How could I? Your mother found me, thin as a noodle,

behind a boarding house I cooked at. She took me home and in an act of Christian charity so wonderfully bizarre, your parents made me one of theirs. They asked no questions. I told them I had no parents, and they fostered me."

"And here I am, asking all kinds of questions."

"But not in judgment, and I'm thankful for that. If Helena or others found out, they might be upset with you for taking me in."

"*Ach,* let them be. There's no need for you to hide yourself. You've paid a terrible price for someone's violating you."

"But that's just it. He didn't really violate me. I was a willing partner. I thought he loved me, and we'd marry one day. But he wasn't interested in marriage. And when I told him of the baby, I never heard from him again. My father, he's the one who took the whip to me when he learned of…the baby. I was big boned then too, and could conceal it for a time."

"Did your mother…?"

"She died when I was born. It was my father and me, and he never did get over her death. He blamed me for it. I made my way alone after that. Until your mother found me and took me in."

"But you decided to work for Keil and to stay there for a time."

She nodded. "Your parents' cabin is small and Johanna takes good care of Lou, and your brothers are a help to your mother. So Kitty and I decided to work elsewhere and live elsewhere, to reduce the burden on them. But there are so many people at Keils' now, with those arriving from Bethel and still so few houses built."

"The scars…from your father, then?"

"It was his way of letting me know how deeply I had sinned." She dropped her eyes, her demeanor that of a scolded dog.

"In my view, *he* performed the greater transgression. You sought to fill up an empty place with love, Christine. More than one of us has done the same and later wished we hadn't acted in quite the way we did. I have." She looked up at me, her eyes pooling with tears. "Yes, I did something that turned out poorly. I'm sure Helena will fill you in if you ask. Maybe my parents told you." She shook her head no. "I refused the help of other people, and married poorly after my husband died. Grief can be a veil against good reason. All that happened next wasn't good. In part, my sons no longer live with me because of how I managed my empty place."

"You didn't leave them on a doorstep."

"No, I didn't." *But I put them in peril.* I paused. "Did you see someone pick your baby up and take him inside?" She nodded yes. "Then you know the baby was safe. You tended him... Was it a boy?" She nodded yes. "You tended him to the very edge and then you went no further, giving him what you couldn't give him yourself just then. But you did not deserve the flogging by your father. No one ever deserves beating. Ever. There is always another way to solve a problem. Always." I took a deep breath. "And you don't need to keep covering your wounds behind your girth either. You're a lovely soul."

"I don't believe what you said, yet; but they are nice words to hear."

"One day you might." I patted her hand. It was cool to the touch, and she didn't pull it away from me. "Sometimes if we act as though a thought is true, it becomes true. We can work on it together."

18

The Hatching House

Christmas Eve. Belsnickel left treasures for the boys. My girls got another doll each that I made myself with extra clothes. I sewed them after the girls went to sleep at night so I saw the moon rise and sometimes dawn appear before I was finished. Comfort came in the stitching.

January 6. I checked on my smoked hams. Andy tells me that Henry T snuck into Keil's smokehouse and took a chunk from the biggest ham that had Brother Keil's name on it. That boy took a risk, indeed. Yet it's good to see that he's not intimidated by power. Still, I appeared appropriately appalled when Andy told me. One mustn't minimize theft, even if it appears as a prank.

The Advent season came and went. Christmas Eve arrived, and we women gave one gift each to one another at our "plotting place." The boys spent the afternoon with us, and later, after we'd walked through a melting snow to my parents' to bring them their gifts, Martin came to my home and sat with us in the parlor while we drank hot apple cider. He said the boys could spend the night if they wished to.

I didn't have the courage to ask if they wanted to, so I told him simply that they would. So they were with me on Christmas morning, and with the sounds of their laughter and even a few arguments between them and their sisters, I could pretend that all was as it should be. I thought of the verse in Hosea about lifting the yoke from our jaws, and God bending down to feed us. I felt fed.

The day went too quickly, and then I knew Martin would be coming for them, so I told the boys to get ready. "Are we going home?" Christian asked.

I thought of Martin's presence as their home now and realized that home for me is where those we love reside. "Yes," I said. I brushed his straight hair out of his eyes. "You're going home."

I walked over to Karl Ruge's hut a few days later. Since the weather kept the school closed from December until spring, he'd gone back to his toll bridge booth. Po bounded up to me as I knocked. I squatted down. "Doesn't your papa let you stay inside in this cold weather?" I asked. An old rug twisted where the dog had been sleeping out of the rain and snow beneath the dripping eaves. Karl opened the door. "Poor little thing. He'll freeze out here."

"He's too warm inside. Down, Po," Karl said as the dog trotted in behind me, a big black spot wagging back and forth on his otherwise white tail. He lay down by the stove as though it belonged to him. I saw a torn-up basket still able to hold kindling, and a once perfectly good shoe, all chewed up.

"Too warm," I said as I bent to scratch the dog's ears. "That's a story."

Karl grinned. "He'd have you believe he's neglected, but he isn't. You can see that. To what do I owe the pleasure of this visit?"

"It's Epiphany. Twelfth Day. And I have one last present to give, to you. I've woven a runner for your table," I said.

"*Ach,* you're not supposed to tell me," he said. He untied the string and rolled it out. "Such bright colors. Purple, red, green. *Ja,* by goodness, this is really good. *Danke.* I have for you a little something too."

He handed me a huge package, so large I had to set it down on the table. I unwrapped the paper, which I'd save for checking my stove heat. Inside the package lay several folds of fabric. Calicos and woolens, cotton blends with wool. All bright colors. Double pinks and cinnamon pinks, chocolate browns, purples known as fugitive dyes that would fade into browns. They were all store-bought material, machine printed, from back East from the looks of them. There must have been fifteen different pieces in all, perhaps five yards of each. One with tiny red stars I recognized as a fabric featured in a dress in *Godey's Lady's Book.* Another was a royal Prussian blue dotted with pink flowers throughout.

"These are…beautiful. I… The girls will love these for dresses."

"*Ja,* maybe for you too." He looked away.

"Oh, look, Karl. This one is one of those 'changeable fabrics.' See, where the light reflects differently against the warp and weft?" It was a rust color but had flecks of gold or yellow. I held it up to the window light, so he could see the shifts in it. "It feels like wool and silk." He nodded. "It must have been terribly expensive, Karl. You shouldn't have." I truly meant it.

"I notice on the ledger sheets that mostly cloth and needles and thread are what you buy, Emma."

"And stoves and chickens and iceboxes." I laughed. "The whole world knows what we do here with those ledger sheets, *ja?*" I wondered if everyone knew that he'd ordered these for me.

"I don't pry," he said. "I happened to see the ledger one time. I looked for my page for the shoemaker to draw my foot onto. I needed new boots. Joe Knight helped me order your cloth from a Portland store."

He was such a good friend. So faithful, so thoughtful in what he offered and gave up, asking nothing in return. "I thank you. And thank Joe Knight too."

Karl busied himself making tea. Always when I spent time with Karl like this, I thought of Christian and our time together. Karl had known me through all my phases. The years with Christian and Karl at Willapa had been good years, and Karl's presence after Christian's death still remained the cornerstone of how we Christian colonists should act to make another's life better than our own. Maybe if I hadn't rushed into the marriage with Jack… I pitched that thought away. "Speaking of Joe Knight, his sister Matilda is much enamored with Jacob Stauffer. You know this?"

"So I hear. And he likewise," Karl said.

"*Ja?* This is *gut*. But why hasn't he asked to marry her? They'd be happy together, don't you think?" I folded the material back up and rewrapped it, keeping my tea set safely to the side. The steam of it smelled of spices.

"He has no way to build a house for her. They'd be far down on the list. And Wilhelm has given his usual remarks that marriage takes one away from the true mission of our work here."

"He didn't think his son Frederick's work would be diminished by *his* marriage," I said. I couldn't keep the sarcasm from my voice.

"It is Wilhelm's way, Emma," he said. "You know this."

Karl's loyalty to Keil was much like my brother Jonathan's. It was a puzzle to me, one I might never solve but, like the labyrinth, might have to walk around.

"What if he and Matilda lived with me until they could get a home built by the colony? Might he ask to marry her, then?"

Karl shrugged. "He might, if he would accept your kindness. Some people are reluctant to accept the goodwill of others, *ja?*"

I felt my face grow warm. "But then we'd have the problem of the ceremony itself. Keil wouldn't officiate."

The dog now sprawled at my feet, and Karl nearly tripped over him. "*Ach,* this dog. You need to take him, Emma. The girls would love him, and he could stay inside all the time, then."

"What if I did take him?" I said. "And in exchange, you officiate at their marriage. Don't you have such credentials?"

"*Ja.* But I would not defy Wilhelm in his own place," he said.

"No. You wouldn't want to do that." I drank my tea. "But what if you officiated at their marriage *away* from here? In Oregon City, let's say. Or even in Portland. Would you consider doing that?"

"In exchange for your taking the dog? *Ja.* This could be arranged."

"Well then. All that's left is for Jacob to ask for Matilda's hand in marriage. Do you want me to push that along? Or will you?"

"I'll talk to him today," he said. "If it means this Po will be one more Epiphany gift I give to you."

———

February 20, 1865, was festive. It felt like spring with warm, balmy air swirling dried grasses as fresh green pushed them away. Green spears of daffodil shot up through the pungent earth. Within a month, they'd give us blooms.

I brought the girls with me, Kate insisting that I let her ride the *Kartoffel* horse that Andy had told her about. "He won't bite anymore, Andy says, and if he does try, I should carry a hot potato with me."

"Andy told you this?" She nodded. "He's a big horse."

"I can do it, Mama." The horses were kept in a long Pennsylvania-style barn, one of the few in the region. Most of the Oregon farmers allowed their stock to graze in the wetness, as it was seldom very cold. But we Germans liked to bring them inside, give them a dry, warm place to know they were appreciated. We saddled the *Kartoffel* horse, and Kate rode beside us in my father's wagon, twisting up the road north from Aurora. We'd placed twists of white bunting on the harness and another on the wagon side to announce that we rode to something joyous.

It had been a while since I'd been to Oregon City. We didn't go as far as those thundering falls but turned off instead onto a wagon road that led through a stand of oak. I'd decided against asking for Andy and Christian to attend, fearing Keil might object. I was pretty certain Martin wouldn't be there, because Keil had not sanctioned the marriage.

But when I saw John and BW's wagon parked by the Knights' home, north of Aurora on Baker Prairie, I wished I had asked for the boys. I said it out loud to my sister.

"BW came because she was a part of the plan," Kitty said. "She wouldn't have missed the results of your house hatching."

"Hatching at my house? That sounds ominous," I said.

Kitty laughed. "Well, isn't that what you do there? I mean, we all do it."

"I guess I hadn't thought of it as hatching, which sounds sinister to me, as though it wasn't natural."

"But hatching is natural, Emma. Look at your chickens. If they didn't hatch, we wouldn't have chicken soup eventually. Or a wedding cake."

"Still, I like to think I was a part of something Providential."

"Wouldn't we all?" Kitty said. "Sorting what's ours and what isn't, there's the challenge. If you remember, you were always kindling your own—"

"I remember," I said.

I was as proud as if Matilda were my own daughter. Fortunately my chickens were laying, since the cake I agreed to provide required fifteen big eggs. Most of them were blue. I used saleratus to add the rise, but with butter and flour and seeded raisins and ground mace and nearly a pint of molasses, and of course, ground cinnamon and cloves to improve everyone's digestion, I ended up with four rounds. Layered between each, I spread a buttery frosting. I cut a small piece of the cloth Karl gave me to make a tiny quilt that I constructed a little frame for. It might have fit in a doll's house, and I told Matilda she could give it to her first girl to play with one day, but it gave a splash of color to the cake top, and it matched Matilda's finely tailored dress.

I'd asked Matilda to go through the material that Karl had given me to choose a fabric for her wedding dress. She picked a printed plaid in greens and reds, the perfect festive colors. The entire Sunday afternoon crowd stitched on that dress. Maybe I should say we hatched it.

It wouldn't have taken much to bring a larger smile to Matilda's face, but on her wedding day, Kitty wove fresh holly in Matilda's hair, and she looked as young as Christine.

"I know I owe this to you," she said as we stood in her parents' bedroom. "Jacob never would have asked me to marry him if you hadn't arranged for Karl to officiate."

"It wasn't me," I said. "Oh, I might have pushed it along, but happiness is from God, and this is too, I'm sure of it."

"A place to live too, though. You've given us that."

"Passing along a gift I was given and hoping to make your lives better than my own. It's the Diamond Rule, remember? Besides, with three other women, two young girls, and one dog he'll share space with, I suspect Jacob will make some noise about moving up on that list for a house. Or maybe even start one of his own before long. But I am pleased to be able to make my home yours. And I thank you for accepting the offer. As Karl once told me, 'You give to others when you let them give to you.'"

Several of the Schuele family attended. Both Almira and Christine said they'd stay home and look after the dog. Of course, all the Knights were there, and the Stauffers arrived from Willapa. They talked of moving to Aurora later since Jacob was planning to remain.

The surprise was that Chris Wolff officiated instead of Karl.

"He was a Lutheran minister in Marietta, Ohio, before he joined with Keil," Karl told me. "And he kept many of the Lutheran tenets while he led the faithful back in Bethel. It's a good thing to do for Jacob and Matilda."

"Doctor Wolff had no problem doing this?" I asked.

"He has never found celibacy to be a critical feature of the Christian faith," Karl said. "He may have had words with Wilhelm over it, but I doubt it. He believes securely in communal ways, in sharing our wealth with one another so no one is in need. He was in charge of marriages and funerals back in Bethel. Besides, the marriage is here on Baker Prairie. What business is it of Keil's, then?"

I raised an eyebrow at Karl's last comment, for it was the testiest thing I'd ever heard him say of Keil.

We had a grand day, and while I was a little weepy remembering the joy of my own wedding day long ago, I didn't stay back there in my mind. Instead, I brought Christian into my present thoughts, reminding him that it wouldn't be long before our sons and daughter would be speaking such marriage vows. On the way home, we tied Kate's horse to the back of the wagon, and Kate rode with us, falling asleep in my lap. I brushed at her hair. *I'll have you in my home for a few more years,* I thought. My mother and sisters rode with us, and I decided we all needed festive days like this, to mix memory with promise. How sad it was that we didn't have more weddings to attend.

It wasn't hatching, I decided, as I carried Kate and then my Ida into the house and handed them into Almira's arms. What we'd done in getting Matilda and Jacob married was to be servants. Chris Wolff saw this marriage as a good thing or he wouldn't have officiated, and Karl had made it happen (so I now had the dog). These were good people, and surely a marriage between them could bring nothing but praise and joy to the faithful. Yes, things could go wrong and often did, but having a partner to walk with through them was a gift indeed.

———

We gave the newly married the south room, the one over the parlor, and Kitty, Christine, and Almira assumed one end of the other upstairs bedroom, with the girls sharing a bed at the other end with me. It took some adjusting. There was now a dog to accommodate as well, and we had our moments. One day, Opal followed Kate, Ida, and Po into the house and jumped up onto the kitchen table, dropping what looked like raisins but weren't. That day we made new rules of who managed the door when animals were about. I asked Jacob if he might convert our back kitchen door into one that could be open at the top and remain closed at the bottom, so we could get fresh air in while keeping animals out. Opal could plop her hooves and head up to look in, but I doubted she'd make the leap over the door to the inside. He said he could, and did.

I always attended the twice-monthly service at the Keil house, in part because I knew that the boys would be there, sitting across the room from me on the men's side. An ache always preceded my seeing their heads come through the door, but it eased as I listened to the music, and my spirits would lift if I caught Christian's eye and he smiled and waved at me, or if Andy nodded to me before I nodded first.

On the off Sundays, the boys came to my home and played with their sisters and the other children who might have come with their mothers that day.

Kitty attended the Keil church with me, but the others often didn't. It wasn't a requirement that people attend the worship at the Keils', at least not a requirement in order to remain living at my house. I should not have been surprised, then, when at a Sunday afternoon gathering in my parlor—on an off Sunday when Keil did not preach—Louisa and Helena arrived too.

I could hardly turn them away, but their presence interrupted the spontaneity of our gathering, as had also happened the day that Barbara and BW had attended. Any change in a routine causes some readjustment. Hadn't we had less spontaneity the first few times that Christine had joined us? And Martha Miller came sometimes too, a quiet, kind girl. Our little grouping felt safe; Louisa and Helena's presence menaced that safety a bit.

"We thought we should have more time with you," Helena said. "We see so little of you, Emma."

"I see you every other Sunday," I said.

"Such interesting things that affect the colony have arisen from your home, Sister Emma." She'd frowned when we first brought out Barbara's Friendship quilt, but when we explained that it would be a gift given away charitably, "as our Lord once healed on the Sabbath," Helena nodded and lifted her needle from her own chatelaine.

"Not all that much happens when we meet here," I sighed. "My boys don't live here anymore, but then you knew that before I did. Little occurs in Aurora without everyone's soon knowing. So there are no secrets, not really."

"*Ja,* but they do well with Martin, don't you think?"

"They wouldn't be there if I didn't think it was a good place for them," I said.

"Well, of course they wouldn't be," Louisa said. "It's a nice arrangement that works out well for everyone. My husband wouldn't have approved it otherwise."

Approved it? He engineered it. These were thoughts I chose not to say. Louisa continued. "Both Martin and, one day, Andy will make fine doctors, and the colony needs that. It's good you understand that, Emma. My boy August has trained himself well in herbs and all too. But he's back there in Bethel. I don't get to see him." She took a deep breath.

I didn't point out that August was a grown man she was missing, while I had young sons who didn't live with me.

"Besides," Helena said, "we wanted to see those cabinets Jacob Stauffer made. I was also hoping you'd returned to your painting, Emma. It was such a comfort to you when you first arrived in Aurora."

"It was my voice then," I said, "when I didn't have one. Now I do feel heard more, even if I don't get my way."

"*Ja,* submission means not always getting our own way," Helena said.

I wasn't ready to say I was submissive, but her definition was one I'd consider.

"Andy will be scientifically trained when he goes to school," Kitty said. "Not that herbs are not healing, but August didn't really have 'the touch.' Remember, we lived in Bethel after you came west. August, well, I don't mean to be critical."

"He didn't? He followed his father everywhere, held the horses for him when he had to tend to an ill person." Louisa sounded defensive.

"Maybe he held horses well," Kitty said.

I wondered what might have gone on back in Bethel, where August Keil had been sent and in the process escaped the smallpox deaths of his brothers and sisters. My parents, too, had found disruption in the arrival of August. But they'd found more dissension with Andrew Giesy, from what I'd gleaned in their conversations.

"Andy will make a good doctor, Emma," Helena said. "He's from our Giesy line. And isn't it nice that the colony will pay?"

The colony pays, but there is always a price.

"And how long do you plan to remain with us, Mistress Raymond?" Helena asked then.

Almira had been quietly stitching, not saying a word, so a question directed to her startled us all. She stared at Helena, who continued, "I mean no disrespect. I'm only making conversation. It must get crowded here. And you've added another."

Christine had a frightened-deer look on her face.

"Jacob Stauffer's been an easy addition," I said. "He puts the dog out at night if need be and has built shelves in the bedroom. They're up above us even now," I said and pointed to the room over the parlor.

"You let the dog stay in the house?" Helena said.

"How heavenly," Louisa said, looking upward to where Jacob and Matilda's footsteps could be heard above us.

"It may not be," Kitty said. "They have the girls up there across the hall, and one of the shelves in their room is storage for Kate's and Ida's stockings and leavings dolls. They rarely get any time alone with the girls' knocking on their door."

"They'll stay as long as they need to," I said. "Almira can remain as long as she likes too. You're of help to all of us here"—I turned to acknowledge that she sat in the room with us—"and when the girls are in school, you intend to add your hands to the work at the tannery, isn't that right?"

"If they'll have me with these knuckles," Almira said. "Though they're doing much better with that salve you gave me, Emma. Otherwise I'll find other work."

"Well, it's good that you and Christine and the new Stauffers have a place to live, with so many other worthy people waiting on houses. You didn't have to wait for long, Emma. Maybe the Stauffers won't have to either," Helena said.

"How fortunate I am, then, to be able to give rooms in this one so generously provided by the colony."

"How fortunate you are."

Everyone smiled sweetly. Almira rose to bring in tea. Kitty looked bewildered, and Christine exhaled. The afternoon proceeded civilly, and I discovered that a jibe gracefully acknowledged frames a picture of success.

———

Spring arrived with a blush of warm air that moved the scented blossoms from their limbs. In March, Mr. Lincoln was reinaugurated in Washington DC, and we hoped his reelection would bring the war to a close. New beginnings occurred for everyone, and we prayed we wouldn't have to worry over any more of our Oregon boys going off to fight.

The bustle of spring planting, of cleaning and sweeping mud from our rugs and doorsteps kept each of us occupied. With so many women living under one roof, the rhythm of our bodies could be seen by the string of washed rags stained by our blood hanging side by side on the line, almost exactly the same days of each month. Jacob took all of this in stride, and we often heard him and Matilda laughing behind their closed door. They didn't seem to mind staying on with us, but they made themselves scarce when the women gathered for those Sabbath afternoons, sharing laughter and pleasantries and speaking prayers for the war's end.

Sometimes Matilda still joined in the stitching. She worked on a "lifelong project," as she called it. The quilt cover she stitched was composed of blocks of yellow diamonds with vibrant dark blue centers sewn onto a backing of angry ocean blue. She'd made a bright red border around them all and called it her Sunflower quilt. The boldness, repetition, and form were things I'd never seen before. It wasn't pieced of leftover material either. Jacob wasn't earning enough money outside the colony to purchase so much fabric of single colors like that. Perhaps her father bought the cloth.

Matilda wanted to quilt it herself too. She placed fifteen stitches per inch, tiny as dots. The quilted pattern stitched into the dark blue formed an intriguing shape. When I looked closely, I could see it was a sand dollar, reminiscent of life along Willapa Bay. The patterns, material choice, and her unique quilting style all spoke of her independence, her history, her love of beauty and life. We women found our voices in our textiles.

I was in my thirties now, feeling the need to do something significant with my life, a lifelong project of my own. I knew a great many women who had died before they turned forty, not of accidents but of what was wearing out. I said as much to what I now called our house church. Helena and Louisa were there that day, but it was a Saturday, so mending was allowed, not just stitching on a quilt for someone else.

"Where do you learn such things?" Helena asked Matilda. "I'll be fifty this December, and I don't worry about doing something grand with my life. Living is enough."

"But it is scriptural, isn't it, Helena? To seek and pursue?" I asked.

"A deeper faith, yes. But not some wild adventure. Heaven knows what that might entail with you, Emma."

We all laughed, and Helena looked startled, as though she hadn't expected to say anything funny.

"It probably does look like I've done more than my share of unusual things. And, now that you say it, those actions have improved my faith. I hated water and river crossings, and I ended up twice living by a river. When we try something we think we can't do, we have to trust more in someone larger than ourselves. More in one another too. Approaching the end of what might be my final decade spurs me on."

"Having children is adventurous," Louisa said. "That should be enough to give a woman pause and deepen her faith. Don't you agree, Almira?"

Almira nodded agreement. "But it's also tedious and can drain a woman's faith. 'Is this all I'm meant to do?' I asked myself that at times, with a broom in my hand."

"Tedious?" This from Matilda, who looked up from her work.

"Washing, mending, sewing, cooking. I know it's important work, but I have this other part of me, as though I had two doors: one open to service and one open to my heart," Almira said. "Tedium gets in the way of both!"

"Those second doors don't get pushed open very often," I said. "I miss adventure. I miss…affection. A son's hug, for example."

Louisa added, "Instead of a son breaking his mother's dishes on the trail before her very eyes. Poor Catherine Wolfer." We all shook our heads in sympathy.

"Though just learning something new, like how to stitch a different quilt block, helps," I said. "Or considering those Greek nouns that Brother Wolff talks about in the evening class. Who knew that 'hearth' was a word that gave birth to the English word 'focus'? That gives what we women do in our kitchens at the fire a certain weight, doesn't it? Warmth and passion for a life."

"Affection only gets a girl into trouble," Helena pronounced. "She has to make decisions she wishes she didn't have to make."

I kept my eyes from seeking Christine's, but Kitty said, "You can only say that if you've been romanced. I haven't, so I guess I'd like to know that for myself. That would be a door I'd like opened. A real adventure."

"Without getting into trouble," Louisa warned, her scissors raised toward Kitty.

"What kind of adventure did you have in mind, Emma?" This from Almira.

"I remember you climbed to the top of the mill in Willapa, for the view. Or so I heard," Helena said.

"This summer, I think we should…climb something higher. Mount Hood." That just came to me, like my thoughts used to, when saying them out loud was the first time I heard them myself.

"Climb Mount Hood?" Christine shriveled into the bench pillow she sat on. Her skirts billowed out around her. "The height…"

"You're so daring, Emma," Martha Miller noted. "I wish I had an ounce of that in me."

"We'd have to find out about it," I said. "Talk to someone who has done it. Maybe not go all the way to the top. We don't want to be foolish."

"I should hope not. It's eleven thousand feet high," Helena said. "It's not feasible for a woman to do."

"It would be formidable," Almira said. She looked at her hands.

"I'm not sure I could hang on to…whatever it is people must hang on to, to keep themselves safe."

"One of us might die there," Martha said.

"If it's Emma, we'll put on her headstone, 'I didn't plan for this,'" Kitty said, and I nudged her with my elbow but smiled.

"Planning is half the fun of it. Few people have climbed that mountain, or so Karl told me. No woman that I know of," I said. "Imagine the view from there!"

"Imagine the snow," Kitty said.

"It's a good three days' ride to the base, and then it would take a day or more to climb it. You'd have to bring food," Helena said. "You'd have to have animals and people to look after them while you went on this whim. You know nothing of mountain climbing. I'm Swiss, Emma. I know about mountains." Helena was adamant. "It would be a foolish, foolish thing for you to do. You have children to think of. *Ach!* Don't spur these younger women to go along with such nonsense. Louisa is right. Being a mother, or for that matter being a woman, is adventure enough."

She took the heat from my pan. "It was an idea," I said. "Something we could all work on together that had some passion in it. Something…invigorating."

"Well, think of another," Helena said. She tugged on her scissors ribbon.

"The men have their band they get to go around the country and play with. The girls' chorus doesn't even get to sing away from Aurora," Kitty complained. She brightened. "Maybe we should push for a joined boys' and girls' chorus."

"Talk to Chris Wolff before you engage in something like that," Louisa said.

"Yes, he might broach the subject with Brother Keil, so you won't need to," Almira said.

"That could be dangerous," Louisa said.

I laughed, and she looked startled but then smiled.

"But at least not life threatening, Sister Louisa," I said.

The afternoon faded with grace. A family gathering, that's what it was. Family, a word that Chris Wolff said came from the Latin *famulus,* meaning "servant." We were sisters, serving one another, serving our families.

Then an interruption as we stitched. "You didn't even knock," Martha Miller said to Mr. Ehlen's rush through the door. She rarely challenged anyone, let alone an elder like Mr. Ehlen.

"Mr. Lincoln's been assassinated," he said, his loose arm flinging wildly as he turned to catch each of our eyes. "Friday last, at Ford Theatre. Telegraph just came through."

A universal gasp stilled the room. We sat with hands across our mouths to keep from screaming.

"Tragic," Almira said at last. "How very, very tragic."

"I'm going home," Louisa said. She gathered up her things, followed by Helena.

Kate waved good-bye at her and asked, "What's wrong, Mama? Who was Mr. Lincoln?"

"He was our president," I told Kate. "And someone took his life."

"What did they do with it?" Ida asked. I pulled her to me.

"Like Papa?" Kate said.

"Like Papa, yes," I said. I felt tears begin, for the senselessness of such a loss, for the uncertainty flooding in that assassin's wake.

"We will lower the flag to half staff," Mr. Ehlen said. Matilda and Jacob stood at the stairwell, having descended at the sound of Mr. Ehlen's voice. "And *Herr* Keil wishes us to gather at his house. The band will play. We will pray, *ja?*"

"I'll tell others," Mr. Ehlen said, swinging that useless arm as he headed out. "At times like this we need to gather close."

The rest of us stayed for a time, bowed our heads in silence, each lost to our thoughts, speaking our prayers. I could hear Kitty crying softly; others too. Then Kate began a prayer for the president's family, for us, for "all people including the man who is making everyone cry." I wished now, more than ever, that the church were finished, but it wasn't. Not yet. So many distractions. I prayed at that moment for my children, that their lives would be full and long. I prayed for Jacob and Matilda, that their marriage would be rich and blessed with children. I prayed Kate's prayer and for myself, that I'd be found worthy as I worked to do the everyday things that kept a family whole, that I'd listen to that voice. I prayed I'd have the courage to let myself be led.

19

Two Doors

That fall of 1865, Captain John Vogt brought in eleven wagons, all pulled by big Missouri mules. Nearly one hundred additional Bethelites increased our population and the demands on our resources. They'd left Missouri shortly after the president's assassination, uncertain about what would happen now in this divided country. The co-conspirators had been tried and hanged in July while the Bethelites traveled west, but their deaths didn't mean that grief was now relieved. I wondered what these latest Bethelites thought when they arrived and found themselves not in a thriving village but bunked down with other families still awaiting housing.

Sometimes the wait for houses here in Keil's town gave me a kind of warped satisfaction. After all, it was for lack of housing in Willapa that first winter that Keil had separated the colony. He couldn't believe we had so few homes prepared for the arrival of two hundred fifty people. Yet there'd been people living in Aurora now for ten years, and out of the nearly six hundred people who now claimed Aurora as their home, only half had single homes to live in. I never said that out loud to anyone, but I felt some vindication when I heard the mumblings of both newcomers and old-timers about what they found once they left Bethel. Aurora was not yet anyone's *Heimat,* that special place of belonging, that I could see.

The apothecary shop, or pharmacy, was nearly complete though, and Martin moved into it with my sons about the time the colony band and many others headed for the state fair that fall. Martin didn't play in the band, but he was busy with his studies, and I asked if the boys might travel with us. I was pleasantly surprised when he said they could. The bile in my stomach had begun to lessen each time I asked for permission to have time with my own sons. We were doing this together, after all, not because I was a failure as a mother, but because it was the best for my sons. Karl would remind me that I had given my heart to my sons, and I did what I did in love for them. "Such love will be rewarded," he said. It was a belief I held on to.

I took the girls with me to the fair that year and convinced my sister Christine that she should come as well. "You can help cook, but you can also enjoy yourself. You work so hard and such long hours, I worry over you," I told her.

"Penance," she'd said and smiled, making her round face open up in warmth like the sun.

"Nonsense. It's time you did what young women do, enjoy themselves."

We began planning yet again for the fair, as much an announcement of seasonal change as the vine maple turning red. Almira sounded enthusiastic at first but then decided she wouldn't join us. She worried about old memories in Salem, she said. While I assured her that time scrubs away much of the edge of sharp memories, she didn't believe it. She'd become quiet of late, and sleeping more, as when she'd first come to stay with us. She didn't seem interested in talking about why. "I'll stay with Po," she said. "Keep him from chewing Opal's ears into shredded meat." She scratched the dog's head. "That's all right, isn't it? That I stay here alone in your home, without you here?"

"Matilda and Jacob are here, and besides, it is your home too. You contribute to the colony," I said.

"I've never officially joined."

"I'm not sure how one 'officially joins,' " I said.

Kitty expressed readiness to pack up for the fair, but she'd been asked to remain behind, to help cook for the bachelors and newcomers at the Keil house. So Christine and my children and Jonathan filled the Wagner wagon. I looked forward to seeing Brita and having time with my children, but I wondered if I was doing Almira a disservice by leaving her behind.

The band was a huge success at the fair. This second year of the new hall crystallized their prominence. There were stories that the governor would invite them to play for a holiday ball, or that they'd be invited to do a tour by someone named Ben Holladay, who was interested in railroad expansion. I suspected our Keil had been having words with him.

I confess to a bit of nostalgia as I walked around the exhibits in the Homemaking and Household Arts tents. There was that Nancy Thornton's name again, signed right on her paintings. She gave art lessons in Oregon City, or once had. The address on her exhibitor's card attached to the landscape read Salem. If it was too far to travel for a class at the university, it would be too far to travel for a private class too. I'd never even taken myself off that Wallamet class list, so even if I did find a way to join, they might not trust that I'd follow through in the future. I didn't trust me either.

Looking into the paintings was a gift I gave myself. A scene of an Indian encampment near a shoreline brought back good memories of a day when Christian and Andy and Kate and I had camped at the Bay. I stopped before a portrait of a woman spinning. She wore a dark green dress, no apron, as though the work she did was for another purpose than just everyday tedium. Window light illuminated her concentrated face. Her hands had large knuckles not unlike Almira's. She was beautiful. The painting was beautiful in its simplicity. I felt my eyes tear up that such a humble subject could make me feel prayerful in the midst of a festive fair.

"You paint like that, Mama," Kate said. I softly brushed at her hair, took in her words as a compliment.

Andy lagged behind as we walked through the exhibits, and at one point he asked if he could go to the horse barns instead.

"Looking at art is good for a future medical person," I told him.

"Why?"

I wasn't sure how to answer. Keil didn't seem to appreciate art; I didn't know if Martin did. "Because healing is knowledge and science wrapped up in experience and heart," I said. "Art helps us reach deeper into the heart, and we experience things we otherwise never could. It tells us something about people, about what they draw on to help a physician heal them. A doctor and patient must work together. There's artistry in that."

He grunted, but I thought he paid more attention to the artists' works.

Most of those exhibiting were women. Louisa had entered her *Fraktur* lettering. I respected the time she'd taken to make the letterings, but even more I admired her willingness to exhibit them and have them judged each year. They'd gotten only a white ribbon, but somehow just seeing them made Louisa stand higher in my eyes. At least she had entered her work. It was an art. Some might call it frivolous, but I could see the careful strokes of her brush, and she must have mixed her own paints. Perhaps she even cut and smoothed the boards she painted on. I suspected that her work took as much time and careful attention as making a sampler, and there were plenty of those on display. Perhaps the work comforted her in her losses. I thought I'd ask her. It might be the reason she urged me to keep painting, a gift she wanted to give me.

Near the exit, a painting of two doors caught my eye. One was a lavish portal with gold-embossed curlicues and what looked like emerald stones inlaid. A rich woman's door. The other was equally intriguing for its spare and splendid nature. No embossing, just fine-grained wood painted white, promising the calm of simplicity behind it. I stood there a long time. The artist couldn't know that I would see it and go to my own inner world of doorways to open, yet she'd conducted my experience, the way Henry C conducted listening experiences for his audiences of the Aurora Band. Music, stories, art, even our quilts and samplers were all products that Keil might deem less important than the compounding of medicines for healing. But like those medicines, the artists' imaginations emerged from the backwaters of their spirits into the stream that the viewer brought to that place, and there they merged. Two experiences. One for the artist and one for the viewer. Both of us receiving something quite grand.

I remembered what Almira had said in our discussion at the house church on the day of Mr. Lincoln's death. We'd talked about two doors: one for service and one for seeking deeper meaning for ourselves as women. We felt completed taking care of others, our children and families, even members of the larger communal family. And yet the demands of others sometimes pushed aside our own need to be creative in more personal ways. Perhaps that was why the quilting time offered so much. It let us open both doors at once. Even Almira, who didn't quilt, found ways to open both doors. She looked after others but was revived when she walked her "lab-rinse" path.

I continued meandering through the exhibit hall, answering questions raised by my children. But I couldn't keep the idea of the blend of richness and simplicity from my thoughts. Simple contentment followed our house church gatherings where we read Scripture, talked with one another of its meaning while we had our hands on fabric. But I always felt as rich as a queen then too. Joy could so easily disappear from our efforts, be as temporary as an aroma. A woman had to nurture what was behind both doors to truly feel whole. And only she can decide which door to devote time to.

It was a thought I'd share with Almira when I returned.

————◆————

Music lightened our steps at this first fair after the end of the war. Christine enjoyed the dancing, once Kitty and I pushed her to it. "I had partners waiting," she said. Her round face glowed with perspiration, her cheeks as pink as watermelon. "One said he didn't think so large a woman could be so light upon her feet. Should I take that as a compliment? Or not?" She laughed.

"We women take good words wherever we can get them," I said. "When I saw Adam Knight after not seeing him for years, he told me, 'You weather well, Sister Emma.' He compared me to a good leather saddle, but I decided to not take offense where none was intended."

"I haven't danced since we came to Aurora," she said. "And not much before that either. It's been lovely. Thank you for making me come."

"You've earned your dancing shoes," I said. "We'd best get back to preparing the sausages. When the horse races finish, we'll have a crowd of hungry people making their demands."

"Like at the *gross Haus,*" she said and laughed.

It was good to see her out with young people and for her to realize that her smile and willingness to move to music brought her young men interested in dancing with her. Several came by to talk later, and I heard a giggle from her that was new to me. She was a woman noticed, and it brought both high color and delight to her being.

Andy and Christian were accustomed to a regular routine, I could tell. Christian especially whined when the evening meal dragged on because we were serving others from the tent. "He goes to bed early," Andy told me. Andy spent most of his time in the science exhibits or walking the barns, talking to the men who cared for the animals. He said they had lots of ideas for mending broken limbs or sore muscles, ideas he thought Martin might find interesting. Jonathan was off talking business somewhere, and some others from the colony were selling food too, though most brought enough only for themselves. Several had something exhibited or were related to the musicians. Despite that, we were heavily outnumbered, we German Americans, and I became conscious of my still-stumbling English when people from outside our colony talked with me.

That night I bundled down with my children. The stars, like silver candles on black silk, formed a canopy overhead. I heard Christine's laughter in the distance. She had not yet joined us in the wagon. And while the cool evening air threatened to bring me a headache, I talked it away. "I will think myself happy," I said and thought it fortunate that Christine was doing the same.

In the morning I looked for Christine in the quilts beside me. I hadn't been awake when she joined us. She wasn't there, and I assumed she'd gotten up early to begin fixing bacon and eggs for the many hungry customers. I needed to remind her that she didn't always have to be the first one up. Jonathan still slept, as did the boys. I sat up, stretched, and looked around. I didn't smell bacon cooking. The fairgrounds were as still as a cemetery. I couldn't see Christine anywhere.

Discomfort accompanied me to the wash tent where I carried my bucket. I splashed water on my face, considering what to do. Christine was a grown woman, an adult. She could certainly take care of herself. If I were Christine, I'd resent intrusion and the assumption that something might be amiss.

Still, she was my sister. When she rushed into the wash tent with her hair pulled loose from its usual swirl of braids around her head, I said nothing except, "Good morning," and put aside that niggling of anxiety that rose there when she answered, "*Ja,* the very best."

Later that day I told the children, "Let's see if we can find Brita." She hadn't appeared anywhere at the fair. Andy and Christian walked with their sisters and me to the livery where we'd last seen her. The Durbin brothers said they hadn't heard from her. I wondered if she'd perhaps left the area completely. Maybe she'd gone to the gold fields near Canyon City, east of here, to make her fortune. I issued yet another letter to general delivery. Andy expressed equal disappointment when we couldn't locate Charles or Pearl or Stanley.

"They moved away," Christian said as we walked back.

"We're the ones who moved, silly," Andy said.

"As it happens, you're both right," I told them. "They moved to Salem, and you boys moved to Martin's. Changes like that happen all the time. But they'll find us in Aurora if they need to."

"You moved too, Mama. To that house. Where you wash the clothes and feed the dog and pick up eggs."

That house. He doesn't call it a home. "That house," I said. "That's right. There are people who have a fine roof over their heads at my home too."

"You're a two-door, Mama," Christian said. "That's what Henry says."

"And what do you suppose he means by my being 'two-door'?" The band instructor's son had quite a lip for quips.

"One for all your friends to come in, and one for your boys to go out."

The words stung.

"There'll always be a place for you there," I said. "Your going out is only from the house, not from my heart."

"But we're the only boys who don't live with our mother," he said.

"*Ja*, well, that's not your fault," I said. "You've done nothing wrong."

"Then why can't we come home to that house?" Christian asked.

I suppose it was time I told a story they might be able to live with. I chose my words. I could give him a door with longing behind it, or one that moved him toward satisfaction, a way to be a good steward of his disappointments. "When your papa died, your uncles thought it best that one of them should stand in for him, take his place to be your papa, to look after you. I didn't think we needed anyone until later, and then I chose one of Papa's cousins instead. Jack."

"Oh, Jack."

"My choice wasn't so good, *ja*, even though I meant the best. Sometimes one's best isn't. So we came here, but still your uncles and others thought it best that you boys live with a man to guide you. When we stayed at Keils', there were lots of men to guide. Then I got that house and they chose Martin, and he's a good man and I agreed. You'll go on to school when you're older. And someday you might be the uncle who helps your sister's children or someone else's child. It's a way of family passing goodness on. Does that make sense?"

"*Ja*. I wish Martin made cinnamon rolls like yours. Then I wouldn't miss that house so much."

"I'll bring them to you," I said, holding him close. "It's the least I can do."

———

In the spring of 1866, Brother Keil announced that several young men would be asked to preach in his stead. He said this at a Sabbath service and gave names. Several were newer arrivals, men who'd come the previous year. John Giesy shifted in his seat with the announcement, but I thought Chris Wolff, Dr. Wolff as many called him, looked pleased. Karl Ruge did too.

The winter months following the fair had been filled with "consternation," as my brother called it. He claimed people were distressed with Keil because he devoted as many resources to the hotel building as to the church, and because few houses had been constructed in the six months since the last group from Bethel had arrived.

Jonathan was a great defender of Keil, telling me, as he ate bacon and eggs at my house, that Keil had authorized the building of Jonathan's house at the north edge of the village. Jonathan complained that people could do more for themselves and not put so much pressure on Dr. Keil to do it for them. "People would rather use their tongues to complain," he told me, "than their hands to take action. The apostle Paul said all parts of our bodies must work together, each in their own unique way, but some of these colonists would prefer to push us all into one single way of doing something."

"Keil did set it up like that," I said. "He wanted to make all the decisions, so he does have to live with the consequences."

"For good reasons, he made these decisions!" Jonathan's face grew red. He'd put on much weight of late, and now he started to gasp.

I got him a glass of water and didn't pursue the subject further. But obviously, others had been expressing their opinions that we needed more leaders, that we needed to expand the work. Those conversations might have been heard by Brother Keil, as he'd announced the change soon after the new arrivals.

At our house church gathering that afternoon, neither Louisa nor Helena attended. The rest of the regulars were there, except for Jacob, who had begun work on a log home. The entire Stauffer family, including Jacob and Matilda, would move into this log home before long. On this house church day, Jacob had ridden out to check on progress.

We opened our gatherings with a reading. Matilda chose a verse of Scripture, and I'd suggested that we talk about where we saw God in such a verse. We'd had such conversations before, and even when

Louisa or Helena came, they didn't seem offended by our exploring how mere women might see God in Scripture. After all, we weren't arguing doctrine, just speaking of our lives. Then one day Martha added that we ought to talk about how we saw God *within* our lives, not only in the verse. That had caused some to shift uneasily beneath their hoops. Kitty rose to get us all more tea. Almira coughed until she had to leave. But then I said what I thought. The verse happened to be about the tax collector Zacchaeus.

I said, "To me, the verse says that even the most ostracized person on the edge could find a place within the love of God. I've seen that for myself, when I felt I needed to leave Willapa. And the verse says, too, that I had the choice to accept the love and healing salve that were offered, but then I needed to do something with it, act outwardly to show that I had been truly changed. For me, that's been the hardest part."

The room had grown quiet. No one else said anything until Almira asked, "But don't you think being brought into something good when one has been at the edge, doesn't that mean one will not make decisions that put one back out at the edge again? I mean, once having chosen to receive, if we make a mistake, it must be because we weren't really healed…right?"

Martha expressed her view. Matilda too. Christine stayed silent. She was with us that day. Since the fair, she'd often been absent on these afternoons. I didn't ask where she'd gone. But it was Kitty who offered comfort.

"That scripture describes grace, Almira. It says we get to start over. We get to be restored. In between, we offer that same grace to others, and that's a way to show that we've been changed. But it doesn't mean we won't have to start again. We have a way back, so we don't have to stay at the outside."

"We start over and over, like in the puzzle path," Kate said. I smiled at her. *She is growing in wisdom, my daughter.*

"I guess it has its one way in and one way out, and we have to keep moving. So yes, maybe that's so, Kate," Kitty said. Kate beamed.

On the following Sabbath, our Scripture verse was from First Timothy, the second chapter, in which all were asked to pray for all men, but especially kings and those in authority, so that there might be peace, and the word of God could be more easily spread.

"It means that when people are at war," BW said, "that it's difficult to spread the love of God to others. Others see only the warring side, and with people of faith fighting on both sides, how can others know the true story?"

"I think it means we have to submit to those in authority. And pray for them," Almira said.

"I didn't see anything about submission," Matilda said. "Jacob and I don't think of our marriage as his having 'authority' over me, nor my trying to get it over him. We're together on things. Most of the time. We talk things out until we are. I think that's what it means."

We stitched for a time in silence, then Matilda spoke again. "I wish we'd have our own house, instead of having his whole family and brothers and sisters live there, but none of them are married. Jacob's the first. It's the charitable thing to do, all live together."

"Who will have authority with all those women living there?" Kitty said. "Have you thought about that?"

"We'll all pray for you," Martha said, "with that many women in one house."

"I'll need it," she said, and we laughed.

"What did you think of Brother Keil's announcement last week?" I asked. "I wonder if this scripture says anything about that?"

"I found it very strange," Kitty said.

Christine said nothing.

Almira, who rarely went with us, had attended that morning. "Are the sermons tiring him? Maybe that's why he's asked others to preach for him. I know my husband worked very hard on his messages each week, to make them faithful to Scripture."

"Too bad your husband didn't *live* faithful to Scripture," Kitty said.

I saw Almira flinch. It might be all right to criticize a family member ourselves, but hearing anyone else do it could be wounding, indeed.

"It wasn't all him," Almira defended. "That girl. And I suppose me. I never did stand up to him the way that girl did. He liked her obstinancy. He never struck her. Anyway, he worked on his sermons. They tired him. That's all I was saying."

"It's a surprise that Keil would allow anyone besides John or Karl to preach. It sounded like even Dr. Wolff might preach sometime," Martha said. She had a chipped tooth that made some of her words sing.

"Maybe some of the younger men will be groomed as new leaders," Kitty said. Her crooked pinky finger stuck out as she spoke with her hand in the air. "Maybe they'll need wives."

"I like listening to Chris Wolff," I said. "He reads Shakespeare and Cicero and classic books that I hope he's introducing our children to in school."

"They're pushing for articles of agreement," Christine said. Her voice was so soft, I had to ask her to repeat what she'd said. Sometimes the loom I'd had Jacob set up in the parlor made a lot of noise. I'd been weaving a blue-dyed yarn made from boiling galls, the pockets of insects that formed on the stems of ragweed. It wasn't Prussian blue, but it was pretty. And we'd give the rug away to Matilda and Jacob when they moved into their house, so we all felt we weren't really working on the Sabbath, we were serving.

"Agreeing about what?" I asked.

She shrugged. "That's all I know for certain. There are snippets of conversations that I hear over the dinner talk. They're more open on the work sites, in complaining about who has gotten what property or how quickly something has occurred. The younger men seem impatient. The hotel will be finished before the church, from the looks of it. Some are excited about the railroad being courted, and others, well, they think it will mean the downfall of our community. The younger men, they want new life. A 'western life,' they call it, where they're free to be independent."

"But they fear risking the wrath of Keil or of doing something on their own and failing," Matilda said. I looked at her. "Jacob tells me. That's why he's building our log home. We'd never get a lumber home. You're very fortunate, Emma."

"Yes, I am," I said. "What would the articles of agreement say? About how money is distributed, or who gets the land? About marriages or not?"

"All of that. And that he'll have a council, a group who will advise him about issues, and he agrees to listen to them. More men in authority, maybe. So decisions can get made, even when Keil is in one of his low moods."

"Goodness. Papa might rejoin if that happens," Kitty said. "Back in Bethel, Andrew Giesy didn't listen. That's what Papa said, anyway. Who knew who was really in authority? Keil was out here, but his son was back there claiming he carried his father's staff. And Andrew made decisions. Many of you were at Willapa... It was very confusing."

"And I suspect not very many new people found a path to our Christian way either, with all that uncertainty," I said.

"Just like here," Kitty said. "Except for Almira, there hasn't been an outsider who has joined us for years. And lots of former members have left. Like the Knights."

"They're still close by," Matilda defended. "They'd help if we needed them. They're helping build our log home."

"They're going to put into writing what we colonists believe," Christine said.

"It's always easier to say, 'Come join me,' when you can say what you truly believe," Almira said.

"*Ja,*" I said. "Kitty's right. It's pretty hard to win souls when everyone is feuding or moving around in different directions. So maybe this is what this scripture is really about."

That and the need to make certain we open our doors wide and that what's on the other side shines light into darkness.

20

Dedication

The colony principles were issued that summer. They emphasized again that all we possessed was to be placed within a common fund, that we'd labor for one another. They spoke of the value of marriage, that the family was to be honored as led by God, and they covered decision making and promised homes for each family. Of course, it affirmed again that Keil was our leader. Our house church women talked about the new principles, expressing surprise that naming Keil as the "president and autocrat" didn't appear until number ten. Even the importance of plain living as number eleven was further down than I'd thought it would be.

We were stuck on number ten, though, as along with naming Keil as leader, it suggested that a vote might take place if big changes were proposed, to indicate "general consent of the community." It was probably too much to imagine such a vote would include women, but one could hope.

"Someone has thought these out carefully," Matilda observed.

Jacob's sister, Sarah, had joined us that day, and she added, "I heard that years and years ago, Chris Wolff and Karl Ruge, maybe Henry Finck, were together in Germany, and they presented a list of principles like this to the Prussian leaders. Then they had to flee, because the prince thought it was a challenge to his authority."

"This could look like that," I said, "if you were a crowned prince."

"At least he put God and parents first," Almira said. "And the family. Family. It's so important. Children…" Her voice trailed off, and she got up shortly after that and went upstairs.

"I like number seven myself," Kitty said. "Maybe if I do find someone to marry, Keil won't tell us we can't. The carpenters are strong and sturdy. I rather like taking dinner baskets out to them. I might find a good man out there."

"Number nine says 'the children' and doesn't exclude girls from the school. Thank goodness for Karl in that!" Matilda said.

"I wonder who the advisors are," Sarah said.

"One thing's for certain, they won't be women," Kitty said.

"At least not up front," I added. "We women might never be official advisors, in authority, but that doesn't mean we don't have persuasion with the men in our lives."

"You haven't talked Papa into having us all live together, though," Kitty reminded me.

"Persuasion takes patience," I said. It was a belief I just realized I held.

The new rules said nothing about widows specifically. And Kitty liked that marriage was supported. She read, "The family is strictly maintained; people marry, raise, and train children." I wondered if it might be an opening for me, to bring my children back into my own personal fold. What might "strictly maintained" really mean? I'd have to ask Karl. He always had insights.

———◆———

That fall, I didn't hear so much grumbling from the workers, so we assumed the advisors now had a voice in the affairs of the colony, at least in the men's affairs, and that our prayers for "all that are in authority" were being answered. The church building stood nearly finished. We learned from Henry C that bells for the belfry had been ordered from Ohio. The hotel's three floors, with windows in the attic, had finishers working into dusk. Ben Holladay, the railroad man, attended a number of our concerts in the Park House, a newly built structure that was nestled in the trees not far from Keil's house. Many new trails had been created through the forest area near the Park House, a building that either Keil (or the advisors) had ordered built for the band's performances. Mr. Holladay and Dr. Keil "took many walks on the paths," she told us. Mr. Holladay was a visionary, as Louisa called him, who would help the colony continue to grow into the outside world. She'd say that because her husband did. Still, I noticed that the band building was finished before the church was.

It bothered me, too, that we weren't recruiting any longer, as Christian had done in the old days, using the light of faith and the comfort of communal efforts to bring people into our fold. Instead, our production lured people in: our fine leather goods, our medicinal wines, our turned furniture and textiles. It wasn't the same to me. People bought our products, but they weren't drawn to our ways of looking after one another and tending to the less fortunate. Our colony grew mostly through the arrivals of those from Willapa or Bethel, rather than through new, invigorated blood. I guessed that like any group, we wanted people to join us, but then we resisted the changes they brought with them. Even our house church changed with each new addition. Change was in the nature of the people who gathered together, whatever the original purpose. Trying to keep a group the same proved a futile effort. But when my mind began muddling over perceived injustices and uncertainties, I tried, as Karl had advised, to find God in the changes and walked my puzzle path of thinking right back to God's power to influence everything, when we allowed it.

The shoemaker and saddler had picked up so many new accounts that they ran short of materials. Whenever Keil or one of his advisors learned of a stand of oak needing to be cleared, our men would be volunteered to do the clearing, so they could take the bark from the trees, so important to the fine tanning that we did. Ashes from the burned bark were blended with water to remove the hair from the deer and cow hides.

This was work Almira found she could do: stuffing the hides into the trough, punching them down with a stick, then waiting three days and currying the hair off. It wasn't "careful work" as she called it, so her hands, large knuckles and all, could keep up. Since she'd been going out to work on tanning, Almira acted happier. She didn't as often leave us, to go upstairs alone to read or outside to walk. Sometimes she even joined us at the Park House for a concert.

Our house church had to change its meeting times, since the band played in the park so often on Sunday afternoons. I wondered whether it was anything deliberate on Keil's part, this taking away from our Sabbath meetings. Maybe he'd changed the Sunday band times in order to keep our house church women from sharing our complaints with one another. He also announced that from now on, the Sabbath celebrations would begin on Saturday at noon. All work would stop then. We'd have music and eat together. Worship would begin on Sunday morning with yet more music and a meal on Sunday afternoon.

Maybe he thought there was power in our women's meetings, power needing curtailment. It was an idea that hadn't occurred to me before.

We women adapted and began meeting midweek.

I almost felt sorry for the men, who lacked this place of comfort to work and talk. We'd try new recipes out on one another, to see who could make the best Scatter Soup with the thinnest dumpling batter carrying the greatest taste. I loved watching how the ribbon of flour and eggs formed odd shapes as they were swirled into the hot soup. "It must be your Clara's blue eggs that give yours that fine flavor," Matilda told me, smacking her lips in a most unladylike manner after she'd scooped up the soft-cooked forms.

"*Nein,* it's her meat broth," Louisa told her. "What do you put in that, Emma?"

"I'll never tell," I said. We almost never told our cooking secrets. My mother made a meatloaf dish with a rare flavor, and she had always hoarded that recipe and probably would until her dying day.

While we stitched, we shared our burdens and prayed for one another, and in between, we sang rounds, a venture begun by Kitty. I have to say I found it refreshing to hear those repeating loops of women's voices, singing psalms and sometimes tunes Kitty said came from Shakespeare's time that children sang around the Maypole. The second group began while the first went on to higher tones. It was like a dance of voices, and I could join in, the lilt of others' voices carrying mine along, even though I sang out of tune.

"Henry C said that to lose one's temper means to be out of tempo in a song," Helena said when we finished a round. "I find that quite comforting."

"You've never lost your temper, ever," Louisa told her. "Have you?"

"I've had my moments," Helena confessed.

No one lifted an eye from the quilt spread before us at this surprising admission.

"Isn't it nice to know, then, that you're simply out of balance?" Kitty offered. "That makes you a lot more like the rest of us."

"I have to say that being called unbalanced has never seemed so...embracing," Helena told her.

Nothing subversive occurred at our house church, just piecing and patching. Acceptance of the way things were fell more easily on my shoulders when we gathered as we did. The distance from my parents, the loss of my sons, the uncertainties for my daughters' lives, even the fate of a world where war once raged became weights carried with me by my friends. Maybe Keil's decisions weren't meant to demean us women; rather he and the advisors simply didn't take our interests into account. We'd long ago taught them that they didn't have to; we knew so well how to adapt.

Louisa would say the men "had the economy" on their minds, so they didn't consider a woman's needs. But I remembered one day when Kate came home and told me she'd learned something in Greek. *"Oikos,"* she said. "It means 'household.' "

"That's nice," I told her, and continued to beat at the rug hanging over the line.

"But, Mama, it means two things, like our two doors. It means... econ...economy too. Dr. Wolff says that in the household, we look after one another and share, and that should be the basis of our lives. He says we shouldn't try to get too big or try to do too much without helping one another. We should all live like it's our house, and in the kitchen, where the cooking stove is, that's where the econ..."

"Economy," I finished for her.

"That's where everything is. In the kitchen. We get fed, and we give to others and make our weavings and trade them, but we see one another every day. That's our *oikos*," she said. "The Greek is easier to say."

She was right. We women had the greatest place to be: at the hearth, the center of it all. The men had their own pressures, and a part of me almost felt regret for them.

From my upstairs window, I could see one of their big pressures: the hotel, looming tall and large. The stage stopped there, but to justify such a huge building we'd need many more customers. We'd need the railroad to bring them. But even there, it was the kitchen *oikos* that mattered. Food sustained us. Without many outside people purchasing our food, the building would be like a boil on the back of the colony, instead of a precious pearl worn to embellish the colony's bodice.

Our colony was defined by colony principles that in truth were established more for the men than for us women. We women had our own principles, I decided. We continued on as we had: tending our families, sprinkling the mundane with occasional song, interrupting our trials with a bit of laughter, and welcoming the acceptance of friends. Keil's rule had never changed that. A woman's *oikos* threaded its way through the ages to this century, in this place. A place I now called home.

———◆———

Matilda and Jacob prepared to move into their family home during the fall of 1866. They announced they'd be moving soon and that Matilda was with child.

"I guess my house was private enough," I teased, and Matilda's face burned red. How I'd miss them! Yet again, another change.

At one of our house church gatherings, Matilda told us that Martin, who was attending her instead of a midwife, had heard two heartbeats through his stethoscope. Louisa said well, of course: hers and the baby's, any midwife would know that. But Matilda said he'd heard two

very fast beating hearts in addition to her own, and they must belong
to two infants.

"Twins!"

"Will they have two biblical cords?" Ida asked. We'd looked at each
other and laughed.

The prospect of twins set us all to spinning and knitting, and we
agreed how good it was that Matilda would have sisters-in-law living
with her, and wasn't it interesting the way things worked out sometimes, the very thing you thought you didn't want turned out to be
something you didn't know you'd need. She'd have good help with two
children being born at once. She was older to be having a first child—
children—so being attended by someone with medical training was a
gift as well.

Many of us at the house church had taken turns sitting at the loom
through the rainy months, and now we rolled out the rug woven with
braids of color: purple and blue and a pink hue. I'd quilted a Nine
Patch pillow top, and Kitty and Christine had begun two cradle quilts
for Matilda's twins. They chose an Old Maid pattern that Matilda
chuckled at. My own mother joined our gatherings now since I'd made
a special effort to invite her. She brought Johanna and Lou with her.
My mother pointed out that we could mark the place for stitches on the
quilt top with soap. It made the needles go through easier and would
wash out. All of us stitched the quilt pieces that Matilda had created
during her first year of marriage, a new quilt she'd worked on since
completing her Sunflower quilt. She backed this new covering as she
had the other, using strips of flannel or whatever she had, including
pieces her mother had brought from Pennsylvania and a striped piece
from Bethel.

A quilt, I decided, allowed us some control in an often-powerless
world. We could put pieces together in the way we wished, with no one
grumbling much about how we did it. Even the mistakes could be fixed
with little thinking, unlike in life sometimes. Quilting was better with
the presence of older women like my mother to dribble little bits of
wisdom into the room as we worked.

"I'll remember this time of family," Matilda said, "each time I look at this quilt."

Matilda didn't think she'd be able to join us very often after her move so far out from the village, but after the babies came, she thought she could. They were expected in the spring of 1867, and she promised she'd bring them along to meet us all just as soon as she could.

"For me to play with?" Ida asked.

"*Ja.* So you can check on their biblical cords," Matilda told her.

We kept Matilda from lifting a thing, while Jacob and his friends carried the furniture he'd built for them down from my home, placed the bed and dresser in the wagon, and drove south a few miles to what we now called Stauffer Farm.

Despite the rain and mud and our own loss at having them go, we made the move memorable. Jacob had planted apple trees near the split-rail fence and maple trees to line the rutted road. The log house boasted two stories and offered a beautiful view of the prairie land surrounding it. I suspected that from the second floor window, you could almost see the steeple of the church that rose one hundred fourteen feet into the Oregon sky. Facing east, I wondered if on a clear, clear day one might see the snowy cap of Mount Hood, the way I could from my home. A clothesline stood ready to catch the wind and the quilts Matilda would air there.

Stauffer Farm was what I'd always imagined Christian and I would have one day. Yes, we'd had a small cabin on the Willapa, but that was only to have been the beginning. I found myself wistful, watching Matilda and Jacob begin their new lives. It was never easy for me to say good-bye to routine. I took a deep breath and walked up the steps. Being hopeful for them scrubbed the dust of change off of me.

———

"Maybe we should move back into their room, now that they've gone," Kitty said. "We could have more privacy that way." We were in our usual stitching place, starting a new project of some table runners. It was just the four of us plus my girls.

"I've gotten used to having everyone in the same room," Almira said. "My husband and I had a small cabin, and the children all slept within breathing space of one another. This has sort of reminded me of that. It's comforting."

"You really miss them, don't you, Almira?" Kitty asked.

Almira lowered those gray eyes. "More of late. I wonder if I did the right thing in leaving him. Them." No one interrupted. Then she said, "I've thought perhaps I should ask him to take me back."

We cast questioning looks at one another, not sure what to say.

"What would be different?" Christine asked then. "Don't go doing the same thing and expecting a different result. That makes a person crazy. Trust me. I know."

"I'm wiser, that would be different. What do you think, Emma?" Almira asked.

She walked on slippery rocks, as far as I was concerned. Our situations were too similar, and yet I knew she felt she'd failed her faith by securing a divorce. That was one reason I hadn't sought a divorce from Jack, that and not wanting to bring yet one more issue of disgrace for my family to deal with or for wagging tongues to talk about. No one divorced quietly in these western places.

"You could forgive him," I said. "Because to not do that will only hold you hostage. But I'm not sure you should forget what he did, or try again unless there's evidence you both have changed. You're welcome here for as long as you like."

"He's still living with the girl, well, she's a woman now, isn't she?" Kitty asked. "He hasn't realized how much he hurt you, or showed that he wants it any different. You'd be going back into the same situation."

"I don't know if he hasn't. I haven't seen him now for years. But it wouldn't be the same. I'm different, even if he isn't."

"Don't you want tenderness from him now, though?" Kitty asked. "If you don't get it, you'll wish you had, and be upset all over again."

"Your older children…?" Christine said.

"They say nothing's different." She sighed. "I miss them all so much." Her voice caught. Across the room from her, Christine's lip quivered too, and so did Kitty's. Soon we'd all be crying. I imagined that Almira cried for the lost joys and for the separation from her children, as much as from missing her husband. But one didn't know, not really. When she cried, we just cried with her and for our own losses as well.

"Don't decide now," Christine said. She patted Almira's hand. "It's winter, and the rains weigh you down, and everything smells musty and damp, and even old ways look better in memory. None of us makes the best decisions then. Although I don't always make the best decisions when the sun's out shining either." She wiped at her eyes, gave a wry smile to me.

"I don't want this to be all there is to my life," Almira whispered. "Not that I'm not grateful to you all. I am. But—"

"You want to feel useful," I offered. She nodded. "To your family. I do understand."

———◆———

We decided to keep Matilda and Jacob's room open, use it as a dressing room but make it easier to invite others in to stay. We'd keep our bedroom constellation, so we could hear our sleeping breaths come out like stars in the quiet of the night.

It was while Christine and I were dressing together before going to Keil's church one morning that I noticed that she did not need a hoop beneath her skirt. As she turned, her body formed the flow while the cloth settled over a woman who was very much with child.

———◆———

Helena appeared at our house church gatherings after the church building was finished but before it was dedicated. Word was that the dedication would wait for the bells to arrive. We wouldn't worship in the building until then. Louisa Keil, the senior, did not come with her that day. The group always changed a bit when they attended; it was much more difficult to talk about them when they were present! I wondered if I added more to a conversation when I was absent than when I was present. I pitched that thought away.

Helena asked if any of us had been inside the new church, and I expected a chastisement when no one said they had.

"We await the dedication," Christine said. She held a pile of fabric lumped over her stomach.

I'd peeked through the women's door while the church was being built. Yes, I had suggested to my brother that they didn't need separate doors for men and women, that we were together all week long; why did we have to be separate at church? But he said it wasn't his decision to talk about doors. Someone else had already decided.

"The sounds inside are splendid," Helena said. "A speaking voice makes one think they are in those limestone caves back in Missouri, where a single note resonates, filling it full. You'll hear a whisper at the back of the sanctuary all the way to the front."

"So we'd best not be chattering during services," Kitty said.

"Not what I meant," Helena said. "I meant that it's going to make all voices sound as though they sang in a heavenly choir."

"That choir ought to have both male and female voices," Kitty said.

"I'm sure they'll let the girls' choir perform, as well as the men's," Almira said. "So long as they remain separate."

"But imagine both men and women singing…together," Kitty said. Her persistence surprised us all.

Helena straightened her shoulders, and Matilda, who had joined us this day, said, "Let's sing one of our rounds. You haven't been here for those, have you, Helena?"

"Yes, I have," Helena responded, but Kitty started us out anyway, by dividing the room into threes, telling us the song, and then leading the first group. We didn't even need to watch each other; we could just sing. Kitty had the finest soprano voice.

"That was lovely," Helena said when we finished. She'd stopped working while we sang, folding her hands over her scissors in her lap.

"A community of voice," I said. "Covering up the individual flaws, *ja*?"

"Kitty," Helena said, "it might be a better dedication chorus if we joined our voices *with* the men's. Since the bells have not arrived, we'd have time to practice."

I stared at her. Was this the Helena I knew, who thought we women should all remember our places, live only for Brother Keil's directives? And she'd made a suggestion that Louisa would probably object to if she'd been present. "Helena," I said, "I can't believe you said that."

"*Ach*. What could be a more beautiful statement of dedication of our worship house than to express it in music of men *and* women, girls *and* boys?"

"Do you think *Herr* Keil would allow that?" Kitty asked. "I've always wanted to sing in a mixed chorus. And not just to have time with the men," she defended herself, as though anyone had challenged.

"Ask the advisors," I said. "See if they might really advise."

"This is a possibility," Helena said. She turned to me then. "But maybe you'd do the asking, Emma?"

"I can't carry a tune in a candlestick holder," I said. "Kitty would be more convincing."

"*Ja*, but you carry a tune with your words." Both Kitty and Helena spoke at the same time. They laughed while the rest of the group agreed, "*Ach, ja!*"

"You think I could influence *Herr* Keil in this way? I don't know."

"You have much more persuasion than you might think, Emma," Helena said.

"*Ja*? Just not about what really matters."

While I considered when would be the perfect time to ask Keil about the music, I also wondered about the best time to speak to Christine. One evening, she and I were upstairs in what had been Matilda and Jacob's room, changing from our modest hoop skirts into the straight lines of our nightdresses. Almira and Kitty chattered with the girls in the room beyond the hall. I tied the soft ribbon at my neckline and checked the stitching on the patch I'd had to sew on after Po jumped up in greeting, tearing a corner piece with his sharp claws. I stared at it much too long, looking for words. I knew I couldn't wait much longer.

"Christine," I said, not asking, but thinking out loud, "you're expecting a big change soon, aren't you?"

I heard her intake of breath.

Her shoulders sank. "I'm not sure what to do," she said. "I'm nearly four months along."

"I'm sure no one else has noticed," I said. "I wouldn't have except, well, we share a changing room here."

"One advantage of being a big-boned girl, as my father used to say. My real father, not yours." Her eyes watered. "I'll leave, Emma. I don't want to put you into any difficulty with having an unwed mother staying with you. I didn't know how to tell you. My becoming…this way…while I stayed under your roof could bring criticism to you." She sat on the rocking chair now, at the edge of the seat. It didn't rock or soothe.

"You remain as long as you like," I said. "Don't even think about my reputation. I've done enough things to it myself." Her lips loosened into a sad smile. "What have you thought about doing for yourself?"

"Going to Portland, where no one knows me. I'll have the baby and place it in a basket. I'll leave it on the doorstep of someone kind. There are many kind people in the world. I'm sure I can find one of them. I thought at one of the churches. That's what I did last time."

She's been through this before. I forgot that.

"Dare I ask about the father?"

"I'd rather not say."

"From the fair," I said.

"Oh no." She looked up at me. "That gentleman was a gentleman. We only talked and danced. I know you thought I wasn't well behaved, but I was."

Had I judged her with my eyes?

"No, it was, well, someone closer." Her face turned beet red. "I suppose I didn't resist his advances as I should have. I thought being at your house would help. I could be alone, away from temptation in the evenings after my chores were complete. Being my size, I didn't expect any man to pay attention to me. I hoped none would after what happened, well, before. Then you invited me to the fair, and I found it was pleasant and I didn't have to be afraid. But I didn't know how to sort out a friend from someone... Before long, things just happened." She looked up at me. "But that's no excuse. It's not his fault. He was only being playful, he said. I knew from the beginning." She sighed. "But I was hopeful that he might really care for me."

"I've told myself similar stories with sad endings," I said. I pulled a small stool up to her and sat, taking her hands in mine. "Does the man know there were consequences to his...playfulness?"

She shook her head no. "But he isn't a candidate for marriage." I waited for her to continue, but she didn't.

"You deserve better anyway," I told her. "I wonder if there isn't some other path for you to take, besides leaving your baby on a doorstep and having to find a new life somewhere far away."

"It's for the best," she said, "my plan. The loss of this baby will be just penance for what I did, twice now. I don't deserve anything but punishment, for not learning from the first mistake."

"*Ach,* Christine, the size of our infractions doesn't matter, at least I don't think it does. Little acts can be as devastating as big ones." I thought of my little indiscretions that had resulted in the colony removing my sons from me; at least I still believed my actions were the primary reasons. " 'Take us the foxes, the little foxes, that spoil the vines' is a scripture right in the middle of one of the Bible's great love stories. We can have wonderful romances, but then small things can spoil it. I've made my own big mistakes, but it's the little ones that have caught me in the end. God is somewhere in this, Christine. In the big and small of it. We have to let ourselves be found."

"If that's so, I wish God would show Himself," she said.

"That's just what we'll ask for, then."

We sat quietly for a time. I could hear the sound of her breath coming in and out steadily. The other women made noises in the next room, muffled as a child's sleepy chuckle. I heard Po bark once in play. I knew, in these wilderness places, that's where we'd find grace, but it was still so hard to accept it. I ached for Christine, sent my arrow prayers. I stood up and found her a handkerchief in the hanky drawer of the cabinet. She wiped at her eyes and sighed.

"Sometimes I'd like to go to sleep and then wake up and have this all be over with. Be a sleeping beauty who never gets kissed again into wakefulness." She smiled a bit.

"No prince is going to come along and wake us up, I agree with you about that," I said. "I tried to make a man into a prince who wasn't. At least you haven't done that. I fell asleep all by myself, and unlike that Grimms' tale, I was the only one who could decide to wake up. That's when I accepted Karl's help and came here. You're my sister, Christine." I took her in my arms. "The good news is once we do wake up, we find out we're really not alone."

21

Sweet Scents

Together, a few days later, Helena, Kitty, and I made our way to Henry C. Finck, to see whether he'd consider conducting a joined choir of both boys and girls, men and women at the dedication. We chose him first in our plan of action. I considered the consequences if we failed at this. Keil would have another black mark to put against my name. He could use this to move me from the house or, worse, take my girls from me so they wouldn't be exposed to such a "contrary woman." But Helena's part in this gave me hope. And working with her and my sister made the risk worthwhile.

"But of course," Henry C. Finck said, exuberant. "It's good Wilhelm has approved such a novelty."

Helena and I looked at each other. I wondered if her need to be precise and correct in all things would force her to explain that we had yet to talk to Brother Keil.

"Well, he hasn't exactly—," Kitty began.

"Yes, yes," Helena interrupted. She explained rapidly that she thought it was a splendid idea. "Wouldn't it sing great praises to our Lord, who had to wait so many years for this church to be finished?"

Henry C narrowed his eyes. "Wilhelm hasn't approved such a thing, has he? He's not that...inspired in his thinking these days." I swallowed. "But I am," he went on cheerfully. "So we'll rehearse, and if Wilhelm complains, we'll explain that boys and girls singing together are no worldlier than having the railroad come to our hotel. He certainly wants that to happen."

"We'll get full approval before we do this," Helena told him. "We'd not put you in a compromising situation. You can be certain of that."

The three of us giggled like schoolgirls as we walked from there to Karl Ruge, basking in our first success. I didn't even go over the details of what had just transpired, for fear Helena might have second thoughts about a sin of omission. At Karl's house, I led with our request as though Wilhelm had already approved.

"Karl," I said, "Professor Finck tells us that having a mixed boys and girls' choir sing at the dedication would be a glorious thing."

"I've heard nothing about it," he said.

"But there's nothing scriptural to preclude it, is there? Surely Wilhelm would note such a thing, *ja*?" I said. "Or John Giesy would."

"*Ja*, well, I see no problem. It might put the dedication back if we need long rehearsals, though. Wilhelm would like to proceed quickly now."

"Henry didn't seem to think there'd be any delay," I said. "We'll be ready when the bells are." I bent down to scratch Po's head. He had trotted along with us, as much mine as my children's now, to visit his old master.

"I bet he's spoiled by the girls, but then every dog in the village is spoiled by someone."

"The dogs see us as we are and never complain about it," I said. "Who could be a better friend than that?"

He put tobacco in his long pipe, then grinned at me, and we chatted a bit longer about the weather and wondering when the bells would arrive. Then we marched off to Chris Wolff.

"Dr. Wolff," Helena said. "Is there anything scriptural to preclude having both boys and girls sing together in the church? Say for a dedication?"

"Or even elsewhere," I added. Helena frowned, and I realized I might have overstepped my bounds, pushing into a field before we'd gotten the gate open.

"Handel's *Messiah* is composed for orchestra and the voices of men and women. Why would Wilhelm question the scriptural nature of it? Or is it you women who are worried over such a thing?" We looked demure. "Well, nothing to worry. It would be a lovely thing for our dedication, to go with our bells. I'm sure Henry has something properly arranged, *ja*?"

"He's probably working on it right now," Kitty said.

From there we took our list of support to Wilhelm.

"Do you think we should talk with Louisa first?" I asked as we walked up the hill.

Helena shook her head. "I don't want to involve her, for if we fail in winning Wilhelm's support, she would have to bear the brunt of his refusal. He might forbid her to come to…your gatherings. She wouldn't want that," Helena said. "She enjoys coming to your home, Emma."

"Does she?"

"We all do. Well, every now and then."

I took that compliment in.

It had been some time since I'd seen Keil's workroom next to the root cellar. The earthy smells would always remind me of nursing Ida, seeing Brita for the first time, the day I faced off with Jack. Here, too, I'd learned that Keil had arranged my sons' lives away from mine.

"To what do I owe this visit of three lovely *Fräulein*?" Keil asked as he waved us in.

Kitty said, "Emma's not a *Fräulein*, she's—"

"The question has arisen as to the appropriateness of having both men and women sing for the dedication," Helena cut her off briskly.

"What? Of course both choirs can sing," Keil said. "The human voice is a gift from God and one that must be given back. First the boys will sing, then the girls."

"*Ja*, my thoughts exactly," Helena said. "But Karl and Chris Wolff and Henry Finck seem to think it would be quite a feather in your cap if we blended the choirs for the first time. Not unlike the great German composers combining voice with instruments, men and women, together."

"Only if you approve, of course," I said.

"Or maybe you already approved it, and that's the reason they're so enthusiastic," Kitty said. *My sister has possibilities.*

He paused, frowned. "I might have approved it…*ja*. I think something was said a while back." He pulled at the gray strand of beard below his chin. "You women needn't worry yourselves over it. It is for a worshipful event. We men will take care of the theology of things. Men and women can sing together, *ja*. Sometimes you women are so simple in your thinking."

Kitty opened her mouth to speak, but I squeezed her arm with my fingers. She looked at me while Helena nodded sagely. We said our good-byes and stepped outside the root room. The sweet scents of earth and a warm March breeze greeted us.

"Why didn't you correct him?" Kitty said. "His thinking we women are such simpletons of thought."

"Sometimes it's good just to be happy, rather than being right," I said.

"Let's sing a round to celebrate," Kitty said as we started down the hill.

"There's only the three of us," I said.

"You can do it, Emma," Kitty said.

"She can do most anything," Helena agreed, but she put her hands over her ears when I sang my part, because as always, it was quite out of tune with the other voices.

The bells at last arrived. One large bell and two companions of graduated size had been shipped out of Ohio from the Buckeye Bell Foundry, by ship down the Ohio to New Orleans, then around Cape Horn, up the Pacific coast to the Columbia, up the river to the Willamette, to a landing area not far from Butteville. Then a new road had to be scoured out all the way from the river to Aurora, because the terrible weight of the bells would have ruined the existing road. Jonathan and my father and brothers joined the workers laying down boards for the wagon to skid across. My father acted familiar with the landing site, suggesting the best way to bring the vehicle up the bank's grade, talking to Wilhelm and John as though they were old friends, pointing, directing.

The children made an adventure of it, and all other colony work stopped as the wagon with four ox teams slowly made its way from the Willamette toward the Point, where the church stood with its empty belfry, awaiting those bells.

Several of us rode out in regular wagons, bringing food for the trip that took two days. The work group and those who served them rested midday. Now, returning to the effort, the labor took on a festive air, with singing and laughter and shouts of direction and joy when the wagon skidded forward. There were several pauses for ham slabs, water, and rolls.

"It's an everyday feast," Kate said as we served.

"An everyday feast. Yes. As each day should be," I told her, then sent her off to give Christian and Andy special cinnamon rolls. I'd seen them in the distance with a group of boys and made sure there were enough for all of them, even that quipping Finck boy.

It would be quite an event, lifting the heavy bells into the belfry, but it was a reassurance to us all that they'd actually arrived. At last there'd be the dedication. Helena giggled like a schoolgirl, skipping along beside the flat wagon pulling the heavy bells.

"They're so perfect," she kept saying.

Extra teams were added to bring the heavy load up the hill past the *gross Haus*. That night, the bells were left covered in the wagon, while the men planned the next day's work. They talked of using pulleys and teams of horses and boys who were willing to ride up with the bells to help set them in place.

Andy volunteered.

"It's dangerous," I told him.

He shrugged his shoulders. "It's not as if I'm going to stand on my head on it," he said.

The next day we watched with held breath as the huge bells were lifted into the belfry, a slow pull using a team of horses, thick ropes, and dexterous young men who guided the hooks into the specially built rafter. In the end, no one had to ride up on the bells, which were cradled in a web of stout ropes. I was grateful for that. When the men reached the opening to the belfry to receive the largest bell first, several pulled it toward the iron hooks. A cheer rose up as the clanger rang out. After lifting the second and third into the belfry, they set them on the floor, no time left to hang them until the following day.

People slapped one another on the back, and the men cheered the food we served them, as though we feasted at a cotillion. Even my family participated. My brothers came back from Oregon City to help. My mother brought *Aepfel Raist,* a toasted bread and apple pudding I remembered from my childhood. Geraniums bloomed a flashing red in a bucket on the table. My brother William grew them. How he got such huge flowers was a mystery.

"It's nice, isn't it, Mama? William's flowers are so large! I wonder how he does that." I sighed. "It's just so nice to have everyone happy together, like when we were in Bethel."

She didn't say anything at first. "I didn't think you were ever happy back there, with Christian gone so often. Isn't that why you left us to come west?"

"I was happy. I wanted to be happier," I said. "To go where my husband went."

"And did you get what you wanted?"

I looked at her. My mother had rarely offered to be reflective with me. She sounded like I'd abandoned them by leaving with Christian. Maybe she'd expected that she'd have a daughter close by, to help with the raising of my younger brothers and sisters. I hadn't thought of that before.

"Not everything. The boys…but I've made the best of what's happened. It took me a while, but I think my choices have been better. At least they've been mine, Mama."

"They haven't always turned out well."

"Things happen, whether I make plans for them or not," I said, "but I decide how to react. That's always mine to choose."

"You weren't raised to think with such…self-centeredness."

It was the most she'd said to me of how she felt about anything in years. I wished I didn't have to disagree with her. "Not self-centered,

Mama," I said gently. "Maybe in the beginning, *ja*, I stumbled and fell, but I let others help me up. I walked my way back from that dark time." I paused. "Maybe it is selfish to want a good life, a meaningful life formed of a simple one. You're one of the kindest, most generous women I know. You took in Christine. You tend my sisters. You've brought many babies into the world as a midwife. You've done those things for others, but didn't they bring you happiness too? That doesn't make you self-centered. It makes you...loving. I'd like to think I've honored how you raised me. I'm truly sad if you think I haven't."

She picked up the bowl that had once held her pudding. It was empty now. She stared at it, then said, "I might have spoken out of turn, Daughter. You'll have to forgive me."

She walked away before I could think of anything more to say.

———

After everyone had gone home but the sun still hugged the horizon, I asked Kitty if she'd like to take a walk with me.

"To the labyrinth?"

I shook my head no. "To the church."

"We'll be there all day tomorrow with the bells getting set," she said.

"There's something I want to do there," I told her. Christine agreed to watch the girls as we made the quarter-mile trek, across the village and up the ravine toward the church. The sunset burned vibrant orange, and the trees formed perfect scissor cuts, like *Scherenschnitte* against the sky. Po trotted along beside us, sniffing at the history that had passed that way hours before.

As we walked by John Giesy's home, Kitty said, "I never noticed before, but John and Barbara's house has two front doors, like yours."

"My house was built first, so he copied me," I joked.

"Isn't copying a way of saying they like what they see?"

We carried our lanterns high—we'd need them later—and hiked up our skirts, tucking them into our apron bands so we could take longer strides. Once outside the church, we stopped to catch our breath. Crickets chirped now and swallows swooped, already finding a place in the belfry to claim as theirs. I thought a bat might have dipped from out of the firs and swirled back, waiting for the moon. The windows were framed in a Gothic look, with arches that flowed away from the point in graceful ways. I didn't know who had designed the window frames, but they looked artful. That pleased me, to see our little colony weaving art into useful things.

"So what is it you want to do?" Kitty asked. "Now that we're here."

"We're going up into the belfry," I said.

"What?"

"Think of the view."

"I'm not going up there. I don't like heights."

"You won't be alone," I said. "We'll do it together, for the adventure of it. Don't you sometimes want to do something just because you can?"

"Not really."

"I do. There's so little in my life I can really make happen, and this is something I can. Come on." We went inside, but Kitty refused to climb the stairs into the belfry. So I wrapped twine around my skirts at the ankles and climbed up by myself.

The flight up reminded me of the mill in Willapa, how I looked out over the landscape to see a whole new world that awaited me. I'd made a mess of that world not long after, but I'd come through it. I was here. Safe. My children were safe. They had futures. Even my parents had joined me, and our relationship held promise of change.

As I caught my breath, I ran my hands over the medium bell sitting on the belfry floor. The bell came up to my chest. Fortunately, it stood next to the smallest bell. I set the lantern down, took off my shoes, and used the smaller bell to climb up onto the medium bell. The metal felt cool, the top slick with condensation from the cooler evening, but my stocking feet eventually took hold. Careful not to bump my head on the bell already hung, I bent over and put my hands flat against the metal. I pushed myself up like a caterpillar unrolling and lifted my feet skyward. It had been years since I'd done such a thing! Then I looked out through the open portals into the sun-settling night.

"What are you doing up there?" Kitty shouted up. "Let's go."

Blood rushed to my head, and my skirts slid up my legs against the twine, but I could see the sunset reflect against the smaller bell. "Just a little longer," I whispered more for me than for Kitty. Out through the window openings, the world was upside-down and bathed in a kind of smoky grace, a quiet confusion that had its own order, just not what one expected. I'd done this sort of thing as a child, stood on my hands upside down to see the world a new way. It was who I was, I decided, always looking at things from a different angle, standing on a precarious edge. The view was new and unique.

I looked down at my hand. The crooked fingers would always be a reminder of Jack. But they'd remind me, too, of my strength, my ability to take necessary next steps for my family. Maybe I wouldn't bring a dozen people to the faith the way Christian had; maybe I wouldn't tend a large family as my mother did; maybe I'd never be as faithful as Helena and Louisa, but I was who I was; I would leave a legacy of everyday devotion both to my family and to the delights of life, including standing upside down on a bell.

I let my feet come down, then slid to stand upright. I panted. My arms were still strong, but they quivered from the exertion. I looked out through the openings. The landscape wrapped around me. Beauty from mountains to rivers. Fir-lined paths leading to prairie flowers spread like petals at a wedding on the grass. This was a place of belonging. Christian had never been a part of this, and yet he was. I'd brought him here through his children, through my growing, changing faith. I didn't have to go back to where he was or to what had been; I'd taken him here, just as I could keep finding myself here, in this place.

"Get down here," Kitty shouted up at me.

I looked for a moment at the smallest bell, holding the lantern high above it, and laughed.

"What are you laughing about up there?" Kitty said.

"Come up and see," I shouted down.

A pause, then, "Oh, all right."

It took her a while. "Don't tell anyone we were even up here," she said, panting. She held the sides of the room as though it would fall apart if she let go. "Now, what's so funny?"

"There are cherubs carved into the bell. At least the smallest bell. See?"

She peered. It was growing dark. "Well, that's fitting," Kitty said. "For a church bell. What's funny about that?"

"They're naked cherubs," I told her.

She looked aghast. "I wonder if Keil noticed!"

On our walk back in the dark, I told her I'd stood on my hands on the bell. Kitty asked, "What made you do that?"

I swung my sister's hand. "Something Andy said when I tried to caution him about the dangers of riding up on that bell. He said, 'I'm not standing on my head on it,' and I thought of how often I get upset or worried over things better left to Providence to manage. Everything isn't dangerous, but I make it so sometimes. In my mind."

I could stop fighting to get my sons back and fight instead to ensure they had all that they needed, that my daughters had what they deserved to live good lives. In the meantime, I'd enjoy time with them all as I could. "Instead, I could enjoy life," I told her. "Kick up my heels on a bell, nice and safe."

"And only a little strange."

◆————

The men finished hanging all three bells. Helena said that the light of the Holy Spirit had visited those bells in the night; she'd seen a light coming from the belfry. She called it a miracle, though others told her it must have been the moonlight reflecting against them. They tolled the bells then, one after the other, mellow, rich tones that reached across the valley and would in time be the hallmark of our village, announcing the need for firemen, ringing in celebrations, and mourning a colonist's death.

A spring storm threatened throughout dedication day but never materialized. It seemed a fitting sign, since so often I worried and agonized over things that never came to pass and could lose the joy of what was before me while I lamented "what might be later."

The bells rang out, calling everyone together. The Aurora Band played, standing on the platform that circled the top of the steeple. The Pie and Beer Band warmed up at the lower balcony, and sometimes the bands played back and forth to each other, as though across a mountain valley. Inside the church, large pillars rose up on both the men's and women's sides. We'd made one inroad this day with our blended chorus.

The oldest women sat toward the front and at the center, with the rest of us graduated on either side of them, as though we were those smaller companion bells. Barbara Giesy had the front row. Helena settled between Giesy nieces. My mother sat in the row with me and my girls. Midway up the center aisle stood a large wood stove, with a steel drum to help spread the heat in the winter. Behind it and a little higher rose the altar. It wasn't ornately carved as I'd expected. Instead it reminded me of a swan's neck, graceful as the turned pillars. Two lovely candelabra held oil laps, and the wooden benches were as smooth as a baby's bottom.

"What do you call these?" Ida whispered as she patted the bench.

"A bench?"

"Kitty calls them stinks," she said. "I told her that was wrong."

"Oh, pews," I said. "That's another name for them. Not stinks, but pews."

The pillars in the center had been turned by Jacob Miller, and they were elegantly spare, much like the other crafts of the colony. Today Oregon grape leaves had been pasted around the pillars, giving them a festive air. And from the tables set along the back, we could smell the food that we'd be consuming when the service was complete.

I looked to my sons, sitting on the other side of the church with Martin. I really didn't know what they thought of this church building, or what they thought of the spiritual life that would go on within it or outside of it. I'd done my best to introduce them to experiences of faith, but my own journey had been so garbled at times—and still was—that I found few ways to even talk about it with them. I saw things differently; but I kept seeking, questioning; and that seemed an important part of one's faith journey. It couldn't be wise to become so certain of how God worked in the world that we stopped seeing evidence of divine surprise.

That was probably heretical thinking—frivolous. Perhaps that was why Keil and Martin and John thought I wasn't competent enough to raise my sons. They might think that the spiritual life of girls wasn't nearly so worrisome and that I could muddle my way through guiding them. But Martin said the separation was more for the benefit of the colony and my sons than for a punishment of me. I'd hang on to that.

Then the girls and boys rose and stood together. Even Ida at five years shuffled forward, turned to face us. She opened her mouth wide as an apple to sing, proclaiming the "wonders God had done." For today, that was really all that mattered.

Andy and Christian stood in the back rows, Andy already so tall. John and BW's girls stood in the row before them. A dozen others filled out the choir. Then the combined chorus raised their voices to sing that great German hymn of tradition, "Dear Christians, One and All Rejoice," the first verse perfect for this day:

> And with united heart and voice
> And holy rapture singing,
> Proclaim the wonders God hath done…

I patted Christine's hand and leaned forward to catch Helena's eye. She winked. At least I think she winked. She might have been blinking back tears.

———◆———

We learned later in the week that yet another group from Bethel had headed out for Oregon. Seventy-five more were to arrive in the fall of

1867, in a mule-team train led by yet another old friend and former scout. Land deeds were being given over to some of the earlier arrivals, so they now had property in their own names. I think Keil did this because the younger men urged the advisors to do so and they'd listened. It was rumored that those coming from Bethel had lost the guiding purpose to make another's life better than their own. They wanted to be like others in the West, independent, earning something to leave to their children when they died. In many ways, I saw Aurora becoming less of a colony and more of a village, no longer distinguished by its expression of faith, just one with a common treasury. I was surprised that I felt sad.

One spring afternoon, my girls and I unrolled a blanket at the Park House while the Aurora Band played. Then Kitty walked with the girls through the forest nearby, and my parents and younger sisters joined me on the blanket. I hoped they'd start coming to the church now so I'd see them more often. I'd asked them specifically to eat with us that day.

"I hear you're thinking of climbing Mount Hood," my father said.

"*Ach,* who told you that?"

"It would be a silly waste of time," my mother said. "I thought you'd outgrown some of those things."

"It was just an idea." *I wonder where they heard of it?* "We were looking for things to invigorate our days."

"Raising children isn't enough?" my mother asked.

"They stimulate in a different way," I said. Andy would be fourteen this fall, and he already stood taller than I. Martin said Andy knew all the ins and outs of running the pharmacy when Martin was away at school. He expected to finish up before long and had promised me again that Andy would be sent off to Wallamet University once he turned eighteen. Wasn't that the greatest work of a mother, to help her children achieve what they could?

"Andy will be tall like his father," my sister Johanna said. She looked out to where Andy was warming up his clarinet. Johanna had weepy eyes, maybe from the spring blossoms, for she constantly wiped at them.

"He's a nice young man," my father said. "I see him at the pharmacy at times, and he's always very polite to his uncles when they come in. Christian's quite the storyteller. Both fine boys."

I couldn't help myself from smiling.

"And my girls?"

"They're fine too, Emma."

"Don't you miss the boys?" my mother asked.

"Of course I do." I always felt a pang of guilt whenever anyone mentioned that my sons weren't raised by me. With my parents, it was worse. "But they are well tended by Martin." I was too tired to fight it again, and maybe not be able to give them the life that they obviously have had there, the good life. "Andy will study medicine."

"*Ja*, we hear that Henry Finck's son will go to that Harvard school when he's old enough. He might be the first from Oregon to attend," Johanna said.

"The boys have learned Latin and Greek and had excellent teachers," I added to my sister's comment. "The girls, too, are receiving such instruction. At least the promising students are." Ida had begun classes, and Kate hadn't said anything about Latin as yet. "I wouldn't have been able to offer that to them as a widow—as a woman alone—if I hadn't come back here. And I've tried to do my best to give back all that's been provided."

My father patted my shoulder. "I heard about your house church," he said. "Will you stop that now that there is at last a real church?"

I fidgeted on the blanket, smoothed a wrinkle or two with my palm, gaining time for my answer.

"Keil still only plans to meet every other Sunday, and some of us do remember the fourth commandment to honor the Sabbath and keep it holy."

"They say it's as important as the fifth," my mother said.

Again I felt that twang of guilt. "Have I not honored you?" I asked. "I offered my home to you, but you didn't want to move in with me. Or live in a house that Keil provided? Was that it?"

"We understood the offer," my mother said. "We just miss seeing you. You rarely come by."

"*Ja,*" my sister Lou said, "it can be pretty invigorating when I have one of my fits." She smiled, and I thought how hard it must be for her, for all of them. I did have a very blessed life. Maybe I stayed away from seeing them because I couldn't give to them in the way Johanna and my brothers did. Maybe I anticipated parental barbs and didn't feel strong enough to hear them without having the words sting me like wasps.

"We miss Christine too," my mother said. "She used to come by every day on her way back from the Keil house to yours, but she hasn't of late. I don't see her here today, either. Kitty keeps us filled in on you, Emma, you and your gaggle of women."

"I bet she does."

"What's this strange path you have the girls walking? Some kind of witchcraft or voodoo?" This from my father.

I laughed. "If Kitty told you that, you'd better question the other tales she tells you. It could be a quilt design, you know, Mama, like that one you made that looks like a carpenter's square, with a path in be- tween going toward the center. Or Walk Through the Wilderness."

"Someone said it was like a labyrinth," Johanna said.

"Your very own brother is the one who told us about labyrinths," I told my father. "They're ancient ways of praying, that's all. They put feet to our thoughts and our words. I find it very soothing."

"First you want invigorating, then something to calm you. You have two sides to your wishes, don't you, Emma?" Johanna said.

"We all do," I said.

"She has two doors to her house," Lou said. "Why not two doors to her heart?"

I looked at her. She was right. There were many doubles in my life: two husbands, two boys, two girls. Twice I'd allowed others to raise my sons. I could be morose and sad and wallow in my headaches, or I could behave in ways that gave encouragement and hope, too. I could be pushy and prophetic.

"Maybe two doors means you need twice the opportunity to get something right," my mother said.

"Or when I get discouraged, there's always more than one way out." I was surprised to see my mother nod in agreement at that.

———◆———

Someone knocked on the kitchen front door while the moon was still up. I grabbed my robe, looked out the window to see if I could recognize a wagon, but saw only a lone horse hitched to the front rail. I raced down the steps, throwing a knit shawl over my nightdress, and opened the door to Andy.

"Martin sent me. He's gone on ahead. Matilda's babies are coming early, and Jacob says she's having a hard time of it."

"I'll get dressed and come with you."

"No, he said to pray for them, for him too, to get the women together to do that."

"I'll gather the women, but as soon as I'm dressed, I'll come out there. Have you told Louisa and Helena, those at the Keils'?" He nodded. "Good. Go then. Let your grandmother know. She's a good midwife. I'll see you there."

I awoke the others, and they talked softly as they moved to the room that had been Matilda and Jacob's. "Maybe praying for them in here will make the prayers more powerful," Kitty said. I told her I didn't think it worked that way, but that wherever they gathered would be fine. "You're not going out there without us, are you?" Kitty added.

Maybe I didn't have the right to tell them they should stay home or to go. "I'm going," I said as I dressed. Then I remembered the girls. "But if you'd stay with the girls…"

"I will," Almira said. "I wouldn't want anyone thinking that my presence there brought about bad spirits."

"I can't believe they would, but thank you," I said.

Christine said she'd remain behind too. "Matilda will have her family there," she said.

Kitty's shoulders sagged. "You go, Emma. Martin sent Andy to tell you about it and for us to pray. We'll do that. You ride careful."

At the barns, the stableman was already up. He'd saddled the *Kartoffel* horse for Andy and gotten Martin off in his carriage. Now he saddled a big roan that murmured to me as I touched my head to his nostrils and sighed. I pulled up the hem of my skirt and tucked it into my apron, then stepped onto a stump and swung my leg over the saddle. I pressed my knees, and the horse took off at a fast but comfortable canter.

As I rode, I sent up prayers that Matilda would be all right, that her children would arrive healthy and alive. Many babies came early and lived. My mother had told of keeping a tiny infant, in a box no bigger than for knives, behind the stove where the water usually heated. That baby would die of old age, she'd said on his first birthday. And she was right.

But there were so many that didn't. Matilda and Jacob had had a late start on their happiness, and in my mind, these babies were to help them catch up with joy. *Please let them be all right.*

By the time I tied the reins to the rail in front of Stauffer Farm, the sun poked its head over the treetops. I heard the buzz of bees already at the apple blossoms. The morning breeze brushed cool against my sweaty face. I saw Andy's horse tied beside Martin's buggy, tail switching. I recognized Jacob's father, a former scout, standing on the porch, a pipe in his hand. John nodded to me. "Emma," he said. "It's good you've come."

"*Ja,* I will do what I can to—"

Jacob burst through the door then and stumbled toward the porch rail post. He clung to it as though if he let go, he would sink like a rock into swirling water.

"Jacob?" I touched his shoulder.

He turned to me. His eyes were like caverns deep in his head. I knew what lay behind the door he'd just exited.

22

Sweeping in Front of the Door

April 10. Maybe the 11th, 1867. Whatever days, they run together. Matilda Stauffer gave birth early to her twins, and then she died. One twin survives, though like a tiny stitch in Matilda's sunflower quilt, so fragile, so easily she could yet be snipped away. The twin girl was buried in her mother's grave. Jacob's sisters, Sarah and Rosana, care for the baby they named Matilda, for her mother. One day she'll have the quilt her mother made, but it will never comfort as would a mother's love.

"But we prayed," Christine said, "all of us did, that they would be all right. How can that not have happened? Didn't we do it right?"

Her lament set us all on edge as we gathered at the house church. It had been two weeks since Matilda's death, and I'd made several trips out to Stauffer Farm. Opal was tethered at the post there, giving milk for the baby. I came to comfort those grieving Matilda and her infant, but also to soothe my own sadness. I carried another worry too, hidden like a small child, hoping no one would notice the broken milk pitcher. I didn't want Jacob to become an angry man, to blame himself for moving toward a marriage that instead of giving him joy now left him empty. Jacob hadn't talked to me, and his sisters said he spoke to no one, just sat in the room and stared. He didn't seem able to look at the baby much either when they brought the infant to him.

"We did what we could do," Almira said. "It isn't ours to decide such things as life or death. The things in between, yes, those belong to us. Doing something worthwhile. Giving back to others. That we can control, but not life or death."

"Amen to that," Louisa said. Since the dedication of the church, Louisa had been a regular at our house church. Once or twice she even asked an opinion about how to talk to her daughter-in-law about the way she kneaded bread dough, or what we thought of a new *Fraktur* design she'd made. Today she continued, "I know something about death. My son Willie died, and I could do nothing for him. I prayed for them all. The same with my girls and Elias."

"Gloriunda, Aurora, Louisa," I said, not sure why I wanted to hear the girls' names spoken out loud.

"All such good girls," Louisa nodded. "And I prayed that they'd live, or that I might die instead."

"Your prayers weren't answered," Christine said.

"So we go on. Don't we? It is what makes us human, to live and endure the deaths of those we love. Maybe if we're young enough, we try again to have children. Maybe if we lose a husband, we try again to marry, *ja,* Emma? That doesn't always work so well, *nein,* but we try to find, if not a reason, a comfort in what happens. We find God in it, eventually."

"Why pray, then?" Christine asked in her tentative voice. "If we can't make things happen through our prayers, then why bother?"

"Our faith overcomes death," Almira said. "That is our hope. At least that's how I see it."

It occurred to me in that moment that this was a way we found Providence within the trials, within these expressions of grief and wonder, of uncertainty and hope. We meandered on our faith paths, not only through the Scripture readings and our leaders' interpretations, but through hearing of how others lived through tragedy and trial. I'd once thought it took great courage to live isolated and alone, but living with one another took more. Our reward was hearing words that rang a bell within our souls. We'd be encouraged by the toll.

"I think prayer is how God moves us, more than how we get God to move," I said. "It's as with any friend or husband or wife: you talk, you share, you don't always understand, but you are there and you feel them there, and somehow you can live inside the loose threads of life because of that. Prayer, for me, is like a basket filled with love from which one draws courage for the next step forward."

"That's a lovely thought, Emma," Helena said. She stared at me. I couldn't read her expression.

"Is it?" I hadn't known I knew that until I'd said it.

"Though I'm not sure how scriptural," she added.

"It sounds scriptural," Louisa said. "I'm sure Scripture promises we'll be fed and filled up. In Hosea there's a verse like that."

"In Malachi, it says people who fear the Lord hearken together, and that our prayers are heard. They create a scroll of remembrances."

"What's 'hearken' mean, anyway?" Kate asked.

"To listen attentively with one's heart. The verse gives support to the times we gather here, on our own, without one of the advisors to guide us in spiritual discussions." I expected Helena to protest, but she didn't.

A spring rain surprised us and patted against the windowpanes. Matilda's death, and her baby's, had left us subdued as we sewed. We'd brought Matilda's Sunflower quilt back with us and were reinforcing the hex wheel pattern, as though doing so would make the quilt stronger and last longer for her surviving child.

"When I knew the rest of you were praying, I guess it did help some," Christine said. "I didn't feel so alone."

"It's what I like about all of us living here together," Kitty said.

"We don't all live here," Martha Miller pointed out.

"I know that," Kitty defended. "But we all live in this place together, this Aurora, and that has the same...I don't know, comfort, I guess. People know one another and care about one another, even if there are skirmishes now and then. There always are in families."

"I've wondered if I should have...meddled," I said. "Getting them married and all." I'm not sure why I confessed such a thing. But saying it out loud gave relief. I took in a deep breath. Perhaps my wayward ways could be curtailed by confession now and then.

"My husband has good reasons not to permit marriages," Louisa said. She held her needle up in the air, making her point. "There is pain within those vows. You ought to remember that, Emma."

"Yet if we avoid making a commitment to someone else, hoping to avoid pain, that doesn't work, either," Almira said. "Separation is just another sort of pain."

"I suppose there are wounds outside of marriage too," Louisa said. "But listening to my husband when he refuses permission to marry can prevent a good share of such discomfort."

"Who's to say that I might not have had even more pain in my life if I hadn't married Christian? We had more than five years together, and they were good years."

"Apparently not enough to last a lifetime," Louisa said. "You married again."

"Even the apostle Paul said it was better to marry than to burn," Kitty said. She pooched her lower lip out the way Kate sometimes did. "You'd think God would send someone my way, so I wouldn't burn up."

"I remember reading Goethe, our old German poet," Martha said. " 'Love and desire are the spirit's wings to great deeds.' " I didn't know she read the classics. "You made a way for Jacob and Matilda. I suspect that for a time, they soared."

"Thank you for that, Martha." My words came out as a whisper.

"We all pushed it along," Kitty said. "And Matilda was happy for it. You helped give her that happiness. And baby Matilda's life testifies to their love. And who knows? Jacob may marry again one day since the first time was a joy for him." She looked up at the rain coming against the window. "Maybe I'll bake a special torte for him. I'll take it out there myself, and I'll just hearken to him."

"Goethe also said that 'a useless life is an early death,' " Martha continued. "Matilda's life was far from useless."

We talked more about who was to say whether Matilda's few short years of happiness with Jacob were enough to outweigh her youthful death. My girls listened intently, their eyes moving back and forth between the speakers, but staying silent as though they understood the importance of this discussion. Po yawned in the corner near the fireplace, got up, turned around three times, and plopped back down.

Christine said, "She had a loving husband, months of knowing she would give birth to twins. She had a family caring for her. She had a beautiful home. She had us. She gave away gifts to friends. She laughed often. She quilted with such truth and beauty. And she had her faith. One of her babies survived and is being loved by many. I'm not sure there is more to a full life than that, even if she'd lived to be one hundred."

We all nodded, hearkening together.

———

Private conversations were difficult to have at my home.

"Christine," I said when she'd returned from work at the Keil house. She pulled her straw hat off, set it on the table beside the door. "I wonder if you'd care to take a walk with me." I was tired from working at the new hotel myself and then coming home to help Almira with the wash. Kitty and Christine had said they'd do the ironing tomorrow. It had grown hot in the dip where our village settled, but at least near the river we had a breeze in the evening, and often it pushed away the mosquitoes and other insects too. Mount Hood loomed white and lustrous in the distance. Christine put her hat back on, and I locked my arm in hers as we walked down the steps side by side. "Have I done something wrong?" she said.

"No. But it's nearly your time and—"

"You're wondering what will happen," she said. We'd found the path, but it was now unmarked, except for our own worn footsteps from the season before. The pine cones and branches the girls lined the paths with had been brushed away by winds and animals, including Po.

We walked around the path in silence for a while, following the footsteps of others. Po sniffed at twigs and lifted his head from time to time to assure himself that we stayed close.

I'd told Christine that praying for ourselves as we walked toward the center and praying for others on the way out was a good practice. It's what I did now, hearing only the crunch of our feet on the pebbles and last year's leaves. Crows called to us. When we made it back out, I could smell the cooking fires from homes near my house. Bacon and bean and sausage scents drifted in the air.

"So let's discuss this plan. You're going to leave us and go to Portland?" She nodded. "I wonder when you thought to do that, or how you planned to get there."

She shrugged her now broad shoulders, picked up a long stem of grass, and chewed on it. My father often did that as he thought. "I'll catch a ride with someone. Maybe take the stage?" She sounded tentative.

"Before the baby arrives or after?"

"Oh, before."

"So you have somewhere to stay, to deliver the baby once you reach Portland?"

"No. But I can find someone, someplace. I did last time."

"Christine, I want to say this kindly, but I believe you're in this situation because you really didn't think things through the last time. And now you're avoiding thinking of things again."

"I'm not avoiding it, exactly," she said.

"Planning ahead does remind us of times when we didn't do it before," I said. "I know about that. But remember those little foxes that can spoil the fruit? Well, putting off important things can spoil the vineyard too."

Christine raised her voice. "Matilda and Jacob planned a life, and see what happened? Maybe we're meant to float along and let fate take us where it will, like a leaf in the stream."

"Christine, waiting for things to occur—"

"He didn't overcome me. I was willing," she blurted out. "That's what I feel so terrible about. It means I'll probably do it again. And maybe again, because I don't know how to judge what's genuine affection or not. I don't know how to say no to something I should."

"You said he wasn't the marrying kind. What made you say that?"

I hoped her answer wouldn't be, *"Because he's already married."*

"He likes his ale, and he goes to Portland at times, and he says he plays cards there. He isn't a musician. He doesn't have anything to really fill his time after he works, except to be flirtatious, to find willing girls, I guess. A man serious about finding a wife wouldn't do that. Jacob Stauffer never did those things. What Matilda said about him, why she liked him, that's what I'd like in a husband one day too, though after this, who would ever marry me?"

"Any number of good men might marry you. But you might never find a husband, Christine, and it would have not a thing to do with your worthiness for one. A lot of women don't marry and not only because they're a part of a colony where the leader frowns on weddings. After wars, when so many men die, there often aren't enough men available to marry every willing woman. Some women prefer alone time and not having to ask permission or explain." These were good things I found about not living with Jack, especially that not-seeking-permission part.

"I'll meet someone in Portland," she said. "Or maybe I'll curl up after the baby comes and…" She shrugged.

"You've been walking on a path that takes you to the same place, all the while telling yourself you aren't there. When you can trust yourself to act in your best interest, Christine, then you'll have a full life, even if you never marry."

"Are we supposed to think so much about ourselves? Isn't that self-centered? Our mother often mentioned that."

"Scripture says to love our neighbor as ourselves. We can best care for others if we truly care about ourselves. A healthy person has more to give than one who thinks of curling up and…disappearing."

"What do you think I should do?" she said.

"I'm not sure, but leaving it to chance isn't wise. Sometimes we have to lean on friends and trust them for the next step."

"I worry about Almira," Christine said after we'd walked in silence. I assumed that Christine had had enough of "planning" for one day.

"You know the German poet Martha mentioned, Goethe?" She nodded her head. "He also wrote that when we sweep in front of our own doors, then the whole world will be clean. Don't you worry about Almira. You have just one door to worry about, but how well you sweep in front of it will help the rest of this world get tended to as well."

———————

I stopped at the pharmacy to talk to Martin about Christian celebrating his birthday with us at the end of the month. The only birthdays the colony really celebrated were the Keils', in March. Most of us didn't make any fuss over our children's birthdays or our own, but even after Christian turned nine, I still wanted a little celebration for him. And I wanted something more for my headaches too. The headaches had increased after Matilda's death, and my own cycle of living made a change in flow. I knew I couldn't be with child but wondered whether I wasn't too young for such bodily changes so early. Or maybe they weren't early. Maybe this was the sign that my own body was slowing down. What would be left for me to do, once my girls were raised? Would I find a life as Helena had, at times strident and other times serene, just being in service? Whatever might have passed between Helena and Wilhelm Keil had apparently ceased, for I saw no evidence of special treatment or even the distant looks of longing that I'd once thought I'd seen. Maybe my skills of observation were fading along with my body, my flow being replaced by headaches, pinched eyes, and an occasional cough.

Andy was there. His back was to me, and he concentrated so intensely on his work that I startled him when I spoke from across the counter. He dropped the mortar he'd been holding. I apologized; he cleaned up what had been spilled and then asked how he could help me. *I'm merely a customer to him. Where is that tenderness I thought we were finding?*

"I need to speak to Martin, about headache medicine," I said. "I wanted to ask him, too, if he had anything for weeping eyes. Your aunt Johanna has that trouble."

"Martin sent a poultice to her," he said.

"Did he? Well, that was thoughtful. Did she come by?"

"Often. But I noticed it, too, when I visit."

"Well, that's good, then." We stood awkwardly, my head throbbing, and a strange ache settled in my heart. "I never see the family unless I go there," I said. "They never visit me. I run into them at the Park House sometimes. Well, it's good she gets out, then."

"He has powders for Aunt Lou too. Aunt Louisa, I mean. She prefers to be called Louisa, did you know that?" I hadn't. "I'll tell him you were here."

I almost raised the question of his coming to our home for my little party for Christian, but another customer walked in, nodded to me, and asked Andy if he had something for an aching tooth.

"A hops pack works well," I said.

Andy frowned. I'd intruded. This was his place, not mine.

"It'll have to be pulled," Andy told him, as he looked in the man's mouth. "Martin told you that before."

The man looked sheepish but nodded his head. "*Ja,* I dread that. When should I come back, then, Andrew? May as well get it over with. I can't go seranatin' with a bad tooth, now, can I?"

My son set up an appointment for him, and I saw in the interaction a strong young man, capable of garnering confidence from his elders, though he had few years and much yet to learn. But it saddened me that he didn't smile at the man whose tooth hurt him so; it saddened me that he was growing older and would soon have no need for a mother's influence, even from a distance. And I grieved a bit that he didn't call me Mother when he said good-bye.

I found Christian at the Ehlen house. Mr. Ehlen and his daughters cooked good meals, Christian told me. He looked torn when I asked him if he'd like to come to dinner, a late birthday celebration at the end of the month. "We was going to go up into the mountains and do some fishing," he said. I let his grammar error go, and he continued, "It'll be a good time of year, won't it, Mr. Ehlen?" The older man nodded. "Can we do it some other time, Mama?"

"Of course," I said. "You can all come, Mr. Ehlen, if you'd like." Everyone nodded agreement, but they didn't offer up a date.

I walked back slowly toward my house. Keil or the committee had ordered signs made for the streets, and one day we'd have addresses like when we lived in Bethel. But for now if anyone came looking for another, they'd simply knock on any door and be directed.

I wasn't ready to go home yet. My head hurt, but the sun felt good on my face, so I kept walking. My boys had their own lives. Soon my girls, too, would find pursuits with friends. They'd marry and be gone, and how would I fill my time, then? Stitch clothes. Put up preserves. Cook and bake. Karl said there were women hoping to change laws, so they could vote and keep their own earnings. Maybe my persuasive talents could be applied to such work. Making a meaningful life as a single woman was a challenge for more people than Christine or Kitty or Almira. It was my challenge too, even though I wasn't a single woman.

I walked past the Park House. The late afternoon shadows were like ripples of changing light across the green. It reminded me of the material Karl had purchased for me, the one that changed colors as you lifted it to the sunlight. I walked the paths for a time, then came through the trees to stand before the church. It was open and I went inside. Christine sat there. I didn't make a sound, but I wondered if perhaps the answer to her need was with me.

———◆———

"There's something I want to tell you all," Christine began.

The four of us remained in the parlor: Kitty, Almira, Christine, and me. I'd not spoken to her that day in the church. Instead I'd gone back through the paths at the Park House and spent that evening with my aching head out beneath the stars, wrapped in my Running Squares quilt. The longer I stayed there, the better I felt about telling Christine that I'd take her child and raise it as my own. It would be my renewal.

I knew about babies. What could anyone do to me if I suddenly appeared with a child in my arms? No one would ever have to know where the child came from, and I could simply say that I was acting on the Diamond Rule, making another's life better than my own.

So when Christine spoke, I thought she would tell the others of her dilemma, and I could offer my solution.

"Almira is going to take my baby," Christine said instead.

"What baby?" Kitty asked.

"The one I'm going to have sometime soon. It's a very long story," she said, silencing questions already forming on Kitty's tongue. "She's made plans to return to the Clatsop Plains to be closer to her children. I'll go with her."

"You have?" I turned to Almira.

She looked back serenely.

"But won't people wonder where you got this child?" Kitty asked. "Won't they say despicable things about you, Almira, arriving as a divorced woman, with a baby?"

"They might," Almira said. "But I'm stronger now because of my time here. And this baby needs a good home that I can provide with my son and his wife. They've invited me to return to them, since I finally wrote and told them where I'd been. It will be a good thing for me to do, to care for their children and for this one."

"I'll have the baby there, Emma. At Almira's children's home. No one here will need to know, if everything goes all right."

"Your first child, it could be difficult," Kitty said. "Mama was a midwife for first-time mothers, and she said it was always a surprise what might happen."

"Don't you think it's a good idea, Emma?" Christine asked me directly now. "I planned it out, just like you said I should. I worked out the details with Almira."

"Yes. Of course. I thought you'd…stay here. Have the baby here. I'll be sorry to see you and Almira both leave."

"There'll be someone else to take my place," Almira said. "I couldn't be moving on if you hadn't rescued me."

"Wagners do that," Kitty said. She looked at Christine. "But you don't even look like you'll soon have a baby."

"You don't have to see to believe."

"Is the father someone we know?" Kitty asked.

"It's better if I don't say. Almira will be the baby's mother, and she can make up whatever story she wants."

"Well, I am flummoxed," Kitty said. She put the yardage she'd been stitching in a heap on her lap. "So much going on, and I didn't even know it. You knew, Emma?"

"I knew that Christine worked out a problem. I didn't know that she'd found so...agreeable a solution."

"It's just the beginning," Christine said. "I've been thinking of what you said, Emma. I've thought of sweeping in front of my own door and keeping it clean."

"You don't have your own door," Kitty said.

"Little foxes can spoil the wine. That's what you said. But if small things can bring spoilage, then perhaps minor changes made each day can bring goodness to the wine too."

"I thought you were talking about doors," Kitty said.

"I'll make day-by-day changes in my own life, so I won't complicate another infant's life in the way I have now tangled up...other lives."

Christine spoke further about the baby, Almira's move, and her travel plans when that time came. She'd be gone for a time; she'd have to be. Almira's departure would leave a gap in my days, as Christian's and Matilda's deaths had. As my sons' leaving had. Christine was right: little things done daily could bring good changes. I'd been thinking of a bigger investment in change, having Christine's baby to raise, but that was not to be. I sat listening to their words, thinking of brooms and making sweeps in front of my door. I had two doors to tend to. Family stood behind each.

23

Let Us Get Together

Running Squares. A piece from my own quilt made in honor of Christian.

Blue fabric. My mother made a dress for me as a child using this material. She said the Germans discovered indigo blue, and we should be proud of our heritage. My mother brought it with her. I'm glad I have the fabric swatch at least, a fine reminder of the gift. It's not enough to wrap my string of pearls in, though. Just a swatch.

Calico with blue flowers and yellow centers. Matilda's baby clothes. The swatch makes me think of Matilda's quilt with the vibrant sun colors. With leftover material I made a sleeping dress for Christine's baby. Maybe I should call it Almira's baby in case someone should ever see this fabric diary.

Christine planned to leave with Almira within the week. We talked of how we'd explain her absence and Almira's too. "I'm mostly concerned about our parents," Christine said. "They'll be so disappointed in me if they know the truth, if they learn of what I've done. I'm not sure they'd forgive me."

Knowing my family, there might be strain. I was living evidence that something could strain and there could still be stretch in the tension. Christine's leaving could trouble my parents, unless we created some story that would make it understandable to them and even to the Keil household. She wouldn't be working there anymore.

Then there was the father. I couldn't help but wonder who he was, and I found myself picturing any number of men who'd find Christine's company acceptable. But for all I knew, the father didn't even live in the colony now. The bachelors came and went. I hoped that her earlier plan to travel toward Portland hadn't been based on some string of interest in him she still clutched.

Kitty had a few pennies saved from her potato harvest last fall. Christine, too, had resources from her savings from before she came to Aurora. We sewed a wardrobe for the baby, but in an effort to keep the secret, put the cloth aside whenever Louisa or Helena or BW or my own mother attended our house church. We considered offering ourselves to area farms to help with spring plantings for pay to accumulate the last that we'd need. But then Almira's children sent money for the stage and fare for the ship that would take them on the Columbia River to the Clatsop Plains.

"I had peacefulness about the final fare the last time I walked the puzzle path," Almira said. "I knew what we needed would be provided." She purchased the tickets to take them north. She was going back stronger and with a purpose, to raise another child well.

The day of their departure, my daughters were at school. I thought of letting them come with us to say good-bye, but they'd said those words the night before, and I didn't want them to miss any of their studies.

I held Almira in my arms, then stepped back to take her hands in mine. I felt the stiffness of her knuckles. Martin's creams had helped her, but not as much as I had hoped. "You have a safe journey now. Write when you can. Be sure to tell us about Christine. Maybe send a telegram and say 'Strudel' for a girl and 'Kartoffel' for a boy." She nodded, hugged Kitty. I gave Almira a traveling desk that I'd built, using the same lumber that I'd had to make the curlicue addition to the porch supports. The inside was lined with the fabric that we'd pieced together to back Matilda's Sunflower quilt. "Small pieces of fabric to help remind you of your time here," I told her.

"It's been good time, Emma," Almira said. "I've watched how you dealt with your sadness over your sons by finding ways to give to others. Your generosity to me, I can never repay you. I'll remember the Diamond Rule. You are the sparkle in that rule." I started to protest, but she silenced me with her finger to my lips. Her finger felt warm and tender. "I know. The rule grows from your beliefs. But still, you live the rule. I see it. I'll remember."

For Christine, I'd sewn a wrapper from the yardage Karl had given me. I put tucks across the bodice and made it look somewhat opulent, with special stitches and a few tiny beads I'd put on the ledger book account at the Keil and Company Store. Those who might notice these two women would decide the larger of the two had gotten that way by overeating, indulging in life's riches, rather than harboring a child beneath the folds.

"You'll visit our parents?" Christine asked as we loaded her bag onto the stage. "Tell them I'm helping Almira. They'll understand that, won't they?"

"It's the perfect story," I said. "And not a lie either. In a few months' time you can return and no one will be the wiser."

"Helena won't like that explanation, I suppose," Christine said. "Or Louisa either."

"Let me worry about them," I said. "You get to the Clatsop Plains before that baby arrives." The last I whispered, so that the other riders on the stage couldn't hear, and neither could the driver.

"You've been a good sister to me, Emma," Almira told me. "I was a washbucket of nerves when I met you, not worth the soap it took to clean me up."

"You were never so worthless." I laughed.

"Yes I was. I slept and took and didn't give much back at all for months."

"I had room and resources, thanks to the colony."

"Thanks to your faithfulness too," she said. "I could restore my own." She straightened her hat; a flourish of Clara's blue feathers clutched the top and side of her head, making her look stylish and festive. Her skin glowed pink with the flush of a new adventure. If her husband saw her like this, vibrant and alive, he might well wish her back in his life, if not his bed.

"You be careful now," I said. "Don't do anything rash when you see him."

She blushed. "What makes you think I'll see him?"

"Oh, they always show up. I've never understood why people think a divorce will separate one from a difficult relationship; it just changes the circumstances under which those conflicts appear."

Almira grimaced, and I realized my thoughtlessness. "I didn't mean… I shouldn't have said that, Almira. I'm sorry. I know you didn't want to take that route. I only meant that men—"

"I know what you meant," she said. "It's a sign of my grit that I can hear that and not wither away with the words. Especially because what you say is right. He is the father of my children, and I loved him many years. That's the truth. And so is how that truth could be shattered, and everything I'd once loved vanish." Christian came immediately into my head…followed by Jack. There'd be another encounter with Jack, I was sure of that. "When I do see my husband," Almira continued, "I'll remember that I don't have to endure any of the humiliation he might bring. I can look for the small, good things that time might have allowed into our changed lives. And if there are none, then he can't humiliate me unless I allow it. And I won't."

Christine let out a rush of air, and I turned to her. "Are you all right?"

"I just need to get off my feet," she said. "They've swollen to the size of spittoons. If I don't sit down soon, I'll have to make another trip to the privy."

Almira stepped up into the stage, then turned to take Christine's hand. I pushed from behind. She truly had become a very large woman. She settled onto the smooth seat with a heavy hushed sound of the material swishing on leather. The scent of lavender rose up from the sachet pouch Christine wore. Almira squeezed in beside her. There were three passengers crowded together on the opposite side. Christine stared at them. She looked back at me with a grimace of someone who'd watched a snake crawl across her foot and was too frightened to shout. "It'll be all right," I told her. "It will."

"Let us go a May-ing, let us go a May-ing, one and all a joyous time," Kitty began. She sang the round from behind me. Christine laughed then and let out a long sigh. Almira patted her hand. No one sang the second stanza.

I hoped the jolting of the stage wouldn't create an adventure for those passengers or, worse, cause complications for Christine. At least Almira had birthed babies in her life—nine in thirteen years—so she'd know what to do. Christine was in good hands, and so was Almira. Kitty and I stepped back.

The driver closed the stage door. He pulled himself up onto the seat, lifted the lines of reins for the six-horse team, clicked his tongue at the animals, and off they went.

I might never see Almira again, but she was a part of who I'd become. Christine was family, fostered into the Wagner clan, and I was certain she'd return; but Almira was family too. Family had enlarged to include those I'd served. I added it to my gratitude list as the stage rattled across the bridge, taking them to their new lives.

Summer came on fluffy white clouds whose shadows played hide-and-seek with the fields. There were the usual changes in the months that followed. Keil agreed to a few more marriages but prevented others, and no one seemed to know why. He moved his workroom to the top floor of the *gross Haus,* sending the bachelors to bunk more closely together on the far side. In his workroom, he composed music along with several other colony men. A demand for traveling trunks increased, and furniture and workshops were built to accommodate the interest. We women painted them our colony blue, the color of the summer sky. The turners formed spool beds on a lathe, and people as far away as Seattle and San Francisco heard of our work and placed orders. Jacob Miller's turned work on the church attracted attention each time we entered, and there was talk of building another Keil house for Frederick and Louisa, with Jacob doing the railings and the pillars.

After Almira and Christine left, I took it upon myself to visit my parents daily. At first it was to tell them that Christine had traveled with Almira, that she wanted to see more of the territory and so had gone along.

"I'm surprised the Keils would let her go like that," my mother said. Jonathan was having breakfast there, and I realized that though he lived in a small house on his own, he must spend a fair amount of time with our parents. He had dirt under his fingernails, so he'd also been farming, a task added to his ledger keeping.

"She's an adult," my father noted. "Guess he can't tell adults much what to do. Unless they let him." I took that to be a swipe at my allowing Martin to raise my sons, but I didn't say so.

"Now, Father," Jonathan chastised. "Keil's mellowed. You ought to give the man another chance, truly."

"I don't despise the man at all," my father said. "I like being in charge of my own destiny. But this place has become more an economic community than a religious one. Saddens me."

"Me too," I said. "There are many in need of the Lord's love expressed through communal ways. Ways that Christian believed in, and you."

My father grunted his pleasure.

"I hope Christine comes back soon," my sister Louisa said. "She always brought candies from the Keils' house."

"I happen to have some peppermint sticks," I said. "Would you like one?"

She did, and that became my opening each time I stopped. It was a small act that brightened their day and mine too. Sometimes Kate and Ida were with me, and once Andy delivered a cone of medicine to my youngest brother, William, while I was there. With all the people around, I hoped no one would notice my awkwardness in my son's presence. He was old beyond his years, my son, and chattered easily with my father about world affairs and local politics. He tipped his cap at me when he left and said, "Mother."

I don't know why the gesture brought tears to my eyes, but it did. Maybe with more time, we'd find a path, or perhaps form a new one, one like Almira's puzzle path, which required no decisions about right or wrong ways, just the courage to enter in.

Helena and Louisa weren't quite so forgiving of Christine's departure. I invited them to the house church especially, offering dry plate cakes. They had to be served hot to stay crisp. While they brushed sugar from their faces, I told them that Almira had left and Christine had gone along to assist for a time.

"Who told her she could leave without letting anyone know?" Helena said. Then, more kindly she added, "She has a lovely voice, and I thought she added much to the choir."

"She told me," I said. "And it was time for Almira to go back. She felt that she should take care of old things, and Christine agreed to help her."

Louisa harrumphed. "Christine ate enough for two while she was here those last months. Honestly, she blew up like a mushroom. Took more than her share at the grain distribution. That's what my dear Wilhelm said, though I don't know how he'd know for certain. He didn't attend the distributions."

"She baked for the colony," Martha Miller said. She'd joined us, and though she didn't know the details, she had a conciliatory way about her. She was neutral. Probably why the elections were always held at her father's home. "So it might not have been that she ate it all."

"Maybe her time away will help her put things into better proportions," I said.

"Just as well that Almira's gone," Helena said. "I never liked those paths she had. It's like something from the druids, walking in certain ways through the woods like that." She shivered.

"It's simply a way of praying," I said. "Didn't you pray as you walked across the plains?"

"We came around the Horn," Helena corrected.

"*Ach, ja.* I forgot. But didn't you walk about the ship and pray? I find it restful. Almira and the girls do too, to walk those paths."

"Prayers aren't supposed to be restful," Helena said. "They're supposed to humble us and make us think about the errors of our ways."

" 'I think myself happy.' The apostle Paul wrote that. Surely one result of a prayer ought to be happiness and hope. Isn't hope the whole message of our faith?"

Helena whisked her hand at me as she said, "*Ach,* sometimes I don't know where you get your ideas from, Emma. No wonder Wilhelm didn't want the boys exposed so much to your thinking."

After all this time, her words still stung.

I took a deep breath, offered her another cake. "Fortunately I had early years with them, and isn't there another scripture that says if you raise your children up in the ways that they shall go, when they are older they will not depart from them?"

"*Ja,* it may be too late."

"Or just enough time," I said.

I could hope.

Christian arrived at our door one morning a few days after. "I'm running errands for the telegraph," he told me proudly. I invited him in for breakfast. The girls were both up and dressed and welcomed him like a lost relative. Well, I suppose in a way, that's what he was. He scooped up the cornmeal pancakes, added molasses and dried berries, and said, " 'Member when I ground the corn for you, Mama?" I said that I did, and any time he wanted to come back and do that, he sure could. He beamed. "Do you still keep the water bucket cool in the root cellar?" he asked but didn't wait for my answer. "This water tastes better than at Martin's and Brother Keil's houses. Oh, here's the telegram," he said, pulling it from his shirt. He patted Po, whose tail pounded on the floor beneath the table.

"I have a telegram? And you just now gave it to me?"

"I was hungry," he defended.

I read it. "It's from Almira," I said. "Remember her?" Christian still scratched at Po's head, shook the dog's ears, and nodded yes that he did. "I remember Opal too," he said. "Is she tied up out there?"

"She's in a pen," Kate said. "We lent her out until Jacob got his own goat. But she has to stay tied now, or she'd come right inside here and eat everything on the table, dirty knees and all. She came upstairs once."

"In my room?" Christian asked.

"Po chased her out. He grabs at her ears," Kate said. "And we have to watch him with Clara too."

"She stayed with us," Ida said, bringing us back to the telegram. "Almira did. She's family, *ja*, Mama?"

I nodded, then read to myself.

"What's it say, Mama?" Kate asked.

"It's about food," Christian said.

"You read it?" Kate said. "That's not nice, is it, Mama?"

"It's nice that Christian can read, but you ought not to read other people's private words," I told him.

"Not many words to worry over," Christian said.

"That's not really your place to decide," I said. "Kate's correct. If you want to keep your job as a telegraph man, you'll have to keep the words they give you very private."

"*Strudel* and *Kartoffel*. That's all I remember, Mama. I won't say it to anyone else, except when I want to eat it." He grinned.

———◆———

In August, Barbara Giesy, my mother-in-law and widow of Andreas, passed away. She was old by the standards of so many women. She would have reached seventy-four in December. It spoke to the good care she'd had all her life, despite the hard work she was asked to perform. In her later years, Helena had tended her, as had her daughter-in-law BW. Andy acted as a pallbearer, and the band played the funeral dirge that Keil had composed for his Willie those many years before.

The large bell began the funeral procession from John's house, and then the next size bell, and then the smallest, the tolling going on until the casket reached the church. The bells pealed again when we headed toward the cemetery where she would be buried. I decided that day, as I stood off to the edge of the gravestones, that when I died I wanted to be buried here too, but not near the Giesy plot. Somewhere off to the side. Somewhere at the edge. Maybe with my daughters' families. That's where I belonged.

Fall brought harvest and news that some of our "boys," who had been staked by Keil and headed to the gold fields near Canyon City, had made good of it. They came back for the winter to report. Few had found gold, but they'd tried their hand at storekeeping and cobbling shoes. They noted a market for hops and encouraged us to plant more land in that crop, assured that we could sell it to supplement their "meager fare," as they described it. I remembered that we'd sold oysters to the California gold market years ago and thought those men ate well. None of our colony boys looked as if they'd had to skip a meal. Most just said they were tired and cold and didn't want to spend another winter in the Blue Mountains, surrounded by miners with nothing better to do than drink and fight and lament their lost loves while they waited for spring. They were happy to be home in Aurora.

The Oregon State Fair had come around in October, as it always did. The band rehearsed its pieces, seranatin' us (as some called it) well into the night. We had more horses to enter in the races, and our cattle looked sleek and prime. I thought it might be due to our huge barns made to care for the animals and keep them out of the weather.

Most of the colony found a reason to attend the fair that year.

I decided to enter something I'd made after Matilda died. Using scraps of fabric, I pieced the odd shapes and sizes, with stark angles and curved edges, onto a fabric backing. But instead of quilting it as I'd always done, I made tiny replicas of some of the shapes and stuffed them with bits of wool so they rose up off the fabric. I hand-tacked the patches and used a small buttonhole stitch over the raw edges. I'd seen a woman working on a quilt like this when Christian and the scouts and I had ridden across the west those years before. The quiltmaker had hailed from Virginia, and she called what she did appliqué.

Mine, when I finished, I framed. It was more a picture than a quilt that could bring comfort or warmth, though I hoped it brought rest for one's eyes. I gave it depth with the stuffed pieces. I wanted people to touch it, to feel the give within the appliqué, to know that it was made of sturdy, discarded stuff but could still be purposeful.

I'd made a landscape scene, bucolic some might say, composed of blue sky and clouds hovering over a log home. A river skirted the edge, and trees soared above the white painted fence circling the yard. Four children, a goat, a sheep, and one dog lounged about. The house had two doors, and I made them with cloth flaps so that the doors could actually be opened if one took the time. Behind one door a tiny candle glowed, an effort of creation that had kept me up well into the night. Behind the other, against a dark wall, a bowl of apples, made with French knots of embroidery thread, graced a table. It had taken me many hours, and I'd shared my efforts with my girls. Both had a fine hand with the needle, and I thought back at how I would otherwise have filled my time if my boys had been daily in my life. Maybe I never would have found quiet encouragement within fabric. My entry hung in the Household Arts exhibit tent.

The girls slept by our wagon now. Po snored at my feet, his long, skinny tail flapping the floor any time I said his name. This wasn't the life Christian and I had planned, but it was a good life. I'd woven meaning into the loose threads that had taken me from Bethel to Willapa and now to Aurora. It dawned on me that I'd found my *Heimat* at last in Aurora.

I'd urged my parents to attend the fair and bring Louisa too. Johanna didn't think I understood how much work it would be, but I offered to stay with them, to bring my girls, and even cook up enough for all of us. That way we could enjoy ourselves, or they could, while I fixed meals over the open fire. I rather liked the informality of fair cooking, where no one complained about the extra dirt that might make its way into their potatoes, the way they did at home if they found a dog or goat hair in the mix.

They agreed to go. Jonathan drove a wagon and so did my father, though neither Christian nor Andy was allowed to accompany us— Martin had his classes, and Andrew covered the store. I wasn't sure why Christian had been kept back. Some things just happened. We had all the rest of our family there—the girls, Kitty, and my younger brothers, who didn't stay with us but who at least took their meals with us. They bunked at the horse barns, and I suspected they made wagers on the outcomes of the races.

Christine, too, was absent, but it wasn't upsetting. There was an ebb and flow to this family; sometimes it supported and sometimes it tore at the edges, as our colony could.

We ate and walked and listened and took in the smells of the fair and the fall. A cluster of people slowed our meandering through the Household Arts exhibit, and it took a few minutes before I realized that a crowd was standing in front of my entry. My mother peered around a woman and took a long look. She said she thought the little doors a clever stitching.

"A scene with cloth," my mother said. "But small enough to hang on a wall, and those pieces that rise up. How interesting." She leaned in, touched the puffy clouds, and ran her hand over the texture of the fibers. "Appliqué," she read. Then she saw my name on the ticket. She gasped. "I had no idea you did such work, Emma. That's my daughter's work," she told anyone around her. I beamed. "Will you show me how?"

"We can begin today if you want," I said.

"*Nein*. We will have that be a winter project. You bring the girls, and we'll sit around the fire. Maybe Christine will be back by then, and you can teach us all."

There were tucks in our relationship that might never be smoothed out, but that didn't have to mean we could not go on sewing up new memories, stitching otherwise-frayed hems. I could imagine myself sitting with them, talking, my showing them a stitch and their telling me of their day. Papa might smoke out on the porch. I'd bring Po along, so he could walk me and the girls home at the end of the evening. Maybe they'd ask us to spend the night, which we'd decline because of the tiny space, but it would feel right to have been invited. The home art, as my piece was called in the fair, would be a good place for our experiences and imagination to intersect. We'd create an artifact that might take on a life of its own.

We walked out into the sunlight, and I squinted, nearly stumbling over a shovel leaned against the side of the exhibit barn.

"Are you all right?" A small, callused hand reached out for mine. "I didn't mean to leave the shovel aleaning there. I hope you didn't get hurt?"

I recognized the voice and smiled as I looked into the eyes of Brita. "I daydreamed," I said. "It wasn't your fault at all."

24

To Provide For

October 6. Received my second ribbon at the fair. I appliquéd but a small portion. Instead, I used red thread to outline every piece of fabric regardless of its color or texture. It reminded me of the veins I see in the back of my mother's hands, only I have made the color red instead of blue. My mother said it looked confused, but I didn't mind. It looked organized to me.

Brita's eyes were pinched, and dirt filled in lines around them that I hadn't remembered.

"Where are the boys?" I looked around.

"They are finding work, staying with farmers who can feed them and give them a warm bed at night. I never could make it once we left the livery."

"I'm sorry. Why didn't you go back to the Durbin brothers or come to Aurora?" I asked. "We'd have made room for you. Did you never get my letters?"

"I wanted to do it myself," she said.

I remembered my own difficulty in reaching for hands that could keep me from falling. "You can come now," I told her. "You'd be welcome."

She shook her head. "I work here, at the fair."

"But you always said you would never go back to the carnival."

She bristled, straightened her back. "I'm not in the circus. I pick up things. I guess they thought I was so close to the ground, my back wouldn't hurt with the reaching and bending. It's good work. I tidy things up."

"Well, of course it's good work. Tidying is what we women do, and usually no one even notices unless we don't." She smiled, her shoulders relaxed. "Would you consider coming later? The fair doesn't last but four or five days. Then what? I have a home. You could bring your boys."

I saw it all in a flash: There'd be the sounds of boys in my house again. We'd find reason to laugh in the midst of our work. "The girls will love seeing Pearl again too," I said.

Her eyes filled with tears. "I'd best return to my station. It was good to see you again, Emma. Tell your boys and those girls hello for me." She looked away.

"Where is Pearl?" The boys were old enough to have been farmed out to hopefully kind couples, but Pearl was a young one. "You never said."

"She didn't make it," she said. A sob broke from her throat. "It was a silly plan, my ahomesteading. Pearl got ill. We were far from the town. She died before I could get her to a doctor." Her grief caught in her throat. "We can't always do everything we set our hearts on, can we? I risked it all, and in the end I had to give up."

Her words bored like an ocean drill into the oyster of my heart. So much of what I'd hoped for hadn't come about either, no matter how much I longed for it, prayed for it. Yet my life was full. All of my children lived. My sons stayed healthy and would go on to school one day; my girls skipped with activity, were being educated with the warmth of family to surround them, and they, too, would pursue their *Sehnsucht*, their dreams and desires. I didn't get to see my boys daily or influence them as I might like, but I still saw them. I wished they'd choose to see me more often, but my own parents felt the same way about me. One could never seem to satisfy that longing for a visit by a child, except to live with them. Or live so close that it felt as though one did. But families then had to suffer the irritations of familiarity rather than the agonies of perceived neglect. There was no perfect solution.

Brita and I moved out of the way so others could walk around us. I touched her shoulder. "I'm so sorry, Brita. Losing a child…" I remembered when Christian died, how my time with his mother after that had been when I'd felt the closest to her. She'd lost a child; I'd lost my husband. But they still weighed unequally; losing a child weighed more.

"My heart has a slice right through it," she said, drawing her wide palm like a sword across her small chest. "I don't know what'll ever be a-mending it. She might have lived if I'd been less stubborn. I thought I could keep her fever down. I couldn't. I don't think the boys will ever forgive me, either. But then, I'll never forgive myself."

"Oh, Brita, we all do things we later regret. It's another thing you and I have in common with everyone else who admits it. But Pearl would want you to forgive yourself. I just know it."

I'd done so many things that I regretted. But I'd also taken steps to change through the years, to cherish what I had, to nurture hope, and to use new brush strokes to bring vibrancy to the painting of my life. I wanted that for my friend too.

"Brita. Get the boys back and come stay with us. If only for a time. We could feed you…not out of pity, but because we can, and you could give back, get restored until you know what you want to do next, truly."

She shook her head. "It would only be a temporary fix," she said. "Like putting a tack where a nail is needed."

"What's wrong with that?"

"It's a coward's way out."

"Oh, Brita, how can you say that? You once lived in a cave; you didn't plan to live there forever, did you?"

In the distance I could hear the band playing. At the end of the piece came applause. If we'd been sitting there watching and listening, we'd have heard the musicians talk briefly to one another, the movement of music papers, and then they'd clear the spit valves on their horns, that little whistle of sound that Henry C, the conductor, said wasn't really spit but pure water formed from their breath as it condensed on the metal. The band began again. My sisters and parents had moved on to stand outside the dance hall door, leaving us alone.

"I never planned a long time in the cave or to stay at Aurora, but I did think the homestead would be forever," she said. She poked at the ground with her picking-up stick. "I thought my purpose was to save those boys, build a home for them and Pearl, and have a place no one could ever take away from us."

"Maybe it never was to be the house," I said. She frowned, looking up at me. "Your purpose. Maybe it was to be with them, wherever that was, however that might be. Maybe that was the goal, and where you did that, or the adjustments you had to make, the kind of shelter you provided, standing tall for them…as tall as you could, maybe that's all that really matters in the end. For any of us."

"Maybe," she said. "But I failed there, too, then."

"It's only one step. You can take the next one. I'll walk with you."

I couldn't convince her, any more than my relatives and friends could have convinced me those dark days in Willapa. But what I'd said to her, what I'd thought out loud before I even knew it, that was what I planned to piece and stitch and frame one day to remind myself: "It's not the house but the shelter." That's what truly mattered.

Christine returned in November. I hardly recognized her. She was thinner than when she'd first come to Aurora, long before she'd danced at the fair with an interested man. But it was more than her physical change that I noticed: she had an air about her, a spirit of anticipation that drew others to her. She said she'd waited to return until after the fair, not wanting to see any old friends just yet. "I'm learning to live inside this new person," she said. "Sometimes I can bend over to stoke the fire and stand back up without even leaning on a staff. I can move without making waves."

"You were always light on your feet," Kitty said.

"I eat and work the same," she said. "But I feel filled up now. The time with Almira was good. We walked new paths, ones she made at her son's house. Maybe it was the walking," she said. "But I did plenty of that here too." She shrugged her shoulders, seemed to accept the change in her life without absolute explanation.

"You look...different," Kitty said. "Happier."

"I am that. I remembered things you said, Emma, about being worthy, from the inside out. That's the door I've opened."

When we were alone, she told me about the delivery of her twins and her sadness when she said good-bye to them and returned here. "But Almira is good to them. And her children are good to her, the older boy and his wife. I didn't meet Almira's husband, but I don't think she's even thinking of returning to him. She said she'd find happiness every morning when she looked in the eyes of those children. I named one Emma," Christine said, "and the other one Karl."

"Not..."

"Not for his father, no, no. *Nein*. For Karl Ruge. The teacher. He was always so kind to me. When my son grows up, I want him to be like Karl. And my daughter, well, Almira's daughter, I'm hoping she'll be generous, like you."

"*Ach*, no," I said and waved my hand in dismissal.

"You ought to let a compliment come your way now and then," Christine said.

Twice now I'd been described as generous, and that thought surprised. My sister Johanna, through her love for my parents and brothers and sisters, stood much higher on the ladder of compassion than I did.

"When you take a compliment in, you do your children a favor," Christine continued. "Almira said letting her children watch their father demean her was one of the worst things she did to them. She didn't realize that until she'd had time here to heal. She's going to let me be a part of the children's lives. I'll be like an aunt to them. It will be best for us all."

"You've exchanged wisdom for your weight," I said. She grinned.

At the harvest dances, Christine had her share of beaus inviting her to *Schottische* or to do the webfoot quickstep. She appeared to enjoy herself, but she told me one day, as we kneaded dough together preparing for the Christmas celebrations of December, that she didn't think she'd ever marry. I cajoled her, telling her she was yet young and any number of things could happen to her that she didn't now think possible. But she said she couldn't tell any potential husband about her three babies, and she couldn't imagine beginning a marriage without telling someone she loved the whole truth. It was a sacrifice she thought made sense.

"I'm sure there are useful things for me to do. And I can be happy knowing I've done good work, apart from caring for a husband or children."

"Jacob Stauffer said something like that a few weeks back," I said. I sprinkled flour onto the table and folded the dough over yet again. "He said he'd done good work in providing for Matilda, giving her a good home and happiness for however short a time. I was so glad to see him thinking that way."

"He'll marry again sometime," Christine said. She patted her dough into shape, then placed it in the tin and sprinkled salt across the top. "Maybe Martha Miller."

"Are you matchmaking?" I said. "I thought that was my job." She laughed. "You may be a little late anyway," I said. "Jacob told me that Christina Wolfer had brought him a chocolate cake with that coconut on it. His eyes lit up as he described it. She served it on that blue plate her mother rescued on the trail."

"I hope her brother doesn't find out his mother still has that butter plate," Christine said.

"Food is the elixir for grief," I said. "That's something we know, *ja?*"

"But it's not all that fills us up."

I echoed Karl and made her laugh when I said, "*Ja*, by goodness, that's right."

I washed the girls' hair on Saturday before the Christmas gathering began. I wondered if this schedule of limited worship was Keil's way of being sure we didn't get caught up in ritual. If he'd done it to halt our house church, that hadn't worked. We still met, and we worshiped as we worked. And on the off Sundays, when the church was empty, I often went there in the mornings myself and would find Helena there, sometimes Karl Ruge, or others of the colony worshiping. *Maybe that's Keil's intention after all, that we worship on our own without a named leader.* Certainly no one was really being groomed to replace him, except for the advisors. But I'd never known a church to be run by a group without a named leader.

Despite the kindling in the kitchen stove, the room felt damp and cool with all of us having our hair washed. We heated the water in big copper pots on the stove, had the girls lean over another blue washtub, and poured the water over their hair first. We collected the wastewater and would reuse it for the next head of hair. Kitty scrubbed with our soap; Christine rinsed, keeping fresh water heated. I dried Ida's hair, rubbing her curly strands between the flannel towels before continuing the routine with Kate, who was young woman enough she could do it on her own. But I liked the ritual as much as she seemed to. After all of us had wet hair and were hoping it would dry before it froze and broke off, someone rubbed our heads as dry as they could, and we'd begin running the comb through our tangles, making the best of the some-times tearful pulls against our scalps. Kitty introduced another round to sing that acted as distraction.

I did like this time together. I inhaled the aroma of the soap and hair rinse, which didn't really seem to help with tangles all that much but did make our hair smell grand. I liked knowing that simple water and soap would make another feel good, and that my children and sis-ters had clean and mended clothes to put on later. It comforted me knowing we had wood enough for the winter, stacked up beside the wash house, and that both Po and Opal were happy inside it during cold nights like tonight. *Ja,* I'd brought Clara into a cage at night so she could be safe inside too. Our flock of colony chickens had their roost house to stay warm in. We women had boots to wear and gloves with sheep's wool lining and knitted hats to go over our wet hair. We'd be lucky if the long strands dried by morning, tucked inside braids. Still, it was a satisfying time. Kitty's music made it almost a time of worship.

We'd all go to the dance at the Park House later that evening. Some children would swirl with their fathers; women would chatter and talk, the older ones bringing their stitching to sit on the side, the younger ones eyeing the bachelors with hopefulness in their hearts. There were still so few marriages. People from the Shaker community in the East had visited us last summer, and they felt celibacy had great merit. But after they left, I heard one of the advisors say he was glad to see they'd gone. "They never laughed or smiled and were plain as white cows. A few frills never hurt anyone."

The Pie and Beer Band was frills. They might play that night (being paid in pie and beer), or sometimes the Aurora Band if they weren't engaged for money by a noncolonist group somewhere else. Both Ida and Kate loved to attend the dances. Often they'd see their brothers there, which was always the highlight for me too.

I'd been unable to convince Brita to return with us, but she agreed to give me her address and promised to write back. I wondered if there was something yet I could do to bring her boys to her.

On a dance night, back when Jacob and Matilda still lived with us, Jacob would make sure we all had our gloves on and knitted mufflers at our necks and heads before stepping out into the night. The sound of a man's voice could soothe, and I missed that. A once happily married woman never forgot the pleasure of hearing a man's voice say her name. She never forgot the pleasure of a lover's touch to her lips either, but that was something I could do little about. I'd have to content myself with having my brothers come to dinner more often, to hear their voices and feel the brush of beard on my cheeks.

We five females made our way through the light-falling snow the quarter mile or so, up toward the Keils' and then through the trees to the Park House. We reminded one another to carry our lanterns high. My hair still felt wet as we walked, and I wondered what would happen if I cut it short so it could dry overnight in the winter. That would raise some eyebrows. It probably wasn't worth the upset it would cause, though I noticed any number of girls and women now wore their hair straight back, or with braids at the sides and not just parted down the center. There'd been clicking of tongues when I'd first changed my hairstyle to pin my braids in circles above my ears. As a young wife, I'd found it amusing to introduce such an insignificant onion into the colony stew.

Christine got asked to dance almost as soon as we came through the door. My parents had come that evening, and as I greeted them, I saw that Louisa and Johanna were there too. While I feared it might happen, Louisa never had one quaking episode. Like Christine, she was asked to dance and did so, despite Johanna's frown when her sister took the gentleman's hand and began gliding around the floor. I looked around for Andrew and Christian. Both boys were standing with others, the Ehlen children and a Will boy. I watched my older son move over toward Rosina Stauffer, who had Jacob and Matilda's baby in her arms. He peered into the blanket, looked up at the baby's aunt, and said something that made her laugh. He'd been there for the delivery. He'd had to witness death and life within the same scene at such an early age. It was part of a doctor's life, I supposed, and Andrew had come to it early. His interest in medicine would stick. Martin had nurtured it well.

I took a cup of hot cider. Martin Giesy talked quietly with Martha Miller. Did I see something pass between them? No one had asked me to dance, and that suited me fine. I was one of the ineligible women who wasn't interested in romantic love and assumed I never would be again. I'd had my one great love. Family and friendship warmed me now. Karl might say it was *philos* love, the word the Greeks used to describe friendship and sisterhood. Once, I felt isolated even in the midst of a crowd, but not now. Perhaps taking in this kind of love was necessary to work our way through that bewilderment of living, the uncertainties of seeking through murky water. One needed time to mend and stitch together a life that gathered friendships and that other kind of Greek love, *agape,* a selfless love where one gives without expecting anything in return. A spiritual love. A mother's love.

"Would you care to dance?" It was my father.

"It's a *Schottische,*" I said. "We need three."

"I've already cornered Andy," my father said, motioning for my older son to join us. *He still calls him as a child, 'Andy' instead of 'Andrew.' Maybe a mother can call him that but still let him grow into a young man too.* I took a deep breath. "And Christian's been commandeered by his sisters. Ida's been dogging him all evening, so we Wagners will take the floor together."

We wove our way through the hops and skips and arm circles while the band played the slow waltz tune. It had been years since I'd danced with my father...maybe at my wedding. Yes, we might have danced on that day. I smiled. And here was Andy on my other arm. He grinned. My mother and sisters clapped their hands in rhythm, and then William had our mother on one arm and Johanna on the other.

What I needed was a way to continue the dance of my life, to take small steps that would keep me light on my feet and moving forward into meaning. Maybe whatever new spirit Christine had returned with I could discover without having to go through more misery to find it. I could still offer my home to the homeless. I could weave and make quilts, make peppermint candies and sell them, form shelves out of scrap wood. My appliqués held promise. I cooked and served at the hotel. I could wash my girls' hair, scent it with the finest herbs I could find, and give them and my mother and sisters time and the benefit of my experience, such as it was.

My father and Andy swung me around. I sensed there was something more to do in my life, a new kind of yearning. I didn't know what it was. For this evening at least, I'd live with that not knowing, trusting that like most emotions, it would not last forever.

Christmas celebrations came and went. I always thought of Jack at those times, wondering if he'd travel to Aurora. He hadn't. The girls at least had stopped asking if he'd be coming. Kate remembered him vaguely. When I saw the boys, neither mentioned their stepfather. I had a kind of settledness about Jack that took little from me now.

The new year arrived to firecrackers, and in March, the Keil birthday celebrations took our time. I turned my almanac to a new year of my life and read with interest in the *Oregonian* that a woman, Fannie Case, planned to climb Mount Hood. The summer moved to its usual rhythm, and in August, Karl told me there was another article that said Fannie Case had done it, had climbed Mount Hood.

"She's a music teacher," Karl told me. "Climbing that big mountain." He shook his head in amazement. We stood outside the schoolhouse. "I wonder what made her want to do that?"

"The adventure of it," I said. "Being in front."

"*Ja.* I know some women who like being first," he said with teasing in his voice.

"Now that I think of it, I bet there were Indian women who climbed it before she did," I suggested. "We always forget about their firsts. I'll ask the woman who brings us huckleberries and salmon to find out what the real story is."

"You were the first woman to come west for our colony," Karl said.

"*Ja,* no matter what happens, I will always have that."

On Christmas morning 1868, it came to me, my new *Sehnsucht.* I suspect it was the aroma of baked bread and the goose dressing and the pies I'd had in the oven since well before sunrise. Or it might have been Kate's words, interrupting my humming as I worked.

"Mama." Kate put her arms around me while I bent to the oven.

She was nearly thirteen and already as tall as I. "I will always remember you best in the kitchen."

"Will you? Why's that?"

"Because food mends everything, before I even know I need a stitch to tie me up."

I laughed. "Food and sewing. You've put those together in a funny way." I turned to hold her to me, brushed the hair from her braid, tucking the loose strands back in. Her nightdress smelled of lavender, a scent I'd put into the soap. Her body was changing into a young woman's.

"Not sewing, Mama. Doing what Andy's going to do. Mending people. That's what you do too."

"Do I?"

She nodded. "Almira's hands were better when she left because of that cream you gave to her."

"Uncle Martin mixed that up for her," I said.

"But you asked him to do it. And Aunt Christine looked so different when she came back. Her eyes sparkle more. You did that for her, didn't you, Mama? I saw you had a present for her when she left. It had magic in it. Foooood," she said lengthening the middle of the word as though it was a song.

"It wasn't food, though."

"No? But food is best." She grinned and motioned by lifting her eyebrows toward a cinnamon cake cooling on the table. "People who cook are good menders," she said. "And people who clean are good workers. We need both, right, Mama? I'm a cleaner."

That much was true. When she was younger, she'd lose things; but since we'd been here in Aurora, she was the tidier of my two. Her eyes lifted to the cinnamon cake.

"*Ja, ja.* You can have a slice, but just one. We save it for the gathering. We're going to your *Oma* and *Opa's* today. We need enough for Auntie Louisa and Johanna and William and Jonathan—"

"They're not aunties! Not William and Jonathan," Ida said, coming into the room.

"No, they aren't. I meant we must save enough for everyone to have a taste."

"So they'll come back for more?"

"*Ja,*" I said. "Satisfaction is only for a time. People always want more."

I hugged her to me, gathered Ida up too. It was human nature to always want more. But it was also part of who we were, to desire being filled up, to be satisfied. People did that in different ways. I felt full when I walked the paths in prayer, when I painted, or when I cut those strips of fabric and formed them into shapes. Music filled me. Dancing gave me delight. But I felt most satisfied when I could listen to the stories people told me while I fed them, stories of their everyday but also of their hopes and dreams of someday. Even if I couldn't fix what it was they wished for—I thought of Brita—I could always listen and I could serve sprinkling words of hope, like cinnamon, to bring out the flavor.

That was my yearning, I decided, that seasoning I needed. And I thought I knew now what to do to achieve the sweetness that is promised in the proverb about desire. I just had to get Keil to agree.

25

Restored to a Former State

December 31. Today we prepared to celebrate the new year. My young Christian brought a goose for me to stuff. Mr. Ehlen took him to the river, and they brought the large fowl back through the heavier-than-usual snowfall. Imported turkeys sell for thirty dollars each in Portland, so he might have made good money selling rather than giving the bird away. I invited him and his brother to eat with us on the first of the new year, but they chose to eat with the Ehlens, and I could understand why. Teaching a boy to hunt was nothing I could do, and neither could Martin. So Mr. Ehlen filled that order with aplomb. Kate said she wished to visit her brothers and so headed there after our meal. But it might be more her interest in a certain Ehlen boy, Lorenz, that drew her early from our table.

At the house church gathering in January 1869, I posed my idea. "What if the colony built a restaurant at the fairgrounds?" I suggested. "We have a dance hall, and that earns a fair penny. We have a hotel here that people love to come to, to eat our food, and the stage always stops for a meal. Why not build a place where people can sit and eat and enjoy a little rest while they're at the fair?"

"Build another building? *Ach*," Helena said. "Already people write back to Bethel that they're hardly in Aurora, they're off doing band performances or building somewhere else. The crops need tending. We are farmers first here, and have always been. It worries me how we get so extended and distracted from our purposes."

"How do you know people are writing letters of complaint?" Louisa asked her.

"Andrew, my brother back in Bethel, tells me. He says the Bauer boys are not happy here. He notes a number of confusions about land issues, both in Bethel and Aurora, and people don't like that kind of bewilderment. This is a religious colony. That should be our foundation. Not all these other money ventures."

Louisa's face looked blotchy and red. "The things my husband proposes help us pay for things we need here, so we can give to one another, Helena. I know you meant no criticism, but these ventures, as you call them, help us keep this a Christian community, able to meet the needs of so many. It helps pay for things like…church bells, among other things," she said. "We couldn't make a trade for those. We had to have cash."

"*Ja, ja.* So you say."

It sounded to me as though they'd had this conversation before.

"What would you serve there, Emma?" BW asked. "Everything we serve at the hotel?"

"Party foods," I said. " 'Restaurant' is a French word that means to 'restore to a former state.' We'd return people to a satisfied state. It means providing food for someone too, of course. But people come to the fair and want to be restored, to find something to distract them from their troubles or give them a way to walk through them in the weeks ahead."

"The way art can restore," Kate said.

"Or how our stitching restores us," Martha Miller said.

They were moving from the fair. I brought them back. "Sore feet, late evenings, talking to strangers and friends at length can get their rhythms out of step when they're at the fair. They don't eat as well as they might, so they end up not feeling well and going home early. Maybe not even buying tickets for the concerts or other events. If we gave them a place to sit and served them sumptuous food, they'd be rested. Make them feel special. Food is love, and love is food," I said, as cheerfully as I could. "We can show them that love, and they'll remember where they received it and maybe come to the hotel for more after the fair is over."

"Maybe even join the colony." Louisa sighed.

"That seems presumptuous," Helena said. "I doubt food would bring about conversions."

"But who's to say that feeding people isn't of the highest spiritual work a person can do?" I said it out loud, something I hadn't realized I believed. "It's what women have done since…the Garden of Eden."

"Let's not discuss what happened as a result of that," Helena chided.

"We could have a Fourth of July event with special food we'd serve on that holiday. Or do a Thanksgiving Day at the fair," Kitty said. "Or maybe a German American day with all German foods, nothing else."

"Why not a May Day event in October with a Maypole and everything as we do here?" Kitty said. "We could have a chorus singing while we served."

"That might compete with the band performances," Louisa said. "We wouldn't want that."

"But music while we work, people would love hearing that," I said. "We could roast one of our beef in a large pit, bring our dried fruit, make dishes with all our own produce, and tell people they could purchase such things at the hotel. Not everyone who comes to the fair has even heard of Aurora. This way, they would."

"Several of us would have to stay there the entire time and work," Louisa cautioned. "They've extended the fair time now to more than four days. It wouldn't be much of a respite for the women." She sighed. "I've always enjoyed the fair, making things to exhibit and all. There'd be scant time for that if we had a restaurant to run."

"We could still go to the dances," Christine said. "We could spell each other."

"*Ja,* you like dancing, don't you?" Louisa said. She smiled at Christine as though she were her daughter. "Aurora did too."

"We could display our quilts," Kitty offered. "And tell people about our tailor shop. And our wines."

"For medicinal purposes only," Louisa added, raising a needle to the air.

"Is beer medicinal?" Ida asked. No one answered.

"It might be fun," Martha said. "Your girls could help serve, right, Emma? They'd meet interesting people. Practice their English. And I'd prefer to be doing something other than wandering around looking at exhibits." That last word sang out through a chipped front tooth.

"We might just rival the band," I said, "with people knowing us for how we feed our friends."

"This must not be a competition, Emma," Louisa said.

"Emma doesn't know how to do things any differently than that," Helena said. "Not that competition is a bad thing, you understand. But always being first. It can be troublesome."

They still didn't understand me. I didn't want to be first; I wanted to be remembered for something worthwhile, for something even adventurous at times. Christian had understood me and never tried to take the wild from me. He knew it wasn't meant to be disruptive or arrogant. It was to take in life and savor it fully.

"Everyone should either ring the bells or stand upside down on them," I said and grinned at Kitty. Louisa looked up, confused. "Besides, 'Small cheer and great welcome makes a merry feast.' That's from Shakespeare," I said, hoping to redirect the subject yet again.

" 'Fools make feasts and wise men eat them.' That's what Benjamin Franklin wrote in his almanac," Helena noted.

"I'm willing to be a fool on behalf of the colony and let the wise men eat our dishes. Wise women too. We'll give them a great welcome when they enter our building," I said.

"Don't you think a tent would be sufficient?" Helena said.

"No. A building. As permanent as the dance hall. People could as easily remember Aurora for a fine platter of roasted meat or a delicate cake frosted with cream or even ice cream as they remember Aurora for the band's songs. Our biggest challenge will be finding enough ice on a hot October day. A structure says, 'We're here to stay,' while a tent, well, it can be taken down and forgotten."

"Ice cream makes my mouth water," Kitty said.

"Which is exactly what we want for fairgoers. But we don't want to sell them food only. We want to serve them. To be hospitable, provide what people need without making them feel…well, like they're needy at all. We'll help them rest and take in the benefits of a lovely meal and the music, so they will be filled up. We'll offer our best manners."

Christine stood up to declaim, " 'Being set at the table, scratch not thyself, and take thou heed as much as thou canst not to spit, cough and blow at thy nose; but if it be needful, do it dexterously, without much noise, turning thy face sidelong.' " She giggled and sat down.

"Wherever did you hear that?" Helena asked.

"In an old book about manners and such that Almira read to me."

"She truly was a woman of suspicious experiences," Helena noted. She stuck herself with her needle, moaned a little, then sucked at the puncture.

"Just like Emma used to be," Louisa said. "And she's turned out quite well, I'd say, with our influence."

I didn't wait to let Louisa's goodwill gather moss. "So should we approach the advisors or Brother Keil or—"

"I'll approach Wilhelm," Louisa said. "And let him know that we have a way to bring more people to our hotel. This is for a good cause, Helena. And all it requires is an investment of lumber and effort."

"I might even ask my father if he'll donate some of the boards," I said.

"*Gut.* That would be *gut,* Emma. The more people we involve in this, the better. But let me smooth the way with my husband first."

"*Ja,* you'll need to grease this well," Helena said.

"And while you're talking to him, Helena and Kitty and I will do our rounds with the advisors," I said. "We combined the male and female chorus that way."

"That was Wilhelm's idea, I thought," Louisa said.

"*Ja*. It was, but we women know how to grease things," Helena said. "After all that time in the kitchen, it's something we know how to do."

I tried not to get my hopes up too high. Wilhelm could still be unpredictable. BW hadn't disagreed with any of our discussion, so if Wilhelm did, there was always another door we could go through to John or the advisory council. A mixed chorus required little investment; a building did. So far, buildings had been built only at Wilhelm's behest.

I wondered about Louisa's ability to make her case with Keil. But she was his partner, at least as much as Keil would let her be. She had entertained Ben Holladay, the railroad mogul, so she must support the plan for the hotel to become a train stop one day. And her words had silenced Helena on the matter and given support to the restaurant idea. But this idea came from a woman, and that could make it suspect in Keil's mind. We'd just have to wait and see.

When we gathered next around the quilt frame—we were completing one for Elizabeth, John and BW's daughter, to put into her dowry (we'd be stitching one for my Kate next)—Louisa brought good news. Wilhelm loved the idea of a restaurant at the fairgrounds. He knew the ropes he had to pull to get permission to build, and he'd try to keep the colony as the only business offering full meals there. He had an idea of design, or so he told Louisa, but we all knew what it would be: a rectangle with a fireplace at one end and perhaps a good cooking stove, if we insisted. It would be furnished with rectangular tables with benches, so people could sit with friends but also might slide down to make room for strangers. We'd paint everything blue, all the benches and the tables.

Keil's only reservation, according to Louisa, was that we women would have to spend our entire time at the fair working. "He didn't think that was, well, fair. He wants meals to be available at all hours, but that means constant duty for us."

"He didn't think our working all the time was equitable?" Kitty asked. "But we work here all the time. Why would he care about our doing so in Salem?"

"Maybe he didn't want others to think poorly of our men," Martha said, "letting us cook at all hours like that. Maybe he wants some men to cook?"

"Most men don't cook a thing," Christine said. "Maybe when they're out hunting, but we're always packing things up for the bachelors to take, so they don't have to do much about feeding themselves."

"Fairgoers wouldn't expect to see men cooking. They wouldn't trust it," Helena said.

"The great chefs of the world are all men," I said. "My uncle in France writes of exquisite dishes, and once he even asked my father to send him a barrel of buffalo tongues he planned to prepare."

"Did Papa do that?" Kitty asked.

"I don't think so. It wouldn't be an easy order to fill. We won't have it on our menu since we won't have a fancy chef to prepare it," I said and laughed.

"Well, you see. Men can cook, if they get the recognition for it," Louisa said.

"It's the everyday preparation that they shy away from, the things we have to do constantly, deciding the night before what we'll have to eat for the next day, based on what we know is in the larder. Men don't have to think that far ahead. I bet those French chefs have women underlings to do their dicing and chopping and shopping the markets for them," Christine chimed in.

I thought of Kate's comment about everyday feasts and how it was fine women's work.

"My Wilhelm has been meeting with Ben Holladay. He took over the contract for the railroad development last year, and..." Louisa hesitated, perhaps because she wasn't sure whether we knew of this transaction, but everyone already did. It was the talk of the colony. "My husband sold him a strip of land, right through the middle of Aurora, to bring the rail line south."

"How ironic," Helena said. She continued to stitch as she talked. "We leave Bethel because the railroad comes so close it might contaminate our young people, and now we'll have the railroad in our own backyard."

"We don't have that many young people to contaminate," Kitty said, "because we don't have many weddings."

I saw Martha cover a smile behind a cough.

"Wilhelm only wants the best for us," Louisa defended. "Mr. Holladay has invited the colony band to go on tour. He'll send them up to the Puget Sound area, where you were married to Jack Giesy, Emma. Wasn't it up there somewhere?" I nodded as she continued, glad Ida wasn't here. "Then they'll cross the country on the train, and he'll pay them five hundred dollars for their concerts and pay all their expenses while they're gone."

"No one's going to pay for replacing their work here, though," Helena said.

"I wish I could go on an excursion like that," Kitty said, her voice dreamy.

"Not even the Pie and Beer Band will be going," Louisa said. "The tour will bring in money for many things the colony needs, things we can't trade for, and it will publicize the railroad and our hotel. And there's no reason why we can't announce as they tour that we'll have our restaurant at the fair. Despite the fact that Mr. Holladay is paying them good money, my Wilhelm is willing to allow this, to build a building that will be the first restaurant at the Oregon State Fair. As you suggested, Emma."

"You didn't tell him it was my idea, did you?"

She blushed. "*Nein*. I let him think it was mine."

There was a time when I'd have been annoyed by Louisa's admission, but this time I thought she'd done the wisest thing.

———◆———

It was the talk of Aurora as spring grew near. The colony men were selected to build, and the material was hauled in large wagons over the road to Salem. Meanwhile, the contingent of musicians went off on their tour, and those of us left behind assumed additional responsibilities. We planted seed potatoes, including those I'd kept in my basement, far away from Opal. I'd heard that several goats over by Needy had eaten raw potatoes, and all had died. So had some pigs.

"Potatoes have got to be cooked if they're to be fed to animals," my mother told me when I visited and reported the Needy livestock deaths. She had a number of what Americans called old wives' tales about things related to food. She was frequently right. I vowed to listen to her more.

My father had donated money for lumber for the restaurant building, and in return, Wilhelm said he'd put a sign up saying, "Contributed in part by Wagner and Heirs."

"I like it that you didn't tell Keil to say 'Wagner and Sons,'" I told my father. I still stopped by their small home nearly every day, if only for a moment. It surprised me how much we had to talk about when I saw my family often, instead of the occasional crossing of paths near the park. I could ask about my sisters' samplers or about the tree they'd planted that didn't seem to want to grow. It was a lesson to me, that the frequency of interactions might carry as much weight as their length. Despite my discomfort in seeing my sons at Martin's, it was what I needed to do with them too, to make my presence known regularly so they wouldn't forget who I was. Perhaps it was already too late, but I'd at least see if more regular contact tied us together with a stronger thread.

"Well, I have more than one son and more than one daughter, and whatever is left after I die will go to all of you."

"To your daughters too?" I asked.

"And your mother, of course," my father continued. "If it's in the will that way, the law can't take it from you." A puff of smoke lifted up from his corncob pipe, and I coughed.

I cleared my throat. "But most would say, 'and Sons,' rather than include their daughters as heirs. Thank you, Papa."

"I've disagreed with the lot of you at one time or another," he said. "But you're still all my heirs."

I coughed again and felt the closeness of the bodies in the room, the clutter and lack of places to take in a deep, filling-up breath. Kate's tidying up our house took on new importance as I reflected on how well organized our space was. Clearly, we had room for them all.

"Have you given any more thought to perhaps moving into my house?" I asked. "I could spell Johanna and Mother too. We'd all be there as one family, and there's more room there than here. I'm a good cook."

"Bragging doesn't become you," my mother said. "Humility, Emma. Remember. Not so self-centered."

"It isn't bragging to state a simple truth," I said. "I do cook well. And you sew well. And Johanna takes care of Louisa well, and she's a fine dancer. William raises fine crops of flowers. I wish my geraniums had such blooms. And so it goes. We don't have to discount our talents, do we? That isn't humility."

"I can tell you William's flower secrets," my mother said.

"Humility is knowing where your talents come from," Johanna said.

"And I do," I told my sister. "I may have had some crossed paths a while back. I may even have gone astray for a time, but I do know where my strength comes from, my imagination, even my—"

"Wildness?" my mother said. She grinned, though.

"High spirit," I corrected. I also knew that it was part of who I was, to take a few steps back before I could go forward; that I hadn't always honored the pearls of wisdom that had come into my life, nor known how to accept them. "Our talents are gifts. I didn't think anyone would want to receive mine, but now I know that demeans the One who gave them to me. It takes the meaning right out of them."

Johanna said, "Though that wasn't what we were talking about."

"You had invited us to come live with you. Again," my mother said.

"But we'll decline again," my father told me.

"I like how we're all mushed in together in this house. It's…cozy," my mother said.

"Not that we don't appreciate the offer," my father continued. "But your house is still owned by the colony, and that means at any time, well, changes could be made."

"Change comes anyway," I said.

"I'll stick with Martin's way," my father said. I must have looked confused. "He's been paying for that apothecary shop himself. Out of what he's earned, helping people who weren't colonists but who needed care."

"Martin owns the building?"

"He does. And I suspect it's because he didn't want to be surprised by anything that Wilhelm might decide. He intends to have his practice there, and I'm sure he didn't want Wilhelm intruding."

"He never said…"

"What happened to you made a change in Martin's life, in more ways than having two boys around to raise. Help raise," he added. My face must have asked for that distinction. "He's done well by your sons, but I think he wishes you were more in their lives, even though he knows it must be hard for you to see them there with him. He wanted that education, but somehow he got caught up in your life with your boys too."

I hadn't thought that Martin might have felt like a pawn of sorts, who'd had to decide, like me, whether to argue with the powers that were or make the best of it, hoping I would make the best of it too.

And I had.

It wasn't the best arrangement for raising a family: brothers and sisters separated, the boys not living with their mother. But it was better than when they'd lived with Jack, and it was probably better than our trying to homestead, the way Brita had, and bearing the consequences.

"I didn't think Martin felt I neglected the boys," I said.

"Oh, not neglect so much," my father said. "He knows it must be painful to come by and then have to leave them behind. He understands. But they miss you. They do."

"I should make a greater effort," I said.

"Parents push beyond what is comfortable for themselves, in order to provide for their children. It's what's required," my father said.

"*Ja*, and my sons are a part of the Wagner and Heirs, and I don't want them to forget that either."

———————

I'd thought Wilhelm would go along on the band tour, since he'd composed several of their pieces, but Henry C conducted while Wilhelm supervised the building of the restaurant. The band members would have many stories to share when they returned, which was supposed to happen in September, so they'd have a few weeks to rest up before their scheduled return to the fair.

I'd decided to put my newfound plan for more frequent visits to my sons into practice, so one day in late September, I made my way to the apothecary. Po trotted along behind Ida and me. Kate was at the Ehlens', helping the girls, she'd told me. Po rubbed his nose at the back of my knees.

I hoped to see Martin as well and ask him about his owning his own building. I could always use that as the reason I was there, if my sons appeared standoffish. I had to overcome those distances to stay in their lives, though I could see how disappearing could be easier than facing the uncertainty of what each new encounter might bring. I took a deep breath. I was doing a good thing, a mothering thing.

I had Ida in hand. We found Andy playing the clarinet.

"Are you rehearsing for the Pie and Beer Band?" He shook his head, with the instrument mouthpiece clamped between his teeth. "Well, maybe next year," I said.

He didn't say anything, didn't release the instrument.

"Play something," Ida said.

He ran a scale. His eyes smiled at her, but he still didn't say anything to her. She told him it sounded nice, and he played a tune that might have accompanied a round. Silence filled the room when he stopped.

I couldn't stand that silence. It was like a bell that clanged 'poor mothering,' ringing to the village. "Is Martin here?" He shook his head again. "Can *you* talk with me?"

He took the mouthpiece out of his mouth, ran his hand through his blunt-cut hair. He was getting too old to have such a boy's cut. "If you want to have me cut your hair sometime, I will," I said. "Into a man's cut. You're a young man now. Both you and Christian."

He lowered his head. "Martin cuts it. He said his mother used to cut his, so he does it pretty much the same way for us. Sometimes Martha Miller comes by, and she cuts it too. It's all right."

"Martha? Oh, well, that's nice. But I can cut hair for all three of you. Would you like me to do yours now? I'll go home and get my scissors."

"Nope," he said. He used the word the way Lorenz Ehlen did, popping the *p*. "But you can come back tonight. Martin will be here then, and so will Christian. I really need to practice now."

"I'd like to sit and listen if that's all right. Ida won't be a bother. And look, Po is already asleep at your feet."

"It makes me nervous for people to listen," he said. He bent to pat the dog's head.

"But when you perform, you let people watch you," I said. "You're quite talented, I can tell."

"Goethe says that our talents are 'formed in stillness; a character in the world's torrent.'"

I brushed the hair from his eyes. He didn't flinch away.

"I've had plenty of torrent," he said. "Besides, I like my time alone. As you do, Mama."

"Of course," I told him. "We'll give you what you're used to, then." I picked up offense, where perhaps none was intended, but I couldn't stop it. I still had so much to learn. I took Ida's hand, whistled to the dog, and left, carrying offense with me.

I wasn't sure what had annoyed me so. Maybe the mention of Martha's cutting his hair, but I didn't know why it should. Maybe there'd always be this space between my son and me in the musical score of our lives. Maybe harmonious chords would never follow, no matter how I set myself to make it happen.

26

A Swept Porch

While I was outside checking on my chickens, Andy came out through the back door, breathing hard. "You need to come," he said. "It's *Opa*. Something's wrong with him. Martin's out helping someone else." He caught his breath, and I grabbed my shawl. "I'll let Kate know to stay and look after her sister."

Andy and I fast-walked down the main street, passed by the hotel, and nearly ran down the grassy slope to the mill site where my parents lived. In the distance the sulfur steam rose off the hot springs on the property, giving the site an eerie look in the afternoon dusk. Andy said Jonathan had come for Martin, then ridden on, while Andy headed to my house. "He said to get you. He'd try to find Dr. Keil if he couldn't locate Martin."

"They're still at the fair, building," I said. "Have you seen your *Opa* yet?"

He shook his head that he hadn't. "But Jonathan says he wanders in the room. He doesn't talk. His eyes look like he sees far in the distance but can't focus when you say his name."

"Not at all like *Opa*, is it?" I said. *He's too young to be dying.*

"Will he drink tea?" I asked my mother when we came through the door. I didn't need but a cursory look at my father to know that something was very wrong. Jonathan had given a good description, though he'd left out that haunted look of confusion that framed my father's face. His skin felt strange to the touch too, clammy but not feverish.

"I don't know," she said. "I don't know." She clasped her hands together. My mother had midwifed and helped mend any number of people and was always a calm presence. But things changed when the person needing mending was someone you loved.

I gave directions to my sisters to heat water for tea. To Andy I said, "See if there are sunflower seeds anywhere around. Grind them up and we'll try to get him to take them."

My father looked disgusted when I asked him questions and brushed his hands at me as though I intruded. William, my youngest brother, stood off to the side, chewing on his cuticle. "Go out to the hot spring," I directed. "Bring in a bucket of the sulfur water." He dashed out without questioning me, grateful, apparently, to have something to do.

"What'll you do with that water?" Andy asked. "It smells terrible."

"It will help purify the blood," I said. "That's what he needs. Mama, do you have potatoes here, raw?" She nodded, so I set her and Johanna to peeling several. William returned, and I told him to bring in the apple press. "Leave a good half inch of potato on the peels," I said. "Get a carrot; do you have raw carrots?" With the peels in a pile, I told them to squeeze them in the apple press and then pour boiling water over them. "As soon as it's cooled enough, we'll try to get him to drink it."

Raw potatoes could kill a goat, but their juice, I knew, could help clear the mind of a bewildered person. My mother had told me that once, long ago. She'd just forgotten it in her distress.

"You'd think I'd remember that," she said as she watched.

"Our minds don't always think too clearly when there's a catastrophe looming. Not that this is," I added quickly, to her widening eyes.

Andy coaxed my father into drinking both the sulfur water and then the potato juice. He resisted the sunflower seeds, but when Andy ground them with the pestle and put the paste onto his grandfather's lip, he licked it.

"What'll I do now?" my mother asked, as she patted his hand. My father had sat down at last. He looked from left to right, a wild animal fear in his eyes.

"Do what you're doing, Mama," I said. "Talk softly. About everyday things."

"He picked up an armful of wood to bring in for the fire. We don't even need a fire yet at night, though he's always so cold. The fire nearly sweats us out of here in an evening, even when a cooling breeze shows up. I couldn't talk him out of it. So he went out. William said he'd do it, but you know your father. He had to do it himself. You must get that independent streak from him, Emma," my mother said.

I opened my mouth to speak but thought better of it.

"And then he dropped them on the floor, just let the kindling roll out there. I said to him, 'Mr. Wagner, what are you doing?' and he looked at me like I was some sort of idiot. That's when I saw his face. But he wouldn't settle down, he kept moving about, stumbling over the kindling until we got it picked up."

Martin arrived with Jonathan then. The trained physician knelt in front of my father, and I saw in him the kind man who had once sent me healing herbs to help my ailing son, the compassionate man who had brought my sons to me before he took them as his own to raise. No, before he *accepted* them as his own to raise.

"The side of his face," Martin said. "Did you notice?" I had. Andy nodded. "I think he's had a kind of stroke," he said, as much to Andy as to me. "The left side seems affected."

"He drank some of the sulfur water, in the tea. And the potato and carrot juice," I said. Martin nodded agreement. "Andy got him to take the sunflower-seed paste."

"That was good, the potato juice. It will help the body take in the sulfur. And the mineral water's a good idea too. What made you think of that?"

"I don't know," I said. "I smelled it as we made our way here, and I was saying, 'Help him help him help him,' and then I thought maybe the water would be a healing thing."

"You'll have to cut back on that rich food you feed him, Mrs. Wagner. And maybe we'll hide his pipe too, so you can all get a good breath in," Martin said. He told Jonathan to be in charge of hiding the pipe. "You might hide your own as well," Martin said. "You could be next, making your heart work that hard."

"Why doesn't he talk?" Louisa said. "It looks like he wants to. He moves his mouth like a fish."

No words came out.

"We'll hope his speech comes back. I see it happening at times. But he may not get the use of his arm back," Martin said. "I don't know. We'll have to wait and see. In a few days, we might try lifting that arm. We'll need to keep it moving, so it doesn't atrophy…shrink from lack of use," he explained to Louisa's frown.

He listened to my father's heart, and then he told Andy that he'd mix up some powders and have him bring it back for my father. "I don't think he's in pain, so no laudanum. That's really all we can do for now," he said. "Except if you can get him to drink a little of the sulfur water every day, that might be good. Might help a few others around here too. It never occurred to me. Quite inventive, Emma. But then you always did see things in unique ways, though some of us failed to appreciate it."

I stayed with my parents that evening and waited for Andy to return with the powders. Johanna left us long enough to tell my girls where I was and that I'd spend the night. Before she left she said she'd stay the night with them. I thanked her for letting me be here to tend this tail of my family. Christian, we learned, was staying at the Ehlens'.

The room felt warm with so many people in it, and I wondered why my father had even thought he should build a fire. Perhaps he'd been growing ill for a time, and tonight's load of wood had been the kindling that had set his heart aflame.

I tucked my mother into their bed, assured her I'd stay awake to be with my father should he need anything in the night. He'd fallen asleep in his chair. The breaths of my brothers and sisters eased into the room as they drifted off to sleep. They slept peacefully, and I thought that it was something I could do, give rest to them by simply being there to sit beside the hearth.

Andy came back with the powders Martin sent, and he asked me if I thought my father would die.

"Some day," I said. "But I'm not sure about now. He's breathing easier; I can feel his pulse, and it's steady though weak."

Andy accepted what I said and then sat with his knees open, his hands clasped between them. He didn't look up at me when he spoke. "I'm glad you were home. I guess I should have gone to find Dr. Keil, but I thought you would want to know about *Opa*." I assured him that he'd done the right thing, especially since Jonathan was finding Martin and Keil was off in Salem.

"The sulfur," he said. "What does it do?"

"I'm not sure. But that water is full of minerals. People soak in such hot waters back East. Even the Indians do, I'm told, so it has to be healing."

"That was good, though, thinking of that."

"Thank you," I said. "One day you'll be in school and learning about all kinds of new treatments for people. But you'll bring things from your experiences too, and those can be just as helpful."

"I do want to go to medical school, Mama," he said.

"I know that. And you will. We'll all make sure that can happen. You found the sunflower seeds and got him to eat them. So thank you for that."

"We both did good, then," he said.

I decided not to correct his grammar. I put my arm around him instead and breathed gratitude when he leaned into my chest.

———

In the days that followed, I let my mother know what I was planning. I knew they wouldn't move in with me, but they'd need help now, and I could give it. Our father wasn't going to be able to operate the mill, that was clear.

"Papa could sell the mill property," Jonathan told me. "It would be enough for him to buy land somewhere else, with a house on it. Maybe down by the Willamette. He likes that place, though he's never gotten the owner to agree to sell."

"I looked at property across the Pudding River in Clackamas County," I told him. "When Andy and I were out homestead hunting those years. They might sell. It has a larger house on it now. We could plant the fields. Everyone could work at that together."

"You'd leave your house? Your two-door house?"

"I would. For them. I'd still work for the colony, but Papa's going to need a different way to do things. Will you help me do this? Handle the land sale for him and make the purchase?"

"*Ja.* It's a good idea, Emma."

"If there's not enough with the sale of Papa's land, I have a string of pearls. Mama gave them to me. If we need them…"

"Let's wait and see."

———— ◆ ————

It had happened quickly, as life does. John Giesy bought my father's property. My brother David Jr. returned from Oregon City to help my parents move. He wore a long beard, grown since I'd last seen him months before. I worried some that making such a huge change might delay my father's recovery, but I could tell almost at once that he liked the landscape.

"It's not the river place Jonathan said you liked, Papa, but maybe later we can sell this one and go there. For now, the boys will keep busy planting fields, and Mama will have a good garden, and before long, I'll bring the girls and we'll move in with you. I'll be home each night to see that you're all well. When school starts, the girls will come with me to Aurora each day, so it'll work out. It will."

His vacant eyes brightened, I thought, but I couldn't be sure.

———— ◆ ————

Helena said that Christine did a fine job cooking for the workers at the fair, but she was constantly fending off young men. "That's not anything you'd have to worry over, Emma," Helena added. She chuckled and gave a snort to her laughter.

"*Ja,* we senior women know when we've passed our prime."

Helena nodded and patted my arm, still too engaged with her joke to speak.

We were at my house. Baskets filled with fabric and the many things I planned to move sat like stepping stones around the walls.

"You were serious when you said you'd restore things at home. But what about us?" Christine said. "Will the colony let us continue to live here? This was your house, Emma. Everyone knew that."

"I'll talk with Jonathan," I told her. Then in deference to Louisa's being with us, I added, "He can confer with Brother Keil. I thought I'd covered all the pies, but I guess not."

"But if we can't stay here, where will we meet for our house church?" Kitty asked.

"We can go back to our house," Louisa said. "Though there's been something pleasant about getting out and about. Well, I'm getting older. Maybe staying at home would be just as easy."

"You can come to my house," Martha Miller said. "Mine and Martin's." She cleared her throat. "We're getting married in September."

———◆———

When Christine and I were alone again, churning butter at the new hotel, I told her how the house had felt so empty with everyone gone at the fair. The girls found friends to be with, and I'd been the only one rattling around in the house until Andy's fateful knock on the door telling me of our father's illness.

"I thought maybe you'd use the time to paint while we were gone, not move away."

"I walked the path. And visited my sons. And took the girls on a picnic. They were troubled I hadn't gone along to help cook so they could go too."

"The burdens of life fall unfairly," Christine said, and she laughed.

I told her I'd sat out under the stars with the girls; we'd checked the hams hanging in the smokehouse. I'd showed them how to make a special knot on the sampler I'd drawn for them, and Kate made progress on hers, stitching in bright colors, "Not a house, but shelter." "I'll sign it 'Catie Giesy,'" she said, a twinkle in her eyes. "That's what Lorenz Ehlen calls me."

I'd gone through my fabrics, hoping Christine would choose what she'd like for a quilt.

"Maybe a Friendship quilt," she said. "But I don't need one for a dowry to attract a future husband."

"Apparently Martha didn't either."

"Kitty might. She so wants to get married."

"It may not happen for her. Sometimes it doesn't, and it's better than making a bad marriage, just to say you could," I said.

"Are you...saddened by Martin's marriage?"

"Why would I be sad? I'm still married," I said.

"I know. But I guess I always thought that you and Martin, well, he's been such a part of the boys' lives."

"And continues to be. It might actually be better for them, having a woman around all the time. Even if it isn't me."

"We share that in a way, don't we? Giving up our children for their benefit."

"I still need to have a conversation with Martin about it." He was caught up in this web too, as I was. But we had our own parts in the stretching of it.

"I've decided to return to the Keils' to live," Christine said. "It'll be easier staying there than coming in from so far out in Clackamas where you'll be. I don't like riding horses much, and you'll need to from there. But Kitty told me she'll move in with you all, if that's agreeable."

"Of course. Jonathan said he could convince Keil to let you both stay at the house, though."

"It wouldn't be the same without you. That house was what we needed for a time. But now we don't. Someone else can move into it and be happy there. The way we were."

"I guess that's the way I felt about it too. I'll miss it...but it was just a house." *I can't believe I said that.* "So tell me about Kitty, when you were building at the fair. Did she have a good time?"

Christine told me that our sister was witty and warm as she spoke to fairgoers. Despite not being invited to dance when the band practiced at night, she smiled, tapped time to the music, and chatted with young children who'd been brought along to listen.

"At least she has her choir to keep her occupied," I said. "And she's good with little ones, so it's nice that they had someone to talk with while their parents danced."

We churned awhile more, and then she asked, "Will you ever… divorce and remarry?"

"I've no plans to," I said. "Where would I find a husband who could put up with me?" She laughed with me. "No, I have my sons. I have my daughters. I have my goat and chicken and dog, and I have you all! I have Providence to guide me. What more could I want?"

"I'm glad you're not disappointed about being left behind," Christine said. She stayed silent for a time, and then she told me why it was good I hadn't come along, a reason that had nothing to do with my father and mother's needing me. "This man stopped by," she said. "It was late. He was loud and boisterous and asked for you. Wanted his wife to serve him. I didn't know who he was, but Louisa did, and she tried to calm him. Kitty acted rattled. Has she ever met your husband before?"

I dipped my head yes. "But Kitty holds a fantasy about Jack Giesy. He was someone she thought she fancied, when he was back in Bethel. She hadn't seen him since he'd come west. And I didn't think she believed me about the reason I left him years before. Unfortunately, he still is my husband."

"It was good that you weren't there," Christine repeated.

"If I go next fall, at least I'll know to expect him," I said. The thought didn't frighten me, as it might have once, or keep me from doing what I'd decided.

"Oh, and that little *Zwerg*, your friend Brita asked for you," Christine said.

"How was she?"

"*Gut.* She had her boys with her. She said she'd come to see us here one day soon, but she had work she did now 'year around,' as she put it. I was to tell you that you were right, things always did change, and she could look for the people who'd be around to help. She had, and they did."

"I wish she'd come here," I said. "We have plenty of room. Or we did. I won't be able to be so free with my invitations now, will I? I'll have others to negotiate with."

"That's a family. It ebbs and flows," Christine said. "Maybe next year we'll have more people out from Bethel or new immigrants, people who might need a place of rest for a time. Confederate soldiers heading west, freed slaves. Widows and orphans. They might all show up at your doorstep. It's pretty certain that the railroad is coming through, isn't it? That'll bring visitors."

But I hadn't wanted to just have visitors. I'd wanted my home to be a place to offer an everyday feast, as Kate put it, for those needing mending, as I'd needed it once. That would change now too.

" 'The help of God is closer than the door,' " Christine said. "Brita said that."

"She's apparently swept well in front of her own."

27

Stitching Pieces of a Family

On October 4, 1870, the wood-powered steam engine roared into Aurora with its passenger cars and stopped in front of the hotel. The men had laid a wooden bridge across the track for easier walking, so while the Aurora Band played a welcoming tune, women from the outside lifted the hems of their long skirts and managed their hoops to climb the hotel steps and look back. They waved at the welcoming Aurora crowd.

I stood on the hotel porch, ready to slip back inside and finish serving that first train car full of guests. We had fifteen minutes to deliver this meal and somehow not let the guests feel rushed, while the train hissed and heaved outside the door, waiting for their return. Hospitality had its challenges.

But we accomplished it! Potato salad with warm vinegar, roasted beef, sliced hams cured with sugar, and a large fish that one of the surviving Calapooias had caught that morning were served beside greens plucked from the gardens behind the hotel. Nuts and dried fruits, plumped up with spring water, and mounds of whipped cream that Kitty and others had beat up minutes before the train's arrival, provided the finishing touches to our gastronomical scene. Flowers from my brother's garden made bright bouquets for the table. While we cooked, we sang—those who could carry a tune—and then we sent them satisfied, we hoped, on their way.

We cheered ourselves along with guests who weren't being carted away to Portland by train. Those guests who'd come by buggy or ridden in could be more leisurely in their eating. Back in the kitchen, Kitty began a round, and the rest of us joined in as we scoured pans and opened the back door to let out some of the oven heat.

"Did I tell you," Kitty said at the end of the song, "that the Indian who brought the fish in this morning asked if his girls could take singing lessons here?"

"From Henry C?" I asked.

"From me." Her face turned the softest shade of pink. "He heard me singing. I guess he's heard me before, and he said his daughters wished that they could sing like the White Bird."

"You'll have something to look forward to this winter," I told her.

"Do you think I should ask permission from Brother Keil or maybe Henry C?"

"You're using a talent of yours." I thought again of Goethe, with talent formed in stillness and character in storm. Kitty had had her share of storms too. Not being married when you wished you were was a storm. It might not compare to the loss of children, but it was character-building just the same. Yet she had talents to offer and did. I looped my arm in hers and put my head to her temple. "You're making someone else's life better than your own. Who could argue with that?"

"*Ja*. That's what I'll tell them if they ask."

The fair that year was the biggest ever, and I was called to cook. It was the first of a new decade. Men on stilt legs ambled around as I imagined giraffes must walk, shouting about demonstrations, markets, or products to buy. The horse barns boasted a record number of equines, and the races promised to be close. The Household Arts exhibit was twice as large as before, with dozens of samplers and quilts on display, flowering plants, and preserves lining the shelves like perfect children dressed in pinks and blues. Dr. Keil had his wine there; Mr. Ehlen's tightly woven baskets stood out, and he had several clarinet reeds for sale. Some were purchased by visitors from New York, who said they were of the finest.

Christian had made a basket to enter in the fair. He grabbed my hand to show me as soon as Martin and Martha and the boys arrived.

"It's been a while since you've been to this fair, hasn't it?" I asked him after we'd admired his fine work. We made our way along the grass-beaten paths back to the restaurant. It was after the band's performance, and most of the restaurant patrons had eaten and left. Martin drank his coffee, and Martha sat with her hands clasped in her lap. Her hat shadowed her face in the lantern light. Po lay on the floor by the door, being good by staying outside but not running off whenever another dog sniffed by.

"We came one time when Brita was here," Christian said. "Remember, Andy? We rolled rings and had a kite." My older son nodded, as he swirled a spoon into a coffee drink he'd added sweet cream to. His brother was twelve and could be annoying, I was sure, but Andy treated him with respect. "I like the fair."

"I do too," I told Christian. "Thank you for bringing them along." I nodded to Martin and Martha.

"It's our pleasure," Martin said.

"You know, you could invite them yourself, anytime you want, Emma. And come visit them more often too." Martha still had that sweet, youngish voice of women her age.

"It's an awkward thing, isn't it?" I said, deciding not to step over the discomfort. "I did talk with Brother Keil, and he says the current arrangement is working well, with the boys on track like a steam engine to go on to the university one day. That's what I've always wanted for them. Medical school for you," I said as I turned to Andy. He didn't look at me. "With us living a distance from the colony now, it isn't always easy to work out times to come by."

Kate, Ida, the Ehlen boy, and several others huddled together, walking near the dance hall. They stopped chattering when they saw us sitting in the restaurant with the door wide open. "It's time you settled down," I said. They groaned, their pleasant plans so rudely interrupted. "Lorenz, I thank you for escorting my daughters safely here," I told him.

He clicked his heels and said, "I'm heading to the bachelor tents right now, Mrs. Giesy." Then, along with several other young men who had been with the mixed young people's group, he did.

"You could come visit us anytime," I continued to Andy, telling Martin too. "I would love to have you waking up every day at your grandparent's home, to fix your breakfast, to…cut your hair. But I know that staying where you are, you're of help to people."

"The same way you are," Christian said. "That's what Martha says."

Martha blushed, and I felt my own face grow warm with the compliment.

"I'm helping *Opa* and *Oma, ja.* Maybe Johanna too, so she's not the only one who can look after your aunt Louisa. And I believe I'm helping both of you, because you'll be able to go on to school. And your sisters are getting a good education. The hotel will make money; the money can go to pay your tuition; I work at the hotel; it all comes around. Like that. We're all busy doing."

"Andy is good help to me," Martin said. He patted Martha's hand. It must be difficult for her to take on the raising of boys.

"And you too, Martha, are certainly helping make another's life better than your own. I'm grateful to you," I added.

"Are you? I assumed, well, that you'd be upset. It's why I didn't say anything about our getting married any earlier than I did. I didn't want to have to explain why I wasn't coming to the house church anymore."

"But then you offered your home," I said.

"And you've rarely come."

"I'll make a point of it. Next Sunday."

"Good. We'll see what we see," Martha said. It was a phrase I remembered from my friend Sarah Woodard, back in Willapa.

"Let things flow as they will. *Ja.*"

We heard the scrapes and thumps of the band putting their instruments away in wooden cases. The hawkers at the carnival sites had settled down. Even the dogs had stopped barking.

"I'd like to live with Mama and *Opa* and *Oma,*" Christian said then. He looked at me. My eyes must have shown great surprise. "Uncle Martin?"

Andy stared at his brother, his thoughts, as usual, well hidden.

"I don't know," Martin said. "Maybe you could. You'd have your *Opa's* influence, and things have changed here with Keil. Emma, you no longer occupy the house… He might feel that having one of your boys live with you and your parents is warranted." Martin looked at me. "Would you like me to speak with Wilhelm, Emma?"

"*Ja,*" I said, when I got my voice back. "I'll accept all the help I can get."

A few days later at the end of the fair, we were packing up when Almira came by. She had the children with her, which gave Christine delight. Almira's eyes sparkled as she accepted a child from Almira's daughter-in-law. Christine and Almira shared a one-arm embrace. We welcomed Almira and her daughter-in-law to rest on one of the blue benches we'd brought with us. Kate got the women jugs of water, and we sat for a moment, catching up.

It was then that Jack Giesy sauntered through the grounds. Almira gasped when he stared at us from a distance. My own heart had started to pound. "Do you know that man?" I asked.

She shook her head no. "He looks so much like my former husband," Almira said. "Those brooding eyes, that clenched jaw." She shook her head again. "I'm relieved it isn't him."

"I know him," I said. "That *is* my husband."

He'd aged since I'd seen him last. As he moved closer I saw the lines that drained what had once been a handsome face. He looked worn as old shoe leather. Thinning hair robbed him of some of his height, though when he stood in front of me, I still looked up at him and felt myself step back from the force of him.

He put his hands down on the table in front of us and pushed his chest toward me, his face close. And while my heart pounded, I didn't feel the terror that had once caused me to cower or run. I knew I wasn't alone.

"Is there something I can do for you?" I asked.

"Serve me," he said.

"I'm sorry, but we've closed down for the season."

Po had stood up at the sound of Jack's gruffness, but now he lay back down, and that encouraged me. I had friends and more, an attitude refreshed.

"Aren't you the hospitable one?" He sneered the words, then sat. He leaned back and tossed coins at me. "Brother Keil would object to your turning away good cash," he said. "Figure something out to feed a man. You're good at figuring." A coin spun on the table, the only sound besides my own shortened breathing. "How much hospitality will this coin buy me?"

"More than you deserve," I said. "If you weren't the father of one of my children, I wouldn't give you a cup of water. But then I'd give a poor dog even that."

A dark cloud of disgust shadowed his face, and I knew I'd gone too far. *I still have much to learn.*

Quick as a snake strike, Jack grabbed at my wrist. "You'd compare a Giesy to a dog?"

I pulled back as Ida interrupted. "There's a sausage left, Mama," she said. She came from behind me and handed it to me. "Would the man like it?" *I hope Ida didn't hear me say what I did about his being the father of one of my children!* I wondered if Jack would recognize his daughter. He was in one of his dark moods that could sometimes leave as quickly as a squall passing over the Willapa firs. I prayed that would happen now, but it didn't. Instead, he took the sausage, tossed it on the ground. Po grabbed it and ran off.

Jack swung his arm to signal to someone. "Bastian! Mary! Come see your rel-a-tive Emma—my dear wife." He dragged the words to remind me of my status.

I hadn't seen Mary and Sebastian Giesy since the day they left Aurora after bringing me the rocker that matched Jack's. And leaving me that Compass quilt. *Compass. I know the direction I'm going now.* I hadn't known they were even at the fair. Mary had probably kept Jack away, hoping to spare me of this.

"Look what I've found here," Jack shouted.

"Let's go, Jack," Sebastian said. He stood nearly as tall as Jack, and he held Jack's arm, attempting to turn him from the small crowd growing around us. "No need to make a fuss."

"Make a fuss? The way you make fusses?" Jack said. He pushed at Sebastian.

"Sebastian, let's go," Mary pleaded.

"Women should be seen and not heard," Jack shouted at her, choosing to confront a woman's pleas as opposed to Sebastian's. Jack swayed. *He must have been drinking.*

Mary pulled on Sebastian's suit coat. "Let's just go. Please."

It all happened so fast! Sebastian pushed her out of the way, not in protection but with the familiarity of force, and Mary stumbled, her hooped skirts catching on the side of the table. Her straw hat was askew, and the reticule she carried at her wrist had tightened with obvious pain above her glove. I caught her before she fell, and she gave me a look. I saw in her eyes understanding mixed with my own former fears.

It has happened to her. I'd never known. We'd kept the secrets all those years ago in Willapa, and in so doing I'd disintegrated, the way caustic chemicals tender the finest cloth.

"Mary," I whispered as I held her arm, untwisted her purse. "I didn't know. We could have helped each—"

"Feed me, Wife!" Jack shouted over Sebastian's shoulder as he was being pushed away.

Andy intervened then.

"Jack, we'll get you something to eat," he said. "Won't we, Mama?" His voice was calm and assured. He didn't try to touch Jack, and while my son was nearly as tall as his stepfather, he stood sideways to him, nothing to intimidate, a young man using his wisdom as strength.

Jack shook off Sebastian's arm. He straightened. "About time someone maybe could pay attention to what I need," Jack said to the crowd.

My son was right: Feed the man what he asked for. Don't challenge him straight on. Let him save face and move on.

"I'll help you," Mary said. She moved with me to the wagon.

Beyond earshot I said to her, "You don't need to put up with—"

"No, no, Emma. It's all right. I'll be all right. It's only happened once. Really. Jack urged Sebastian on one time. But Jack will settle down. I was afraid this would happen. It's why I didn't want Sebastian to come by the restaurant. I thought Jack might recognize Ida or be angry if he saw you happy. Boshie wouldn't have pushed at me except that he knew I'd been right to try to keep Jack away."

"My fears have always been for Andy," I said. "That he and Jack would—"

"He did good, Emma. You did good to take him away years ago, give him tools to deal with such men. He's a good man, a good Giesy, your son. So is my Sebastian. My husband doesn't..." Her eyes dropped to the bread she cut. The knife shook in her hands. "I'm safe there; truly, I am."

"If you ever aren't, don't do what I did. Ask for help before it's too late. You have a place to call home. In Aurora."

We served the cold potato salad and big slices of bread with Aurora pear butter to my husband. He ate in haste while he and Andy spoke of the weather and crops as though they'd often talked of such men things. Then he succumbed to Sebastian's encouragement, and the three of them left. Mary turned back to me and mouthed the words, *I'll remember.* I prayed that she would.

"That's my father, isn't it?" Ida asked. "I knew he was your husband, Mama. I just didn't know that he... You said he was the father of one of your children. It has to be me."

"He is," I said. "And there was a time when he wasn't as he is now. His behavior is no reflection on you, Ida."

"Why didn't you tell me?"

"I didn't know how. I didn't know how to say that I'd made such a mistake once. All I knew and know is that you're the best thing that ever happened between us. A gift I didn't deserve."

"Will you tell me about him?"

"As you wish," I said. I held her to me. I'd have to face those times, but I could be hopeful now about the stories of strength I could tell. "You had many fathers who cared for you in Aurora, Ida. Just remember that. And a sister and brothers, too, who showed great love for you." I rocked her in my arms and looked at Andy.

"You did well, Andy," I said. "So well." I wanted to take my son in my arms and hug him, but I didn't want to risk his rejection, and my arms were full. "I'm so proud of you. Jack's a sad man, but he's no threat to us now. I almost challenged him into something unnecessary, bringing out his worst traits. You brought out his best, helping him calm down and go away again in calm."

Andy nodded. I thought he might have moved just a little closer to me. I released Ida, holding her with one arm, then put the other around Andy's shoulder and patted the striped shirt he wore. He let me.

"There are always safe ways through the wilderness, *ja*? I kissed Ida's head, leaned into Andy. "Your mother just needs to keep learning the paths."

28

Life Exhibits

March 26, 1871. Yet another year passes. My hair is graying just as Po's is, at the edges. Karl brought by my annual almanac. "And step by step, along the path of life, there's nothing true but Heaven," Goethe wrote. Like the old friends we are, Karl and I sat and talked of promising students he had, my son being one. He smoked his pipe while I stitched. My older son will be eighteen this year; Kate, Catie, my beautiful older daughter, has turned sixteen. My two youngest fill me with delight. The dreams I had to raise my family are coming true, though not as I had planned.

At Easter, we gathered together to etch eggs. My Clara, the Araucana chicken, laid three blue ones and one olive green egg, whose colors made the perfect backdrop for our etchings. I loved making these sculpture paintings, and while no one outside our family would probably be interested in them, I did consider entering them at the fair this coming fall. That's what I was thinking about, more than "the plan," which my brothers and sisters and mother hadn't mentioned for some weeks, knowing plans take time to implement. I carried a basket of eggs from the chicken coop to my parents' house. In Aurora, I knew that the apple trees were in bloom at Henry C's orchard; the millrace water rushed pleasantly. Building continued but things were calm there, the pause before spring squalls blew through.

At my parents' home, I saw progress too. My father was talking again, though with a slight slur to his speech. His mind was good, and when we failed to understand him quickly enough, he'd write his thoughts down. He directed my brothers in their work, using his one arm mostly.

We sat at my parents' blue table, each of us lost to our thoughts as we etched. Jonathan had found a buyer for my pearls. I kept back the one small one from Willapa Bay that Christian had given me, but the remainder had been a gift from my mother. She'd agreed to the sale; even though it was now my gift to give away, I wanted her approval. With the cash, we'd add the rooms we needed to the house, pay off the property, and buy seed for our crops. One day my father would deed all to Wagner and Heirs. That was what he wanted.

Oak and fir trees clustered at the edge of the property, and some land had already been cleared and planted in crops. We'd harnessed the spring, so fresh water welcomed, and much of that early demanding work had already been done. We'd made a puzzle path beneath the trees, a place for quiet thought.

We'd carried on from someone else's broken dream, turning it into our own hope. For frosting on the cake, it had a fine view of Mount Hood to the east. We'd all left the Aurora Colony, all except Andy and Christine and Jonathan; yet we were still connected. Even Kitty had decided to come back home to live.

My sisters and I worked at fixing and serving, continuing our commitments to the colony. At our new home, my father sat in the rocking chair that matched Mary's, and when my brothers weren't clearing ground or getting ready to plant crops, they built fences for the chickens.

"Always farmers," my father said. "Stay that way."

Kitty and Christine and I would still work at Aurora, especially now with the railroad bringing in hundreds of guests. We still made our way as a group every other Sunday to the church. We walked past my old two-door house. Someone else lived there now. I didn't miss it, not really. I only missed seeing my son.

———◆———

The fair in the fall of 1871 outdid the previous year's. New performances and a larger carnival brought people out from their simple homesteads and small villages, as well as from cities far away. Some fairgoers still packed their own baskets of food, but many more made their way to our place of restorative meals. I cooked the entire time and found it always brought me joy.

Jack Giesy showed up again. At first I felt that same rush of fear and outrage, but then I remembered Andy's ways with him, and I did the same, not provoking. He could only have power over me if I allowed it. Jack asked for food. I served him. He ate. And when he saw that I still had friends to stand beside me, he left. I was never sure what Jack wanted besides power. I gave him none over me or my children. I rested in the confidence of my community, my family, my God.

Andy had begun classes at Wallamet. Henry T. Finck, that wise-mouthed boy, headed off to Harvard. Both boys had been well prepared by their good teachers Chris Wolff, Henry C, and Karl Ruge. I stopped by to see Andy in his classroom, since I was there at the fair. He turned a shade of radish when he saw me, and I waved, then slipped quickly away. No young man wants his mother hovering while he follows his desire. Even I knew that.

Kate walked hand in hand with Lorenz Ehlen when they thought no one was looking. I could see the two of them marrying one day. I wouldn't allow Keil to interfere, should he consider it. That year, I also saw Brita! She brought me laughter and reminded me that I could bring hope to myself, as well as to those I love.

One welcome change was that Johanna joined the festivities that year without Louisa. Kitty and Christine had remained behind and agreed to help our mother look after her. Johanna surprised us all by participating in the first art classes that Nancy E. Thornton had ever offered at the fair. My sister was quite gifted, but she'd had little time to paint. Now that Kitty and I lived at home and could help, she would.

Ida entered an apple pie and earned a ribbon. Next year she said she'd make a quilt to enter—if I'd help her.

Oh, and I made a drawing of my two youngest children, transferred it to cloth, cut fabric pieces out, and appliquéd them. It did not win a single prize, except in my heart when Christian said, "It's different, Mama. I like especially those bright colored pieces along the edge. They're from a quilt you made me, aren't they? Can I take it with me when I leave your home to go to school? So I'll always have pieces of my family with me?"

Of course I agreed. What more could any mother wish for? What more could any woman want?

———◆———

I visited Wilhelm Keil one day in the spring of 1872. It was a journey I needed to make. I rode through the landscape of colored leaves and crisp air. Even though we no longer had a house in Aurora proper, I knew now I'd never live far from here. Willapa had been my test; Aurora, my new beginning.

Keil looked tired that morning. He wore one of his finely tailored suits, but crumbs from his breakfast biscuit dribbled on his vest. An old pair of slippers covered his feet, and he shuffled them as he made his way to the workroom door, answering my knock. I was a bit winded by climbing up all those stairs, breathless, but not because I feared the man as I had back in Bethel as a young wife begging to convince him, but simply short of breath, as a woman growing older.

"Ah, *Frau* Giesy," he said. "It's been a long time."

"I've been busy at the hotel."

"*Ja.* Louisa keeps me informed, from your little house church gatherings at Martin's." He shook his head. "It offered something inconsequential for you women." He waved his hand as though brushing at flies. "And no harm that we men could see. Otherwise I'd have put a stop to it."

He'd gone from considering our meeting at Martin's house to a previous time, when it was my house church that he must have struggled with, if only for a time.

A part of me wanted to point out to him how many good things had come from our little house church: a safe harbor for abused women, new lives for a young girl's twins and their mother, the beauty of a mixed chorus, a place to grieve the death of a friend and her child, countless quilts and coverlets and baby clothes, not to mention ideas for a restaurant at a fair. In that little house church, lives were comforted and shaped in ways none of us would ever know. But trying to inform him would have distracted me from my mission.

The windows were open, and a breeze moved some of the papers lying on his workroom desk. He turned to the rustle and set down a wide-bottomed bottle to keep them from fluttering. Silently I handed him my gift, my special pork fruitcake, knowing he'd like the salt and lard mixed with fruit. Like Karl, he had aged, and he might welcome those intense tastes that rose from fermenting fruit in flour.

"*Danke,* Emma. Your parents are well?"

I nodded agreement.

"Honoring the mother and father, *ja,* this is *gut,* Emma. But you did not need to move to do this. You could have had them move in with you. Right into your two-front-door house."

"They wanted a place to call their own. Just as Martin has. And others that you've deeded a house to. I didn't think you'd deed my house to me."

This wasn't something I'd intended to bring up, but I thought, *Why not ask?*

"You're right. I would not. If anything, it would need to go to Jack Giesy. You are still married to him."

"This is something I'm likely never to forget," I said. "But what you could do, that would help my family, is deed that house to Jonathan. I'm sure he'd make room for guests, if the hotel overflows. He'd use it for the good of Aurora."

"Jonathan wants to live in your house?"

"I haven't asked him. But it would be good for him to have that assurance. He's worked hard for you through these years."

He took a fork full of the cake, poked into one of the cherry preserves. "*Ja.* This could be arranged," he said at last.

He'll deed it to a man but not a woman. Some things will never change.
"What matters now," I continued, "is that you will honor our original agreement. That's why I've come to see you." He frowned a bit, and I thought he might have actually forgotten it. "That you would educate me and my family in return for my using the house for the good of the colony. Does that still stand?"

"Should it?"

"What more could I do for the colony than what I have?" I said. "I came west with my husband for it; I gave my sons to it, to be raised by someone within the colony who is not their father. Andy lives now with others even though I have room for him in my home, in my life. He'll be a doctor here one day. I've made the colony my second family. I've worked and done what I could to live the Diamond Rule. If you keep your word, you will truly be making my sons' and daughters' lives better than your own. I can die an old woman, knowing I, too, did something to make others' lives better than my own."

"It will be a long time before you are an old woman, Emma Giesy," Keil said. He had a glint in his eye, which I ignored. I waited in silence. He sighed. "A long time before you'll die too, I suspect. Like me, a streak of ornery keeps our blood flowing." He lifted my chin with his fingers, stared into my eyes. "I saw what Chris saw in you, and I thought he should tame you. He never did. You might have been easier to manage if he had." His smile held a tint of sadness. "But you might also then still be there in Willapa with Jack on your hands. You might not have endured. Instead, you are here and you have brought…interest. *Ja.* Fascinating interest to our colony." He sat down stiffly.

I stepped back a pace, reflecting. I understood now some of Keil's own ways in our long struggle. I had more power than I'd thought.

"You have suffered, Sister Emma. I know this too."

I had suffered. Some of it of my own doing; some of the torrent that I hoped built character, deepened my faith. "*Ja,* but suffering is a part of living. Karl Ruge reminds me of the many kindnesses I've received in my life. He quotes a German master who wrote, 'One who suffers for love suffers not and his suffering is fruitful in God's sight.' "

"*Ja,* that is Meister Eckhart. In that, I believe he was right."

He folded his hands on his desk top and sighed. "Ah, Emma, Emma. You did suffer for the love of your sons, but you have been fruitful from it. *Ja,* of course we will do our best to educate your sons, all the way through. Like his father, Christian serves and adds much to Brother Ehlen's life when he visits. Andy shows a singular talent for medicine, for tending others instead of forcing them to certain things."

"Beyond talent, I believe he is a compassionate man," I said. "Maybe his suffering has helped him become that."

"He's been a good match for Martin's work, *ja*? He does well in school?"

"People will choose a hopeful approach to life, if they're allowed," I said, "rather than being pushed into it or, worse, scorned into it."

He stepped over that. "Your girls, too, may go on to school. That's happening more now. Girls going." He picked up his pipe and tapped the tobacco from it, drew on it to make a little whistle sound.

"If they don't marry, they can contribute in other ways, *ja*? We women have our plans."

He didn't seem to notice my slight to his history of marriage restrictions.

"You and your plans. Those fancy chickens," Keil said. "You want to do something more with those, I suppose, on your new farm."

"*Ja.* Chickens and sheep. We Germans are farmers at heart." I sat down.

"Your father's place always had the best flowers," he said.

I laughed. "*Ja.* My mother finally told me how that happens. William carries out the thunder bucket every morning and dilutes it with spring water, then feeds the plants with it."

Keil laughed at that. "I'll start doing the same," he said.

The breeze moved across my face, cooling me. I sat amazed at my calm when once this man had frightened me so. Here we sat talking almost like equals. After all was said and done, in Aurora, I'd found my *Heimat,* what we Germans called the home of our hearts where we put down roots and were free to be as we were created to be. "There is this art class," I continued. "That one I wanted to take years ago. I would sign up again. I'd like you to pay for it."

He raised an eyebrow. "It's always something with you, Emma."

"I'm learning there is always a new desire. It is who we are, we Germans. All of us have dreams, or should have. You did long ago."

He nodded. "I dreamed of a second Eden," he said. "Here in Aurora. Other societies, back East, they dreamed it too, but ours is still here, *ja*? We did something right." He had a faraway look in his eyes.

"Have more cake. Eat your fill," I urged. He took another bite, then laid the fork on the edge of the snow white plate.

"An art class. Taught by a woman, I suppose." I nodded. He lifted his fork, took another bite, then used the fork to point at me. "Well, this I approve," he said. "We colonists are known for our craftsmanship. You're entitled to improve such…talents. Women do have them, or so my dear wife keeps reminding me. I saw that Sunflower quilt *Frau* Stauffer made before she died. An engineering marvel." High praise coming from Keil, and too bad that Matilda didn't live to hear it. "I'd prefer a man be your teacher," Keil continued. "You need strong reins, *ja*? There is a boy in Bethel with such skills. Perhaps I'll ask him to come west. He could teach you—"

"I'll not wait that long," I said.

"*Ja*. Well, better an art class than climbing some mountain."

I smiled. "Oh, I'd never do anything so dangerous as that. At least not before I turn fifty."

"You could get hurt risking such things," he said.

"*Ja*. I could suffer," I said. "But I'd find my way through it, I'm hopeful of that."

He held up his empty plate like a small boy, seeking more. "This is very *gut*, Emma. Excellent taste. A bit of sweet and sour. Just right. I will tell Louisa. You could stay for supper at the *gross Haus*, share with her the recipe? You could serve as you did of old, when you first came and huddled outside the door there with your children and that little *Zwerg*."

"I do have good experience in cooking and serving," I said.

I took the empty plate from him, stood. "But tonight I have my family to go home to," I said. "Thank you for permitting the class." He brushed his hand to the air, dismissively, as though his permission and payment were nothing. Or perhaps he was telling me I hadn't even needed to ask. I pitched that thought away. We'd come a long way, Brother Keil and I. Both of us, still changing.

"I'll bring the recipe when I come next time," I told him. My ruffled petticoat swirled against my legs as I turned to leave.

"*Danke. Danke.*"

"I can only hope it will appease your hunger," I said. "As I'm hoping that the art class will satisfy mine."

"That will be good, Emma. You are a good woman, a good servant."

I blushed with his compliment but knew I didn't need it. I nodded good-bye, then went out through the root room door, whistling a tune as I left, already reworking that recipe.

Author's Notes
and Acknowledgments

It's difficult for me to leave Emma. In part, I am reluctant because so many have made her journey come alive for me, including many readers. The Aurora Colony Historical Society opened its archives, and the board, staff, and volunteers gave of their time and stories to bring this woman, her community, and her journey to life. For this reason I've dedicated this final book in the Change and Cherish Historical Series to them.

Many have assisted me, but special appreciation goes to curator Patrick Harris, executive director John Holley, and staff members Janus Childs, Pam Weninger, and Elizabeth Corley. Board members Norm Bauer, Gail Robinson, Jim Kopp, and Annette James continued to offer wise counsel and encouragement throughout the series. Volunteers Irene Westwood and Roberta Hutton opened doors to history that would otherwise have been closed, and I'm grateful beyond words. Each of these people gave of themselves in the way the colonists did, helping make someone else's life better than their own—in this instance, mine.

I am indebted to direct descendants of Emma: David and Patricia Wagner (Emma's great-nephew through William's line), Mike and Ariana Truman (Emma's great-grandson through Catie Ehlen's line), and Louise Hankeson (Emma's great-granddaughter through Christian's line), all of Portland, Oregon, who shared their homes, letters, photographs, fiber arts, musical instruments, and even recipes handed down from Emma and her daughter. Members of the Jerry Giesy families (descendants of Emma's first husband's brothers) provided treasured looks at calling cards and opportunities to explore the lives of the descendants who have peopled my life for the past three years. I'm deeply grateful to them all, especially for their willingness to share family stories, including the ones related to Christian's death and Emma's spirited life, and for allowing me to speculate to fill in historical gaps.

Erhard and Elfi Gross again offered advice and suggestions related to the German language used by Emma and others, though any errors in usage are mine. Their years operating a bed-and-breakfast in Astoria, Oregon, helped inform me about the wonderful German cuisine that I hope reflected well on Emma's own efforts in this book. Most of the recipes mentioned came from either the *Aurora Colony Heritage Recipes* cookbook or from the 1915 *Kenilworth Presbyterian Cook Book* that included recipes from Emma and her daughter. Author and quilter Mary Bywater Cross introduced me to Emma through her book *Quilts of the Oregon Trail.* How could I ever thank her enough for that?

Retta and Steven Braun, owners of the historic Frederick Keil House, allowed us to visit, to photograph, and to get a feel for the root cellar and the flow of life in the early *gross Haus* built close to the colony church, neither of which still stands. Frederick did indeed marry Emma's niece, Louisa Giesy, and they lived in the house, which is said to have the same floor plan as the *gross Haus.* I'm grateful for the Brauns' hospitality and their continued efforts to maintain this piece of Aurora history. Suzie Wolfer, a colony descendant, loaned me period books on herbal healing that both Keil and Martin Giesy might have used, and shared tea and stories with me. Descendants of many of these families—Keil and Wolfer, Will and Stauffer and Steinbach in Aurora and Portland, Oregon; in Ohio and Pennsylvania; and Lucille Bower back in Bethel, Missouri—shared photographs and stories that brought insights into the telling of this community.

In previous books in the series, I included a suggested list of reading material related to communal societies and the Aurora Colony specifically. For this last book, I relied heavily on Eugene Edmund Snyder's book *Aurora, Their Last Utopia: Oregon's Christian Commune 1856–1883;* as well as drawings done by Clark Moor Will, a descendant of a colony member, and his remembrances; those published by the Aurora Historical Society; and those included in the Marion

County Historical Society newsletters. In step with the incredible memory of Patrick Harris and the volunteers, colony archives, and descendant records and stories, I did my best to stay true to the historical record. I did, however, diverge for some story elements, and I want to convey those detours now.

From the record, we know that Emma returned to the colony in 1861, and from a divorce petition she filed thirty years later, in 1891, we learn of the circumstances under which she left Willapa and returned to Aurora. We know she didn't initially have her sons with her, but it is not clear why. From a letter Emma wrote to her parents in 1862 from the Aurora Colony (reproduced nearly verbatim in the text), we learn that she did have all four of her children with her by then since she comments on that. Her father has a ledger page in November 1862, telling us when they arrived; but there are few entries after that date, for either her parents or for Emma herself. It is noteworthy that Emma is the only woman with a colony ledger page in her own name. After 1862, most items for her sons are listed under Martin Giesy's name, so something happened that meant Emma's sons were no longer with her. This is verified by later census records. Did she have her own funds and thus didn't need to use the colony communal supplies? Did Jack provide resources? There's no evidence of either. Yet a house was built for Emma sometime around 1864–65. It still stands. Did she leave the colony in the interim? Did her parents live with her in that house? Did she go with them, if in fact they left? If she had a house, why were her sons with Martin still living in the *gross Haus*? Was she banished for some reason? These are all speculative questions, and I have tried to answer them while staying true to Emma and the rest of the historical record. These questions became threads for the fabric of fiction.

There were tensions between her family back in Bethel and Andrew Giesy the manager and August Keil, Keil's son who was sent there to encourage dispersing of property so the Bethelites would come west. But letters suggest that the Bethelites were quite happy where they were, and the more primitive conditions in Aurora forestalled the migration. The difficulties between Emma's parents and the Giesys of

Bethel appear to be related to personal property ownership, and this would indeed have created conflict in what was to be a largely communal society. Whether this was the source of tension between Emma and her parents is speculative. But when Emma's father died in 1873, he did have an estate to leave to "Wagner and Heirs," and it was a portion of this estate that in Emma's 1891 divorce petition she claimed as money used to purchase her property that was hers and hers alone. She was apparently hoping to prevent Jack Giesy from making a claim against her property, telling us that he continued as a force in her life, one I believe she managed well over time.

A newspaper account in the 1870s suggests that Emma lived with her parents near Aurora at least for a time. Following her father's death, Emma and her mother and siblings "officially joined the Aurora Colony," according to colony records. Up until then, Emma had apparently kept herself at the edge, separate, even though she lived and worked there, perhaps as a final statement that the Willapa group was indeed its own entity, much as Bethel was.

Jonathan Wagner helped negotiate the purchase of property along the Willamette River in 1874 for his mother and siblings. The property acquired belonged to George Law Curry and his wife, Chloe Boone. Curry was Oregon's territorial governor from 1854 to 1859. The property remained in the Wagner family until becoming the development of Charbonneau, which is how it is known today. David Wagner did own a grist mill in Aurora, and the flour sacks were stenciled with "Wagner and Heirs," just as Emma had noted.

After her father's death, Emma took her inheritance—something unique for a woman to even have in that period—and bought property. Two years later she sold it, doubling her money. She later loaned money to her son Andrew, who did indeed go on to become a physician, though his original schooling was provided by the colony. In census records he is recorded as a helper at the pharmacy. He continued to live with Martin Giesy and Martha Miller after their marriage until he left for school.

Andrew graduated from Willamette University in 1876 and did

postgraduate work at Jefferson Medical College in Philadelphia, earning his MD degree in 1882. He returned to serve as a colony physician for three years. Andrew was named assistant physician at the Oregon State Hospital in Salem in 1885. In 1886, he married Ida Harriet Church. They had one son. Andy eventually opened a private practice in Portland, in the new specialty of obstetrics and gynecology. It appears likely that the loan to him was for the additional training, so Emma did continue a relationship with her son.

Christian married Louisa Ehlen, and his sister Catherine (Kate/Catie) married Lorenz Ehlen, thus blending these two families. The Ehlens were known for their basket making, weaving, reed making, farming, and carpentry skills. In later life, Emma lived for a time with her son's family and still later with her daughter's family in Portland, Oregon. Census records also show her living for a time with Ida's family, the Beckes. Emma stayed connected to her children. On May 17, 1916, Emma died. She had lived with Catie for some years and was a member of the Kenilworth Presbyterian Church in Portland at the time of her death. Incidentally, Catie did change how she spelled her name, as evidenced by a sampler contained in the colony's collection of artifacts.

Emma did make one visit back to Willapa after she left there in 1861. She was well into her eighties at the time and was described as being alert and knowledgeable. She visited Christian's grave and recalled fondly her journey across the continent with the scouts in 1853. She said little else about her time in Willapa.

Ida, the daughter of Jack and Emma, married Henry Becke, a farmer, and the families all remained within the Northwest for many years after the dissolution of the colony. Ida and her daughters were known for their quilting, a continuing family tradition. Some of these quilts, as well as a sewing machine said to belong to Emma and likely used by Ida, are often on display in the colony during the colony quilt show held each fall.

A house, with two front doors, was built for Emma. We know of such a house from a photograph with the notation that it was built by Jonathan Wagner "for his widowed aunt and her three children." We know where it was located in Aurora proper, and it probably had a view of Mount Hood. The notation errs in that it was not Jonathan's aunt but his *sister,* Emma, for whom the house was built. We believe she had only her daughters with her, but she may have had Christian as well, at least for a time, which would account for the "three" children mentioned. The house built for Emma became the home of John and Elizabeth Kraus, the daughter of John and Barbara (BW) Giesy, and in the 1970s the house was given as a gift by the Kraus family to the Colony Historical Society. It was moved from its original site on Liberty and Third to its current site next to the ox barn on Second Street and is known today as Kraus House.

Whether Emma used the house to welcome others like herself, who lived at the edge, is also not historically certain, but I wanted to convey the essence of care and community that the Aurorans were known for through the years. Serving and restoring through music and good food were hallmarks of the colony, and through such work I believe Emma found peace and meaning. Stories relate that no one in need was turned away, and I felt that Emma might well have been at the center, living the art of hospitality and spiritual understanding within a family setting, and in so doing demonstrating how profoundly an ordinary life can touch the lives of others.

Almira Raymond was an actual historical woman who endured the trials mentioned, and she might well have known Emma, or Emma might have known about her, given the notoriety of her divorce. We also don't know whether Emma and the others found comfort in walking paths, but reports from the Rapp Society of Pennsylvania, of which her parents were a part, describe several such labyrinth paths, and it was likely Emma would have enjoyed their replication and perhaps used them as a way to keep her from falling back from hope.

Whether or not Emma found that the gift of music soothed her soul is unknown. But the old German proverb, "Music washes the soul of the dirt of daily living," is a sampler included in the Bethel Colony Museum in Bethel, Missouri. Emma might well have heard this proverb spoken and taken its message into her heart. We do know that workers in the colony—as did many workers of old—sang as part of their everyday experiences in the potato and bean fields or while bathing their children at home. We also know that the Aurorans, including Emma, were deeply attached to the landscape, seeking *Heimat,* that special homeland where roots could grow deep. They likely found solace at the Park House nestled beneath the trees, where paths meandered and people picnicked as the band played.

Christine was fostered by the Wagner family. Her name appears on a special accounting of residents of Phillipsburg, listing those in the David Wagner home. The translation, *1833 Residents of Phillipsburg (Now Monaca), Pennsylvania,* was compiled by Dr. Eileen Aiken English in 2004 (Skeeter Hill Press). Many colonists did adopt or foster children as a way of expanding their population. That's all we know of Christine; the rest of her journey is purely fictional. None of Emma's sisters married; only her youngest brother, William, did. Emma did move with her family in 1870 to a property not far from Aurora, though she remained connected to the colony.

I also detoured in my storytelling regarding the marriage of Matilda and Jacob Stauffer, placing it just outside of Aurora, rather than in Willapa where it likely took place. Whether they lived in the house with Emma as portrayed is unlikely. What happened to Matilda and her babies is documented, as is her incredible creativity with needle and thread. Quilts of hers have been handed down, and her descendants have graciously permitted them to be displayed during quilt exhibits of the colony. Jacob Stauffer did build a two-story log home outside of Aurora in 1865, which today belongs to the Aurora Colony Historical Society. I wanted to explore Keil's restrictive marriage policy and the way it was sometimes thwarted by marriages performed away from the colony, and so I used Matilda and Jacob to do that. (One factual story concerns a couple who dated each other for thirty years, marrying only after Keil died. That way, when the colony assets were divided, the man received his portion and the single woman received a portion that amounted to half of what the man received. A married couple only received the man's portion; a wife's contribution to the colony effort was not counted.)

We don't know the actual date of Matilda and Jacob's marriage, but we do know the dates of their children's births. Jacob Stauffer later married Christina Wolfer, the sister who watched her brother break all those dishes along the trail. The rescued butter dish was handed down through the family along with the story. In 2007, the dish was given to the Aurora Colony Museum by a descendant, where the story continues to be told.

Every year, thousands of school children learn about early colony life by spending a morning at the Stauffer Farmstead. They cut fir branches to make candle holders, dip into wax to make their own candles, piece together swatches for quilt blocks, knead biscuits and watch them being baked in the old cast-iron stove. Children also make cedar shakes and write their names on them, recording their journeys into the past while taking some of that past with them when they leave. The shakes were originally used to side the smokehouse and other colony structures. Making primitive crafts that children can hold in their hands may be the finest way of bringing history alive in this technological age.

Life did seem to revolve around the Oregon State Fair, which was usually held in October after harvest. The colony's dance hall and the first restaurant at the state fairgrounds brought them wide renown. Many items are listed in the *Oregonian* records as being exhibited by the Aurora families, though Dr. Keil's are the most prominent. The Aurora Band toured at the expense of railroad magnate Ben Holladay. The band was known throughout the region, performing at Butteville, Oregon, as they first performed in the 1850s, and at the colony's elaborate three-story hotel, especially when the train brought in its first travelers in October 1870. The Pie and Beer Band played second fiddle, so to speak, to the Aurora Band. After a remarkable discovery in 2005 of original compositions of music, the historical society has begun the work of restoring and performing this music, including introducing it to schoolchildren. Already two public concerts of the works have been performed. Many of the instruments were handmade and of unusual designs. The Ehlen family, which Emma's daughter and son married into, was known for their skill at making reeds for wind instruments.

The colonists were also known far and wide for their food, served at the fair and at the hotel. Though the hotel was but thirty minutes by train from Portland and the end of the line, for years the train stopped in Aurora for meals "served within 15 minutes." Many other patrons took leisurely Sunday rides to the colony to participate in the restoration promised by fine German cuisine.

Most of the growth of the colony occurred through arrivals of Bethelites and the Willapa residents coming south to Oregon. By 1867, nearly all of the Willapa Giesys related to Emma had come to Aurora, except for Jacob/Jack Giesy and Sebastian and Mary. Interestingly, other Giesys came to Willapa from Ohio after the Civil War. The Giesy clan continued to look after the stockade that Christian and the scouts built in 1855–56, until it crumbled with age. They also tend the cemetery where both Willie Keil and Christian Giesy, among others, are buried. Willie Keil's burial site is marked by Washington State highway maps. Joni Blake graciously assisted in early readings of this series.

The pharmacy, the Keil and Company Store, and the colony church were some of the later buildings to be erected by the colonists in Aurora. The church was dismantled in 1911, and the lumber used elsewhere. The pews, however, found a home in the Aurora Presbyterian Church, which stands across from the ox barn, and some of the hand-turned pillars became part of the museum's changing exhibits. Several original colony buildings are identified by markers for visitors taking a walking tour of Aurora today.

Changes in the economy of Aurora and the eroding of communal life are well documented. Keil may have wanted his people to be self-reliant and to find spiritual strength through their work and their arts, or perhaps he wanted to stand out from neighboring religious practices and thus did not preach except twice a month. The record shows he did stop preaching for a time and that the deaths of his children caused an enormous change in his demeanor. With the arrival of Christopher Wolff, colony youngsters gained a more consistent school experience. After that, younger men were invited to preach, and perhaps these same young men became the advisors when the agreements (included at the end of this section) were developed. Henry C. Finck was the music instructor, and his son Henry T was the first Oregonian to matriculate to Harvard. Karl Ruge continued to live at the *gross Haus,* tend the bridge as toll keeper, and teach.

Descendants report innuendos about inappropriate relationships between Keil and some of the women, and with certain families in the colony. I did attempt to incorporate some of that uncertainty, which can occur in communal groups where there is but one recognized leader and where that leader fails to prepare anyone else to take his place. Sexual innuendo is about power and its use. I hoped to convey the misuse of Keil's power through a variety of means, without denying or minimizing the genuine commitment of the colonists to demonstrate the Diamond Rule by making others' lives better than their own, as they believed they were called to do by Christ's words. They were loyal Unionists during the War Between the States. They were communal in the sense of carrying out their Christian beliefs from the book of Acts, that each should give to a common fund and draw whatever was needed from it. They hoped to demonstrate the power of Christian love, operating within the larger world, by living compassionately and with joy, working well with one another and with their neighbors. A further discussion of these issues and others affecting the communal nature of Aurora can be found in Dr. James Kopp's book *Eden Within Eden: Oregon's Utopian Heritage,* to be published in 2008.

Wilhelm Keil died suddenly on December 30, 1877. By then, many colony properties had already been placed into individual hands, but much remained deeded in only Wilhelm Keil's name in Aurora and in Bethel, in the name of his holding company. His family might have claimed it all, in both Bethel and Aurora, but Louisa and her surviving sons did not. Louisa died in 1879, and negotiations continued uninterrupted to dissolve both colonies and to distribute the monies in an equitable manner. Willapa was not included in any of these negotiations, so we can assume that it was indeed a separate colony, as Emma had always hoped; or that by the time of Keil's death, nearly all of the former Bethelites who had stayed at Willapa had found their way to Aurora and were thus a part of that final distribution. While there were some disagreements during the years of negotiations, the colony was successfully dissolved in January 1883 with no lawsuits. A Bethel Colony Heritage Society continues in Bethel, Missouri, with a fall celebration each year to commemorate the colonists' lives there.

The Keils are buried, along with Helena Giesy and other selected colonists, in a small cemetery not far from where the church stood in Aurora. The headstones of Wilhelm, Louisa, and Willie, their oldest son, who died as they were leaving Bethel to come west and who was brought across the continent to be buried in Washington Territory, have the motif of weeping willows; the other Keil headstones do not. Emma is buried in the Aurora Community Cemetery, not with the Giesy family, but at the edge of the Ehlen family plot.

The community of Aurora continues to be on the National Historic Register, and some of the original buildings are maintained as a part of the museum, where visitors can see a rotation of exhibits centered on various families, a range of colony artifacts, the herb garden, and the annual October quilt show. Many communities claim connection to this colony: those from Bethel, Willapa, and Aurora proper; surrounding communities where names like Knight are prominent; and descendants of those who interacted with the colonists, purchasing their tin lanterns and medicines, trading pottery for tailored clothing, attending events at the Park House or the fair, worshiping at the colony church, whether they were colonists or not. Should you visit this historical village where six hundred live today, you'll find antiques stores in old colony buildings, pleasant walkways lined with flowers, and much of the same gentle hospitality that made it the most successful communal society in the west. Your visit will likely make you a storyteller too, just as it did for me. In 2009, the National Communal Society will meet in the Aurora area to correspond to Oregon's one hundred fiftieth anniversary of statehood and to continue to explore stories of this remarkable group of German Americans in the west.

Many other helpers, from the editorial and production team at WaterBrook Multnomah Publishing Group to my neighbors not far from Starvation Lane, contributed greatly to this story and gave aid and comfort in remarkable ways. There are too many to name them all. Carol, Judy, Susan, Blair, Laura, Nancy, Gabby, Kay, Sandy, Dudley, Erin, and of course, Jerry, must be mentioned for their constancy in my life. Thank you.

Because of my own visits in researching the life of Emma Wagner Giesy, I have new stories to tell. Some will be included in a nonfiction book that will celebrate the quilts and crafts of the colony, especially their fiber arts, music, food, basket making, and furniture. *Aurora: An American Experience in Quilt and Craft* will be released by WaterBrook Multnomah Publishing Group in the fall of 2008 and will feature Emma's quilts and many of the eighty quilts made by colonists during the colony period.

For further information contact www.auroracolony.com, Aurora Colony Historical Society, P.O. Box 202, Aurora, OR 97002, (503) 678-5754; or you can follow progress on this latest project at www.jkbooks.com or jane@jkbooks.com. Thank you for helping me keep stories of remarkable historical women and their families alive. I hope you're inspired to record your own family stories and the rich legacies they left behind.

Jane Kirkpatrick, 2008

DISCUSSION QUESTIONS

1. Emma writes, "I questioned whether expectation was a virtue one could nurture, or if once lost, would never sprout again." Can hope be learned? Can we change how we feel, or must we depend on others to behave in ways that bring us nurture? Did Emma find a way to nurture expectation over anxiety?

2. The Jan Richards quote in the front of this book speaks of community rhythms. What rhythms did Emma discover in Aurora? How did grief and loss interfere with her acceptance of those rhythms?

3. In your own communities (book groups, professional associations, faith communities, etc.) have you ever felt at the edge? What was that like? What strengths did you gain from being in "the backwaters"? What were the trials? How did the women in Emma's house church, and Brita, represent people at the edge?

4. Most novels begin with a character having a desire. What did Emma desire? Did she achieve it? How did the author show Emma's desires changing? How do our desires change as we enter new communities or face new trials or opportunities?

5. What roles did landscape, relationships, faith, and work play in the telling of Emma's journey? Can you identify how these four threads are woven into the fabric of your own life? Do they bring you strength or threaten to bring tendering to the experiences of your life, causing disintegration from exposure to caustic material, rather than nurturing?

6. Did Emma work hard enough to bring unity to her family? Did she rely on her own strengths, rather than trying to "see God" in the situation, as Karl advised her often? Were there steps she didn't take that she could have used to bring her family together? What surprised you, if anything, about her decision to allow her sons to remain with Martin?

7. What outside factors began to change the communal aspect of the Aurora Colony? Did Emma's activities contribute to that change in any way? What role did the deaths of the Keil children play in how the colony changed?

8. Communal societies are marked by tension between individual needs and community desires. While most of us don't live in communal societies, how do we experience those same kinds of tensions? How do conflicts get resolved without the presence of a communal leader to dictate what will happen for the good of the community?

9. What role did quilting, painting, singing, even making glasses provide in Emma's journey to find meaning? What role do the arts and crafts play in our lives? Are they undervalued as sources of mending in our lives? How might their status be enhanced? Or should they be?

10. What impact did the absence of a church building have on Aurora's development and in the lives of Emma, Louisa, Helena, Matilda, and the other colonists? Why do you think Keil waited so long to build the house of worship? And why did he limit services to twice a month? How does a person of faith continue to grow spiritually when a religious leader restricts curiosity and exploration of faith issues?

11. Where did the house church women draw their strength from? What do you think the verse from Malachi, presented at the beginning of this book, has to say about hearkening together and creating books of remembrances? How do you experience that happening in your life? How could you?

12. If you speculated about future relationships between Emma and her children, how might you characterize them? What about her relationship with her siblings and her parents? Are there times when tensions with immediate family cannot be resolved? What hinge can keep us together, agreeing to disagree, perhaps, while remaining engaged? What hinders those resolutions in families today?

13. Are women the brooms of the world, as artist Alison Saar observed in the initial story quote? How do ordinary women find meaning within everyday life? How does the Goethe observation (page 300) that Emma makes about sweeping in front of our porches relate to this artist's quote?

14. What *restored* (as in the French for "restaurant") Emma? What restores you? Can you teach and share those skills, experiences, behaviors, and actions with those you love? What support would you need in order to find that restoration in your life?

———◆———

The author is available at predetermined times to join book groups by speakerphone. To find out more, visit her Web site www.jkbooks.com and click on Book Groups. She welcomes your comments and questions on the public guest book located there. Schedules of when she may be in your community are available there as well.

THE AURORA COLONY ARTICLES
OF AGREEMENT—1867

1. All government should be parental, to imitate the parental government of God.
2. Societies should be formed on the model of the family.
3. All interests and all property are kept absolutely in common.
4. Members labor faithfully for the general welfare and support.
5. The means of living is drawn from the general treasury.
6. Neither religion nor the harmony of nature teaches community in nothing further than property and labor.
7. The family is strictly maintained; people marry, raise, and train children.
8. Each family has its own house, or separate apartments, in one of the large buildings.
9. The children of the community are sent to school, open year round.
10. Dr. Keil is president and autocrat. He has selected advisors to assist in the management of affairs. When vitally important changes or experiment is contemplated, nothing is done without the general consent of the community.
11. Plain living and rigid economy are inculcated as duties from each to the whole: Labor regularly and waste nothing. Each workshop has a foreman. The fittest comes to the front. Men shall not be confined to one kind of labor. If brick masons are needed and the shoemaker is not busy, the shoemaker makes brick.

Glossary

aber	but
ach	oh no!
Ach, Jammer!	an expression of frustration
Belsnickel	a traditional Christmas persona bringing gifts
bitte	please
Frau	Mrs.
Fräulein	Miss
Fraktur	unique printing designs; a German calligraphy
gross Haus	large house
gut	good
Herr	Mr.
Heimat	more than a house, a place of belonging
Hinterviertel	seat or a person's backside
ja	yes, pronounced "ya"
Junge	boy
Kartoffel	potato
Kinder	children
nein	no
Oma	grandmother
Opa	grandfather
Sehnsucht	a yearning or longing (of the human spirit) for something of meaning
Schellenbaum	A bell-like instrument known in English as the Turkish Crescent. Popular in the eighteenth and early

	nineteenth centuries, the large instrument combined music with a symbol of authority or standard of allegiance. The colonists hand-crafted their *Schellenbaum*.
Scherenschnitte	German folk art; cutout paper pieces are glued together to create objects, such as trees, flowers, animals, or decorative elements for certificates.
Schottische	a dance with three
Scatter Soup	made with a slim batter similar to Chinese egg drop
Tannenbaum	a tree, especially at Christmastime
Zwerg	dwarf

A Sneak Peek At…

Aurora
An American Experience in Quilt and Craft

*The True Story Behind the Change
and Cherish Historical Series*

by Jane Kirkpatrick

On Sale Fall 2008

Craft
Past and Present Intertwined

Spare and splendid, the quilts and crafts of the old Aurora Colony still comfort and inspire as treasures of identity and legacy. Their presence, collected by descendants and those passionate about former stories, are preserved inside the properties owned by the Aurora Colony Historical Society at the Old Aurora Colony Museum and the Stauffer-Will Farmstead near the present day village of Aurora, Oregon. Additional quilts are owned privately and often shared for exhibits. Aurora is Oregon's third national historic district, where the society has preserved nearly one hundred quilts and textiles, as well as baskets, furniture, tools of tin, and wood and other artifacts, all connected with the colony period (1856–1883). They're showcased in an 1862 ox barn or an 1865 farmstead or an 1876 log cabin. These artifacts reflect the simple passions of a faithful people.

In Oregon's verdant Willamette Valley, between 1856 and 1883, lived a cluster of German Americans seeking something more, something splendid at both a spiritual and secular level. They found it in their Christian communal society, one of the only successful such communities in the West founded in the mid–nineteenth century.

Not unlike the Amana Society of Iowa or the Harmonists of Pennsylvania, the colonists expressed their values and traditions through their interactions with the world around them. In contrast with this twenty-first century when people are often disconnected from the work of their hands, from extended family, and from faith, these colonists demonstrated who they were by their unique artifacts and traditions, their food, music, furniture, and fiber arts—and by living out their Christian faith in community. They passed their stories down from one generation to the next through their quilts, crafts, and traditions. Unfortunately, they did not always talk about them, so descendants and curators must interpret their meaning and allow the works of their hands to be their voices.

We are privileged 153 years later to experience a part of their lives in our contemporary world and consider how we are bound with them through threads of art and community, faith and healing, past and present intertwined by the works of their hands.

I began seeing quilts and crafts as stories while wandering through antique stores and imagining how people once used a strange-looking tool or how many hours it took to quilt a now-worn Ocean Wave. Then several of my novels were chosen to be interpreted through quilts by various quilting groups in the Northwest. The beauty and uniqueness of these fiber "stories" made me more conscious of quilts as narratives and how such crafts reflected the women who had made them.

My interest was cemented a few years later when I was invited to be the guest scholar for a weekend retreat of quilters. Though I have never quilted, they asked me to speak of stories and how they inform our lives. While I talked, the women from around the country sewed and stitched, having brought their material and machines with them to the Willamette Valley.

During a break, I paged through a book by retreat leader Mary Bywater Cross and there found a story of a quilt made by Emma Wagner Giesy. Her story, and the story of the colonies she came from, led me to Aurora and its roots in Germany; then to Indiana, Pennsylvania, Missouri, Washington, and finally to Oregon. Her fiber art served as her legacy.

The Change and Cherish Historical Series (WaterBrook Multnomah Publishing Group) chronicles this woman's journey to celebrate her voice in a society that often acted tone deaf to its female members. In the process of researching and writing, I fell in love with the stories and the way the community stumbled and righted itself as it chose to carry out its faith and philosophy in an everyday world.

It is my hope, and the hope of the Aurora Colony Historical Society, that telling the stories of these treasures through text and pictures of artifacts and crafts will inspire a reader's own exploration of family, legacy, and community. Perhaps these artifacts will allow a new look at family objects, especially the crafts that enrich our lives and help memorialize the triumphs and tragedies of our ancestors. I invite you to join me on this journey of another place and time, as we explore the landscapes, relationships, work, and faith of these German Americans and their wish to live a simple, meaningful life in the American West. May the work of their hands bring you comfort.